WHAT IF WE BREAK?

NY SWEETHEARTS
BOOK 1

JOELINA FALK

What If We Break?

Copyright © 2024 Joelina Falk

All rights reserved. No part of this publication may be reproduced, distributed, or transmitted in any form without written permission of the publisher, except for brief passages by a reviewer for review purposes only.

This is a work of fiction. All names, characters, locations, and incidents are a product of the author's imagination and are used fictitiously. Any resemblance to actual persons, events, or things—living or dead—is entirely coincidental.

Copy Editing: Kayla Morton

Proofread: Cassidy Hudspeth

Cover designed by @andersartig_designs

eBook ISBN: 978-3-910980-05-1

Paperback ISBN: 978-3-910980-11-2

Alternate Cover ISBN: 978-3-910980-10-5

You can find me here:

https://www.instagram.com/authorjoelinafalk/

https://www.joelinafalk.com

DISCLAIMERS

The use of the NHL in this series and any of its teams is a work of fiction. In no way does it reflect the policies or opinions of the actual organization.

Names, characters, businesses, Universities, places, events, and incidents are either the products of the author's imagination or used in a fictitious manner. Any resemblance to actual persons, living or dead, or actual events is purely coincidental.

While I stuck as close as I could to the NCAA (in regards to ice hockey), NHL, and competitive figure skating guidelines and rules, I took creative freedom with certain details because this is fiction.

TRIGGER WARNING

This book contains topics that may be triggering for some readers.

For a full list, please head over to:

https://www.joelinafalk.com/what-if-we-break
or
https://www.joelinafalk.com/books-content-warnings

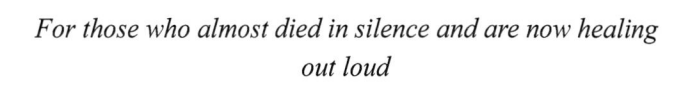

For those who almost died in silence and are now healing out loud

Playlist

Nervous — The Neighbourhood
Who Do I Call Now? (Hellbent) — Sofia Camara
Again — Noah Cyrus, XXXTENTACION
Gives You Hell — The All-American Rejects
Constellations — Jade LeMac
Bed Chem — Sabrina Carpenter
nasty — Ariana Grande
Reflections — The Neighbourhood
If I Lose Myself — OneRepublic
Earned It — The Weeknd
My Blood — Twenty One Pilots
In A Little — Alec Benjamin
True Love — P!nk, Lily Allen
i hope you're miserable until you're dead — Nessa Barrett
Perfectly Wrong — Shawn Mendes
12 Notes — Alec Benjamin
Till Forever Falls Apart — Ashe, FINNEAS
Breakfast — Dove Cameron
Under Pressure — RILEY, Chase Atlantic
Polaroid — Jonas Brothers, Liam Payne, Lennon Stella
DIE FOR ME — Chase Atlantic

DICKTIONARY

For those of you who'd like to find and/or avoid the smut quickly, skip to/avoid the following chapters:

Chapter Five
Chapter Six
Chapter Nine
Chapter Twenty
Chapter Twenty-Seven
Chapter Thirty
Chapter Forty-Four

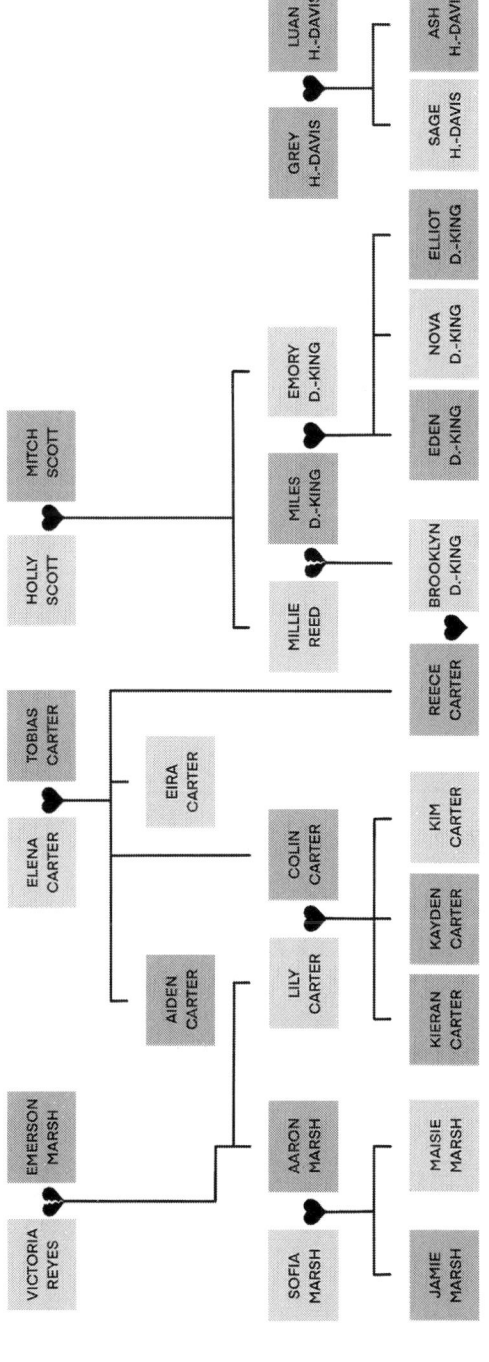

Prologue

Brooklyn

Seven Years Earlier – Age 13

"Brooke, we need to talk," Reece, my best friend in the whole wide world, said as he came marching into my bedroom without so much as a knock.

To be fair, Reece never knocked because I was used to him showing up out of the blue, and on normal days, I didn't mind it. I had nothing to hide from him except maybe my feelings.

Even now, I didn't mind him barging in here as if it was his right to be inside of my bedroom. However, the moment your best friend walked into your room without warning, saying the words *we need to talk*, that raised concerns.

So I sat up in a second, and my hands started to shake at the thought that he was about to say what I feared he would for a while now.

I couldn't lose Reece. He was the only friend I had. Literally. I wasn't exaggerating.

"Sure, what's up?" I tried to play it cool, but I knew he could hear the tremor in my voice. He always did.

Reece was next to me in the blink of an eye, his hand

linked with mine. "First, take a deep breath, *mi princesa*. Stop worrying about me leaving because that's not going to happen."

My heart smiled at the nickname. It wasn't the first time he called me that. In fact, he said it at least a couple of times a day ever since we were like six. Yet it still made me smile every single time.

I did as he said and took a deep breath. In theory, I knew there was nothing that would ever make him run from me. Our shared history was enough to secure me a safe spot in his heart for the rest of our lives, but try telling my anxiety the same thing. No matter how often Reece would reassure me we'd always stay friends, I'd always find a way to doubt it.

"Better?"

"A little." A smile crept onto my face when I looked at him, and my heart pounded so heavily in my chest when he returned the smile.

I think I might've liked him for a while now, but I never wanted to tell him. I still refused to tell him because, again, I didn't want to ruin our friendship. I saw what admitting feelings to your best friend did to all the girls in my school. They always broke up after a while and never spoke again. Or the other person didn't feel the same, and now their friendship was ruined for nothing. I simply couldn't risk that.

"So, what's up, *mon soleil*?" I asked, regretting it immediately.

I never called him that before.

"*Mon... soleil?*" he repeated as his eyebrows shot up. Reece didn't speak French, but I taught him a few things a while ago.

"I didn't say anything." My cheeks felt hot all of a sudden.

Reece's older brother once told me that the nickname *my*

sun was like a trophy in their family. Reece never felt like he earned the right to call me his sun because he was barely alive when Aiden—Reece and Colin's older brother, who had sadly passed away way before Reece could form coherent thoughts—told his siblings about the meaning of the nickname.

Reece wasn't going to use it on me, so he came up with his very own, very important and meaningful nickname for me. I figured the significance of *my sun* in the Carter family couldn't die with Colin. So whether Reece wanted me to or not, I was going to pass it down for him eventually. Our kids would—oh... right. We weren't a couple...

I had no right calling him that just yet. Or ever.

Reece took a deep breath, his hand loosening in mine. Was he pulling away from me? So, was he lying? No, Reece never lied to me before. He wouldn't now, either.

"Demi told me what happened between the two of you yesterday," he said carefully, changing the subject.

I rolled my eyes immediately. Demi, that cunt—sorry, I wasn't allowed to swear. My father would quite literally have a heart attack if he heard me say that aloud.

"Can she ever shut up?" I pulled my hand away from Reece and moved a bit away from him. He followed me, though, his thigh pressed right against mine.

A tingle formed where our thighs met, and I wished I had magical powers to make these feelings go away. Some of the princesses in movies had cool powers or at least some kind of wand or a witch or fairy supporting them. Why didn't I?

"You told her she couldn't speak to me ever again, Brooklyn. That was so not cool."

He used my full name... Reece only ever did that when he was mad.

A tear rolled down my face almost immediately.

Confrontation and I weren't really good with each other. Others got angry or defensive when confronted with anything, and well, I cried.

"She was getting on my nerves. Demi wanted to ask you out, and I couldn't—" I couldn't tell him why I was incapable of allowing her to ask him.

Reece would've said yes, and seeing him with her would've destroyed me.

But what if I was taking his one big love away from him that way? Could I really have been this cruel to him? What if they were meant to be together?

"I'm really sor—" I never got to voice my apology because Reece cut me off in a way I never thought he ever would.

He kissed me. So quickly that I barely even realized it. One second, his lips were pressed to mine, and the next, they weren't.

It was my first kiss ever, and I wanted him to do it again. And again. And again. And maybe… maybe once more, just to be sure that really happened.

But instead, I sucked in a breath. My cheeks heated up, and I immediately brought both of my hands to my face to hide the blush that was probably as red as a warning sign right now.

My stomach was fluttering, and I had goosebumps all over my body. Perhaps it was my anxiety. No, actually, I knew it was, but it wasn't as scary as it normally was.

Sure, some part of my brain was running wild with theories.

What if Reece just kissed me as part of a bet? But Colin and Dad would decapitate him if that was the reason, and Reece knew that.

What if he just lost balance, ended up with his mouth on mine, and never meant to kiss me? Sounded plausible to me.

What if... just... what. If.

Then suddenly, Reece jumped off my bed, and I finally removed my hands from my face to see why.

Both of his hands pushed right into his hair as he pulled on the ends of it while he paced up and down my room. "Your dad is going to *kill* me!" He didn't even look at me.

I wish I was able to form words, but I couldn't. I was so shocked and confused by what just happened that not a single word was present in my vocabulary. None except for: "*Je veux être ta petite amie, idiot.*"

He stopped pacing and looked at me. "Fuck, Brooke—"

"Don't curse." I pointed my finger at him warningly. He might've not had any younger siblings, but I had. The last thing I wanted was for them to learn bad words at a young age.

Reece chuckled for a split second, but then the amusement died before he said what I refused to believe he did. "I want to kiss you again."

Still, I stood and walked up to him. Reece was taller than me, even though I was older by a little over a month. I was never intimidated by his height until this moment.

He stood about one and a half heads taller than me—I inherited my birth mother's height. He had to look down so our eyes met when my chest was pressed to his body. His hands found my waist immediately, holding me.

"I think I've wanted to kiss you since we were like... three." A humorless and embarrassed chuckle left him. He didn't notice, but my eyes slowly filled up with tears at his admission. "I never did because, God, could you imagine what your dad would've done with me if I ever did?"

I nodded because, yes, I could imagine what he would've

done. Dad was very protective of me. Of all of his kids, actually.

Both of my hands found Reece's jaw as I enveloped his face. "Are you still mad because of Demi?"

"Mad?" Reece laughed at that. "I was never mad to begin with, Brooke. If you didn't threaten her, I—shit, Brooke, I don't think I ever would've kissed you. And you have absolutely no idea how badly I want to do it again. And again. And aga—"

I pulled his face down to mine and pressed my lips to his.

Truthfully, I didn't know if I was doing this correctly. Was there a thing such as the right way to kiss? If so, I did it wrong, and that worried me.

What if I was the world's worst kisser?

No... or maybe?

As we pulled apart, Reece brought his forehead down to mine. His eyes were still closed, even when he asked, "Was that your first kiss?"

I sighed. "Was I that bad?"

His eyes finally opened and the brightest, yet deepest shade of blue stared back at me. "No," he said. "And even if you were, I wouldn't know. You were my first kiss, too, Brookie. Besides, I'm asking because I need to know how deep I dug my grave just now." *I was his first kiss, too.*

While I knew everything about my best friend, there were things we never talked about. Like kissing.

I laughed while my hands clutched tighter around his shirt. "Very deep."

He nodded to himself. "Well, so another kiss won't hurt, right?" Reece smiled at me and stroked a thumb over my flushed cheeks. "You're so cute when you're blushing."

"You can kiss me whenever you want," I said and regretted it immediately. I pressed my face right against his chest, groaning in embarrassment. *Why are you so stupid, Brooke?*

His arms wrapped around my body and held me in a tight embrace. "Like a permanent consent pass?"

"A what?"

"A few months ago, Colin told me there's a permanent consent pass for kissing, but I think it comes with marriage."

Chapter One

Brooklyn

"HAPPY BIRTHDAY, BROOKIE!"

I internally rolled my eyes as my ten-year-old brother shoved his present into my hands. I didn't even have a second to wake up yet. All I wanted to do was go grab a snack. Trust me when I say that I fully planned on going back to bed to wallow in self-pity.

The thing was, I loved my birthday. It was one day of the whole entire year that was dedicated to me *only*. With a family as huge as mine, birthdays were a *constant* occurrence, especially in September. My father always made sure all four of us felt special on our birthdays.

So, what made today different?

The Brooke from two days ago was jumping with joy at the thought of her birthday, but today-me would've rather been left alone altogether.

Just two days ago, I gave Dad a huge list of last-minute items I wanted for my birthday party, and despite the huge eye-roll I was met with and the groan in protest, I knew he got right to it. Today was my twentieth birthday, a pretty special one. Twenty-one was more special, but I liked twenty.

And still, the pain in my heart that had been there ever

since my boyfriend and I broke up was ruining all the excitement for me.

For the longest time, I thought Reece and I were endgame. I bet so did everyone else in my family, his family, and anyone else who was around us. We grew up together and started dating when we were thirteen. And everything was great… until it wasn't.

I didn't know what happened, but at some point, occasional fights became frequent, and frequent turned into daily. No matter what we did, every time we resolved one problem, another occurred.

I honestly couldn't tell you when those problems started or what they were even about. As it seemed, everything was against us, and though I agreed that taking a break from our relationship was the best decision, it didn't hurt any less.

Could you blame me? Reece had been there from the moment I could sit up straight. He was my only friend for the longest time imaginable. How could I not love him?

Losing him as my boyfriend also meant that I lost my best friend because he was everything to me. He *is* everything to me.

The worst bit, I'd still see him daily. Luckily not at school, but at home.

No, he didn't live with us, but my father and his three best friends somehow decided to move into one apartment building together, and a couple of years ago, they all moved into separate houses on one street. We were still neighbors. Next-door neighbors.

Reece moved in with his older brother a year after we started dating because their parents moved to Spain. He could've left with them, but he wanted to stay here with me.

He helped Lily with the kids whenever Colin was gone,

and I'd be lying if I said it didn't make Reece just that tiny bit more lovable.

Urgh. Shut up, brain.

I still lived at home, too, because honestly, I might have been a tad too afraid to leave yet. Also, why would I move into a college dorm or find an apartment—in the middle of New York City, mind you—when I had a perfectly fine bedroom here at home?

"Brooke?" Elliot tapped my shoulder a couple of times, then waved a hand in front of my face. "Are you there?"

"I don't know, am I?"

"I don't know, are you?" He raised an eyebrow at me. "I *see* you, but you're doing this whole staring-ever-so-dreamingly-into-the-distance thing again."

"I wasn't *dreamingly* staring anywhere. I was…" about to bawl my soul out one more time at the thought of Reece.

My family didn't know about our breakup yet, mostly because I feared what would happen once they did. It wasn't like my father would've *physically* hurt Reece, but there was a little voice in the back of my head telling me that this breakup would have more negative effects on my father and Colin's relationship than it had on Reece and me.

Maybe not, but I didn't want to risk it.

"Whatever." Elliot shoved his present against my stomach now, practically forcing me to pay attention to it. "I paid for it with my own money this time."

"Oh, so you didn't steal something from my room two months ago just to give it back to me now?"

He shook his head but laughed. "Nova did." Of course. "Open it, *pleaseee*."

"Fine." I finally took the present from him and ripped it open. Usually, I would've opened the present all neatly and carefully, but as we have already established, today was *not* my favorite birthday.

Once the present was open and I got to look at it, I felt like the most horrible sister known to humankind.

For the past three months, I had asked my dad to buy me these new skates. Mine were still good, so he said no. Apparently, if I wanted something new while I still had at least three unused items of the same kind, I could use my own money to buy it.

But skates were expensive, and I honestly didn't feel like spending hundreds of dollars on skates. So when Dad said no, the skates I had seemed pretty good to me.

"Elliot." My voice was choked with tears.

"I only saved half of the money, Brookie. But Reece gave me the rest so I could give them to you. Are you happy?"

Reece gave him money. God, could he get any more perfect?

"Reece helped you with this present?" The tears swelled more and more in my eyes. Now no longer because I was touched by the fact that my ten-year-old brother decided to buy me the skates that I had wanted for a while, but also because apparently, my ex-boyfriend helped him.

Elliot nodded. "Yeah. He's pretty awesome."

Just when I was about to thank my brother for the gift, someone rang the doorbell. There was only one person who would've rang the doorbell instead of simply marching inside.

All of my uncles had a key.

"Oh, I think Brooke's still asleep," I heard my dad say.

"Did that ever stop me from coming in?"

My breath got caught in my lungs the moment I heard his voice. My knees were moments away from giving in, my head spun, and the tears that threatened to leave my eyes now rolled down my cheeks.

Why did breakups have to hurt this much?

To be fair, I'd never been in any other relationship before, so I didn't actually know that breakups were *that* painful until... well, until Reece.

"Brookie?" Elliot took the skates from me and set them down on the floor. He then grasped my hand in his. "Are you okay?"

I nodded without wanting to.

I couldn't remember a single day in my life when I genuinely lied about my feelings to my family. Well, okay, I could count a few times when I lied to my *siblings* about them. They were all much younger than me and shouldn't have to worry about their older sister and her stupid boy drama.

But I had never *not* told my dad about what was going on in my life. In fact, Dad was always the first person I went to when things got tough. Now look at me: lying and hiding my emotions to avoid a possible war between the only people who truly meant something to me.

While I knew that my father would've always taken my side, Colin would've always taken Reece's.

The last huge fight we had, Colin and my dad got involved and it wasn't pretty. They didn't talk for a week. Once siblings and kids get involved, even the longest and strongest of friendships break.

I couldn't do that to my family.

"Should I get Dad?" Elliot asked.

I gasped for air, but my lungs were burning and no oxygen seemed to make it inside of my body. I could feel my heart pound inside of my chest, and still, with every breath I took, I took another one a second later because nothing was filling my lungs.

Tears were rolling down my face and I had no control over it. My head filled with unidentifiable voices, as always.

Every thought of mine screamed at me at a volume that nobody should ever have to hear, and yet while one thought yelled, another did, too. And another. And another. It got so much that I couldn't hear a single one of these thoughts because they all shouted at the same time as though they were fighting for my attention.

While everything was so loud inside my head, I still couldn't hear a single thing. All I did was feel.

I felt how my heart was beating at the speed of lightning. I felt how my lungs were burning. I felt how the tears dripped down from the tip of my nose, and how my hands were shaking.

"DAD!" Elliot yelled, and the only reason I heard it was because he was a tad too close to my ears. It shut up the voices in my head for a hot second. "DAD! BROOKE IS—"

Two hands lay on my jaw a moment later, and blue, comforting eyes met mine.

"Brooke?" My father swiped his thumbs underneath my eyes, not being put off by the way my eyes kept rolling back when I felt exhaustion creep up on me.

People back in high school made fun of me because of it a lot, but I had Reece there… he always made sure I was okay. He was *there*. Always.

Dad took my hand and laid it flat on his chest. I could feel his heartbeat against my palm, and because this wasn't the first time he had done this, I knew he wanted me to focus on the beats. It was too fast for me to count, or maybe I just wasn't in the right headspace to really count this time, but it definitely served as a distraction.

"Come on. Take a deep breath with me, Brooke." He breathed in, and I felt his chest rise beneath my palm.

It usually worked for me, but not this time, it seemed.

I tried to mimic him as best as I could, but while he managed to hold his breath for a while, mine drew out of me within a second.

We tried again and again, and probably a couple more times, until my lungs finally accepted the oxygen. Despite that, they were still burning.

"You're okay, baby. Nothing's going to happen to you, okay?" Dad looked right into my eyes, conviction was in his while I was sure all he saw in mine was doubt.

Nothing about this was ever going to be okay.

I had been struggling with anxiety for as long as I could remember, and while I was glad my father could never understand how I felt, I sometimes just felt… alone.

Lily was the only other person close to me who knew what it was like, but I didn't want to bother her with any of my silly problems. She promised she'd never think I was disturbing her when I decided to seek out her help, but I just couldn't take it.

Chapter Two

Reece

Guilt washed over me as I watched Brooke gasping for air, her body trembling.

I had memorized all of her triggers and knew exactly what pushed her to the edge of a panic attack. And yet here we were… and I just couldn't help but feel as if this was all my fault.

I knew crowds scared her, and when we were still together, I'd always make her walk through them with her eyes set on me. She trusted me enough to guide me, enough to know that I never would've let anything happen to her. She could've closed her eyes, walked through a mall by my side, and knew she would've never bumped into a single person or object.

I knew that keeping secrets from her father made her anxious, and she never disobeyed him either. It was because Brooke feared losing him if he found out she did something she shouldn't have. Miles would've never pushed Brooke away, but I understood where her thoughts were coming from.

There hadn't been a single person I knew better than Brooke Desrosiers-King, and there would never be a person

I'd know better than I did her. Which was why I felt as though I was to blame for everything that was happening to her.

Brooke kept a secret from her dad, and then I showed up as well. Of course, she was freaking out.

If I hadn't lived with my brother then perhaps I wouldn't have had to show up this early in the morning, but I had no other choice.

Colin was already suspicious when I told him I wasn't going to stay over at Brooke's last night. He thought it was strange, especially since it was her birthday. And he got even more worried when he found out I wasn't going to stay over tonight either.

Last year, I took Brooke on a birthday trip. Granted, our families followed because she wanted her family with her on her birthday. But my point is, we'd spent three whole days in one cabin together—separated from everyone else. The year before, I slept over at her place for the entire weekend. As I did all the birthdays before.

When she looked up over Miles's shoulder and her eyes laid on mine, my heart broke for the second time today. The first time it broke was this morning when I opened my eyes and realized that I wasn't going to spend Brooke's birthday with her in my arms. That I wasn't going to hear her giggles or sneak in kisses when nobody was watching. That I couldn't drag her away from her guests or bring her up to the top of their roof to watch the sunset.

And then now. Seeing her cry and panic broke every piece of me. And knowing that I couldn't just touch her, pull her close to me, and hug her tightly until she was okay again, it was painful.

Years ago I had promised myself, and Brooke, that I'd

never be the reason for her tears. And I loathed myself more than ever knowing that I failed.

Colin taught me to be better than that.

When I realized Elliot was looking at me funny, I did what I knew I shouldn't but would've done had Brooke still been mine. I asked Miles to step back for a moment, which he did, and then I sat down in front of Brooke. I enveloped her face with my hands, and her eyes closed as she leaned into my touch.

With every ounce of strength in me, I managed not to shed tears myself. And when I opened my arms, and Brooke fell right into my embrace and swung her arms around my neck like always, I was praying to every entity out there not to let me break.

It is better this way, I tried to tell myself. But it didn't feel *better this way*.

Her body was shaking, sobs broke free like I'd never heard before. It pained me to know I was the reason for those tears, those pain-filled sobs. If I could've made it right, I would have, but I had no idea how to.

"I'm sorry," I whispered into her ear. "I'm sorry. I love you, Brooke. So much. I'm so sorry."

Seven years. We'd been dating for seven whole years, and suddenly it didn't work anymore. Juilliard was messing with Brooke. Her figure skating partner got in the way. *Hockey* got in the way. Our lives got in the way. But I shouldn't have had to sacrifice her just to get closer to my dreams.

She shouldn't have had to sacrifice me just to keep working with her figure skating partner. He always thought of me as a distraction, I knew that. Brooke knew that. Neither of us cared until that man constantly threatened Brooke to end their partnership.

She needed him though…

And she shouldn't have had to break up with me just to show her stupid college that she wasn't "too distracted" by me.

"Don't…" Her arms closed tighter around my body. The strain in her voice told me exactly how much she hated me at this moment, how much she wanted me gone but couldn't quite find the strength to let me go.

I looked up at Miles, just to figure out if he was mad at me. I told him about what happened yesterday because I knew Brooke would cave eventually and then feel bad because nobody told him immediately. So when my eyes met his, I expected fury, but instead, he just nodded his head toward Brooke's bedroom door.

I shouldn't have. Honestly, I knew I should've said no and left, but I couldn't bring myself to run away from her. No matter how much Brooke would despise me, I'd always love her.

So, I stood and pulled Brooke up with me, then lifted her, and carried her back into her bedroom. Miles must've closed the door behind us because when I went to do it, the door was shut.

Brooke now sat on her bed, her face hidden behind her hands, shoulders shaking.

"Brooke," I said and stepped toward her.

Before I got to continue, she already shook her head. "I don't want to talk about it."

I stepped closer. "We should."

"No." Her voice was muffled by her hands, but the thing was, Brooke didn't even need to use her voice for me to understand everything she was trying to tell me. Ever. I'd always know.

"*Princesa*—"

"Don't, Reece. I swear… just… please, don't." She finally looked up. Her eyes were red, her nose too, her face tear-stained. She was still breathing heavier than usual, but it was slowly regulating itself. "Can we just ignore everything today?"

"Why?"

"Because if we tell my dad we…" her voice broke again, but she tried her best to continue "broke… up—" she gasped for air "—there *will* be this huge fallout. The last thing I need is losing you *and* half of those who mean something to me."

I couldn't tell her that Miles already knew because it would just make her worry more, so I kept it to myself for now.

"You didn't lose me, Brooke," I said. "I'm right *here*." I pointed at myself, then closed the last couple of steps between us. When I took her hands in mine, I expected Brooke to fight my touch, but she didn't. "We'll figure this out, we always do."

"We never broke up before, Reece. This is different."

I sighed. "Then just… let's not."

Her eyebrows drew together with confusion. "Let's not what?"

"Break up." I knelt down to her and cupped my face with her hands.

"We have no other choice." The tips of her fingers tapped against my skin. "Your coach will bench you. Erik will leave me. The New York Rangers are probably thinking about drafting you already, and you haven't even entered the draft yet. And with a little more training, I could make it past nationals again after three years of not even making it past qualifiers. And I'm pretty sure Juilliard will kick me out because I'm too distracted. We can't risk our dreams for a relationship."

"Let them kick you out. You hate that school," I said, my voice thick with anger. "Juilliard's killing you. You're not even interested in ballet anymore, and you don't plan on making it your profession. Why stay?"

"It's an elite school. Do you know how di—"

"Yes, I know how difficult it is to get accepted. But you've also been accepted to Harvard, Columbia, *and* Princeton, Brooke. Juilliard is only beneficial if you want to make dancing your full-time job, which you don't." My hands slid down to her wrists, holding them. "Transfer to a different college, *mi princesa*. Not for me, but for yourself. You can go to NYU, and major in dance or fine arts or something like that. Or you can transfer to St. Trewery. It'll be so much less stressful for you. You won't have to work out fifteen hours a day anymore, plus somehow attend classes and find time to sleep."

Brooke pulled her hands away from my face, from my grasp, and rested them on her lap. Her eyes stayed on mine, though I knew she wanted to look away.

She stayed silent for a while, that beautiful mind of hers working overtime. If there was one thing Brooke hated more than crowds, it was change. Transferring from Juilliard—a place she already knew—to St. Trewery, where she didn't know a single person beside me, I knew the thought of it scared her.

Eventually, Brooke blew out a heavy breath at the same time as her head nodded ever so faintly. "Do you think St. Trewery would accept me?"

"Definitely." St. Trewery would be stupid not to take her. Besides, the second they read her last name, she would be granted some sort of extra-acceptance shit. I knew the only reason I got accepted was because of my last name, not because I had good grades.

The St. Trewery hockey team had been doing pretty bad, so naturally, the college accepted anyone *great* who could potentially help out with that problem. They probably read *Carter* and were like; "Oh, Reece Carter, that's the kid who lives in the shadows of his NHL superstar older brother." Or maybe not, who even knew?

Brooke slid a hand down her face. "Okay, let's say I transfer to St. Trewery, then what? I have a little more free time and less obnoxious professors. That doesn't change the fact that your agent thinks I'm keeping you from going pro and that Erik will quit being my partner."

"I'll fire Pike."

"You can't," she snapped back at me. "He may be a prick, but last year alone, Pike got ten NYU college graduates into the NHL, most of them into their dream teams. By the time you graduate, Colin will have retired, and even if he hasn't, that's not a guarantee the NHL, or more precisely, the New York Rangers would take you. You'd rather die than play for any other team, the AHL, or ECHL."

She had a point. My agent was my secure ticket into the NHL, into the NY Rangers. Sure, I could've asked Colin for help and he would've asked his management or whoever to pull some strings or even got me hooked up with *his* agent, but I wanted to do this on my own.

It was bad enough that my father used to coach the NY Rangers up until a couple of years ago. And my brother had been one of their best players pretty much since he got drafted. I wasn't even six years old when Colin went pro.

People already had expectations of me thanks to Dad. If he could coach the pros, surely he wouldn't allow his son to be bad at ice hockey, right? And ever since Colin became an NHL player, the spotlight was on me more than ever before.

Any coach I had, no matter how old I'd been, would say the same thing; "You'll make a great player one day. Like your older brother."

It was *always* me being good because of my brother. It was never *me* being good because I just was.

If I asked Colin or our Dad for help to get in, I'd never be able to prove that it wasn't my name that defined who I was.

But despite that, if going pro with no help meant losing Brooke, I'd be plastering my name all over the goddamn country and using my connections to get into the NHL.

No dream could ever be more important than my future together with the girl who'd stolen my heart from way before I could form coherent sentences.

I took a deep breath, let the air linger in my lungs for as long as it took me to come up with my next words. Carefully, but mostly afraid of her reply, I asked, "Do you truly want to break up, Brooklyn?"

Brooke's eyes widened instantly while filling with tears, lips parting slightly. She sucked in a sharp breath at my question. "No." Her voice was small, filled with sadness.

I held my hand out for hers which she hesitated to take. "Then let's not."

"But—"

"We'll just have to keep it lowkey for the next two years. You'll have time to find a better partner or somehow make Erik understand that you're allowed to have a boyfriend while still being a figure skater. And Pike won't quit on me for being 'too distracted.'"

It might not even be two years. If I enter the draft this year and get drafted early, I'd rather quit college and play hockey than attend stupid lectures about stuff that didn't interest me. Colin thought that was stupid and irresponsible of me, but I didn't need a degree.

Besides, if I somehow ended up getting kicked out of the NHL and had to take an everyday job, I could always become a coach like Dad.

Chapter Three

Reece

"You look like shit," Fynn commented as I walked into the locker room.

Fynn had been a great friend to me since college started. For a while, I considered him my best friend on the entire team, but Ming took the spot shortly after as Fynn appeared a bit different sometimes. He was a good friend, though, at least I thought so.

"It's seven in the morning." I dropped my heavy bag on the ground in front of my cubby, then took a seat to take a breath.

"Dude, practice didn't even start yet. How are you already exhausted?" Ming chimed in, laughing. He sat down beside me and nudged me in the ribs with his elbow. "Had a long night, huh?"

"You could say that." It was long, but not for the reasons he had in mind.

I barely closed my eyes as my thoughts were running wild with possible solutions of how Brooke and I could fix our relationship.

If my brother taught me one thing in life, it was to fucking fight for her, no matter what. I couldn't disappoint him by giving up on Brooke and me, and I didn't want to disappoint myself by doing it, either. But most importantly, I sure as fuck wasn't going to disappoint Brooke by not fighting for us.

I just had to figure out how we were going to do this.

I was supposed to spend the night at her place like I did every year for her birthday, and I didn't do that. Perhaps that was also a reason why I just couldn't sleep last night.

Colin already thought that was strange, and he asked like a million questions, neither of which I replied to. He looked so defeated when I wouldn't talk to him, and I was sure he had assumptions as to why I was so closed off. So, I'd have to work extra hard to convince him that Brooke and I were fine.

We were, in theory… well, almost. Kind of. To an extent.

I called Brooke's dad last night and told him we sorta broke up because I knew Brooke would've wanted him to know. Miles didn't say much, but I could tell he wasn't very pleased with it. So I suppose he told Colin by now. Or maybe he kept it to himself because he knew the breakup was temporary.

Brooke agreed to give it another try. We'd have to pretend we weren't together for the next two years so Brooke's professors and Erik would leave her alone. Also so that my agent would be pleased and actually help me get into the NHL.

The only people who'd see how much she meant to me were her and our families.

I knew we weren't over, I could feel it, but fuck, it felt like it anyway.

Hiding her? I'd never done that before. I never *dreamt* of doing that.

Acting like she meant nothing to me was a nightmare, and even though it was my suggestion, I wasn't sure how it was going to affect our relationship.

How could I watch her go out with her Juilliard friends and forcefully flirt with other guys, while I had to stand on the sidelines and couldn't fuck up the guys' faces?

How could I not run right into her arms after my games?

How was I supposed to *not* attend her ballet recitals, figure skating training, or competitions? How was I supposed to not kiss her in front of everyone? Congratulate her on her wins, or console her for her losses?

I'd have to wait until we were back home to show my girlfriend any form of affection. That couldn't have possibly been good for our relationship.

But… it was the only way I could keep her. At least until I found another solution.

"How could anyone possibly be this cranky after fucking their girlfriend all night long?" Fynn suddenly took a seat on the other side of me, slapping my knee.

I sighed.

"Right?" Ming sounded as cheerful as ever.

"Man, I'd probably be in a coma, but it'd be so worth it. And this guy here—" Fynn slapped my knee once more. "—he's all groggy."

Did neither of them realize that I wasn't *exhausted* but moments away from losing my goddamn mind?

My eyes stung with tears and I rarely cried. My heart was racing as if I was currently running a whole ass marathon. If they looked closely, they were probably able to see my hands shaking as well.

"You know, I've always been wondering; does it ever get boring?" Fynn asked, sounding as cheerful as never before. It was almost as odd as his question. "Like, haven't you been fucking the same girl since you were like… thirteen? That's six years man. I'd be bored out of my mind."

"Seven," I muttered. "It's seven years." Actually, it had

only been five years, but only because Brooke and I hadn't been intimate until we were fifteen, not that it mattered.

"You're nineteen," Fynn scoffed.

"I turn twenty next month, Sherlock. That's seven years." I stood up, ready to change, but my two idiotic friends scootched closer together and blocked my cubby entirely. Knowing they wouldn't let it go, I sighed again. "No, it's not getting boring. Now, could I please get changed before Coach kills me? I'm already late."

Ming moved out of the way immediately, Fynn didn't.

"So if it's not getting boring, why the long face?" Fynn asked.

"Who said this was about sex in the first place?" I reached for my bag and dropped it on the bench. "And honestly, even if it was, you two would be the last I'd ever discuss my sex life with."

"But we're your best friends?" Fynn said with an offended undertone in his voice. He'd been even more offended if he knew I did not consider him my best friend anymore.

"Yeah, two very sad virgins who'd tell me shit like 'be happy you're getting laid.'" As much as I'd hate myself for it, I'd even rather ask my brother for advice about that than these idiots. But I'd have to be more than frustrated to go to Colin for *that* topic.

Brooke would've killed me if I ever spoke to my brother about our sex life. And I was pretty sure Colin would've killed me as well because he didn't want to hear about that.

"Exactly. Like what's there to complain about?" Fynn was suddenly on the other side of the room, rummaging in his bag. "Your girlfriend is hot. If I had the chance to fuck someone like her, I wouldn't give a fuck how bad the sex is. Actually, if you don't want Brooke, I'll take her."

I was just about to pull my shirt over my head but stopped halfway up my torso at his words. My eyes snapped to his, every ounce of anger that I'd been trying to suppress these past days was boiling up.

"Say that again, Fynn. I dare you."

"Woah. You know I was just joking." He held his hands up, laughing.

My shirt dropped down again, and in the blink of an eye, I had my hockey bag swung over my shoulder and I made my way over to the exit doors. "Jokes are supposed to be fucking funny."

I stormed out the door, past the ice, ignoring Coach calling out my name.

I could handle my friends taunting me about my relationship, making fun of how stupidly in love I was with Brooke. All of those jokes weren't harmful, they were *jokes* and I knew that.

What I couldn't handle was my supposed friend talking about my girlfriend as if he'd *ever* have a chance with her. And the fact that he thought saying that nonsense aloud was a good idea showed me how much of a great friend he was.

Why was Fynn thinking about Brooke in that sense in the first place?

Chapter Four

Reece

Juilliard was bigger than I remembered. I'd picked Brooke up or dropped her off for her classes a few times before, so I'd seen the place multiple times. Still, I had this image of a small building with like ten rooms in mind.

Everyone made Juilliard sound like this magical place, put it on a pedestal, and made it out to be the *hardest* possible college to get into.

I knew it was difficult to get accepted, that they were very picky about their students and had high expectations of them, so that probably fed into the false image of the school in my head.

In reality, it was a pretty awesome, huge-looking building. A definite upgrade from St. Trewery, though that school wasn't much worse.

Walking up to the building, I slipped inside with a couple of other students. There was no way they all knew each other, but I tried my luck anyway.

"Can I ask you something?" I asked one of the girls who just entered the building with me.

The brunette girl looked at me, eyebrows raised in an arrogant manner. "Make it quick."

"Ignore her," another girl with a heavy Irish accent said as she took my hand and pulled me away. "That's Valery. She's kind of a bitch."

"I see." I pulled my hand away, not wanting to be touched by a random girl.

"I'm Rina." The redhead smiled at me brightly. "Whatever question you have, feel free to ask me instead."

My eyes wandered down Rina's body, taking note of her jeans overall that were covered in paint. She even had paint in her hair, on her hands, and a few splatters on her face.

Could've been a wild guess, but she was probably not here for ballet. But whatever, she could still show me to the classrooms, right?

"Do you know Brooke?" I asked.

Rina furrowed her eyebrows. "I know lots of Brooke's. Well, okay, I only know three, but either way, you've got to be more specific, pretty face."

"Brooklyn Desrosiers-King," I answered, refraining from rolling my eyes. "Little blonde girl with a temper. She's a ballet dancer, and she should be in class right now, I just don't know where."

Rina laughed, though I didn't know why. "Do you even go to school here?"

"No."

"Then what are you doing here?"

"Looking for my girlfriend."

"Ah." She nodded, her grin widening. "You must be Reece, then. Brooke talks a lot about you."

"She does?" I mean, I knew Brooke wasn't hiding me, and it was pretty difficult to do when we hung around each other daily, so it shouldn't have surprised me. However, ever since we'd been going to different schools, I barely knew anyone who was in her life anymore. I was going to meet her friends for the first time later at her birthday party.

"All the time." Rina nodded for me to follow her, so I did. "It's so nice to finally meet you. I used to think she was making you up because Brooke refused to show us a picture of you, and I didn't want to believe someone could be as perfect as she's been making you sound."

"I'm not perfect." Which was quite obvious, seeing as our relationship was slowly making its way down the drain.

I'd only come here because I needed to talk to Brooke. For some stupid reason, my friends' comments affected me more than I wanted to admit. Neither of them knew what it was like to be genuinely in love with someone and how that affected everything you did. I shouldn't have listened to them.

I shouldn't have let their comment about *my* sex life shoot me down a black hole, spiraling about whether Brooke was feeling the way Ming and Fynn believed they would. Brooke and I had been together for almost seven years. We'd been friends for almost our entire lives. So I knew if something bothered her, she would've told me.

Still, I couldn't help feeling like a piece of shit about the whole situation.

I was seconds away from pulling out my phone and giving my brother a call just to beg him to tell me how to stop those awful thoughts I was having. Colin would've been honest with me. I was sure about that. However, speaking to him about this was the last thing I wanted to do.

He gave me the talk at fourteen when I already knew most of the things I needed to know, and that was bad enough. For my own sake, I couldn't have added another awkward conversation.

Before we rounded a corner, Rina stopped in her tracks

and looked at me with guilt etched in her features. "I lied," she said.

"About what?" If she lied about knowing Brooke, I was going to lose my mind.

"I knew you were Brooke's boyfriend from the very first second."

My head lifted and fell slowly in a nod. "Okay?"

"She posts a lot of pictures with you in them online, you know? It's difficult not to know who you are."

"Yes, I know. I follow my *girlfriend* on her accounts." It'd be strange if I didn't.

Her smile returned. "Great. I just wanted to be honest."

Truthfully, I hadn't even thought about that until she just mentioned it. It didn't matter, anyway. All I cared about was getting to Brooke.

Rina led me down a long hall and some of the classrooms we were passing by played music so loud that I was surprised the other professors weren't complaining about the noise.

Suddenly, I remembered that Juilliard was supposed to be a performing arts school, so why the fuck was this girl covered in paint? Did they have art classes here?

"It's fairly early, so Brooke should be in either ballet or modern. Unless she's on a break, that is," she told me. "I don't know her exact schedule because I'm here for music, not dance, but I've picked up on a couple of things."

We stopped in front of a door, and Rina told me to step aside before she quietly opened the door and peeked inside. A moment later, she pulled back and closed the door. "Yup, like I assumed. She's in ballet."

"How do I get her out of there?"

"Our professors don't like interruptions, but it's not like they're going to stop Brooke from just walking out of class.

Free will and all. I could go in there and ask if she could come out, but it's going to cost you."

I sighed. "What do you want?"

"Actually, I'll do it for free because I smell drama, and I'm eager to hear Brooke complain about you for once." That said, Rina opened the door again and headed inside.

The classical music I heard a minute earlier stopped, exchanged by a voice that sounded almost mad. Man, was I glad I didn't walk in there.

Another couple of minutes passed until the door opened again, and Rina came back outside, followed by Brooke.

Brooke had her bag swung over her shoulder, and when her eyes laid on me, I suddenly wished I never showed up here. She'd never looked at me with this much anger in her eyes before. Sure, she'd been mad at me before, but this was like she was about to burst into flames.

"Could we talk somewhere private?" I asked.

"Uh-huh." Brooke grasped my wrist, holding me tighter than ever before. I could swear my wrist was about to snap off as she led me down the hall.

Every door that stood remotely open, Brooke peeked inside until she found one empty room. She pushed me inside the room, closing the door behind her as she followed.

"What the fuck, Reece!" she snapped. Brooke dropped her bag and then took a few steps away from me to bring some distance between us. "You know they're already giving me a hard time, despite the year having barely begun, yet you're pulling me out of class?!"

"I'm sorry..." She never used to care when I pulled her out of class in high school, but I supposed college was different.

"You're sorry?" She laughed. "Do you know what you just did? I should be in class until shortly after twelve, it's not even eleven yet. How am I supposed to prove to my teacher that you're not a distraction when you're quite literally making me miss class?"

"You could've told Rina you weren't going to come outside."

Brooke shook her head, taking a deep breath as she turned around and walked toward the windows. "I was kicked out because she interrupted."

"I'm sorry."

"But even if Ms. Dubois hadn't kicked me out, I still would've left and you know it." She pulled on her hair tie, letting her hair down. "When Rina told me you were outside, asking to speak to me, do you know what went through my head?"

"No." I wanted to walk up to her, but I wasn't sure if she wanted me to, so I remained in one spot.

Brooke turned around, tears pooling in her beautiful green eyes. "I thought something *really* horrible must've happened, like... I don't know. You were going to tell me my dad died or something. You never showed up here before, and if you had, it was only to pick me up. You're supposed to be at school yourself. The only reason for your presence here could be that you have awful news to share with me."

Screw standing in one spot. With long strides, I made my way over to my girlfriend and cupped her face with my hands, forcing her to look at me. "All I wanted was to see you."

"So look at a picture of me!"

"I should've waited, okay? I know that now, and it won't happen again. But I just... Brooke, I just really needed to see and talk to you."

A heavy breath drew from her lungs as she relaxed into my touch; the anger in her eyes slowly draining. Her hands covered my own, but she didn't remove them. "What happened?"

"Why do you think something happened?"

She leaned into me, sneaking her arms around my torso as she rested her head against my chest. "Because you never skip hockey unless you have a great reason to do it."

"Something so ridiculous, it honestly shouldn't even have bothered me enough to get you in trouble for it." I wrapped my own arms around her body, holding her close without having plans of letting her go again.

"Tell me." Brooke sounded much more like herself now, her voice no longer radiating anger.

"Fynn said he wanted to fuck you. Well, he said he'd take you if I didn't want you, which is basically the same thing."

"That's gross." Her fingers clutched around the material of my shirt. "Reece, you know I'd never sleep with anyone but you, right?"

"Yeah." The word left me in a whisper. I really tried to fight the question that was lingering in my head, but after a minute of silence, I couldn't do it anymore. "You'd tell me if you were getting tired of it, right?"

Brooke pulled away from our hug, eyebrows drawing into yet another frown as she looked up at me. "Tired of you?"

"No. Sex with me."

Slowly, her lips pulled up into a smile. "You know, it's adorable when you're worried about things that you should know would never be true."

"What's that supposed to mean?"

"It means, why would I get bored? Why are you worried about me getting bored of something that *nobody* would ever be able to do better for me? We've had so many years to learn what we like and what we don't. Just because something isn't as adventurous as it was in the beginning doesn't mean it's bad or boring," she said. "Think about all these couples out there that have been together for decades. They're doing just fine with having that *one* person for the rest of their lives."

Brooke reached for my face, enveloping it with her hands. "Do you remember our first time together?"

"I try not to," I admitted, earning myself a chuckle in return. Oh, how I missed hearing her laugh.

"Exactly," she laughed. "It was awful and—"

"Hey," I interrupted, pretending to be offended. "I tried, okay?" Though thinking back to it, I wasn't sure what I was trying. Nothing good, that was for sure.

Brooke hit her forehead against my collarbone, shoulders shaking in a silent giggle. "I'm just saying that we went from truly awful and mortifying to something magical, Reece. That's not boring." She pulled away from me again, narrowing her eyes as a slight smirk pulled on the corners of her lips. "But if you do want something exciting… this room should be free for at least another twenty minutes."

"Oh."

Chapter Five

Brooklyn

Reece lifted me up and sat me down on the piano, not giving me a chance to breathe before his lips slammed down on mine. My arms swung around his neck as I deepened the kiss, only for a whimper to leave me when he slipped his tongue into my mouth.

He was such a good kisser. My knees would've given in hadn't I already been seated. His fingers dipped into my hips like they always did before one trailed over my body and snuck between my thighs. He grunted into my mouth when I sucked his bottom lip between my teeth.

"Anyone could walk in," he reminded me when his fingers traced along the seams of my bodysuit underneath my skirt, toying with the buttons before ripping them apart to bare me to him.

"I don't care."

"Don't you usually wear underwear underneath those things?" he asked as his fingers slipped through my wet lips.

I nodded, kind of anyway. "There's no underwear in ballet, especially if we're wearing leotards," I said. Since I wasn't wearing a leotard, I added, "Besides, I was busy crying this morning."

Reece planted another hungry kiss on my lips, removing his hand from me. "Me too, yet I'm wearing underwear."

"Reece," I groaned with frustration. "Don't play with me."

He smirked as he sat down in front of the piano, spreading my legs. "But I like playing with you."

A surge of excitement rippled through my body, causing my skin to prickle with goosebumps.

I leaned back and rested my weight on the sleek, black piano as he settled between my legs. Our eyes met as Reece waited for my final approval. When I nodded softly, his thumb began to trace slow, tantalizing circles over my exposed clit.

"Reece," I whimpered, trying to close my legs, but he instantly pushed them open again.

Every inch of my skin was on fire, craving more of his touch.

"You've got to keep them spread, *mi princesa*." His lips lay on the inside of my thigh, trailing kisses farther up my body. His teeth grazed my skin, nibbling gently. "Unless you don't want my mouth on you after all."

I loved his mouth on me.

"Please," I begged, but before he could make another snarky comment, I reached a hand into his hair and pushed his head slightly forward, letting him know exactly how much I wanted his mouth on me.

Reece let out a low chuckle as he dragged his fingers through my slick slit. The warmth of his touch spread through me like wildfire, igniting every nerve ending in my body.

His touch caused a shiver to run down my spine as he slowly slipped one finger inside of me. "Ah, shit," he muttered under his breath. "You're so wet for me, baby."

My body instinctively responded to him, my hips involuntarily shifting toward him as if drawn in by a magnetic force.

Without hesitation, Reece pulled his finger out and plunged two back inside. My lips parted, releasing a silent moan that I quickly covered with my hand to ensure no sounds would make it out.

If there was one thing I couldn't afford, it was getting caught having sex in a classroom.

Then again, I really didn't give a fuck.

Every stroke of his fingers evoked flames that sparked in my stomach. And when he lowered his face and brushed the tip of his nose against my clit before his tongue darted out and licked me, every inch of me felt as if it was on fire.

My cheeks were burning, my skin ablaze. It took everything in me not to come this instant, which Reece knew.

I was fortunate, yet unfortunate enough to come quickly the first time, then take forever to have a second orgasm, a third was almost impossible. But Reece always found a way to work around that little problem, even if that meant torturing me in the run.

And I knew he loved teasing me, trying to see how long he could drag out my first orgasm.

It was practical for a situation like this, where we had to hurry up, but impractical at other times. Like this. When we needed to hurry the fuck up yet Reece still refused to give me less than two orgasms.

His mouth vibrated against my pussy as he altered between wet slides of his tongue, sucking, and carefully grazing his teeth along my clit.

The tips of his fingers dipped into the skin of my hips as he held me down, restraining my movements. His other hand was busy thrusting two of his fingers in and out of me at a steady rhythm that made me whimper.

His name fell from my lips, muffled by the force of my own arm covering my mouth.

He pulled his fingers out of me, replacing them with his tongue.

"Fuck," I cried out, falling back on the piano as I lost strength in my arm. My back arched as he licked his way up to my clit again, sucking hard. "Reece, I-I…" I moaned out loud, feeling my legs starting to shake. "I can't."

"Yes, you can."

My skin was prickling, eyes closing as the knot in my stomach tightened with every swipe of Reece's tongue.

His hand moved up my body, cupping one of my breasts over my clothes, squeezing.

When he pushed his fingers inside of me again, moving faster than before, and brushing his tongue over my clit over and over again, my body went limp.

Something blissful spread through my body, veins igniting with a thousand fireworks as my orgasm rippled through me.

"Reece," I cried out, my hands pushing into his hair and pulling at the strands.

He didn't give me the chance to take a breath or calm down from the high before he pulled me up to sit. He stood up, leaning down as our mouths collided in a frenzy. His tongue pushed into my mouth, and I could taste myself on him.

"I need to be inside of you," he spoke quietly before reconnecting his lips to mine.

My heart was racing, nerves squeezing my throat and robbing me of the ability to talk.

It wasn't the first time we'd done something reckless like this and toyed with the chance of getting caught. But something about being on campus—in a classroom where anyone could just show up—was far more nerve-wracking than a high school locker room where we knew nobody was going to come walking in because everyone was supposed to be in class.

I wrapped my arms around my boyfriend's neck, kissing him one more time before I said, "Have me."

"I don't have a condom." He looked almost in pain when he said this; eyes filling with regret and something torturing. As if he wasn't fully aware that it didn't matter.

It wouldn't have been the first time we didn't use a condom, and I'd been getting the shot for years, which he knew. Plus, I wasn't due for a renewal for another two months, so we were good.

"Just fuck me already, Carter."

Reece shook his head at me, chuckling. "Just…" He grasped my face with one hand, swiping the pad of his thumb over my bottom lip. "One second."

His blue eyes lingered on mine, lips tugging up into a tender smile.

"You're so beautiful," he said, his voice soft.

"Thanks." I giggled. "But Reece, you have the rest of our lives to tell me I'm beautiful, now's not the time. You want to fuck me, I want you to fuck me… so fuck me, bro."

His eyebrows dipped. "Jesus. You're acting like we haven't had sex in months, *bro*."

"Don't bro me. I'm your girlfriend."

"You—" He took a deep breath, but since I knew he was only going to say something stupid next, I pulled him closer and pressed my lips on his instead.

Chapter Six

Reece

I fumbled with the zipper on my pants, heart racing as Brooke's fingers expertly pushed them down along with my underwear, freeing my throbbing erection.

Her delicate fingers wrapped around my cock, giving me a few long, torturous strokes. She wanted to kill me, at least the grin on her lips and the way she was stroking me were clear indications of that.

Each stroke left my balls aching for more, somehow making me even harder, and sending shivers down my spine. If there was one person who could've made me drop down to my knees in an instant, it would've been Brooke. Right at this moment, I was ready to beg my own girlfriend to put me out of my misery, ready to shove my cock into her mouth and watch her as she sucked me.

Unfortunately, we didn't have the time for that, but that was alright since I had other plans.

As I pulled her hand away from my cock, replacing it with my own, Brooke wrapped her arms around my neck. She shifted her hips as the tip of my cock slid between her wet lips, desperate to feel me inside, and I happily obliged.

"Do me a favor, baby," I whispered into her ear. "Try to be as quiet as possible."

"I'll try," Brooke promised, desire burning in her almost emerald-looking eyes as our gazes met briefly.

I glanced at the door for just a second, making sure it was still closed when I thrust inside her, slow at first. My hands roamed over her body, gliding from her shoulder blades down her spine until my hands were perfectly situated on her ass.

A moan slipped from her parted lips as I stretched her, filling her to the hilt. As she realized the volume of her sounds, Brooke pressed her face into the front of my shoulder, hoping it would mute her.

My fingers dug into her skin, squeezing her ass as I thrust at a moderate pace, enjoying the way she clenched around my cock.

Being buried deep inside my girlfriend was one of my favorite places, aside from simply being in her company. I'd never tire of it, that I was sure of.

"Reece," Brooke gasped before her tongue slid into my mouth as we kissed, her hands firmly tangled in my hair.

"Shh." Her legs wrapped tighter around my hips at the sound of my voice. "You've got to keep quiet, *mi princesa*."

Brooke looked right into my eyes when a soft whimper fell from her lips, her hips jerking to meet each of my thrusts.

I could've died right on the spot at the sight of her lust-filled gaze and her parted lips. She was the most beautiful person ever to walk this earth, that I was convinced of.

Her nails scratched down my back, along my sides before her hands slid underneath my shirt to get a feel of my abs. She loved to touch my abs, God knew why.

I left kisses from her jaw down her neck as I moved one of my hands up her body, cupping one of her breasts over her bodysuit.

Her breath hitched at the sudden change in sensation, her nails digging even deeper into my back. My other hand found its way between our bodies, teasing her clit.

She gasped, her mouth falling open as my hand caressed her breast. Her nipple hardened under my touch, and I could feel the electricity coursing through her body.

Brooke's hands clawed my back, desperate for more contact, but I had to pull away and stop moving, letting her breathe for a moment.

She needed that tension, needed me to build that anticipation. Otherwise, I was going to come in a while, and she could kiss that second orgasm goodbye.

With a slowed pace, I nuzzled my face into her neck, feeling her heart racing against my own.

"Please," she begged, impatient as always. "*Pleasepleaseplease.*"

Chuckling, I placed a soft kiss on her lips before bringing my mouth to her ear. "Are you ready for it, baby?"

My fingers continued to tease her clit, applying just enough pressure to send shivers down her spine.

"Yes." Brooke was panting, her hips bucking against me. "Please, Reece."

Taking a deep breath, I began to thrust into her again, picking up my pace.

My hand between her legs worked a bit faster, teasing her clit.

Her moans filled the room, getting so much louder with each thrust that I had to press my lips to hers to keep them a little more muted.

The last thing I wanted was for any Juilliard student to hear her and then see us walking out of this room. Or even worse, one of Brooke's professors.

"Reece," she moaned again, her hips rocking in rhythm with my thrusts. I could tell she was slowly getting closer.

"I got you, *mi princesa*," I whispered, my voice barely louder than her own heavy breathing. "I'll make sure you get what you want."

I picked up the pace, thrusting into her harder and faster. The sound of our bodies slapping together filled the music room, mingling with the wet, slurping noises as my fingers continued to work her clit.

It was a music room… surely they had some sort of sound absorption panels in here to keep the noises of their piano, violins, and whatever other instruments they played inside this room down.

There was a chance I would regret this later, but right now, I couldn't have cared less if Brooke made any sounds.

I released her mouth, moving my own to her neck instead, driving into her over and over again as I sucked on her skin, making her moan and writhe.

My breaths came out ragged, matching Brooke's rapid heartbeat.

Every day I had to share some part of her with someone else: her words when she spoke, her laughter, even the way she cared. But her rapid heartbeats, her moans, and her kisses were mine and mine alone, and I was determined to make her feel exactly who she belonged to.

I looked at Brooke, my gaze lost in the lustful depths of her eyes for just a moment before I leaned back down and began to trace the delicate curve of her collarbone, leaving soft kisses behind and then sucking on her skin. I wanted to see some marks by the time we were done here.

Brooke let out a shivering breath, her fingers pushing into my hair once more, clutching as if she were holding on for dear life.

"I… love you," she whispered, tightening her hands in my hair when I resumed my thrusts. Each stroke elicited cries from her lips.

"I love you more."

She tried to shake her head, I could feel it, but instead, she moaned out loud. "Harder, please," she begged.

"We're going to break the damn piano, baby," I replied, yet obliged, slamming my body against hers with a primal force.

"I don't care."

Her body tensed, her hands gripping my shoulders, her nails digging deep as her legs began to shake, her walls clenching around my cock in a vice-like grip.

"Oh, God, Reece!" she gasped, her voice barely audible over her moans. "I'm going to come!"

I felt her body shake with each wave of pleasure as it washed over her, her breathing erratic.

Brooke's whimpers mixed with my own groans when my body tensed and trembled with release as well, my muscles contracting as a burst of pleasure rippled through me. As I slammed into her, every nerve ending seemed to light up in sparks, making every thrust feel ten times more intense.

"Fuck," I groaned as I came inside her, my cock pulsing with each spurt of cum.

Brooke fell back on the piano, panting and trying to catch her breath. At the sight of her heavily rising and falling chest, I felt a surge of satisfaction, the warmth of her body still pulsating around my lingering erection.

Unfortunately, I couldn't enjoy the moment much longer as laughter in the hallway outside of the classroom brought us back to reality.

I quickly pulled out, trying to avoid any embarrassing

mess on her skirt or the piano, then tugged my dick back into my underwear and pulled up my pants, zipping them up.

With a sheepish grin, I whispered, "We have to get the hell out of here before someone catches us."

Brooke nodded, sitting up before sliding off the piano with my help. I helped her button up her bodysuit before she flattened out her skirt and double-checked that her bodysuit was in all the places it was supposed to be.

Her face scrunched up in disgust when my eyes laid on hers, and I could barely contain my laughter.

"Please tell me you brought your own car to get here," she spoke, walking away to get her bag while I checked the piano for any stains that we might've left. "God, this is so disgusting."

"Of course I brought my own car," I chuckled. "Colin would kill me if his precious car was missing in the driveway."

"Good, so it doesn't matter if your cum ruins your seats."

I shook my head at my girlfriend. "Oh, you're so sitting on a towel."

Pulling out a tissue, I wiped over the surface of the piano, knowing it did little to really clean anything, but it felt weird just leaving it without at least trying to clean it.

After making my way over to my girlfriend, I quickly pressed a kiss to her lips, then pulled the hair tie out of her hair to redo her bun as her current one was... far from perfection.

The second I finished her bun, the door to the classroom burst open. The person standing at the door must've been a teacher of some sort, at least judging by the stern look on her face.

"Oh, God," Brooke whispered, clutching my hand in hers. When her eyes widened in horror, I knew we were fucked.

What If We Break?

The teacher, a tall, angry-looking woman with a tightly pulled-back bun and a disapproving look on her face, looked through the room with a scowl before her eyes settled on Brooke. She kind of looked like what I imagined Brooke's ballet teacher to look like.

"What are you doing in here?" the woman demanded.

"Uhm... Ma'am, we were just..." My heart was pounding inside of my chest as I tried to come up with an explanation that wouldn't get Brooke in even more trouble. But I had no clue as to what a socially acceptable excuse would've been at a place like Juilliard.

In my mind, this school was like a military school—no room for mistakes. Maybe it wasn't like that, but from what I heard from Brooke, it was.

My professors were chill. You could've told them that you were fucking a random student in their classroom and they would've shrugged and gone about their day. But this place seemed like the complete opposite of St. Trewery. In my mind anyway.

"I apologize, Ms. Dubois," Brooke chimed in. "My... cousin just needed the keys to my house. He's here for the week and nobody's home."

Ms. Dubois didn't look impressed at all.

And Brooke calling me her cousin stung in places of my heart that I didn't know I could feel.

Her *cousin*? Seriously?

"Oh, yeah?" Ms. Dubois sneered, her eyes now set on me. "So you're not that boyfriend who stops Ms. King from reaching even a slightly okay-ish performance?"

My heart broke at the same time as rage poisoned my veins.

Brooke had been saying her teacher thought I was a distraction for a while, but I never knew how badly that woman thought of my girlfriend. That wasn't healthy for Brooke, not in the slightest.

As much as I wanted to yell at Brooke's teacher, I couldn't for my girlfriend's sake. She was going to have to live with the consequences of my actions, and I couldn't do that to her.

So instead, I shook my head. "No, Ma'am. Just her cousin from Canada, wanting to get a good sleep."

She hummed, then looked back at Brooke. "You're not welcome in my class anymore. At least not for today. If giving your cousin a key is more important than class, it's a clear sign of your disinterest, Ms. King. I do not need lazy dancers in my class." That said, Ms. Dubois walked away and probably right back to her class.

Chapter Seven

Reece

I sat down next to Colin, who was putting his daughter's hair back up into a ponytail.

Lily returned home with Kieran an hour ago because the kid hated crowds almost as much as he did talking to strangers. Huge birthday parties weren't his thing, so it was a surprise he even agreed to show up at all. He usually only hung around Jamie, his cousin. He even refused to attend school if Jamie was sick. He really wasn't much of a people person.

"I think I should move out," I told Colin, who almost instantly looked at me.

"Come again."

"I'm just saying. I spend two hours driving back and forth from college five days a week, even more when the traffic sucks. That's at least two hours I'm wasting when I could do something far more productive," I said.

"I mean, I get that." Colin chuckled. "That was one of the reasons I moved out a week before I started college."

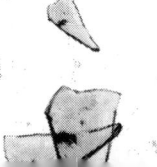

St. Trewery didn't require their freshmen to move into the dorms for their first year, so I thought staying home was a good idea. Guess it wasn't my smartest idea, but it allowed me to see Brooke more often.

Kim turned around on her father's lap, frowning up at him. "You no go to college, Daddy."

"That wasn't me?" Colin hummed as Kim shook her head. "Damn, where'd I meet your mommy, then?"

Kim shrugged. "By the hockey game with Uncle ReeRee."

It was a good theory, but I doubted it was true. I had no idea how Colin and Lily met, I just always assumed it was in class or at a game. Perhaps I knew once upon a time, but I barely had any recollection of my life before I turned five.

I couldn't even remember my brother and sister, which stung a lot more when I sat at a table with my family, and all they did was talk about them. It always made me feel left out because they all had memories of Aiden and Eira, and all I had were pictures that proved I met them before they died.

I sat sideways on the bench, then stole my niece from my brother. "Daddy's just a liar, right?"

Kim nodded with conviction. "And we no lie."

"Exactly. We don't lie in this house."

Kim was the youngest of them all, which, unfortunately, made her the kid in the family nobody played with. She only turned three back in June. The youngest before her was Ash, Grey, and Luan's son, who turned six last May.

Kieran and Kayden played with her sometimes, but they were both way older, so they never knew what to do with her. At least they tried.

"Are you stealing my daughter right now?" Colin asked, giving me his all-famous disappointed look. It didn't work on me anymore as much as it used to.

"It's not stealing when she loves me more. Right, little Kiwi?"

Kim nodded again, giggling when she fell back into my arms. "Down, Uncle ReeRee."

So much to loving me more.

I carefully set Kim down on the floor, watching her wait a whole second before she ran off to find someone to play with.

"Back to the topic of you moving out," Colin said before reaching for his water to take a sip—the pause was for dramatic purposes, I assumed. "When will that happen? Tomorrow or…?"

"Wow, Colin." My eyes rolled. "You should get an award for brother of the year."

"Right?"

I knew he was joking. He never even hinted at wanting me out of the house, and I would've understood if he did. I'd been living with him since I was thirteen, surely he wanted some more time with just his wife and kids. I was only his annoying younger brother anyway.

"It's not going to be tomorrow," I said eventually. "I still have to even look for an apartment. It was just a thought."

"Wondering what I think of the idea?" he asked to which I nodded. As much as I hated being compared to Colin and being called his shadow, I still valued his opinion. "Is Brooke moving in with you?"

Just as he mentioned her name, Brooke's laughter echoed through the air. At the sound of her voice, my eyes immediately started to look around the backyard, searching for her.

When I found her, I could feel my heart beating a bit faster than usual. Just looking at her made my heart swell with so much love for her, it was ridiculous, but I wouldn't have wanted it any other way.

"I didn't ask." I didn't have to either. She wouldn't move over to New City to be closer to *my* university and further away from her own. And the last time we talked about it, she said she wasn't ready to leave home yet.

"And what does she say about you considering moving out?"

I sighed. "I didn't tell her I was thinking about it."

Sure, I was going to talk to Brooke about it, but I didn't know how just yet. The last thing I wanted was to hurt her because we didn't see each other daily anymore. Frankly, I wasn't sure I was going to survive *not* seeing her for a whole day or more.

"What's going on between the two of you?" His voice was laced with sympathy and concern.

"Nothing."

"Don't lie, Reece."

My eyes teared away from Brooke so I could look at my brother instead. He looked almost disappointed, but I was sure he had tried his best to appear indifferent. "I'm not sure I can tell you."

"Why not?" Colin's eyebrows drew together, head cocking sideways.

"Because you'll have a million ideas and know exactly how to help, and I want to do this on my own. I spent my whole life proving to everyone that you didn't make me, and if I allow my superstar older brother to save my ass, what does that say about me?"

"That you're a *nineteen*-year-old kid who is smart enough to know when to ask for help?" he said, making it sound like that was so obvious. "Reece, I really don't know what this is about, but if you're risking your relationship to prove to whoever that you're your own person, then maybe you shouldn't be in a relationship."

"What?"

Something about what Colin said struck a nerve inside of

me. Was I really willing to jeopardize my relationship just to prove a point?

No, that couldn't have been right. That wasn't something I was doing, was it?

Sure, I refused to let Colin help me with Brooke because… well, because I didn't want everyone to think I needed his help to live my life. I didn't want people to think I was depending on my brother, even though I knew he would've been able to help.

"And honestly, I get it. I had, and still have, to deal with everyone saying I'm only good at hockey because of Dad; that I got to where I am because of him," Colin added. "That won't change unless you start not giving a fuck what they say. And putting Brooke on the line just because you feel inferior to me is the stupidest thing I've ever heard you say, and you said *a lot* of stupid things in your life."

Perhaps he was right… in a sense anyway.

Okay, maybe telling him what was going on was better after all. "Pike said my chances of getting drafted are low if I'm in a relationship. Brooke's ballet teacher thinks I'm distracting her from focusing on what's important, which Erik apparently agrees with. Only that he took it up a notch and told her that if she doesn't break up with me, he'll leave her."

Colin remained silent for what felt like an eternity, looking into the distance with no reaction whatsoever. When he did find his voice, it wasn't anything like I expected.

"Pike Anderson, right?" I nodded in response. "He's a manipulator who just wants to ruin your life, Reece. Yes, he gets a lot of guys into the NHL, but *only* if they play by his rules. The NHL doesn't care if you're dating someone or not. As long as you're good on the ice, go after other important duties, and don't let your relationship affect your job, it's none of their business. Aaron and I were both in a relationship when we got drafted. Miles was *married* when he got an offer, so it really doesn't matter. Brooke's ballet teacher can kindly fuck off, and Erik… I never liked that guy anyway."

I always wondered why the NHL would care, but I also never questioned Pike because I feared that if I did, he'd drop me.

"Me neither, but she needs him." My elbows set down on the table, my hands holding up my head so I wouldn't hit it against the wood. "And I need Pike."

"The fuck you do." I could swear he was about to slap the alleged stupidity out of me, but he kept his hands to himself. "I can give Anthony a call and—"

"No," I interrupted. Anthony was Colin's agent and I could already tell where he was going with this. "See, that's what I don't want: you meddling with my career. I know that if I just asked you or Dad, you'd hook me up with someone, but I need to do this on my own. You did it on your own. Why can't I?"

"I didn't," Colin said, now looking at me as if I was even stupider than before. "Dad pulled some strings because I wasn't going to let anyone take away my chances of playing for the Rangers. Do you really think Aaron, Miles, Grey, and I all got drafted by the same team because we got lucky or fought for it?" He laughed. "The likelihood of that happening is basically nonexistent. We had help."

Really? Now I felt stupid. "Don't you feel bad about that?"

He shook his head. "Sometimes, having connections is a good thing and it doesn't make you any less amazing on the ice for using them. Just think about it. Almost the *entire* film industry is based on connections, only a small percentage got to where they are because of hard work. The NHL isn't much different. Besides, they're already having an eye on you because you're part of the Carter family. Our family has been in the NHL for decades. You're genetically prone to be good at hockey, to make it big, of course they're going to watch you. They've been watching you since you were a kid, Reece. *Any* agent you have will get you a spot in the NHL, and the teams will fight for you. They're just waiting for you to enter the draft so they can throw contracts your way and bid you millions of dollars."

"You really think so?"

"I know so."

I raked a hand through my hair as I thought about what he said for a little while. It made sense in theory. There were tons of brothers in the NHL, some who joined way later than the first one. They had expectations either way, and if the brother who joined later played only half as good as the older one, even that was considered a win.

Chapter Eight

Brooklyn

Reece had been pacing back and forth between the bouncy house for the kids—which the adults used more than the kids—and the back porch for the past thirty minutes. I hadn't seen him stop walking even once.

Each time I saw someone approach him to talk, Reece would shut down their attempts and continue to pace around.

Something was wrong with him, and I'd been trying to ditch my friends for a hot second now so I could talk to Reece, but I also didn't want to seem rude.

Talking to Reece when he was upset—or vice-versa—would've led to us sneaking off to my bedroom to talk there and then we wouldn't return until we were no longer covered in sweat from activities other than talking. Whatever was bothering the other person was usually fixed before our clothes came off, but it always ended with us naked.

We had to work on that; I knew that, and Reece definitely knew that as well.

After another thirty minutes, I finally left my friends to speak to Reece because I was sure if I hadn't walked up to him, he would've continued to pace back and forth for another hour or two.

"Reece?" I said as I approached him. At the sound of my voice, Reece stopped and turned around, looking at me with tears glistening in his eyes.

"Brooke," he choked out, closing the few steps between us. "You should be with your friends."

My head shook as I reached for his hands, only then noticing he was holding a piece of paper. "What's that?" I asked carefully as I saw a row of numbers that looked like a phone number.

"Anthony Gillis' number," he told me, blowing out a deep breath. "Colin's agent."

"Okay?" I looked back up, watching for signs of discomfort on his face as I slowly led my boyfriend over to the patio so we could take a seat. "Why do you have Colin's agent's number?"

I hated seeing Reece in distress, his eyes glistening with unshed tears. He was always so strong and composed when there were other people around. Usually, he only showed his more negative emotions when it was just the two of us.

Seeing him upset shattered me. Every fiber of my being wanted to reach out and remove his pain and replace it with something joyful; I wanted to wipe away those unshed tears and bring a smile to his face.

"He gave it to me," Reece told me, clutching my thigh as soon as we were seated. "Did you know Colin used our dad to get into the NHL?"

I nodded softly, though I was sure he didn't notice because his eyes were on that piece of paper in his hand. "Dad mentioned it when I asked about why he quit the NHL to be a chef. I thought you knew, too."

"I didn't."

"But that can't possibly be why you've been pacing around the backyard for an hour, is it?"

A deep sigh drew from his lungs as he shook his head. "All my life I told myself that I had to work hard for my spot in the NHL, that I could never ask my dad or my brother for help because I didn't want anyone to say I'm only good because of them."

I rested my head against Reece's shoulder, rubbing soothing circles on his back.

Perhaps we should've gone inside to avoid our family seeing this whole thing, but when I looked up, I realized that nobody was paying us any attention at all. It was a good thing though.

I knew how much his independence meant to Reece, how fiercely he fought to prove to himself and everyone else that he was good and not just because of his family. I could understand that he didn't want to be just *another* Carter, but that he wanted to be *someone*. Someone who wasn't just part of a family legacy, someone who wasn't just another shadow.

"Knowing that Colin used our dad's connection to get ahead... it just makes me question everything," Reece continued, his voice heavy with emotion. "Like, would it really be so bad if I called Anthony and asked for his help rather than rely on an agent who's trying to sabotage my relationship? Would it really be so bad if I asked Dad to speak to the team managers or whoever's in charge to secure me a spot with the Rangers?"

He kept on rambling for a little while, coming up with scenarios that were so unlikely that I had to fight the urge to laugh.

Eventually, Reece stopped talking, lifted his head, and looked right at me with expectation in his eyes. It was as if he was asking me to decide whether he should use his connections or keep trying on his own.

I couldn't have possibly decided that for him.

"You're not your brother, Reece," I said softly, figuring he needed to hear this. "Colin thought it was best for *him* to get the help, and I'm sure he was still proud of getting drafted by his dream team no matter how he got there. Your last name doesn't define you or give you any talent. Even if you use your connections, without talent, not even the worst team in the NHL would want to draft you. You're an amazing player because you worked hard for it, not because you're a Carter. Whether you fight your way into the NHL or take the easy way out, it won't matter because they'd draft you for how good you are on the ice, not because your family batted their eyes at the team owner and said *pretty please*."

He sighed, his shoulders sagging as the oxygen left his lungs. "What if I don't ask for help and then fail? What if I'm not meant to make it on my own and then I fucked it up because I was too stubborn?"

I reached for his hand, intertwining our fingers. "Then not even asking for help would have gotten you a spot in the NHL. As I said, your performance on the ice and how much work you put into improving makes you a good player, not your last name. But sometimes getting help is a sign of strength, not weakness."

Reece's eyes softened as he looked at me and the downward-pulled lips slowly began to turn upward as my words finally seemed to settle. "Maybe I should call Anthony and just have a chat without signing any contracts or firing Pike."

A small smile tugged at the corners of my lips in support. "It certainly wouldn't hurt."

Reece gently lifted my chin before leaning in and placing a soft kiss on my lips. "God, I wouldn't know what I'd do without you."

Chapter Nine

Reece

Brooke stood in front of her closet, wearing nothing but her underwear while she decided what to wear to bed. Every now and then, she'd sigh heavily and look back at me.

I knew she was waiting for me to give her my shirt, but I was curious to see how long she could continue to wait until she caved and demanded it.

Besides, the view of her half-naked ass or the glimpses of her chest I got every time she turned around for a second weren't ones I was eager to get rid of.

Brooke had plenty of my shirts in her closet, mostly because I spent a lot of nights here but also because she stole a ton of them. She could've just taken one of them, but she always slept in the shirt I was currently wearing because it smelled the most like me. Never mind the fact that she was going to sleep in my arms, so it really didn't matter.

After speaking to Brooke earlier, I decided that I was going to call Anthony just to hear his thoughts, and only then I'd decide what to do next. Perhaps firing Pike was the best thing I could do. Perhaps it was going to be the worst idea. Surely Anthony could tell me, and he wouldn't lie... I hoped.

But either way, Pike wasn't going to destroy my relationship, and neither were Juilliard or Erik.

"I was thinking," I said, not getting a reaction from my girlfriend because she knew I wasn't going to offer her my shirt. "We shouldn't pretend that we broke up."

"So you're firing Pike?" She finally turned around, but covered herself up by crossing her arms in front of her chest. "What if Erik quits on me?"

"Not yet. As I told you earlier, I want to speak to Anthony Gillis first," I replied. "As for Erik… he can't quit on you during the season, can he? Wouldn't he get disqualified or something?"

"I'm not sure, actually. I mean, we're listed as a pair, and if one of us got injured, we could get another partner to carry on with the season, but dropping out is different," she said, turning back around to stare at her closet. "Then again, if there is like a *huge* conflict between the skaters, I suppose terminating the contract mid-season is better than ending the season with a dead body."

Not sure where that came from, but I guess she was right?

"On the off chance that I could walk up to my coach tomorrow, tell him that I refuse to skate with Erik, and it would be fine, what do I do then? I'd be partnerless and can't compete this season."

"Then you're going to have to stand your ground," I said, crossing my arms over my chest. "Because I never hid you from anyone before, and I'm sure as fuck not going to start doing it now."

For Brooke, I could handle Pike even if I didn't fire him. And even if Colin would turn out to be wrong and I wasn't going to get drafted, I would be okay. If I didn't have hockey in my life, I'd be okay. But I wouldn't be okay if I lost Brooke, and I was ashamed that it took Colin telling me I shouldn't be with Brooke if she wasn't my priority to even realize it.

We'd get through whatever rough patch we were facing. I knew that. If Brooke wasn't going to deal with Erik, I'd find a way to deal with him. And the daily fights would stop eventually. I was sure of that. We just had to find our rhythm again.

Guess getting separated for college threw both of us off, and now we had to find a way to deal with it.

We could spend as much time together as we wanted, laugh, kiss, and fuck, but that didn't mean our relationship was strong enough to sustain any more hits. So, from that day forward, I was more determined than ever to find out where the real problems in our relationship lay.

"I don't think we would've been any good at pretending to be exes anyway," Brooke spoke quietly, making me chuckle. "Honestly, we might've made it two hours as fake exes, and then we'd be found kissing in the locker room."

She wasn't wrong.

"Do you remember the first time we 'broke up'?" I asked because what she just said sounded almost exactly like it.

"You mean when we had our first real fight as a couple, and neither of us knew what to do, so it was the most logical consequence?"

"Yup." My head shook at the ridiculousness of that entire day, yet I couldn't stop smiling. "Our idea of a broken-up couple was best friends holding hands and kissing occasionally."

Brooke laughed. "Holding hands in *anger* and kissing occasionally to make up for the fact that we were both angry at each other," she corrected. "Very important details to mention."

"Right." My eyes wandered down her exposed back, and for whatever reason, my dick decided my girlfriend's back was pretty good-looking. "The most important part of the story, however, is that we broke up just to be together anyway. Until two hours later, you realized that perhaps we should just kiss like a couple again, not like exes."

There wasn't a difference in the kisses, obviously, but back then, I was convinced our kisses as a couple were a million times better.

"See, we wouldn't make it two hours pretending to be broken up," Brooke said, still refusing to look at me. "I'm really glad about that."

"Yeah, me too."

We fell into a comfortable silence, but after five minutes, Brooke finally closed her closet and walked over to me. She crawled onto her bed, taking a seat on my lap as if it was her right to sit on top of me. It probably was.

"Can I help you?" I asked, looking right into her green eyes as I pretended not to know why she was sighing so much.

"No, all good." She sighed again, and it took everything in me not to chuckle. "I'm just a bit cold, is all."

Brooke reached for my hand, smiling when her eyes fell on the little heart tattoo on the inside of my ring finger. It was the only tattoo I had, and I only got it because Brooke had the same one. They were like our own version of a promise ring.

Her dad wanted to murder me when he saw it.

"Ahhh. I think I might know a solution to that problem." I reached for the seam of my shirt, watching as her lips lifted into a smile before I wrapped my arms around her body instead, turned us around, and pushed her into the mattress.

Hovering over her, I pressed my lips to her neck, sucking

on her skin to leave faint marks. She was mine, after all, and I didn't mind reminding everyone of it.

"Reece," she gasped, arching her back and pushing her tits up.

"Getting any hotter?" I asked, slowly kissing my way down her body.

"No."

"Hmm…" I kissed my way farther down, trailing soft kisses between her breasts. "And now?"

"Slightly increasing." Brooke smiled at me as I looked up and her hands pushed into my hair, gently scratching my scalp with her nails.

Lowering my face again, I ran my tongue over one of her nipples, feeling it harden before I sucked it right into my mouth while my hand covered her other breast. It always fascinated me how perfectly they fit in my hands, like they were molded for my touch and mine alone.

Her chest rose and fell faster, her delicate fingers tugging on my hair as my cock strained against my pants.

A gasp elicited from her throat, followed by a moan so soft, I could've imagined it.

When our eyes met, her gaze was heated, and her cheeks had a slight tint to them. And when she smiled, the entire world stopped spinning.

I couldn't think of a single day I wasn't in love with this girl, and every time Brooke looked at me, I just fell deeper and deeper.

"Reece," she whispered.

"Yes, *mi princesa*?" I began to slowly trail my lips down her torso. When I reached the elastic of her underwear, I sat up and hooked my fingers into the material. "Do you want me to stop and just give you my shirt already?"

Brooke knew she was getting my shirt eventually, she always did. I'd even stop by and give it to her before she went to bed if we didn't sleep in the same house, but that rarely happened anymore.

She giggled, shaking her head. "No."

I tugged on her underwear, and she lifted her hips to make it a bit easier, then slid them down her legs. "You gotta be quiet."

"I know."

Her legs were on either side of my body, knees spread to grant me a view that was too enticing to ignore. My hand laid down on her pelvis, my thumb stroking from her opening to her clit.

"I could spend the rest of my life staring at you like this," I spoke, watching her lips as they parted and her hips shifted when I began to draw small circles with my thumb. "You're so perfect."

A whimper fell from her lips when I added a bit of pressure, and I knew I had to pull my hand away.

I loved teasing her, figuring out how far I could go, and stopping just before she'd come. I loved dragging out her first orgasm, even if she'd threaten to murder me at least five times in the meantime. And I loved that her coming quickly the first time was like a superpower in situations where we had to hurry up.

Not to forget that I got to spend a lot of time inside of her for a second orgasm, and who didn't like having his dick buried deep inside his girlfriend for as long as possible?

"Take your shirt off," Brooke demanded the moment I pulled my hand away from her body.

Without hesitation, I got off the bed and grasped the end of my shirt, slowly pulling it up my body and over my head, enjoying the way Brooke watched me intently with a mix of anticipation and lust.

Her eyes never left mine as I undressed, taking off my pants next, revealing the body she knew so well, yet still blushed every time she saw me without clothes.

Once I was down to my boxers, Brooke sat up and reached out to trace a finger along the ripples of my abs, her touch sending shivers down my spine. Our breaths mingled as she lifted her face to mine, and I leaned down to press my mouth on hers. The softness of her lips sent a surge of warmth through me as our kiss deepened.

Time seemed to slow down, the world around us fading into the background as we lost ourselves in each other.

One minute I was standing in front of the bed, kissing my girlfriend, and the next, I was sitting on the edge of the bed, Brooke on my lap.

I wrapped my arms around her, pulling her closer as if trying to merge our beings into one. The scent of her hair, the taste of her on my lips—everything about her felt like home.

I could taste the hint of cherries from the fruit bowl we'd shared earlier, and it only fueled the fire that was building between us.

As our tongues intertwined in an urgent, passionate kiss, I reached down and grasped her hips with my hands, positioning her right over my crotch.

The warmth radiating from her skin seeped through the thin fabric of my underwear, and I knew it wouldn't be long before we were both completely naked.

She rocked against my body, her pussy rubbing against my erection through my boxers. Our breaths came out in sharp pants, our eyes locked as she wrapped her arms around my neck, digging her nails into my shoulders.

I knew what she wanted, and there was no denying I didn't want the same thing.

"Reece," Brooke said softly, breathing heavily.

God, how I loved hearing her say my name.

It was dangerous, though, because I was sure if Brooke asked me to do the most out-of-pocket, illegal thing she could think of and added my name, I wouldn't hesitate to do it. It was so ridiculous.

I laid Brooke down on her bed, and I crawled right on top of her. Keeping my eyes locked with hers, I reached my right arm over to her nightstand.

The moment she heard the drawer opening, her lips parted in a silent gasp, eyes wide in horror and excitement.

"What are you doing?" she asked, but I knew she was well aware of what I was about to do. It wouldn't have been the first time we incorporated that little toy of hers.

I began to kiss my way down her perfect body once more —starting at her lips, down her neck and collarbones, sucking her nipples into my mouth before kissing a trail down between her breasts and her stomach.

Settling between her thighs, I nudged her legs a little further apart.

I groaned as if I was in pain when the most perfect pussy on planet Earth came into view, all smooth, pink, and wet. I couldn't wait to taste her, eat her pussy like a starved man as if it was the last time I'd get to do it.

Of course I knew it wasn't. Brooke was my forever, and I'd get plenty of chances to make her come on my tongue, but she deserved nothing but the best performance.

"Look at how pretty you are, baby," I said, lust in my voice, and she flushed.

My eyes snapped to her tits because I knew that she

flushed everywhere when she got turned on, and it must've been in the top ten of my favorite things about Brooke.

The pink flush on her perfect, perky breasts was almost enough to make me drop dead right on the spot.

I reached a hand to her breasts, squeezing one after the other, pinching her nipples to feel them harden a little more before sliding my hand down her stomach.

I dragged my thumb over her lips, spreading some of her wetness onto her clit. I couldn't wait to taste her, to feel her squirm from my touch.

Turning on Brooke's vibrator, I touched it to the skin below her navel just to annoy her a little, slowly dragging it down.

"If you come before I allow you to," I began, making sure Brooke looked right into my eyes as I spoke. "I won't let you come a second time."

That was going to be quite the challenge for her.

"Reece," she tried to argue but was cut off when I slid the tip of her vibrator through her damp lips. "*Oh!*"

"Keep quiet," I said, my voice carrying a warning tone.

Since I knew we didn't have lube here, I was going to get Brooke just a little bit wetter before I could insert her vibrator, but that was no problem at all.

Her back arched, and her hips came off the bed as she sucked in a ragged breath when I moved the vibrator to her clit while pushing one of my fingers into her wet cunt. After thrusting my finger in and out of her a couple of times, I added a second one.

The wet sounds of her arousal filled the room, mixed with the buzzing of the vibrator, and her cries of pleasure that she was trying to keep under control but failed miserably, as always.

Brooke reached up, grabbing a hold of her headboard, and

shifting her hips so much, I had to turn off the vibrator to keep them in place.

"I can't do it," she cried, panting. "I *need* to come."

"Not yet," I replied, a sheepish grin playing on my lips but she was too busy staring at the ceiling and distracting herself to see it.

"You're going to kill me, Reece!" A gasp fell from her lips as I pulled my fingers out of her, deciding that she was ready for her favorite toy.

"I'll make up for it," I promised, slowly guiding the vibrator into my girlfriend's drenched cunt. It slipped inside with ease, her muscles clenching around it as if it were my cock. And God, how I wished it was my cock already, but that wasn't going to happen until she came at least once.

"Look at me," I said, and she immediately tilted her chin to meet my gaze. Her mesmerizing green eyes were clouded with lust, and the rosy blush spread across her cheeks slightly deepened in color. "Once I turn this back on, you're not allowed to make a sound or come until I tell you to, alright?"

She nodded, but it didn't look like she really heard me. Right now, I was sure I could've said I would sell our firstborn, and she would've nodded.

"Tell me you understood, *mi princesa*."

"No sounds and—" She gasped when I pushed the vibrator in a little deeper.

"And?"

"I... I can't come until you say so."

"That's right." I switched on the vibrator, increasing the speed from what it was before, watching as Brooke's eyes fluttered shut.

Her body trembled from the intense sensation, and her head instantly fell back into the pillow. Her fingers turned white from the pressure she was inflicting on the headboard, but that wasn't going to change for a little while.

A few, quiet whimpers made it past her lips, but I chose to ignore them, especially when I finally dipped my head down and sealed my lips over her clit. I sucked it into my mouth before circling it with my tongue, and to my surprise, she only attempted to moan *once*.

Brooke was usually really bad at keeping up with any challenges I threw her way during sex.

The vibrator hummed rather quietly, her hips recklessly shifting as if she was trying to escape her building orgasm.

When another moan left her mouth, I pulled the vibrator out of her as a punishment.

"No, wait, *please*," she begged, her tone frantic. "Please, don't stop."

I smirked at her plea.

The veins in her neck stood out as she tried to maintain control, but her body betrayed her, twitching and quivering. I knew Brooke was close, but I really wanted to see how far I could push her until she broke.

"You want it so badly, don't you?" I whispered, my voice dripping with sarcasm. "You want to come for me, don't you, baby?"

Brooke nodded, her eyes wide and desperate.

I leaned down, teasing her pussy with my breath, and Brooke shivered in response. I ran my tongue from her entrance up to her clit, stopping before I took it into my mouth.

Her breath hitched, a soft moan filling my ears with sounds.

"Please," she begged again, her voice breaking with need.

I smiled wickedly, loving the power I held over her at that moment.

With a flick of my tongue, I traced circles around her clit, sending shivers through her body. Brooke tried to push herself closer to me, but I held her legs apart and stopped her from moving.

"I'll let you come when I'm ready to give you the okay," I teased.

Her body trembled, and beads of sweat formed on her body as she fought to control herself when I slipped the vibrator back inside her cunt, turning it on.

"Oh, God... *please*," she cried, her hips moving more with every passing second.

I couldn't resist any longer. I took her clit into my mouth, sucking and nibbling gently. Her whole body convulsed under my touch, her moans growing louder and more desperate.

Was I supposed to stop when she made a sound? Yes, but it was a miracle she still hadn't come, so I could look past the noises she made.

She squirmed underneath me, her hands now pushing into my hair, holding them tightly.

"Almost there, baby," I murmured, my voice low and reassuring. "You're doing so well."

Brooke started to shake uncontrollably and she let out a series of loud, drawn-out cries, probably a few curse words as well.

She wasn't going to last much longer. This was already as long as I could drag it out with a vibrating toy inside of her.

"Are you still cold?" I asked, earning myself an exaggerated headshake. "Good." I pressed a kiss to her pussy. "Come for me, Brooke."

Her body went rigid almost instantly, every muscle tightening as her climax hit. Her back arched off the bed, her limbs shaking with the force of her orgasm.

Brooke's skin flushed a deep pink as she rode the wave of

her pleasure, her chest rising and falling rapidly with each breath.

She cried out loud, her moans echoing in the room.

When she finally stilled, I turned off the vibrator and slowly pulled it out of her, setting it aside on her nightstand after crawling up her body.

"You did so good, baby." I pressed my lips on hers. "You ready for your reward?"

Chapter Ten

Brooklyn

"Oh, my God, how have you been skating all your life and can't land a goddamn axel?!" Erik yelled while I brushed some of the ice off me.

"I bet it's that guy's fault again, isn't it? What's he done now?" He laid his hands on my shoulders, shaking me violently. "Wake up, Brooklyn. He's an asshole who doesn't want to see you succeed. He wouldn't be with you if he cared one bit about you!"

I pushed Erik off me. "You don't get to talk about Reece that way."

For years, he'd been trying to talk Reece badly, as if Erik even knew him. The only contact Erik had with my boyfriend was an eye-roll when Reece showed up for practice, or when he watched us at competitions. They hadn't exchanged a single word before. At least not that I knew…

They both went to St. Trewery, but it was a big school. They had entirely different majors, and I knew that Reece usually stayed with his hockey guys rather than making other friends.

And if Reece talked to Erik, he would've told me.

"I'm just stating facts, Brooklyn. If you don't want to

hear the truth, that's a you-problem," he spat, skating over to the spot on the ice where our program usually began so we could start over.

A sigh left me, but I didn't bother to continue to argue and followed him.

As we stood in our first position, looking over at our coach to signal to Ilya that he should restart the music, I noticed my father standing next to him. He occasionally showed up for practice, but not as often anymore as he used to because he still had more kids than just me to look after and show up for, and a restaurant to run.

Actually, I asked him to stop showing up so often. I loved my dad, and I wanted him here just in case something happened and I was panicking, but the older I got, the more I realized that he was putting everything on hold just to be here for me. My siblings had hobbies too, and though he still managed to show up for all of us, he, too, deserved a break.

Seeing him here right now helped me regain my focus. At the same time, I was already thinking about the questions he was about to ask me. Dad looked like he was moments away from walking onto the ice, carrying me out of the arena, and as far away from Erik as humanly possible. I wasn't sure if I would've complained or thanked him.

"If you fall one more time…" Erik warned, though he never got to finish voicing his threat as the music restarted, and we had all but two seconds to begin our program.

As I sat in the locker room, cooling my knee from falling onto it ten minutes prior, I grabbed my phone to check if Reece texted me.

He had to stay longer for hockey practice, and he

promised to text me once he was on his way home, but even at eight PM, there wasn't a single text from him. He wanted to call Anthony Gillis today, but I suppose that was a task for tomorrow, then.

Since I was already checking my notifications, I saw that Rina had sent a few messages a couple of hours ago.

> **RINA**
> I just overheard Ms. Dubois and Mrs. Kent talk about you
>
> Well, Ms. Dubois was talking about you, Mrs. Kent was just listening
>
> B, that woman HATES you

Great... like I didn't already know she couldn't stand me.

> **ME**
> What did she say?

> **RINA**
> You finally done with skating?
>
> Welcome back to earth, my dearest friend!
>
> She was saying how your posture is off all the time and that she can't see how you'll make it past Junior year

> **ME**
> It's September... the year literally just started?

> **RINA**
> Right?
>
> She thinks you're the worst dancer in class and she might send your parents a letter to inform them about your "awful dancing"

> ME
> What is this, High School?

> RINA
> Apparently

A knock appeared on the door, and a moment later, Dad came walking inside holding two hot chocolates in his hands. Almost immediately, I felt the corners of my lips lift into a smile.

"Been a while," I said when he handed me my drink.

"I know, I'm sorry." He set his drink down on the bench beside me, then kneeled before me and pulled my foot onto his knee to check on mine. He removed the ice pack and after a moment of inspection, he said, "That doesn't look good."

Dad added a bit of pressure on the sides of my knee. It wasn't even a lot and yet pain shot through my entire leg, making me wince.

"I can't believe he purposefully dropped me," I muttered. I just knew he did it on purpose. "Erik's mad at me."

"I got the sense he might be, but that's no excuse to hurt you." Dad laid my leg back down on the bench, grasped his hot chocolate, and took a seat across from me.

"He wants me to break up with Reece." I instantly felt lighter finally telling him about it. "We did break up… for like a whole day before my birthday."

Dad nodded. "I know."

"You know?" It shouldn't have surprised me, yet it did.

"Brooke, if you're not with Reece, you're hanging around Emory and me all day, every day. For you to spend your entire day in your room is odd, and him not staying over the night before your birthday was even more concerning," he said, then took a sip from his drink. "Also, Reece called that day to tell me."

"He did?!" Why would he do that? "We agreed not to tell anyone because—"

"Because you're afraid it's going to ruin Colin and my friendship, I know, Brookie." He cocked his head at me, eyebrows raised in a judgy-dad way.

"It's scary," I whispered to myself, but he heard it. "What if one day Reece and I *really* break up and... and it's not on good terms? Dad, I know you'll always side with me, and Colin would stand with Reece. There's no way that wouldn't cause some sort of feud between the two of you."

"Brooke," he sighed, his features softening. "That's not something for you to worry about, okay? And you and Reece aren't going to break up, you know that."

"We might. We already did once." I sure hoped it wouldn't happen again, though.

"For fourteen hours."

"We're constantly fighting."

"Because you care," he argued back.

"No, because of stupid things." I tried to get up, but when Dad noticed that I was having a hard time, he was quick to stand beside me, holding me up. "He gets mad at me for not terminating my skating contract with Erik all the time."

Dad sighed, but it wasn't the kind of sigh I expected. It sounded more like he was upset with *me*, not my boyfriend.

"What?" I asked.

"Can you really blame him, Brooke?" he asked in return. "You believe Erik purposefully dropped you, and he does it at least once a week. You're complaining about your skating partner more than you're saying good things about him. Of course Reece wants you to end the partnership with someone who's actively harming you."

"I guess..."

Chapter Eleven

Brooklyn

"So, what do you think I should do?" I asked, ending my ramble about how much I hated attending Juilliard.

Grey and Luan both took a deep breath, probably glad I finally stopped talking, though Grey should've been used to someone talking his ears off without giving him a chance to speak.

Grey was my dad's best friend, and growing up, I used to spend a lot of time with him when Dad and Emory had places to be where I couldn't go. I had the option to stay with Colin or Aaron as well, but Grey was my first choice, always.

He might've been my father's age and best friend since college, but I was pretty sure Grey was *my* best friend more than he was my dad's.

"Do you want something to drink?" Grey asked instead of answering my question. He got off the sofa, making his way over to their open kitchen. "You have the choice between water and… well, water. If I let you touch Luan's apple juice, we're both dead."

Luan snickered, but nodded nonetheless. "I'll make an exception for you."

"I don't want a drink. I want to know what to do!" I

turned to Luan, hoping for a more straightforward answer. I didn't get one.

"Fine. It was a one-time offer, though." Luan shrugged.

Grey poured himself a glass of water and then returned to the living room. Despite fearing neither of them was going to actually give me some advice, I kept on hoping for it.

In theory, I knew it was my decision to make. I knew I had to figure out whether or not I wanted to transfer to a different college, stick out the last two years, or quit altogether. Reece would've helped me talk through it, but part of me feared he would've just advertised St. Trewery to me instead of thinking rationally. I was going to talk to him anyway, of course, but I needed someone else's opinion first, someone who was a bit older than Reece and me, a bit wiser.

When Grey finally opened his mouth to speak, he was cut off by his daughter running into the living room. "DADS!"

They both turned their attention to Sage almost immediately. My problem wasn't half as important as their daughter, so I guess I was going to have to wait and keep on hoping for some advice in a few minutes.

Sage jumped up on the sofa, forcing herself between her parents. "Guess what? I tried to do my homework, right? Because Papa said I have to do it when I know for sure that it can wait another five weeks—"

"If you do it in five weeks, you'll no longer need it," Luan interrupted.

Sage turned around and looked at him, eyebrows scrunching together. "Yes, that's the whole point, Papa." Her eyes rolled dramatically. "Then I don't have to do it anymore. No homework means I get to have more time not stressing about homework."

Grey chuckled, earning himself a more-or-less angry glare from his husband.

"So anyway, I tried to do my homework, right? And guess what? Mrs. Simone is sick tomorrow, so I don't even need it anymore." She fell back against the sofa, and her eyes settled on me. The moment she spotted me, her face lit up. "Oh, my —Whaaaat!" Sage jumped off the sofa and ran right into my arms, startling me for a second. "Where were you yesterday?!"

"On a date with Reece," I answered, picking her up to hold her in my arms. Well, it wasn't a date, per se… we went out to eat at my dad's restaurant. We didn't even talk.

"Ash said you told him you'd come by to play with us, but then you never did."

I couldn't even remember promising Ash I'd stop by. I knew I was over here a lot when Reece, Dad, and Emory were all busy, but that didn't mean I stopped by every day either, so he couldn't have just assumed, could he?

What did I know? Ash was six. He definitely just assumed.

"Brookie, do you know that Ash and I are switching schools?" she asked, which instantly made me look at Grey and Luan with narrowed eyes.

So they could allow their kids to switch schools, but they refused to help me decide? They should be the perfect candidates to weigh out the pros and cons with me.

"Why would you transfer to a different school?" I asked in return. As far as I knew, Ash just started first grade. How could there have been any problems already?

Guilt painted Grey's face, which was more than unusual for him. I was used to his expressions being unreadable, even if he'd gotten better at expressing himself over the years.

His usual neutral, grumpy expression aside, he'd shown plenty of emotions, mostly happiness, but I'd never seen guilt before.

Sage sighed heavily, rolling her eyes. "Because some older guys in our school are making fun of Ash."

"Why?" And why hadn't I ever been informed about this happening? I'd been through a couple of rough days at school, so I could've told Ash exactly how to make them stop. Or tried to anyway.

Sage looked at her dads, smiling at them before her eyes were back on me. She leaned in, whispering, "They're not actually making fun of *him*. I just said that because I don't want Daddy and Papa to know the truth."

"What truth?"

Once again, Sage looked at her parents, making sure they weren't paying enough attention to actively listen to what she was telling me. "They're saying Ash will never be a real boy because he has two dads. I don't think he knows that they're saying it because they're not saying it to his face. I beat one of the boys up."

My eyes widened drastically, coughing as I swallowed the wrong way. "You did what?"

Grey's eyes narrowed at me, clearly having picked up on my surprise.

I was sure they both knew the real reason why Sage wanted to switch schools, which made me wonder if Grey told my dad about what was going on. Did anyone even know Sage and Ash were transferring to a different school?

Sage giggled. "They were being mean, so I was meaner! Daddy always says that we have to stick up for ourselves, so I stuck up for my dads and Ash because they weren't there to do it themselves. Rowan avoids me now."

I mean, it was good to hear she could take care of herself… but Sage was only seven. She shouldn't have had to do this.

I hugged Sage, holding her a little tighter. "You have to

tell your parents, Sage," I whispered back to her. "I know you're very brave, and I know you just want to protect everyone, but we don't hide things from the people we love, okay? Sometimes, you're protecting them more by telling them what's really going on than hiding it."

And she was most definitely too young to carry the weight of something like this.

"I'm going to quit Juilliard," I announced as I stormed into the kitchen.

Dad was frozen in place, stopping to stir whatever he was cooking. It smelled like he was making boursin pasta with roasted tomatoes, one of my favorites.

Mom looked up from her iPad, taking a break from working on her newest project. "Quit Juilliard?" she repeated, concern in her voice. I nodded. "Why?"

I walked over to her, taking a seat by the kitchen island beside her. "Because the professors don't like me, and I seriously can't be bothered putting up with it anymore. I don't care one bit about ballet, and it's just too much unnecessary stress. So, I'll drop out."

"Honey, did you think this through?" she asked, taking both of my hands in her own.

"Yes, Mom, I thought it through."

Emory never officially adopted me because I didn't want it. I loved her dearly, and perhaps until I was ten, I was convinced I'd want her to adopt me, but Dad always said he wasn't going to let that happen until I was at least thirteen and knew what that meant.

I was glad he said no every time I asked because once I truly grasped why Dad was hesitating, I no longer wanted it either. I used to think it was cool that my aunt would be my mother, but the older I got, the more I understood that it was a bit unusual. Still, I didn't care.

After I turned thirteen, I realized that Emory didn't need to adopt me to be my mom. She'd been there for me from the second I was born, so it really didn't matter that she didn't give birth to me, or that we had no legal document saying she was my mother. She was my mom to me, even if I still called her by her first name sometimes.

It was a habit I just never got rid of, so now she was either Mom or Emory.

I didn't know the woman who gave birth to me, though Dad sat me down once I turned eight and told me all I needed to know. Emory and Dad answered all of the questions I had about Millie, and to this day, I couldn't fathom how a mother could do something as horrible as she did.

She faked her own death for five years just so she wouldn't have to raise me.

Now, twenty years later, she was still trying to get in touch with me every now and then, but I refused. If she could give me up that easily, I didn't want to meet this woman. Ever.

"What do you want to do instead?" Dad asked, continuing to stir the food so it wouldn't burn. I loved his cooking, and I always thought it was funny that people out there were praying to eat his food one day while I had the privilege of just coming home and getting a plate handed to me by the chef himself.

I sighed. "Do you think St. Trewery would accept me if I applied for next year?"

Mom smiled, cocking her head slightly. "St. Trewery?"

"Yup." It was the most obvious choice for me—sort of close by and still an elite university. Plus, Reece was there.

Dad narrowed his eyes at me. "Why?"

"Because..." Because it was where Reece went. Because, perhaps, if we were attending the same school again, all of our problems would vanish. Just... because. "I want to see where you went to college and learn all about your legacy."

Reece told me there were tons of pictures of the hockey team from the year my dad graduated, mostly showing off Colin, Grey, and Aaron because they were *huge* names in the NHL now. There were also pictures of my dad since he was on that team, and while he didn't go pro, he was a famous chef now.

"His legacy." Emory laughed. "The only place where you'll find *his legacy* is on the walls of the bathroom stalls."

"So I'll add a good thing or two." I shrugged. "And maybe draw over everything my eyes shouldn't have seen."

"That's wise," Dad said, walking over to the cabinets behind him to take out a couple of plates. "My legacy will appreciate you erasing it."

I grinned at him, but my smile faltered when I turned the topic back to my possible transfer. "So... you think they'll accept me?"

"Oh, definitely," Dad replied, setting the plates down on the counter. "If you ask Colin to talk to the chancellor, they might even let you transfer right away since it's just the beginning of the semester."

Colin was a huge sponsor, sending monthly checks to fund the hockey team because Reece once complained about the arena being too rusty.

They were still working on remodeling certain parts of the arena, but at least Colin knew his money was actually put into the hockey team, not something else.

Chapter Twelve

Reece

Brooke and I had been fighting all morning.

Erik called her at three AM, saying she should get to the ice rink by five so they could continue with practice since she left early yesterday. She was injured, and could barely stand on both legs at the same time, but of course, she went anyway.

That guy was destroying her, and she refused to see it.

Okay, well, she did see it, but she insisted that she had to stick out the season with him. Apparently, she wouldn't continue the contract with him for next season, *if* her body made it until next season. The way Erik was pushing her, injuring her, there was no way she'd be able to continue to skate after this season.

The chances of Brooke having to retire from figure skating were higher than her starting the next season. I couldn't tell her, though, because I feared we'd just continue to fight if I did.

But fighting over this was better than watching my girlfriend destroy herself.

I looked up from the ice, trying to find my brother in the crowd, only to see my parents instead.

They weren't supposed to get here for another couple of days.

Shit, now that I knew they were here, it felt like someone was wrapping a rope around my neck and cutting off my oxygen.

I knew they were always watching my games on TV, but having my father here in person was a different kind of pressure. The urge to win the game and make him proud was stronger now that he was present.

I barely got to spend time with my parents, and the last few times they came to watch a game of mine in person, we lost. So today, perhaps we could celebrate a win for a change.

"CARTER!" one of my teammates yelled as he skated past me.

My head shook as if to shake off unwanted thoughts and focus on the game once more, but it was too late.

One second, I stood on the ice. The next, someone pushed me against the boards so hard that my lungs stopped working for a moment.

"Is Brooke coming to dinner with us?" Dad asked as he and Mom sat down in my car.

Colin was taking Lily and the kids home, so he had no space for our parents, which meant I had to drive them home.

I didn't mind and I didn't see them often enough to be able to complain about it.

My parents came here about once every three months for a week unless it was one of their kids or grandkids' birthday. Sometimes, Lily's if she asked them to come, but she didn't even celebrate this year.

Colin wasn't in New York for his birthday, so neither were they, which meant I hadn't seen my parents since July.

So, driving them to dinner and then home really wasn't a big deal.

"I don't think so," I answered and looked out of the window to watch Brooke as she and Nova, her younger sister, waited by their father's car for him and Emory to get there. "We could just make it a family dinner."

Dad looked out of the window as well, waving at my girlfriend when she spotted us. Without missing a beat, Brooke's face lit up with a smile, and she waved back.

Her gaze shifted over to me for a brief moment, and although the smile stayed on her lips, something just seemed off to me.

I couldn't exactly see her eyes from this far away, but if I had to guess, she was far from happy at that moment.

Our fights were draining the life right out of us, and I hated that feeling more than anything. Something had to change before it was too late, but I had no idea where to start.

"Brooke's like family," Mom said eventually. "Go invite her."

"Can I send her a text?" I pulled out my phone, but Mom already said no before I even got to unlock the phone.

"You *never* invite a lady to dinner over text."

My father chuckled. "This isn't the eighties anymore, Elena. Kids these days handle everything through their phones."

"Yeah, Mamá. We handle everything—"

"Go. Ask. Her. Out. In. Person." She clapped her hands with each word. "Just because she's your girlfriend doesn't mean you get to not put any effort into your relationship anymore. Buy the girl some flowers for a change, Reece. And stop texting her everything when you have two perfectly working legs to go see her and talk to her in person."

I threw my phone onto the free passenger seat beside me, sliding a hand down my face before I got back out of the car.

"And Reece?" Mom said before I could close the car door. I poked my head back inside, waiting. "When do you plan on proposing? I'd love to be alive for your wedding."

"Oh, my God," I muttered under my breath, and without giving my mother an answer, I stepped back and shut the door before making my way over to Brooke.

As I crossed the parking lot to get to Brooke and Nova, I didn't know whether I was supposed to kiss Brooke first or start talking right away. Technically, we were still fighting, so kissing her would've been weird, right?

"You lost again," Nova pointed out as I approached them. While I wasn't expecting to get attacked by a ten-year-old, I did appreciate her starting the conversation so I didn't have to choose. "If you keep that up, you'll never make it to the NHL."

Brooke pressed her lips together to refrain from laughing, but it didn't really work.

I knelt down to Nova. "Listen here, little lady, I only lose because you never believe in me."

Nova gasped offendedly. "That's not true!"

"So you weren't rooting for the Denver team?" I pointed at the jersey she was wearing. "Because it sure looks like you were."

She blushed. "Just because Trevor is playing for them! He has a sister, did you know that?"

"I did not." Nor did I care. "Promise you'll be rooting for my team next time so I can win?" I held out my pinky finger.

Nova sighed heavily, then hooked her pinky with mine.

"Fine. But only so you can stop crying about losing all the time."

I stood back up, meeting my girlfriend's eyes. "Will you go to dinner with me?"

"Dinner?" Brooke cocked her head. "Like a date or with your parents?"

"With my parents."

"Tonight?" she asked, something odd in her voice. She was going to say no, I could feel it. I nodded anyway. "I can't tonight. I promised Erik I'd meet him for practice at eight. I'm already running late because of your game."

I snorted in response, chuckling to myself. "Of course you are."

"Reece—" Brooke reached her hand out for mine, but I stepped back.

"No, it's fine. You enjoy getting fucked over by your skating partner for the tenth time this week."

Chapter Thirteen

Brooklyn

Erik was already waiting for me in front of the arena, but instead of greeting me, he pushed a blue folder into my hands.

"What's this?" I asked, opening the first page. I expected some sort of new practice program, but what I found instead almost made me slap that folder into Erik's average-looking face. "Are you serious?"

He shrugged. "I talked to my doctor and he said it was for the best."

"A diet!" I pushed the folder back into his hands. "Even if I wanted to lose weight, your stupid doctor doesn't know me! He can't just put me on a goddamn diet, and neither can you!"

"You're too fat," he said, gesturing at my body. "I have a scar on my thigh from where your blade cut into my body. If you weighed less, that wouldn't have happened. And lifting you gets more challenging every day because you gain like two pounds a day, which is no surprise. You eat like a pig and you never work out."

Shaking my head at Erik, I stormed past him to get inside the arena. This was going to be a long, painful evening.

He could criticize my skating all he wanted, could drop me and throw me across the ice however he desired for another year, but I wasn't going to let that prick of a human tell me I was fat when I knew very well that I wasn't.

Thinking he could put me on a diet without my authorization was going to have consequences, though I wasn't sure he had enough brain cells to really grasp that he wouldn't get through with it this time. He tried the same thing four years ago when we just became partners, and while I didn't start a diet, he never faced any punishments for his asshole behavior.

Now, I had no idea how *I* was supposed to punish him, but there had to have been something I could've done to make him regret this.

As I walked inside the arena, my coach was already standing in front of the ice, looking more distressed than ever. He was on the phone, yelling at the person on the other end of the line. At first, I didn't understand why, but the closer I got to the ice, the more I understood.

Half of the ice was melted.

In all four years we'd been practicing at the rink, this had never happened.

Reece and I used to go to a different rink when we were still skating together, but then he quit to focus on ice hockey and so I ended up with Erik at this place. To be fair, Reece was never interested in figure skating, he only did it because of me. I really appreciated it, though.

Back when we first started learning how to skate, he joined my figure skating class so we could spend more time together. Sometimes I wished he never quit, but I understood why he did it. Hockey was more important to him, and that was okay.

I used to play hockey for him as well until I was eight, then Dad said I had to choose between hockey, figure skating, and ballet because all three of them at once weren't good for my health or grades. They were all very time-consuming hobbies.

Reece decided for me because I couldn't, and he knew that the only reason I didn't want to quit hockey was because I didn't want to hurt him.

He was okay with me quitting, so when he told me he was going to quit figure skating, I wasn't allowed to get mad. And Reece deserved to focus on what he truly loved, so even if I was upset that we'd no longer skate together, I was happy that he did what *he* wanted for a change.

By the time Ilya got off the phone, Erik was standing with us, staring at the half-melted ice. "What the hell are we going to do now?"

Ilya looked at Erik, sighing. "The dance studio is booked tonight, so you can't practice stunts there, which means your only options are going to the gym or going back home."

"We're going to the gym," Erik said. "But I was more concerned about this whole situation." He pointed at the ice. "It's going to take at least a week until we can skate here again."

"Way longer," Ilya muttered. "They need to replace some pipes and now that the ice is already melted, they'll repaint the lines, which they should've done over the summer but didn't. I've also been told that they're updating the security and the entire cooling system, as well as making some other renovations. This rink will be out of order for at least a few months."

That wasn't good at all.

If we couldn't practice, how were we supposed to get ready for competitions?

"Maybe we could use the rink at Madison Square Garden," Erik suggested.

Ilya laughed. "Yes, and share the ice with the Rangers, great idea, Erik. Do you know their training schedule? Do you know how difficult it'll be to find *any* time for you to have at least an hour to practice? Both of you have classes to attend, so your only free time is in the evening! The hockey season just started, so they'll be at the rink as much as they can when they're not on the road."

He wasn't wrong, but their schedule also wasn't *that* inhuman.

"Okay, but maybe we could get thirty minutes of ice time tonight," Erik said. "Who even cares about ice hockey?"

I pulled out my phone and checked the time. "The Rangers start practice at nine tonight. I bet half of the team is already at the rink, so it'd be useless to check if we could have at least thirty minutes for us tonight."

Erik rolled his eyes, then laid his hands on my shoulders. "Nobody gives a fuck, Brooklyn. Your stupid knowledge about the Rangers' schedule is embarrassing. Frankly, it's creepy, you stalker."

"Fuck you." I ripped myself away from his grasp and left the arena as quickly as possible. He tormented me enough for this week.

Chapter Fourteen

Reece

> **MI PRINCESA** 🦢
> Are you still at dinner with your parents?

I was thinking about not replying.

No matter how many times I told myself that her refusing to go to dinner with my parents, who lived in a whole other country than me, was less important to my girlfriend than a second round of skating practice with that god awful Erik guy.

I understood skating was important to her, but if she asked me to go to dinner with her and her family, I would've canceled any other plans I had in a heartbeat. Fuck, I would've skipped hockey practice for her.

Yet, the thought of ignoring her text was almost unbearable.

A couple of years ago, I ignored her message because I was mad, and the next day I found out that she'd been crying all night long, and all she wanted was to talk to me, but I didn't reply. I didn't even pick up my phone when she called. So when I found out why she tried to reach me, I promised myself I'd never ignore her again, no matter how upset I'd been with her.

> **ME**
> The whole family, but yeah
> Why?

Brooke responded instantly.

> **MI PRINCESA** 💍
> Can I come?

> **ME**
> All of a sudden?

> **MI PRINCESA** 💍
> Reece, I'm sorry.
> I know I should've gone to dinner with you, and I'm truly sorry I didn't
> I wasn't taking your feelings into consideration and I'm really sorry I hurt you with my decision
> I know you're mad at me, and you have every right to be. I would be mad too if I were you
> But please... I really need a distraction right now. So, even if you don't talk to me all night long, being there with you and your family would still be better than being alone with my thoughts

I sighed, using every ounce of strength inside of me not to hit my head against the table.

> **ME**
> What's wrong?

> **MI PRINCESA** 💍
> I'll tell you later, okay? I don't think I could sum it up into one message

> **ME**
> Okay. Do you want me to come pick you up?

> **MI PRINCESA** 💍
> No, it's alright! Rina's driving me

> **ME**
> We're at Gramercy Tavern. Let me know when you get here and I'll come get you

> **MI PRINCESA** 💍
> Okay, thank you
> I love you

For the first second after I read her last message, the world seemed almost okay again.

There was no pain, no anger, no fight. It was just Brooke and me, and our love for each other, and everything was fine. But then the next second came crashing in, and everything fell back into that black hole that was slowly sucking the joy out of our relationship.

> **ME**
> I love you too

"I think he should propose this year," I heard my mother say and a moment later, Colin burst out into laughter.

My head shot up just in time to see Lily slap my brother to shut him up, but he only grasped her hand in his, brought it to his mouth, and kissed her knuckles before he continued to laugh.

Colin was off for another week because Kieran came down with a bad cold which he caught, so he didn't have to go to practice tonight. Suddenly, I wished his doctor let him go back to work already.

"Mamá, Reece is still a kid himself," Colin said, still laughing.

Kieran looked up from his book. His eyes wandered around the entire table, not saying a single word before he looked back down and continued reading. It was a miracle he even wanted to be here.

If Colin knew I had already spoken to Miles about proposing to Brooke, he would've freaked out, as it seemed. I didn't actually plan to ask Brooke to marry me for another few months, but I already had a ring.

I'd been waiting for a good time to propose—a time when we hadn't been arguing the entire week before that proposal.

Was it so hard to believe we'd ever get married, or was this just Colin being a brother and having to tease me? I wasn't thirteen anymore, and even Brooke's dad thought it was a cute idea to propose before we turned twenty-one next year.

Sure, we were young… but a lot of people got engaged and married young, right?

I wasn't a kid anymore.

"That's not true. Look at him." Mom gestured toward me. "He's turning twenty in a couple of days. That's old enough to get married. Especially to someone he's been dating for years. If they got married next year, they could have their first baby by—"

"Woah there," I stopped her. When did our conversations go from 'How have you been doing?' to 'It's about time you knock up your girlfriend'? "Slow down, Mamá. Don't you have enough grandkids?"

It wasn't that I didn't want kids with Brooke, and I knew Brooke was already making lists with baby names, but despite thinking I was old enough for marriage, kids weren't *anywhere* on my mind yet. Colin didn't get married until he was twenty-four, and he didn't have his first kid until he was twenty-seven.

Yes, our parents were older now than they were when Kieran was born, but they should've thought of that before they had me seventeen years after Colin. Just because they were getting older didn't mean they had to rush me into things that I should've been discussing with Brooke, not them.

I was going to propose to Brooke when *I* wanted to. And we were going to have kids when *we* decided to have some.

"Hardly." She rolled her eyes, then smiled at Kayden, who looked at his grandma a little dumbstruck.

"Good luck explaining to Miles why your son knocked up his daughter at twenty," Colin said.

"Like he has room to talk," Dad countered. "If I remember correctly, your dearest friend Miles came to hockey practice at *twenty-two* with a four-year-old in tow."

Yet neither my dad nor my brother took me to Colin and Miles' practice to entertain my best friend. Quite rude of them, if you asked me.

"What does knocked up mean, Daddy?" Kayden asked, jumping off his chair to make his way over to his father.

"It means getting someone pregnant," Kieran answered, not bothering to look up from his book. "Grammy wants Reece and Brooke to have a baby."

Kayden's face scrunched up with disgust. "Like... a human one?" He looked over at his mother, waiting for an answer.

"Yes, a human one." Kieran sighed, flipping to the next page of his book. "Now, stop asking stupid questions so I can read my book."

What If We Break?

"Kieran…" Lily reached for his face, lifting it to meet her eyes. He immediately smiled at his mother. "We know it's really hard for you to be here, and you know we're all so endlessly proud of you for trying, but that doesn't mean you get to be rude, okay?"

"I'm sorry." He closed his book and gave it to Lily so she could put it away. "But I agree with Dad. Reece's Cups is too young for marriage."

Oh, man, I thought he forgot about that nickname.

And again with that *too young*. I wasn't too young to marry my best friend—someone I'd grown up with and known my *entire* life. But what did Kieran know? He wasn't even eleven yet.

My phone screen lit up, and I immediately checked out the notification.

MI PRINCESA 🤍

I'm outside

I stood up from my chair, ready to walk away without saying a word, but I changed my mind. Looking directly at my parents, I said, "If either of you mentions marriage or babies in front of Brooke, neither of you will be invited to our wedding."

Chapter Fifteen

Brooklyn

"Did Reece tell you that he's been looking for apartments so he could move closer to St. Trewery?" Colin asked while slowly feeding Kim.

He wasn't talking to me, yet I spoke before his parents could. "Why didn't you tell me?" I looked at Reece. Some sort of weird pinch squeezed my heart.

When did we start keeping things from each other? He used to tell me everything the moment it happened, and I used to do the same.

I still hadn't told him about transferring to St. Trewery, but that was because I wanted it to be a surprise, not because I forgot to mention it. Moving an hour away certainly wasn't going to be a good surprise.

Reece shifted his weight and cleared his throat uncomfortably. "I was going to," he answered. "But you were so busy with skating and college that I forgot to mention it."

"How do you just *forget* to mention moving out?!" I was busy, yes, but we still saw each other daily. We had plenty of time talking about other things and having sex, but he couldn't mention this? "I thought we were going to move out *together* like we talked about. When did you change your mind about that?"

If he had just told me I would've understood. Driving back and forth between Staten Island and his college was a waste of time, I knew that, so it made sense that he wanted to move out. I would've helped him look for an apartment.

Reece moving out meant we wouldn't have seen each other daily anymore, but I still would have understood why he wanted to move closer to St. Trewery. It just would've been nice if he had told me.

Reece sighed, sliding a hand down his face. "Can we talk about this later?"

"That doesn't sound like she's going to say yes," Kayden said just before he got shushed by every single adult at the table. "Wow." He held up both of his hands, laughing. "So that's why we always sit at a kids' table. We're not allowed to talk here."

"Yeah, adult talk is boring anyway," Kieran threw in, rolling his eyes. "All they ever talk about is money, their jobs, and how Dad always dumps his hockey bag in the living room and leaves it there for at least two days before he *finally* throws it in the washing machine. Then Auntie Sofia says Uncle Aaron does the same thing and it's *sooooo* annoying. And Emory ends up laughing at everyone because Miles doesn't play hockey."

Dad might not, but all three of my siblings made sure to leave their stuff everywhere, so there wasn't much of a difference.

"Oh, and recently, all they ever talk about is Brooke and Reece," Kieran added, making sure to look at me. He smiled at me softly, and I honestly wasn't sure if he just said this to mock me or to inform me about this.

"Kieran…" Colin sighed, pinching the bridge of his nose.

"What? You keep telling me that talking behind someone's back is a bad thing, so if you don't want Brooke and Reece to know you're talking about them, then don't talk about them!" His eyebrows scrunched together in a mad frown as he turned to look at his grandparents. I'd never seen him angry before. "Grammy, you always say how we have to learn to make our own decisions, but you never let Reece make his own. That's not a very nice thing to do. If he doesn't want to marry Brooke, he shouldn't have to!"

I gasped, feeling my cheeks flush with embarrassment. Kieran's words hit me like a slap in the face, and though I tried to tell myself that whatever Reece said, he must've misunderstood, but that didn't make it hurt any less.

We'd been talking about marriage ever since we were fourteen. While I knew most of those conversations we had were just for the fun of it, we didn't mean any of it... our most recent ones were pretty serious to me. I thought Reece felt the same way.

"And now that we're already talking about it..." Kieran looked right at me, sighing. "For the love of whatever's holy, please get rid of that Erik guy you're skating with. Reece can't stand him but he would never tell you this. He keeps crying about how—"

Before Kieran could finish his sentence, Lily covered his mouth with her hand. It was a little too late.

Suddenly, the air felt heavy with tension, and all eyes were on Reece and me, looking guilty and embarrassed. But the only set of eyes I was interested in were my boyfriend's.

His eyes were also on me, waiting for me to react, but I didn't know how.

Colin got up and walked around Lily just to kneel down next to Kieran's chair, probably to talk to him about how what he just did wasn't the right way to approach a conversation.

Kayden was looking around the table all innocently, though he clearly picked up on the awkwardness because he firmly pressed his lips together.

Kim was asleep on her chair, and right at this moment, I wished I was still her age and slept through this entire thing.

Before anyone uttered a word, Reece had pulled me off my seat and was dragging me out of the restaurant.

As we stood outside, all we did was stare at each other for a solid two minutes. Neither of us spoke.

I wasn't sure what I was supposed to say. I knew I couldn't force Reece to talk to me, and I knew that I'd been super busy lately, so I shouldn't have even blamed him for forgetting to tell me about his plans to move out.

Did it hurt that he didn't tell me? Sure, it did, but I couldn't change it.

I should've asked what Kieran was talking about when he mentioned Erik, but I didn't even have to. I knew Reece didn't like Erik, I knew he wanted me to terminate the contract. He'd been pretty clear about that a while ago.

I just wished he told me how deep that hatred really went.

There was so much space between us, space that had never been there before. And we'd never stayed quiet for this long.

The longer we stayed silent with nothing to say, the deeper my heart sank. With every passing second, more pieces broke, and pain surged through every inch of me until, eventually, tears were streaming down my face.

As a sob escaped me, Reece closed the distance between us.

His hands were on my face, thumbs swiping underneath my eyes as if that was going to make me stop crying.

"Do you want me to drive you home?" were the first words that left his mouth. Part of me wished he said something entirely different.

I took a deep breath or tried to anyway. "I'll talk to Ilya first thing in the morning," I forced out. "I'll terminate my contract with Erik."

"You don't have to," he replied. As much as he tried to hide it, I could hear the slight hint of desperation in his voice. No matter what he was going to say, Reece would always want me to terminate the contract. He just didn't want to be the reason for it.

I wrapped my hand around his wrists just to hold him. "I can find a new partner for next season, Reece. I... I knew you never liked him, but I failed to see how much worse your hatred got over the past weeks."

It made sense, though. Ever since Erik told me to break up with Reece if I wanted to keep him as a skating partner, and I actually considered it... I should've known he was worried I'd do it again.

"It doesn't matter," Reece said. "This is your dream, Brooke. You can't make it to the ISU Grand Prix without him. You spent all summer at practice to make sure your program was perfect. You were so excited for this year, and I can't take that away from you. I just..."

"You just?"

His hands slid down to my waist, holding me as he pulled me against his body. "I just can't lose you. Yet every day you spend with him, I can't breathe until you're back in my arms, and I know that we're okay. Every goddamn day you go to practice, I'm wondering if you'll come back home and end our relationship for good. And the worst thing is, I get it. You've dreamt of making it to the ISU Grand Prix way before you were even old enough to participate. Erik is your guaranteed ticket to get there. So if breaking up with me means you'll get there, then I wouldn't even be mad at you. But that doesn't mean I fear it happening any less."

I wrapped my arms around Reece's body, hugging him so tightly to my own that I was almost convinced I was cutting off his air supply, but he wasn't complaining.

"I wasn't thinking," I told him, keeping my voice quiet so we wouldn't attract any more attention from strangers around us. "He got into my head that one time and—"

"Exactly," Reece interrupted. "He did it once and he'll do it again. But I can't complain about it because I want to see you succeed more than I need you in my life, Brooke. You deserve that victory."

My head shook against his body, my tears wetting his sweatshirt. "That victory would mean nothing to me if I couldn't celebrate it with you."

His arms around me tightened, and I honestly didn't even know it was possible. "I'll always be here when you need me, *mi princesa*."

I didn't doubt it.

"Why would Kieran say you didn't want to marry me?" I asked before I had the chance to forget about it and pretend it never bothered me.

Reece and I had to relearn how to talk, so might as well start now.

It didn't surprise me that everyone was talking about Reece and me. They were worried about us, especially since they clearly noticed our fights even if I thought we were hiding them pretty well.

But that didn't explain why Kieran thought Reece didn't want to marry me.

"Because he's ten and he doesn't know that just because I tell my parents to stop asking when I'm going to propose to you, it doesn't mean I never plan to." Reece pulled back just to look at me. "Fuck, Brooke. We're only twenty. If everyone knew I already had a ring for you, they'd think I'm crazy. You don't even want to move out of your parents' house yet, which, I'd genuinely want you to do when we get engaged. To be honest, I'd rather we're already living in our own place before we even get engaged."

He had a good point... though, he was wrong about one thing.

I wanted to move out of my parents' place, but it wouldn't have made sense while I was still going to Juilliard.

Finding an apartment in the middle of New York City was almost impossible. And, okay, perhaps Dad would've paid the rent for me, and I was sure Reece's parents would've helped him to pay for his part as well. But it was useless for Reece to move somewhere close to Juilliard for me just to still take an hour to get to St. Trewery.

It made more sense for him to move to New City.

Then finally, I realized a whole other part of his little speech. "You already have a ring?"

Reece's cheeks flushed a light shade of pink while his eyes displayed some form of shock. Guess he didn't realize he said it either.

He tried to chuckle his way out of the situation, or at least make it a little less awkward or weird. Eventually, he cleared his throat and nodded. "Yeah, I got it a few months ago. It's been burning a hole in my pocket ever since."

My eyes widened in surprise, my breath getting caught in my lungs with my next sharp inhale.

"Why didn't you tell me?" I whispered, my voice barely reaching him over the noise of the city around us.

Reece's gaze softened, his hand reaching up to brush away a tear from my cheek. "I wanted it to be special. I wanted the moment to be perfect when I asked you to spend the rest of your life with me."

Though half of my heart swelled with happiness, the other half was overcome with guilt and confusion.

I never expected Reece to already have a ring, let alone be planning to propose. All these months, we'd been at each other's throats and he still wanted to marry me... he still went out and got a ring.

A shaky breath drew from my lungs as I processed everything Reece had just said. A mixture of emotions swirled inside me, leaving me feeling too many things at once. Happiness, for one, but I was also really terrified at the same time.

Suddenly, his hands cupped my face, and his thumbs gently wiped away the tears that continued to fall.

"Things have been pretty difficult between us," Reece began, his voice soft yet unwavering. "But despite everything, my feelings for you have never changed. You're my rock, Brooke. And I want nothing more than to spend the rest of my life by your side. I want nothing more than to be your husband and love you so endlessly much until our dying days. Cupid would start to think he gave us ten times the normal dose of love."

I swallowed past the lump in my throat and tried to ignore all those strangers who stopped in their tracks to stare at us. This was something we should've talked about in private, not on a busy street in the middle of Manhattan.

"You know, I even asked your dad for your hand in marriage months ago," he added, speaking quietly so those nosy strangers couldn't hear it.

"You did?"

Reece nodded, a small smile tugging at the corners of his lips. "Yeah, I did. Your dad was... well, being your dad. He didn't want to give me his blessing right away just to fuck with me, but eventually, he said he couldn't think of a better person for you to be with."

That sure sounded like my father.

I let out a little laugh, feeling a mix of relief and so much love for Reece. Despite our recent struggles, he'd always been there for me. Reece had always been my biggest supporter, no matter what. The fact that he planned to propose and even asked my dad for his blessing while our relationship was going through heavy ups and downs was just another reason for me to love him.

Reece was everything and so much more than I deserved.

Wrapping my arms around Reece, I buried my face in his chest, taking in the familiar scent of his cologne.

As we stood there on the sidewalk of this super busy street, surrounded by curious strangers, and the most annoying city sounds, I felt a sense of peace wash over me.

I turned my gaze up to meet Reece's eyes, seeing the depth of emotion reflected in them. Bits of fear lingered in his blue eyes, probably because he was scared of the moment I'd finally answer his unspoken question. It was already out in the open, so there was no use saying it again.

"I love you," I whispered, smiling at him. "I want to spend the rest of my life with you, too."

"Oh, thank God," he said, relief flooding his features as he let out a deep breath. The tension in his body seemed to lift off his shoulders almost immediately.

Without warning or hesitation, he leaned down and pressed his lips to mine. He held the kiss for a moment, his lips moving softly against mine before slowly pulling away, leaving me breathless and wanting more.

As I looked at him, my heart was doing a million backflips at once.

We were going to get through this, I knew it. Things that felt this good and this right couldn't have been wrong.

"I don't have the ring on me right now," Reece told me. "Otherwise, it'd already be on your finger." Nonetheless, he took my left hand and spread my fingers apart to catch a glimpse of the heart tattooed on the inside of my ring finger. "This will have to do until we're back at your place."

"Reece?" I said softly, feeling the urge to come clean to him. "I'm transferring to St. Trewery. So… if you still want to, we could look for an apartment for *us* together?"

Twenty different stages of emotions crossed Reece's face within three seconds when he realized what I just said. "You're dropping out of Juilliard?"

I nodded. "I'm starting at St. Trewery next Monday."

Once again, without a single warning, Reece pressed his lips to mine. "Do we have any classes together?"

"Almost all of them… I chose to study sports management because it seemed like the easiest one." And if figure skating didn't work out, I could always become a Coach with that degree; or an agent. "Since I knew your schedule I just picked whatever courses you chose. If I ever need help, I know a guy who can help me study. He happens to be my future husband."

Chapter Sixteen

Brooklyn

Lying on the bed, I held my left arm up in the air, staring at the sparkling diamond engagement ring on my finger.

I still couldn't believe that happened today. Was it the most romantic proposal, no, but it was pretty on-brand for Reece and me, I'd say.

It didn't even matter because, at the end of the day, I was engaged to the love of my goddamn life.

Reece was on the phone with me, walking me through the fifth hypothetical situation of how his family might respond when we shared the news of our engagement.

My dad clearly knew it was going to happen soon-ish, and since he knew, he probably told Emory, too. The only people who could've been surprised when we told them would've been my siblings, but honestly, even they probably expected it.

All of Reece's hypothetical situations were positive, and frankly, I would've been surprised had he come up with a single negative one.

"My mom was *just* telling me how it's about time I proposed to you," Reece told me before he sighed heavily. "I think she might have even placed bets with everyone in my family on when I'd finally pop the question."

He chuckled softly, and the sound of it could make my heart skip beats even though he wasn't in the same room as me tonight.

It was strange lying in my bed without him next to me, especially since we had spent almost every night together since we first started dating. His presence was a steady comfort in my life, and the thought of him not being here made the room feel colder, and emptier.

I missed the weight of his body next to me, the warmth of his breath on my neck as we both drifted off to sleep. I always felt far safer in his arms, even though I had nothing to worry about when I was at home. It was just another level of peace that came with knowing he was there.

"If it makes you feel any better, I'm almost certain my family did the same." I laughed quietly, imagining the knowing looks and whispered conversations between my parents every time they'd catch Reece and me being even slightly affectionate to one another.

On the bright side, it felt pretty great to know that both of our families were more than happy to welcome the other into their lives—not that they had any other choice.

"It does make me feel a little better," Reece admitted, and I could picture the grin that I knew was on his face without having to see it.

"What are you doing right now?" I asked, finally getting up and walking over to my bedroom window, where I took a seat on that sitting nook my father built me when we moved into this house. My eyes immediately began searching for Reece on the other side of the road, but his lights were turned off.

My bedroom was on the front side of the house, allowing

me to look right into my fiancé's bedroom—if it wasn't almost midnight and his lights were turned off, that is.

"It's late, *mi princesa*. I'm just lying in bed and talking to you on the phone," he replied, chuckling. It made sense, but it sounded kind of boring. "God, I wish you were in my bed right now."

"Me too," I sighed, pulling my legs right underneath my chin. "This was a very stupid idea."

After getting the ring from his place, Reece suggested that we should avoid staying in the same house for the next couple of nights. We wanted to wait a few days before telling our parents about our engagement. If my parents had seen us together and noticed my obvious joy, I would've blurted out the news without hesitation.

It was safer to stay apart until we were ready to tell everyone.

"I was just thinking the same thing." He groaned in frustration. "It's alright though, right? It's just until we're ready to tell them."

I leaned back against the window frame, watching the moon casting a soft glow over the neighborhood. It was so quiet out there, so peaceful. Sure, it was a very small neighborhood consisting of four houses in total—all of which belonged to my father and his best friends from college—but it seemed extra quiet tonight.

"I know, it's just until we're ready," I repeated, trying to reassure myself more than Reece. The idea of keeping our engagement a secret for a few days felt like an impossible task, especially when all I wanted to do was shout it from the rooftops.

But as much as I wanted to share the news with our families, there was a small part of me that wanted to stay in this bubble of secrecy. It was our little world for now, where it was just Reece and me, and everything was perfect.

Also, I was a little afraid that if we spoke about it, everything would go downhill from there. The world could be cruel once you were happy, so maybe if we kept what made us happy for ourselves for now, we'd be okay.

A slight movement caught my eye from across the street, and I squinted to get a better look. Reece's bedroom curtain fluttered briefly before falling back into place. A part of me wondered if he was also stealing glances out the window, searching for me in the darkness.

"I wish you were here, too," I murmured, feeling the weight of his absence a lot more now.

As I stared at the house across the street, I suddenly realized how easily Reece could've snuck out if Colin and Lily had been stricter with him. There was a roof piece right underneath his window, and all he would've had to do was slide down the roof and survive the nine-foot jump.

Or he could've held onto the gutters, hoping they wouldn't break as he lowered himself. Reece was pretty tall, he would've survived the maybe three-foot fall to the ground from there.

"Did you ever sneak out?" I asked. He never mentioned doing anything like that before. Colin was pretty easy-going with Reece if he wanted to go somewhere, so there was never a reason for him to sneak out. But maybe there was one before, and he just didn't tell me.

"Not really," Reece answered, pulling his sheer curtains open. I could see his silhouette in the dark, but that was about it. "Did you?"

"No, but it sounds exciting."

I looked at my own window, and for just a moment, I wondered what would happen if I tried it.

I glanced back at Reece's window, and the thrill of the idea sparked a mischievous smile on my face. The thought of sneaking out to be with him, just for tonight, was both exhilarating and nerve-wracking. But the more I considered it, the more it seemed like a daring adventure worth taking.

"Reece, I'm going to hang up now," I told him, because I couldn't possibly have continued talking on the phone when I was sure I needed both of my hands in a second.

I quickly ended the call with my fiancé and quietly opened my window. Perhaps I should've put on some longer clothes instead of staying in my shorts and Reece's T-shirt, but I couldn't have cared less about it at that moment.

A few bruises weren't going to ruin my life.

The night air was chilly against my skin as I carefully climbed out onto the roof, feeling a rush of excitement.

I made my way over to the edge, glancing down at the drop below. It seemed a lot higher from up here, but being with Reece tonight, sleeping in his arms, made me want to keep going.

With a deep breath, I lowered myself down, gripping onto the edge of the roof before letting go and dropping to the ground below. The landing was less graceful than I had hoped for, but I quickly brushed myself off and made my way over to Reece's house.

I could see him waiting by his window, a surprised yet delighted expression on his face as he watched me approach.

Taking a deep breath, I looked around myself, trying to figure out how I was supposed to get up to his window. I wasn't tall enough to reach the gutters from the ground, and there was nothing I could use to help me up there.

Maybe I could climb up on the fence of the porch and try to pull myself up onto the roof, but that seemed like a lot of work. I could also try and use one of the columns to help me get up there.

"Baby, what are you doing?" Reece whisper-yelled, amusement in his voice.

"Shht, let me think."

"I'll come open the door for you.

"No, don't. I can do this."

I smiled up at him before approaching the porch and climbing up onto the fence. My arms were wrapped around one of the columns as I stood on the top rail of the fence, and only then did I notice that I wasn't even wearing shoes.

Whatever, I only lived once, right? And I was never going to do this again anyway.

Once I felt a bit more comfortable standing here, I finally reached up, one hand after the other, and grasped the gutter tightly.

Pulling myself up with all the strength I could muster, I hoisted my body up onto the roof, feeling an adrenaline rush like never before. Reece climbed through his window, then offered me a hand to help me up the rest of the way.

"Are you crazy?" he whispered, a mix of concern and awe in his eyes as I finally made it onto the roof. "I can't believe you actually did it."

"I couldn't stay away any longer," I replied breathlessly, a wide grin spreading across my face as we sat down on the roof, our legs dangling over the edge.

Reece shook his head in disbelief, but there was a sparkle in his eyes as if he had never been happier to see me. "You'll never do this again, though, right? I had like twenty heart attacks just thinking about you slipping and getting seriously injured."

I laughed quietly so that I didn't accidentally wake someone up. "No, I'm good."

"Good, because I don't think my heart can handle that kind of stress," Reece said, wrapping an arm around my shoulders. The warmth of his touch sent a shiver down my spine.

As his hand ran down my naked arm, Reece looked at me with something odd in his eyes. "You could've at least put on some clothes and shoes."

"I was in a hurry," I replied as he cupped my face with his hands. "And honestly, if I thought about it too much, I probably wouldn't have done it at all."

In the moonlight, his features softened, and he reached out to tuck a loose strand of hair behind my ear. "I understand, but, Brooke, your safety is so much more important. I don't want you hurting yourself."

I nodded softly, smiling to myself as I leaned into him, closing my eyes as I let the heat of his body warm me. "I know."

"We should go inside. You're getting quite cold."

Reece stood up, offering me his hand to help me up as well. I took it, and suddenly, a rush of gratitude swelled in my chest at his concern for me. He'd always cared about me, even in the most spontaneous and reckless moments of my life, even when he was upset with me. I could never find anyone better than him.

The Carter's roof was a bit more slippery than ours, or perhaps I was imagining it, but either way, I clung to my fiancé like a monkey as we made our way through the window and into his bedroom.

Reece closed the window behind us before turning to face me with a tender expression. "What will your parents say when they wake up in the morning and you're no longer in your room?"

I shrugged, reaching for his hand one more time before I

pulled him toward his bed. It was still late, and I was getting seriously tired now that I was with him again. Before lying down, I quickly took off my socks.

Days and nights with Reece by my side were so much better than anything else.

"Hopefully, they won't know I climbed through my window to get out." A soft chuckle slipped past my lips. "I could've used the door, you know. It's not the first time they'd wake up to me suddenly being at your place."

"That's true."

The room was cloaked in darkness, only the faint glow from the street lamp outside casting shadows across the walls.

I crawled under the covers, feeling the warmth of the blankets enveloping me as Reece joined me, wrapping his arms around me protectively.

I snuggled into his chest, listening to the steady rhythm of his heartbeat. It was one of my favorite sounds to listen to at night, and I didn't usually appreciate noises as I tried to sleep.

"Brooke," Reece whispered, tracing his hand up and down my back. "I'm glad you're here."

Looking up at him, I met his gentle gaze that was filled with nothing but love, and offered him a warm smile. "Me too."

Chapter Seventeen

Reece

Brooke talked to her coach about ending the partnership with Erik… Ilya advised her to stick out the season with him.

It made sense that he'd try to make them get along for another season, as terminating their contract during the season could cause a lot of issues. It could even hurt Brooke and Erik's reputation and might make it difficult for them to find other partners in the future. It could disrupt their skating schedules, competition plans, and even affect their ranking and qualifications for nationals and other major events.

It was easier and more secure to terminate their partnership once the season was over.

As much as I hated that, I could live with it. Hopefully.

Brooke and I spent all weekend looking for apartments or a small house close to St. Trewery. Most of them were either too small, too big, or just not worth it.

We did come across one house, though; the one Grey and Miles used to live in when they went to college. A couple with a kid still lived there until mid-October, so we'd been told, which meant we wouldn't have been able to move in before November. Still, we applied right away.

As far as I remember, it was a decent-sized house. Two

bedrooms with en-suite bathrooms, a toilet downstairs, and an office space that we didn't need, but I was sure we could turn the space into something useful.

I had a bunch of hockey equipment, and Brooke owned a lot of figure skating stuff, so we could've easily turned the office into a separate closet for skating equipment. Then we'd have our bedroom and a spare one. Sounded good enough for me.

It was only until we graduated, anyway.

I was constantly checking my emails to see if the landlord had made a decision yet, but the only emails I got were sports newsletters that I subscribed to. Only when I heard Fynn's voice did I tear my eyes away from my screen.

"I get it now," Fynn laughed as soon as Brooke and Erik finished their practice skate.

I wasn't even supposed to be here because Erik was throwing a fit when he saw me earlier, but since they were using our ice rink now, nobody could tell me I wasn't allowed to be in here. After all, hockey practice was starting in an hour.

Besides, I didn't give a fuck what Erik wanted.

"What exactly are you getting?" I asked, already regretting it.

"Why you were always hoping Erik would drop her as his partner," he replied, pointing at him. "I mean, dude, who wouldn't fall in love if they were *this* close six days a week for hours?"

I glared at the guy who was supposed to be my friend, shoving a french fry into my mouth. "Professionals."

"She had her cunt in his face like two times, dude. It doesn't bother you?"

It didn't, because as much as he wanted to believe either of them was paying attention to body parts, I knew both of their heads were far too occupied. They had to memorize two entire three to four-minute-long programs; their heads were busy worrying about landing the next jump and keeping their balance. The approximately two seconds that Erik's stupid face was remotely close to my fiancée's intimate area because of a stunt was brushed over like it never even happened.

Their stunts were as natural as hockey players punching one another.

"The only things that bother me are that you keep bringing up Brooke's private parts, and the fact that Erik treats her like shit," I muttered, but I suppose he heard it.

What exactly was Fynn's obsession with Brooke's body anyway? He'd known her since middle school, and he never gave a fuck about Brooke before. He only recently began to sexualize her.

"Why do you care if I bring it up?" He leaned back in his seat, holding both of his hands behind his head. "It's not like you broke up or shit, so chill your balls, dude."

My hands balled into fists, and I could swear if his mouth opened just one more time, I would've thrown them right at his face. But I was better behaved than that, at least I liked to think so.

"I texted her last night, just to see if she'd be down to fuck, but she never replied," he added. "Why do you suppose that is?"

"Oh, no, how ever would I know?" I wanted to break his nose. Fuck, I wanted to break every single goddamn bone in his body.

When did my friend turn into someone I wanted to throw off a skyscraper?

"I sincerely hope the fact that my *girlfriend* ghosted you didn't break your heart of gold," I said, yet somehow managing to keep my voice calm and steady, despite fighting the urge to reach for my skates and slit his throat with the blade.

Just one more hour, and I could punch the guy in the face without getting in trouble for it. God, I loved hockey.

Brooke and I decided to keep our engagement to ourselves for now, just so we didn't have to deal with our friends' judgment. We were going to tell our parents later tonight, though.

"Nah, it's fine, I'll find someone else to fuck eventually." He looked toward the ice again, laughing when Erik dropped Brooke once more.

He did it on purpose. I just knew it. There was *no* fucking way he couldn't have held onto her hand for another second and pulled her up.

Yes, mistakes like this happened, I knew that, but I *never* in my life allowed Brooke to touch the ice when I was still her partner.

If she fell, I threw myself underneath her just to make sure she didn't get hurt. If I knew I wasn't going to catch her because I made a wrong move or for any other reason, even if it was just a feeling, I didn't throw her in the air, didn't lift her, didn't do shit but make sure she was okay. And I held onto her for dear life so she wouldn't get hurt during certain spins like the death spiral.

Fynn spoke again, yet I didn't hear anything but inaudible chatter because I'd been too focused on watching the ice.

Brooke and Erik just went into a spiral sequence when suddenly, Erik slipped. He reached for Brooke and pulled her down with him. Brooke tripped over one of his legs, which pulled it back into a *very* painful-looking position as he hit the ground.

My fiancée's hands shot up to cover her mouth in shock as she sat on the ice.

Erik tried to move, but he stilled instantly when a groan so loud that Fynn and I could hear it on the bleachers sounded through the arena.

Their coach immediately sprinted onto the ice to help, but I didn't think there was much else to do but to call an ambulance.

"Shit, I think she broke his leg," Fynn muttered.

As much as I knew this was wrong, I couldn't stop the laughter from spilling out of me when I realized what this meant.

If Erik really broke his leg, it would take at least six to eight weeks until it healed, and then another few weeks would pass until he could even consider going back on the ice without injuring himself worse than before. And he wouldn't be able to go back to skating at a level he did before for another couple of weeks to prevent fracturing his leg again so soon after the first one.

Two to three months was the earliest he would return *if* it was a minor fracture. However, that one time years ago, when Brooke broke her ankle, she was advised to stay off the ice for at least six months.

She bounced back in three months after tons of physio and with a lot of painkillers as her daily assistant.

But even if Erik was able to come back in three months… the season was over for him.

Chapter Eighteen
Brooklyn

"This isn't your fault," Reece repeated because he probably thought I didn't hear him the first time. He cupped my face with his hands and forced me to look into his eyes. "He tripped."

Reece was supposed to be on the ice right now, but instead, he stood in front of the ice, talking to me while his team was going through some drills to warm up. His coach was furious, eyeing us every now and then, but Reece never paid him any attention.

Ilya texted me ten minutes ago to let me know that I had one week to find another partner for this season and another one to teach him the entire program. If I failed, Erik's two broken legs didn't just end the season for him, but for me too.

I wasn't going to lie, a part of me hoped Erik would've gotten injured so I could get a new partner since Ilya advised me not to end our partnership just yet, but that didn't mean I wanted him to break both of his legs!

One broken leg was torture for a figure skater; two were the epitome of a nightmare.

He probably needed surgery. And what if he never fully

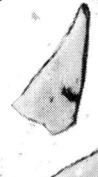

recovered from the fractures? His figure skating career was over.

"You should get changed," I told Reece because I didn't feel like continuing to talk about my misery. Or, well, listen to him talk about how I didn't break Erik's legs and that it wasn't my fault.

Besides, I didn't want Reece to get benched for his next game because of me.

Reece looked at his coach and then back to me. "No way."

"This is important for you."

"Let's get some ice cream." He reached for his hockey bag and swung it over his shoulder, then took my skates from me before interlocking a hand with mine and leading me toward the exit doors.

"Reece…"

"Don't you 'Reece' me." He let go of my hand to open the door for me, then interlaced them again once we were outside. "You're upset, and I know you don't want to be alone right now. You need someone to vent to about needing a new skating partner, and then someone who will help you find one so you're not forced to quit the season. As your fiancé, I have the privilege to listen to you talk about all that while stuffing your cute little face with ice cream to make you feel better."

I completely forgot about needing a new partner. Okay, I didn't forget about it per se. I just didn't bother to get my hopes up about finding someone. The season just started, *if* someone was willing to skate with me because they were partnerless, it was going to come with a twist.

Either way, I wasn't going to make it to the Grand Prix next year.

What If We Break?

We sat in an extra room behind the kitchen of my father's restaurant.

This room didn't exist until I was ten years old, and my dad got sick of all of his friends, Mom, and Reece and I showing up to eat here. He couldn't say no to us even if there were no tables left, which was usually the case.

The restaurant was booked for years in advance, so the only times we—okay, not me and Reece because we used to eat in the kitchen with Dad, anyway—could dine in was if someone canceled their table last minute.

Anyway, Dad then had an extra room built behind the kitchen explicitly for all of us and his staff. That way, we never had to hope for a cancellation and could come in whenever.

So now Reece and I sat in the empty room, eating ice cream. He was right, ice cream did make me feel better about the whole situation. Perhaps not the situation itself, but it distracted me for a little while. At least until I got a message from Ilya.

> **ILYA**
>
> Erik won't be participating this season, even if he bounces back in a couple of weeks. His doctors are advising him to take his recovery slow to ensure he can make it back onto the ice without any problems.
>
> Also, just a heads-up, his mother wants to sue you because she thinks you did this on purpose. I'm trying to reason with her, and even Erik told her it wasn't your fault but she won't budge.
>
> Mrs. Reed insists that you've had it out for her for a while now? What's that supposed to mean?

I sighed, then pushed my phone across the table so Reece could read the messages as well.

His eyes rolled before he looked back up at me. "Do you even know his mother?"

"Nope." I shoved a spoonful of vanilla ice cream into my mouth, but this time, it did nothing to make me feel better.

If ice cream couldn't even make me happy again, then the situation was more than fucked up.

Reece reached a hand over the table, holding mine. "Even if she does sue you, she can't prove that you injured him on purpose, especially since we all know you didn't. If what Ilya says is true, that Erik told her it wasn't your fault, then all she does is harm herself. Besides, accidents happen. It's part of the whole skater experience. And if she really sues you, she better be prepared for all the pictures and videos I have on my phone of him purposefully dropping you just because he was mad."

The first time Erik dropped me, we all brushed it off as an accident because... Reece was right. Accidents happened. Even the second and third time was brushed off as an accident. But the more frequently these "accidents" occurred, the more skeptical Reece got, and so he started to record huge chunks of Erik and I's on-ice lessons.

I knew he had a couple of videos of Erik dropping me where it was obvious that he'd done it on purpose. For instance, there was one video where Erik was supposed to catch me after a jump, but he didn't because he was wiping his nose with the back of his hand.

We were trained to ignore a runny nose during a performance.

"I don't want to start any drama," I said. All I wanted was some peace and quiet, and a skating partner who wasn't anything like Erik.

Reece's thumb brushed over my knuckles, and I smiled when my eyes fell on the ring on my finger.

I hadn't worn it all weekend because I didn't want Dad to see it before we told him, so when I left the house this morning to start my first day at St. Trewery, the first thing I did when I sat in Reece's car was put on the ring.

"You're not starting it, the dick's mother did," Reece vetoed. "But on the bright side, we now know where the dick gets his asshole-like attitude from."

I chuckled, ready to tell Reece to stop calling Erik a dick, even if he was, when my father's voice interrupted me.

"Why did I just get a call from Erik's father?" Dad asked as he came marching into the dining room. "But more importantly, why are his parents reaching out to me for something that happened between the two of you, like you're in middle school again?" He sighed heavily, taking a seat at the table with us. "Last I checked, Elliot and Nova are in middle school, not you. And unlike Eden, I never received any calls about you when you were in high school either, so why are parents reaching out to me about you *now*?"

Dad took my bowl of ice cream from me, stealing a spoon of my comfort food as if he didn't know it was supposed to make *me* feel better.

My eyes narrowed at him. "That's my ice cream."

He shrugged. "I spent the past twenty years of my life sharing my food with you. Let me steal yours for a change."

"Technically, it's yours," Reece threw in. "I mean, we didn't pay for it, and this is your restaurant, so…"

Dad looked at Reece, nodding. "Exactly. It's my ice cream." He stole another spoonful of my vanilla ice cream before his eyes were back on me. "So, why's Erik's father trying to get me to meet up with him to discuss 'further actions'? Whatever that is supposed to mean."

"He broke both of his legs at practice earlier because he tripped," Reece told him, sounding a little too happy for my liking. "Since he pulled Brooke down with him, she tripped over his legs and probably made it a little worse, but that wasn't her fault, yet his parents like to think Brooke did it on purpose."

Dad blinked once, then burst into laughter. He was quick to slap a hand over his mouth, trying to stop himself. "That's not funny, Reece," he said, still having a hard time containing his laughter.

Reece's mouth opened in protest, but he refrained from making a snarky comment, or so I thought. "I apologize, Mr. King. I should be more mature at my age. Even assholes like Erik don't deserve to break a bone or two." He joined my father's amusement, and for just a second, I could feel the corners of my lips pull up into a smile. At least until I remembered what Erik's injuries meant for me.

"Either way," I began to get their attention again. When they both stopped laughing and averted their eyes at me, I continued. "I'm going to need a new partner for next year. Finding a new one for this season is useless. I don't want the leftovers, and even if I decide to settle for one of the skaters nobody wants to skate with, we will never be good enough to make it to the Grand Prix."

It took me a while to get comfortable with new people. To make pair skating look elegant, the pairs needed to have some sort of chemistry and be comfortable with one another. There was no way I'd been able to build a strong connection with a stranger within a week. It took me an entire year to warm up to Erik.

And frankly, I deserved better than a leftover guy or a newbie. I hadn't been skating my entire life just to fail because my partner was awful.

Okay, I knew even new skaters could be good on the ice, but I wasn't going to risk it. Either I would do this season with someone who was at least as good as me, or I wasn't going to participate at all.

Dad started to suggest possible solutions but I was too busy watching Reece to listen to my father.

Reece reached for his phone—which he rarely did when my dad was talking to us—scrolling for a moment before his eyes settled on something that seemed to be interesting enough for a little crease to appear between his eyebrows.

For a moment, he just stared at the screen before looking up at me. His eyes were gleaming with something joyous, and a shy smile formed on his lips.

"What are you so happy about?" I asked, curiosity in my voice.

"Okay, so... don't get mad," he said, instantly catching my father's attention with his words, even if they were directed at me.

Dad leaned back in his chair, crossing his arms as he raised his eyebrows. "If she won't, I will."

Reece pointed a finger at my father. "Have a little faith in your future son-in-law."

"I know your brother, so there's no way I can have faith in either of you." Dad shook his head, sighing heavily. "And I watched you grow up, so I know the only good thing in your head is the fact that you love Brooke."

"Fair enough." Reece cleared his throat. "But I think I have a good idea for once." His eyes met mine again, the unsure smile still on his face. "Since you need a new partner, I was thinking, what if —"

"I'm not going to steal someone's partner."

He cocked his head at me. "Fine, but I have another idea."

"Does it require me having to injure another skater?"

"Not quite."

"Then shoot."

His hand reached over the table once more, holding mine. Without thinking, apparently, because that little move might've been nothing had I not been wearing a ring my father didn't know existed. Until now, when Reece unintentionally drew his attention to the engagement ring. But my dad didn't say anything.

"I don't plan on entering the draft next year, so even if it's going to look bad on me if I do miserable this season, it won't matter *as* much. So, what if I just step in for Erik?" he said. "I'm nowhere near as good as Erik, at least not anymore, but I mean, it's only been four years, right? It can't be that difficult to start back up again, and it's not like I stopped skating entirely. Okay, I might be a little wobbly with jumps now, but we have two weeks to make sure I get this right. Other than hockey, we have the same schedule now so finding time won't be an issue, and I'm sure we can find a place to practice way past opening hours if necessary."

My mouth hung open and a million different thoughts were running through my mind, forcing me to be happy, sad, confused, and a little angry all at the same time.

A part of me was relieved that I didn't have to quit the season. Another part was afraid for him. Even if it was just for one season, if he missed too many hockey games, it could have fatal consequences for him.

I trusted Reece, obviously, and I knew we worked great together... but that was *before*. It was before we got engaged. And it was before we had all these fights.

What if our balance was way off? What if skating together again would bring more arguments?

We just barely made it an entire weekend without fighting.

What If We Break?

What if he couldn't enter the draft in two years because skating with me messed up his stats?

"I've been talking to Ilya to make sure it was okay with him. He just replied and said that if you're okay with it, he'd love to work with us as a team again," Reece added when I stayed quiet because I didn't know what to say.

I wanted to be happy so badly, jump in his arms, and thank him for doing this for me, but I was frozen in place, worrying more about what that potentially meant for us.

"You can say no," he said. There was a note of uncertainty in his voice, something regretful. "It was just an idea."

I swallowed past the lump in my throat. "What if *we* break?" I asked. "What if working together does us more harm than anything else?"

His thumb brushed gently over my skin. "I don't think it will. I'm not skating with you to have an opinion on the program or anything else. This is your dream, Brooke, and I'm just offering to help you get there. You call the shots on everything. If you're not satisfied with my performance, you may yell at me, and I'll do better. Though, a little heads-up, I might get a bo—"

"Careful what you're saying next, Reece," Dad warned.

My head snapped toward my father, only now really realizing that he was still here with us. He'd gotten so quiet ever since he noticed the ring on my finger that I completely forgot he was here.

Reece's eyes widened, and he gulped down an unsteady breath as he shook off his shock. Guess he also forgot my dad was in the same room with us.

"I wasn't even going to say anything bad." He crossed his arms over his chest. "I was just going to say that I might get a bo... bow, and clip it into my hair, then walk around campus with it all day to show Brooke how much she hurt my feelings by yelling at me. If I walked around with a bow in my hair, I'd humiliate myself, and Brooke would then be together with a guy who—"

I cocked my head at my fiancé.

"Fine, okay. I was going to say another *b-o* word, but you can't blame me. I share the same DNA as Colin, so you knew I had to make a dumb comment."

Dad blew a laugh from his nose, shaking his head. "Good, so we agree that we're blaming everything on Colin?"

Reece and I nodded.

My dad got up, stretching. "Great. So, Colin broke Erik's legs. Colin ate both of your ice cream. Colin's at fault for Reece's inappropriate thoughts in my presence. And Colin told Reece to propose to my daughter and not tell me *when* he was going to do it, or that he already did it." He looked from me to Reece and back. "I like it. I've been looking for a new reason to throw a taco at him next Sunday."

While Reece closed his eyes—probably waiting for my father to yell at him or something—Dad walked around the table and stood behind me. His lips pressed to the top of my head just after he said, "I'm happy for you. Congratulations."

Chapter Nineteen
Reece

"You guys are making it really hard for anyone else to find love," Ming said as he took a seat on the opposite side of Brooke and me.

I hadn't seen my best friend outside of hockey practice for a couple of days since I was too busy showing Brooke around the school. It wasn't really necessary since we shared the same classes so she wasn't going to get lost either way, but I still wanted to show her the place.

She wouldn't always be around me so she had to know her way around. Brooke needed to find her own crowd, make her own friends, and not rely on me or Ming too much. But for now, I was convinced I needed her around me more than she wanted to be.

Throughout our entire middle school and high school years, she barely made more than two friends and always just stuck around me. I loved it and I wouldn't have wanted it any other way, but while the past two years had taught me that being separated from her sucked balls, it was good for her.

Brooke had Rina now, and other people she met at Juilliard all on her own. She needed her own people, some she could go to and complain about me without fearing they'd tell me because they were also my friends.

"Why would Reece and I make it harder for *you* to find love?" Brooke asked, setting her iced coffee down. We just got here from Claire's because the cafeteria's coffee was the worst, and so was the food.

Claire's was a little coffee shop close to campus. It had been here for ages, but since the majority of St. Trewery students went there on a daily basis, it was no surprise it was still standing.

"Because every time I look at you two, I'm like 'Aw, I want that too' and suddenly, every single girl I meet just doesn't measure up to you guys," Ming replied before his breath rushed out on a sigh. "Also, so totally off-topic, but, Brooke, you haven't even been here for a week and everyone's already jealous of you."

"Jealous?" She reached for my hand underneath the table. Brooke was getting anxious. "This, uh… this is a huge school, not *everyone* knows me." Her fingers interlocked with mine, holding me tightly. "And there's nothing to be jealous about."

"Are you kidding me?" Ming's eyes almost popped right out of his head. "The second one person saw and recognized you, you became the school's most talked about topic. Your parents are kind of famous, Brooke. Everyone here knows Rêverie and if they hadn't been there already, they're *dreaming* of going there. You could easily become the most popular student at St. Trewery."

"Popular with fake friends," I said, stroking my thumb back and forth over her smooth skin.

Our interlocked hands laid on Brooke's thigh, and I did everything I could to press her leg down and stop her each time it began to shake.

What If We Break?

If Brooke broke down in the middle of the cafeteria, she would've never shown her face here ever again. And if people took pictures and uploaded them online, Brooke would've fled the state altogether, if not the entire country.

She had enough eyes on her already.

Ming was right though, Rêverie was very popular, and not just in the state of New York. However, not everyone who knew the restaurant knew who Miles was or cared enough to find out who his kids were. Still, that already put Brooke in the spotlight in some way.

In addition to that, Emory was a famous illustrator, working with Sofia—the wife of my sister-in-law's twin brother who was also playing for the Rangers—on turning her novels into comics. Three of their comics got turned into TV shows, one of which was still very popular and got a new season just two months ago.

The coolest part about that was the fact that my sister-in-law directed those shows.

Anyway, even if Miles and Emory weren't known, Brooke's figure skating competitions were televised.

There were fan accounts for Brooke online; some of which were talking about how she should date Erik since they had oh-so-much chemistry. Luckily, there were a bunch of people out there who knew Brooke was dating me so they made sure to enlighten as many people who shipped Brooke and Erik on that.

I mean, honestly, it wasn't that hard to figure out. If Brooke ever posted a picture online, I was usually in the frame as well, if only in the background.

"She literally couldn't have a single fake friend with you by her side. I feel like you can smell them from a mile away and would just scare them off," Ming said, propping his elbows onto the table to hold his head up with both of his hands. "See, you're like a German Shepherd when it comes to Brooke. The German Shepherd to Brooke's Great Dane." He sighed dreamily, looking at my fiancée. "You're so lucky. I want to be someone's German Shepherd to their Great Dane. But unless I ever find someone who wants to spend as much time with me as you guys spend with each other, I'll never be that. So, yes, you guys are making it disgustingly difficult for me to fall in love because I'm always like 'Damn, but that's not what Brooke and Reece would do' and 'Brooke would never say this to Reece'."

Brooke leaned her head against my shoulder, chuckling softly. She was still tense, but it got better with every moment we steered farther away from the eyes-on-her talk.

"I say a lot of things to Reece that you'll never know about."

"Nope. In my head, your relationship is as perfect as ice hockey, so don't ruin it." He reached for his phone, rolling his eyes as he read a text. "Sorry, I gotta go. Fynn wants to tell me about some stupid plan. I don't think he wants you to know, but I'll tell you about it later." He nodded at me, then said goodbye and rushed off, leaving me alone with Brooke once again.

Ming running off because someone asked for his attention wasn't strange for him, but it was concerning that Fynn wanted to talk to Ming without me being there as well. But whatever, recently, I didn't feel like wanting to be Fynn's friend any longer anyway.

"Did you tell Pike you didn't want him as your agent anymore yet?" Brooke asked, suddenly finding her confident voice again. She always spoke in an unsure tone with other people. I knew she wasn't the best at socializing, but that didn't mean her voice changing was less funny to me.

I shook my head. "I'll do that just before skating practice later today."

Yesterday, Anthony could finally make some time to speak to me. We'd been on a call for a few hours as he listened to my problems with Pike. He ran me through a bunch of scenarios that could've happened if I chose to stay with him and also things that were possible if I fired him. Anthony didn't hold back at all, which I really appreciated.

However, his ultimate conclusion was that I'd been better off with an agent who cared about me rather than just getting me signed with a team and cashing in a huge chunk of my money.

He also said that Pike was being unnecessarily difficult.

So, I decided to fire Pike despite the possible consequences, and sign with Anthony. He assured me that he wouldn't treat me better than his other clients just because his most successful one happened to be my brother.

He also mentioned that he couldn't promise that I didn't get better treatment and offers from teams because they knew Colin was great and we now had the same agent. A very great and highly-requested agent, too.

I wouldn't have been able to sign with Anthony hadn't it been for my brother, but Colin was right, sometimes, it was better to use my connections.

And honestly, better offers and treatment sounded good to me.

"You know what's weird?" Brooke spoke, lifting her head off my shoulder.

"The fact that I haven't gotten a kiss from you for at least an hour?"

"No." She laughed, slapping her hand to my thigh. "What's weird is the fact that the last time I was inside this cafeteria, I was like four and sharing my animal crackers with everyone." She looked around us, eyes big with curiosity and confusion at the same time. "It looks so familiar but so different."

My eyes fell on the small pack of animal crackers on the table before us, and a smile tugged on my lips almost instantly. She still loved them.

For over ten years, I hadn't left the house without a pack of animal crackers on me just in case Brooke wanted some. She'd always crave them at the most random places with no way to get the ones she liked, so I wanted to be prepared.

"Like, I remember this place but I don't." She looked back at me, her eyebrows drawn together. "It's a really unsettling feeling."

"I can imagine."

She hummed softly. "Maybe we shouldn't get my dad's and Grey's old place after all. I think I'd just try to compare everything from what I remember about the place to what it looks like now. We should find a place that is *ours* so we can create new memories of just you and me."

Chapter Twenty
Brooklyn

Reece's hands were everywhere, trailing along the curves of my body as if he'd never touched me before. As if he had to get familiar with me again, which couldn't have been further from the truth.

His lips pressed to my neck, teeth grazing my skin as he clutched my ass with both of his hands, pushing my back into the blue lockers. Our bodies pressed together just before his lips captured mine, igniting fires on every inch of my skin.

My arms wrapped around his neck, a moan slipping past my lips as his growing erection rubbed against me.

"I need you so bad, Brooke," he half-whispered against my lips, pushing his hips up to create more friction. "I want to fuck you so hard, you won't remember your name when I'm done with you."

He sat me down on his knee to ensure I didn't fall when his hands snuck underneath my shirt, the tips of his fingers tracing along my sides, before inching up to lift my shirt.

"We can't." I forced a hand between our faces, stopping him from kissing me. "Anyone could come in and—"

"Do me a favor, *mi princesa*," he said. "Lift your arms."

"Reece…" Despite my attempted veto, my arms reached

up, allowing Reece to pull my shirt right over my head, leaving me in nothing but my white, lacy underwear. "We're in a locker room," I reminded him, giving him another chance to stop.

His hands were back on my ass, holding me up.

"I don't care." His lips attacked my collarbones, kissing their way down my cleavage until they reached the rim of my bra. "I want you screaming my name, and I don't care if anyone walks in here or if they hear how well fucked you are."

I supposed it was a good thing that we got to the arena two hours before anyone from his team was even going to show up for morning practice. It was about four in the morning, and the only reason we were even awake was because we didn't have a single piece of furniture in our new home except for an uncomfortable, inflatable mattress.

That mattress barely did anything to offer warmth in the middle of October, so it was easier to get in some practice and move our bodies than to freeze to death at our apartment.

We might've decided against the house my dad owned once upon a time, but we found a cute little studio apartment close by. The landlord said we could move in immediately, so we signed the contracts an hour after having been notified that we could have the apartment. Though we probably should've bought some furniture before we decided to spend the night at our new home.

Reece and I were supposed to start working on teaching him Erik and my program today, but I had the slightest assumption that we'd be too exhausted to even put on our skaters later today.

With a final kiss, Reece looked into my eyes, a fire burning in his own. "Nobody's going to walk in," he promised, as if he could predict the future.

I hesitated at first, torn between his words and the reality that we were in an open, public space. It wouldn't have been the first time we'd done something reckless, but it was never as out in the open as this.

Yet when I looked into his eyes, it was almost impossible to resist.

I nodded, giving him the okay to unhook my bra. Reece lowered me down to stand on the floor almost immediately, reaching his hands behind my back and unclasping my bra, letting it fall to the side. His hands quickly replaced it, cupping my breasts and teasing my nipples with his thumbs.

I bit my lip, trying to keep the moans at bay, but I knew I wasn't going to last very long at keeping quiet.

As his lips attached to my breasts, my lips parted in a gasp. I grabbed the back of his head, pulling him closer and encouraging him to explore more.

His tongue darted out, licking and grazing my skin with his teeth before he sucked my hardened nipples into his mouth, one after the other.

My legs trembled and I could feel myself getting wetter, needing to press my thighs together in an attempt to soothe the growing desire inside of me.

Reece's eyes displayed something devilish as he slid his hand down my waist, his fingers dipping past my navel and rubbing them over my covered pussy for just a moment.

My breath hitched as he eased me onto the cold, hard locker room bench, my back arching against the solid surface.

My pulse quickened as he leaned in close. My heart pounded against my ribcage, threatening to burst out of my chest, as his breath tickled my skin and his eyes bore into mine. Our lips were just inches apart, and I couldn't wait to see where our next kiss would lead us.

I knew I should resist him, but that was really hard to do

when the guy you'd been in love with basically all your life used all his magic words and could do very unholy things with his dick.

Reece's lips barely laid on my lips long enough to satisfy the growing need inside of me, but as he trailed tender kisses down my body, past my stomach, I gripped the bench for support. Every complaint vanished in my brain when his hot breath grazed my skin.

He hooked his fingers into the waistband of my underwear, and I lifted my ass off the bench as he slid them down my legs, leaving goosebumps on my skin. With each inch he exposed me, the anticipation grew.

With his hands on my knees, he parted my legs, tracing his fingers along my inner thighs. I gasped, my hips bucking involuntarily when his fingers came in contact with my bare pussy. "Please," I whispered, urgency in my voice.

He smiled at me wickedly, his fingers slipping between my wet lips. His thumb slid across my entrance, teasing me cruelly and I moaned, helpless in his grasp.

"Please, Reece," I repeated, sounding far more insistent this time. "Please, I need you."

I was raised to never beg for anything; if it wasn't supposed to be, then it wasn't. But each time Reece touched me, I just couldn't help it.

His fingers entered me slowly, my back arching at the welcoming intrusion. His thumb pressed against my clit, sending shockwaves of pleasure coursing through my entire body. I cried out, my hands holding onto the bench on either side of my waist for dear life.

"God, you feel so good," he murmured, his voice raspy with need. "But I'm going to make you feel even better, baby." Reece's eyes gleamed with wicked intent.

Pulling his fingers out, he thrust them back inside firmly

and began to move them in and out of me, matching the rhythm of his thumb against my clit.

I choked on my breath, my head falling against the metal bench as my incoming climax started to build deep inside of me.

With every stroke from his fingers and his thumb teasing my clit, I could feel myself getting closer, driving me to the edge of release. My body was shaking, my breath coming out in jagged gasps.

Reece watched me intently, his eyes never leaving mine as he continued to tease me, knowing exactly what he was doing to me.

But I needed more, and I needed it now.

"Please, Reece," I pleaded again, whimpers coming out with my words. "Please, take me now. I need to feel you inside me."

His lips curved up into a smile, his eyes darkening with lust and satisfaction. He removed his fingers from my pussy, leaving me shivering and panting. "Trust me, baby," he began, seduction etched in his voice. He sounded like a smooth melody that flowed through my body.

I sat up, looking at him as my heart was thrumming heavily in my chest, my body aching for his touch. I wanted to trust him with whatever he was about to say or do, even with the risk we were taking. I wanted him more than anything.

Reece leaned in close, his hot breath fanning over my skin as he continued, "I promise, I'll make you feel things you never thought were possible."

Each beat of my heart resounded like a drum in my ears, the electric surge of adrenaline and excitement coursing through my veins.

He wasn't just some random guy, he was Reece, the love

of my life. And the thought of him inside me sent a chill through my body.

Reece stepped back, letting me see the bulge in his pants.

Impatiently, I watched him undress himself; his eyes never leaving mine and that devilish grin never leaving his lips. I watched as he unzipped his pants, sliding them and his underwear down his legs. His erection stood tall and proud, glistening with a bead of pre-cum at the tip. It was long and thick, pulsating with every beat of his heart, and the veins stood out against his taut skin.

When he approached me, my body quivered with excitement. My skin pricked with goosebumps as his hand brushed against my arm before locking his fingers with my own. He pulled me off the bench, taking a seat before I was sitting on his lap, his erection pressing against my pussy.

God, I was so ready for him.

Lifting my hips, I reached a hand between our bodies and wrapped my fingers around his cock, guiding it to my entrance.

Reece's eyes widened at the sight, his body trembling as his tip got coated with my wetness. Taking one last deep breath, I began to lower myself onto his dick, feeling his thickness stretch me.

His breath caught in his throat as I took him in, my pussy adjusting to his size. I sank onto him slowly, savoring the feeling of him filling me completely.

Once I was fully seated on him, I looked into Reece's eyes and saw the passion and love I felt for him reflected back at me.

He wrapped his arms around me, pulling me close, his lips claiming mine. As our kiss deepened, I tasted Reece on my lips—a hint of the coffee we shared earlier, mixed with the sweetness of his breath and the saltiness of his skin.

The smack of our lips meeting echoed in the quiet room, making a soft, wet sound as we explored each other's lips.

I began to move, rocking my hips in a slow, sensual rhythm. Reece's hands roamed over my body, caressing me. His fingers traced the curves of my back and hips, driving me crazy. His grip was firm, possessive.

I felt like I was floating, lost in a dream when our movements increased.

"You feel so good," he whispered between kisses, his breath hot and heavy against my skin.

Reece leaned back slightly, his eyes set on mine as he thrust upward, meeting me halfway. Each stroke was slower than the one before, building the tension between us until it was almost unbearable.

His fingers pressed into the skin of my hips, guiding me, and controlling our movements. I clung to him, my nails digging into his flesh, our bodies slick with sweat.

I could see the flush of arousal on Reece's cheeks, the way his eyes darkened with need as we moved together.

"Oh, Reece," I cried out, my voice barely audible over the pounding of my heart. "Please, harder, faster."

His eyes flared with something dangerous, a sinful grin forming on his lips. With a grunt of effort, he picked up the pace, his thrusts becoming more urgent, more intense. Our bodies slapped together, the sound ringing in the locker room.

The air was thick with the scent of sex, musky and heady, mingled with the light scent of our sweat and the subtle hint of vanilla from our body wash. The slapping sound of our bodies colliding sent tingles through my body, making every nerve ending come alive.

Our bodies moved in perfect synchronicity, our movements mirroring each other with increasing intensity.

His hands were back on my waist, pulling me right against his body, my breast pressed to his chest, his heart beating in time with mine.

With each thrust, the intense sensation of his cock filling me consumed my body, urging my hips to move faster. As Reece's pants grew more ragged and my moans became louder, I knew we were getting closer to the edge.

Sweat dripped from our backs, our bodies glistening in the moonlight, my skin slick against his. I could feel the tension building within me, the pleasure coursing through my veins, making my muscles quiver and my breaths shallower.

"I'm close, Reece," I gasped.

"I can feel it too, baby," he panted, his eyes locked on mine, the intensity of his gaze burning into my soul. "Come for me, *mi princesa*." One final thrust and I was gone. My body shook with the force of my orgasm, my screams mingling with Reece's deep groans.

As my orgasm subsided, I collapsed against Reece, my body still trembling slightly. He held me tight, his own breathing calming down but his heart still racing.

"That was…" I began, struggling to find the words to describe the intensity. "Wow."

Reece laughed softly, the sound deep and rich in my ear. "Just wow?" he asked.

I couldn't help but smile at his teasing, my body still trying to regulate itself. "I mean, wow. Like nothing I've ever experienced before."

"Now that's rude, but whatever." He kissed my forehead, his lips warm and gentle. "I'm glad you enjoyed it, baby," he whispered.

Chapter Twenty-One
Reece

"Do you want me to pick you up or do you think you'll get to the arena by yourself?" Reece asked as he came walking out of our bedroom, now making his way over to the front door to put on his shoes.

"Rina said she'd drive me." I watched as she nodded a confirmation.

"It's on my way home anyway," she chimed in, shrugging slightly.

"Okay." Reece rushed over to me, pressing a quick kiss on my lips. "I'll text you once practice is over."

I nodded, watching as Reece made his way back toward the door, grabbing his bag and keys before saying goodbye and leaving.

Half of our classes had been canceled today, so we spent most of the day building up the remaining furniture that we'd been putting off for two days now and started cleaning up a bit. Up until an hour ago when Reece wanted to take a little break before having to leave for practice.

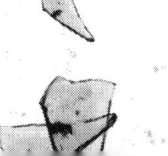

Rina asked if she could stop by and see my new place, and though I was in desperate need of a couple of hours of just doing nothing before having to spend half of the evening at the arena trying to get Reece competition-ready, I agreed.

He was quick to learn the program, which I knew he would, but there were a few things we needed to work on. Some jumps didn't look as flawless anymore, so we had to spend as much time as we could at the arena to fix that. It had only been a week though, so only a few flaws were pretty good in that case.

"The apartment is cute," Rina said as she looked around. She just got here five minutes ago. "A bit bland but cute."

"It's not done yet." We moved in about two days ago. "At least all of the necessary furniture is standing and neither the sofa nor the chairs break when you sit on it."

We could've hired people to do this or asked our family for help, but Reece and I wanted to do this on our own.

Rina laughed, then jumped up and ran over to the sofa, launching herself at it as if she wanted to test its stability.

To be honest, I didn't think there was much to do wrong when setting up a sofa, but if someone was able to fuck it up, it was Reece and me.

She slightly bounced on the sofa and ran her hands over the soft material before falling back, then swung her head around to look at me. "This thing is almost more comfortable than my bed."

"I was going to say the same thing before I checked the price tag," I told her, making my way over to her. "The only reason we bought it was because Reece's brother paid for it."

"Damn. If my brother ever offered to pay for anything in my apartment, I'd immediately assume there was some sort of stipulation for it. Like, I don't know, that I'd have to rob a bank first or steal a homeless person's last two cents." Her eyes rolled. "Something cruel, you know?"

"Your brother sounds like a nightmare." I scootched back a little just to lift my legs and hug my knees to my chest. "But to be fair, if Eden ever offered to pay for anything for me, I'd also assume it came with some sort of condition."

Elliot could be a sweet kid though, so I wouldn't have been too surprised if he ever offered it when he was older. Then again, I was ten years older than Elliot so, maybe it would've been strange if he had to lend me money or something.

"So we agree that Reece's brother paying for this sofa is odd?"

I shook my head but didn't voice an actual reply.

Colin paying for Reece's and I's furniture? Yeah, that was pretty on-brand for him. I mean, he split the cost with my dad, but still.

He refused to let Reece touch his trust fund yet, so Colin even paid for Reece's college tuition.

For a while, I used to think Colin did this because he just felt responsible for his brother since he was living with him. I was sure once his kids were older and ready to go to college and move out, he wasn't going to let them spend their trust fund on things that every parent should've been able to provide for their child in some way.

Okay, perhaps a parent wasn't supposed to pay the rent of the apartment for their kid, but college was almost every person's goal, right? And before you have a kid, you know that stuff can cost you a pretty penny. I suppose that's what a trust fund was for, to pay for tuition, but not really if you grew up in a Carter household.

Nonetheless, he wasn't Reece's dad, so even if Colin didn't pay for Reece's college, their parents would have.

So, the older I got, the more obvious it became that this

was just Colin's way of giving something back to his last remaining sibling. To do something good, though I wasn't sure why he felt the need to, or if that was *really* the reason he did it. I could've been totally wrong.

What I did know was that Reece didn't get to meet his other brother and he never really met his older sister either— they both died pretty young. While Reece couldn't remember them, Colin could and so, in my mind, it made sense that Colin was looking out for Reece like no other; making sure he lived the most fulfilled life with not a single care in the world.

"Anyway," Rina said with a sigh. Her eyes wandered around the room once more. "How could you give up living in Staten Island for... this?" She looked at me again, eyebrows drawn together. "Don't get me wrong, it's cute. But you moved away from a rich neighborhood with peace and quiet to a place that's fifteen minutes away from your campus. I'm pretty sure I saw a Fraternity house just down the road. It'll be a miracle if you get one quiet weekend here."

I rested my chin on top of my knees, sighing so quietly, I was sure Rina couldn't even hear it. "It's only until Reece and I finish college. After graduation, we'll either move back close to our families or find a place near the arena of whichever team he'll end up playing for."

"What if he gets drafted by a team in California?" she asked.

My shoulders lifted into a shrug. "Then we'll find a place there."

"You'd move across the country for a boyfriend?"

My smile collapsed. "Sure. Why wouldn't I?"

I mean, I definitely would've preferred to stay close to my

family, but if I had to choose between going with him or giving up on him, I'd definitely choose the former.

And, yeah, okay, perhaps I was struggling a lot with being too far away from my dad specifically, but I also knew that it was going to be okay. I could always call him.

I was afraid that if I'd been too far away from home and something happened to my father, my mom, or even my siblings, I couldn't make it in time to potentially save them. I was afraid that I'd lose them all; that they'd need me and I wasn't there.

I had always been very anxious about losing people that I loved and not being there when I was needed, but I'd been in therapy for it for like three years. These days, while it still scared me, I could live on my own and I knew that those fears were triggered by a disorder. I could identify triggers and I knew how to calm my anxiety, so it was okay.

I knew I was never going to be alone, and that even if something happened back home, my family was surrounded by people who I trusted and knew would stop everything to make sure everyone was okay.

So even if I left, they'd be fine.

But Rina couldn't have known that I had these fears because I had never told her about them before.

"Isn't Reece your first boyfriend ever?" she asked, caution in her voice. Before I could get defensive at all, she held up one of her hands. "Hold on, I'm not saying it's a bad thing. I actually think it's really adorable, and you guys are the cutest."

"But?"

"Buuut, as someone who moved to a different country for college, I know that leaving your family is a big step. With Reece gone most of the time because of ice hockey, and your unwillingness to make friends, you'll be really lonely."

I held my knees closer to my chest, trying my hardest to suppress the tears from building up just thinking about leaving New York. "Moving from New York to California or anywhere in the country is different from moving from Ireland to the US though."

Rina nodded. "He could be drafted by a Canadian team."

Chills ran down my spine at the thought of potentially moving to Canada.

It would be okay though, I knew that. At the very least, I really hoped that I'd be okay.

"But either way, the location doesn't change the fact that you'll be lonely," she added. "Didn't you tell me that Reece's brother is in the NHL? So you should know how often he's gone and how that might affect his family."

"Are you trying to stop me from living with Reece after college?" It sure sounded like it to me.

Rina shook her head instantly. "I'm a realist, Brooke. I'm just telling you what you know but refuse to acknowledge."

She was right. I knew that if Reece didn't get drafted by the Rangers, another team would want him and he'd have to move. However, I'd always known that no matter where Reece was going to end up, I'd be with him.

His dream was the NHL, and who was I to stop him from making that dream come true?

If I had to force myself into conversations with other hockey girlfriends or wives just so I wouldn't be as lonely, then I could do that for him.

A soft smile pulled on my lips as I looked at my best friend. "He's worth the loneliness though."

"Oh, my God." Rina closed her eyes as she fell against the sofa, holding a hand over her heart. "I take it back. You guys are gross." She opened one eye just to make sure I was still looking at her. "You should break up so I can shoot my shot with you."

"Maybe in another life."

"I'm deeply hurt over this, just saying." She sighed very heavily, very dramatically. "I guess only ever fucking one person has its perks. Though, if you ever—"

"Rina!" Laughing, I reached for a decorative pillow next to me and threw it at her.

Chapter Twenty-Two

Reece

"It looks good," Ilya said, though there was a certain tension in his voice that told me there was a but coming. "But… I just think you could tell a way better story."

Hockey practice had already exhausted me more than anticipated, and Brooke and I had been on the ice together to go through the program for the past three hours. My feet were numb by now, literally couldn't feel them anymore. Every muscle in my body was sore, my head throbbing, and I had zero strength left. Of course Ilya thought we could do a better job.

"A better story?" Brooke brushed off some of the ice on her legs.

I noticed that her bun was hanging lower than before, so I carefully pulled her hair tie out of her hair. Brooke didn't even question me.

She straightened her curly hair earlier, which made it a lot easier for me to gather every single blonde strand and force them all into a ponytail. I had yet to learn how to make buns look good, so I was on the safer side with a ponytail.

"You two skating together had always looked magical," Ilya said, then averted his gaze on my fiancée. "Erik and you were good, but there was something missing. You could never tell a gut-wrenching story. Your routines have been soft and friendly. But soft and friendly doesn't do it for *you*." He gestured between Brooke and me. "Your chemistry is so strong, you could make anyone who watches you feel something. This routine worked for you and Erik, but it's not working for you and Reece."

"So what's that supposed to mean?" Brooke crossed her arms over her chest.

"It means that you can either compete with this routine on Saturday and pray you'll make it through championships, or you start working on a new routine with a more heartfelt song, telling a story so emotional, it'll make everyone who's watching feel like they've been stabbed right through their chest. Because you, Brooke and Reece, have the ability to make that happen. With your current routine, even if you're lucky and make it to the Grand Prix, you're not going to win."

"How are you so sure of that?" I asked. I wasn't convinced we could come up with a whole new routine in two days and make it look perfect.

Ilya looked at me, then at Brooke, and back at me. "Because you two share a love that's so strong, you make people want to throw up. Your connection is visible when you're just standing in the same room; it becomes even more apparent when your hands touch. If you turn that love, that connection, into something painful, it's going to *hurt*. Separating the two of you, even if it's pretend on ice, will make everyone feel that in their guts."

"We can do this, right? You learned this routine in an hour, we've just been working on fixing your jumps. So if we create something new, we could do this," Brooke said as she reached for my hand, interlocking our fingers.

I nodded softly, regretting it immediately. It was better for Brooke, but I already knew I was putting my body through hell with this. "So are you thinking more of a right-person-wrong-time thing or something that started strong, weakened, and found back together?"

Suddenly, I was glad I convinced Brooke to shower at the arena. She'd already been tired before we got in the car, and I knew that if she fell asleep in the car and I woke her up, my head would no longer be attached to my neck. Especially when it was just about taking a stupid shower.

However, I also knew that if I didn't wake her up to take a shower before bed, she'd hate us both in the morning.

Now, we stood in an unmoving car in front of our apartment. I kept the engine running because I feared that if I turned it off, she'd wake up.

A deep breath filled my lungs as I looked at her, wondering how on earth I ever deserved her.

Never in my life had I been more grateful to my brother and Lily for taking me in when Colin and my parents left the country. I never told them how grateful I'd been for that, but just watching as Brooke's chest rose and fell with every breath, her eyes closed and lips parted ever so slightly made me want to call them and thank them. God knew if Brooke and my relationship would even exist if I'd been forced to move to Spain six years ago.

A strand of her hair fell into her face when she moved, so I carefully tucked it behind her ear before I eventually killed the engine of my car, unfastened Brooke's seatbelt, and got out.

The October breeze brushed over my skin but I ignored it.

Brooke used my jacket as a blanket, and I certainly wasn't going to take it away from her just to walk into our apartment building in about two minutes.

I jogged around the car and slowly opened the door to minimize sounds. I took Brooke's purse from the dashboard, then hooked one arm underneath her knees and forced the other between her back and the seat. Without hitting a single body part of hers against my car, I managed to get her out, closed the door, and carried Brooke toward the building.

I locked my car before I could forget about it, and then blindly tried to find the apartment key and unlock the door. It took me a while, but five minutes after leaving the car, we were in our warm apartment, my sneakers off my feet, and I was walking through the dark living room to get Brooke to bed.

I turned on the bedside lamp before laying her down. While I was taking off her shoes, Brooke moved slightly, making the cutest little sounds I'd ever heard before propping herself up on her elbows to look at me.

Setting her shoes down in front of the bed for now, I walked up to her and pressed a kiss to the top of her head. "Go back to sleep, *mi princesa*."

Brooke closed her eyes and plopped back down, yet still shook her head no. "Shirt." Her arms flew up, waiting for me to pull her up to sit.

"You're already wearing a shirt of mine."

"But it's not the one you're wearing right now." Brooke wiggled her fingers, still waiting.

I pulled her up to sit, and while I took off my T-shirt, Brooke managed to take off her sweatshirt all on her own.

Her beautiful, yet very tired-looking green eyes met mine after I pulled my shirt down her body to cover her back up.

Before I could put the sweatshirt away, Brooke had

wrapped her arms around my now naked torso and tried to pull me onto the bed. "We should sleep," she muttered sleepily, pressing her face into my stomach.

I raked a hand through her hair, a chuckle rumbling in my chest. "We need to brush our teeth first now that you're awake."

Brooke groaned. "Only if you carry me."

I picked her up immediately. "I'll carry you anywhere for the rest of our lives if you ask me to, *mi princesa*."

Chapter Twenty-Three
Brooklyn

Reece was waiting in the car outside, and all I wanted to do was pop into Claire's to pick up our coffee orders when all of a sudden, someone tapped on my shoulder.

"Brooklyn?" a rather raspy voice spoke quietly.

I didn't recognize the voice, and since the Barista was just handing me my two coffees I wasn't thinking, let alone looking at whoever tried to speak to me.

"Yeah?" I said, then finally turned around only to stare into a face that was both familiar and alien to me.

She looked sort of put-together, though there was an emptiness in her eyes when she looked at me. Her blonde hair was stuck up into a bun and her outfit was lazy.

All those years, I'd hoped she was doing miserably. Every time she was reaching out, Dad shot her down for me because I never wanted to meet this woman. Someone who'd been so desperate to get rid of me, then come crawling back seemed like a person who didn't know how to live their life in the slightest.

But she looked… okay.

I really wish she didn't.

"Before you run away—"

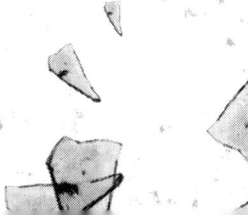

I already turned around and made my way to the exit doors. Luckily, I paid online when I ordered the coffees an hour ago, so I was free to go.

I wanted to forget her voice, wanted to unsee her face.

The only times I saw her face were in pictures when I was younger, but I could barely remember those. Emory threw out the last pictures of her sister when I was ten and confirmed I didn't want to have any memories of her, they weren't mine anyway.

"Brooklyn." Her hand laid on my shoulder again, but I didn't want to cause a scene in a café, so I didn't scream.

"Don't you dare touch me," I said, keeping my voice down.

Millie removed her hand from my shoulder, sighing. "Can we please talk?"

"No."

"But, Brooklyn, I jus—"

"Leave me alone." I took a step back, putting space between us.

It was a miracle she even knew my name. Dad said she never bothered to learn it, and she could've easily asked her parents for it.

I remembered my grandparents to an extent, and up until I learned why I never saw them anymore at some point, I held onto those memories like my life depended on them.

My grandpa died a couple of years ago, but that was okay because the few memories I had of him drowned in the pool of his lies a long time before he passed. My grandma was still alive, as far as I knew anyway, but I hadn't seen her in about fifteen years. The few memories I had of her were also tainted by the reality of what she'd done to my father, even if he definitely never told me the whole truth about her.

Dad never wanted me to hate my grandparents, even if he

and Emory did. He gave me—and Eden—the option to be in touch with them, but when I refused, Eden did too. He never met them anyway.

Elliot and Nova, though knowing the truth, kept saying both of them were dead. They were to our family, that was for sure.

"Please," she begged, her voice much sadder than a moment ago. "Spare me five minutes of your time."

I looked out of the window, finding Reece sitting in his car as he waited for me. He was on his phone, oblivious to what was happening inside the building, and oblivious to who was standing before me.

Though even if he looked, he was a tad too far away to know this was Millie, not Emory.

Mom stopped dyeing her hair ginger a few years ago because she wanted to stop damaging it. She no longer felt the need to prove to everyone that she wasn't Millie.

Now that Mom's hair was blonde again, their resemblance was uncanny. The length of their hair was almost the exact same.

There was one obvious difference, but even if Reece looked, he couldn't have seen it.

Millie had a scar that went down her left eye until the middle of her cheek. It was healed, but still so obvious.

I wondered if it had always been there or happened more recently. Perhaps it was some kind of birthmark no one had ever told me about. It was a strange spot to have a scar of this size.

"I don't know what there is to talk about," I said when I turned my eyes back on her. "I certainly have nothing to say. And if you had an interest in me, you wouldn't have faked your own death just to get away from me. So, no, Millie, I don't even have five minutes of my time to sacrifice for you. That'd be five minutes of my life wasted."

Besides, I had places to be.

Reece and I had been invited to a frat party. It was Friday evening—the first Friday this season he didn't have to be at practice or a game. While we had to get up early tomorrow for a competition, Reece wanted to go to this party because Ming begged him to come. We'd leave before midnight though, so we could catch some sleep.

"I've got to go," I added, but before I could walk away, Millie stepped closer to me once again.

"I'm sorry," she muttered. "I know I've been a bad—"

I snorted. "Don't you dare call yourself my mother."

"But I am."

"You gave birth to me, is all." Anger was slowly flooding my veins. "There's no need to apologize for disappearing. You did me and everyone else a favor by dying. Just because you suddenly feel guilty for something you did doesn't give you the right to corner me in a coffee shop. I have no interest in getting to know you, and the past fifteen years of everyone telling you to leave me and my family alone should've been a clear indicator of that. You can shove your half-assed apology up your entitled ass and leave me, Dad, my mom, and everyone else the fuck alone, got it?"

"Your... mom?" For whatever reason, she looked taken aback by that. "Emory isn't your mom, I am. I gave birth to you, Brooklyn. Emory stole my life!"

I took a deep breath, trying to stay calm. "How could she steal your life when you were trying to live hers?"

Again, I didn't know the whole story, but I knew a whole lot more about my parents' history than Millie apparently thought I did.

"Look, whatever happened between you and my parents

is *your* problem. I'm not interested in getting to know you. You had your chance to get to know me when I was born, but you chose to fake your death instead. That's on you. And you can't even say that *I* ruined your life because I know that you thought if you got pregnant, it'd mean Dad was going to stay in your life forever. You just realized you didn't want the responsibility a little too late. So again, that's on you. It's been twenty years, let it go. I don't want you in my life, Dad doesn't want you in his life, and my mom couldn't give any more fucks about your existence either. Let. It. Go. Move on."

Her mouth opened as she was trying to disagree with me, but the Barista cut her off.

"Mrs. Reed? Your coffee is ready."

Millie turned around, and while she was telling the Barista to wait a second, I took that moment to leave Claire's.

I wasn't interested in hearing her out. When I said she should've gotten the memo by now, I meant it. If I had had the slightest ounce of interest in her inside of me, I would've reached out to her ages ago.

She didn't try to follow me to the car, which I was glad about since I was sure if Reece saw her, he wouldn't have stayed as calm as I tried to. He never met her either, obviously, but when we were younger, every time I used to get upset over my birth mother seeing me as someone who had ruined her life, he got more angry than me.

I didn't want Reece to get mad.

As I reached the car, I realized that *she* reacted to Mrs. Reed. Guess someone was stupid enough to fall in love and marry her after all. That poor guy.

"Claire's didn't look like it had much of a line when we got here," Reece said as I got into his car. "Didn't think you'd be gone for ten whole minutes."

I handed him his coffee without saying a word. I wasn't sure if I could speak right now.

Part of me wanted to tell Reece who I'd just met, the other part was still trying to understand it happened myself.

In theory, I knew she was alive. I knew she tried reaching out before. But for the first five years of my life, I'd been told she was dead.

While I didn't remember much from those years, I remembered being told Millie died giving birth. Then, the next thing I remember was my dad sitting me down at eight years old, telling me how she wasn't dead but that she apparently faked it all just to get out of being a mother.

For the next six months, I'd been crying myself to sleep because I thought I ruined someone's life. I was worried Dad thought of me as a burden as much as this woman did.

I knew that if it hadn't been for me, Dad would've gone to the NHL. He wouldn't have had to spend his college years taking care of a kid he didn't plan to have, and instead could've had fun and been irresponsible.

I thought, if she could hate me for ruining her life, so could he. The difference was that she did something horrible to get out of her responsibilities while Dad stepped up.

Dad reassured me that I'd been the best that's ever happened to him more than once, but on very bad days, even that reassurance did nothing to console me.

A few years later, I found out that Millie got pregnant on purpose, she just failed to tell my father until I was twelve.

Ever since then, I knew she technically wanted me... until she didn't anymore. But by that time, I already resented her, and finding out about that made my hatred even worse.

"Hey, are you alright?" Reece laid his hand on my thigh, his thumb stroking back and forth.

I looked out of the window, noticing that we were no longer near Claire's.

"Do you want to go back home?" he asked.

"No," I replied. "I need a drink."

"You can't drink, *mi princesa*. We have a competition tomorrow."

I turned to look at him, but Reece's eyes were focused on the road.

He styled his hair earlier. Usually, Reece's hair was all fluffy even though he always put gel in it so it stayed in place. Sometimes I'd think he woke up like that and didn't even brush his hair, but it never looked bad.

Today, he parted his hair in the middle.

I kind of wanted to run my hands through his hair just to mess it up again. I liked the middle part, but this so wasn't Reece.

"Now, tell me. What's wrong?" He stopped at a red light and took that moment to look at me. "Who do I have to beat up?"

I smiled softly at his words. He'd never beaten someone up, but I liked that he claimed he would. "I met Millie," I told him, keeping my voice down as if it was a secret.

"Millie?" Confusion flickered in his eyes. "Millie... Scott?"

I nodded quickly then shook my head. "I think she's a Reed now."

"Who the fuck would marry someone like her?"

My shoulders lifted into a shrug. "Someone who's as cruel as her or... they're just really stupid."

Reece's grip on the steering wheel tightened as we sat in silence at the red light. I could feel the tension radiating off him, his knuckles turning white. Despite my own resentment towards Millie, I didn't want Reece to get too upset about the encounter. He was protective of me, sometimes to a fault.

"Did she say anything?" Reece finally asked, his voice low and controlled.

"She tried to apologize," I replied, my gaze fixed on a distant building outside the car window. "Tried to blame my mom for everything."

"Emory?"

I nodded, feeling a mix of emotions swirling inside me. "She claimed Emory stole her life. That she's the victim in all this."

Reece let out a frustrated sigh, shaking his head in disbelief when I looked at him again. "That woman has some nerve."

"I just... I can't believe she had the audacity to tap on my shoulder and try to talk to me," I said.

As soon as the traffic light turned from red to green, Reece shifted the car back into drive and continued down the road.

"What was she thinking? That Dad didn't tell me what happened back then? That I'd just forgive her and hear her out?" Anger poisoned my blood, but I didn't even want to be angry. It was pointless anyway.

Reece remained silent for a moment, his grip on the steering wheel steady as he navigated the car through the streets.

After a while, he spoke, "You don't owe her anything, Brooke. Not your forgiveness, not your time, nothing. She made her choices, and now she has to live with them."

"I know." Hopefully, that was the first and last time I'd see her.

I tried to recite Millie and my conversation to my fiancé. Each time I made a good point, he was smiling and throwing in a sarcastic comment to strengthen my argument, even though Millie wouldn't know about it.

I really appreciated his support.

As we were nearing the party location, Reece said something that seemed almost too comical to be true.

"You know, it's funny how she has the same last name as Erik now. It fits, though, they are both very awful people. She could be his mother for all we know."

Chapter Twenty-Four
Brooklyn

"I started to think you guys weren't coming!" Rina said as she jumped into my arms the moment I got out of the car. "You said you'd be here at eight-thirty PM, not eight-forty-five PM!"

I chuckled. "We stopped for a coffee."

"Well, don't ever do this to me again, Brooklyn. If anyone here finds out I'm not a St. Trewery student, they'll eat me alive."

Reece laughed but he stopped shortly after, probably because Rina was sending him a death glare of some sort. She had a pretty good one.

"I'll meet you inside, okay? Gotta find a spot to park the car first," he said.

Rina finally let go of me, so I could turn around and look at Reece when I said, "I'm not going in there without you."

"You're not alone." Rina sounded offended, or as offended as Rina could get. I'd never actually witnessed anyone offend her; and if they tried to, she simply wouldn't let them.

"Ming's inside," Reece added, slightly cocking his head at me.

What If We Break?

I'd gotten better at handling crowds… but I'd never been in a crowd without Reece or my family before.

Parties scared me big time. The only birthday parties I attended were from my family—including my dad's friends' families.

Birthdays were much different from college parties though, so if I couldn't even do birthdays, I wasn't going to survive a frat party. Sure, Reece was going to find me, but who knew how long it'd take to find a parking spot? Or how long it'd take until he got through the crowd of people who'd want to chat with him or the onslaught of drunk puck bunnies who were ready to drop to their knees right in the middle of the room.

Okay, the puck bunnies weren't actually *that* scandalous, I knew that… in theory.

"Who's Ming?" Rina asked with curiosity, already pulling me toward the huge Delta Chi house. "Is he cute?"

"I… I don't know. I guess?"

Rina groaned, swinging an arm around my shoulders. "Why do I even ask? Your type is Reece and Reece alone."

"Yeah." I looked back toward Reece, but he drove off to find a parking spot.

I couldn't even tell him to drive safely. What if he got into an accident because I didn't remind him? It was unlikely but possible.

Oh, God.

He was going to die, wasn't he?

No.

I took a deep breath, feeling my hands shake and my legs slowly losing strength.

Reece was going to be alright, and I could go into Delta Chi without having a panic attack.

It was a stupid party with people my age—some a bit

older, some a bit younger—who just wanted to have some fun. We, okay, *they* were here to get drunk, or smoke weed, or find someone to fuck, no biggie.

No one was looking at me. No one was interested in me. No one was judging me.

And Reece was going to be alright.

"Yo! Brooke!" someone screamed over the loud music as Rina and I entered what looked to me like a living room. A big one at that.

I looked around the room, trying to locate that voice.

The living room was surprisingly underwhelming. For its size, I expected fancy furniture and expensive artwork, but it was all so bland.

They didn't even have a fireplace, but then again, perhaps it was a bad idea to give a bunch of eighteen to twenty-something-year-olds a fireplace.

"Who's that?" Rina pointed across the room at a guy with black hair who was waving his entire arm back and forth to make himself noticeable.

"Oh... that's Ming."

"*That's* Ming?" Her eyes widened drastically. "Man, I thought you and Reece could pull some strings for me and hook me up with his friend so I didn't have to flirt with tons of guys tonight... but that guy's a virgin."

"What's wrong with being a virgin?" I asked, genuinely curious.

"Nothing, per se, but did you ever—wait, no, you didn't. Honestly, I'm not even sure why I thought you and Reece could be my wingman and woman. You guys don't even know what flirting is."

I stopped walking in the middle of dancing bodies just to look at my best friend—lips parted and eyebrows raised at her obvious attack.

"What's that supposed to mean?" I spoke over the loud music.

Rina laughed but I couldn't hear the sound of it as the music was swallowing it entirely. She leaned into me to make it easier to hear her. "It really shouldn't offend you. You chose one dick and decided that's it for the rest of your life. That's one guy you ever kissed. One guy you *flirted* with. And I bet you didn't even flirt with each other until you were like sixteen. You just dated at some point. You don't know the dating struggle."

My eyes rolled as I stormed past Rina and made my way over to Ming.

She wasn't wrong, I knew that, but it sure sounded like she was judging me for the choices I had made.

Why was everyone so annoyed by Reece and my relationship? How was it any of their problems?

Fynn was constantly making fun of Reece for only ever having dated me. He'd been trying to stir up drama in our relationship for no goddamn reason, and I bet he aimed to break us up.

I had no idea why he even cared in the first place.

Even if he had a thing for me—which I doubted—that still didn't guarantee I was going to start shit with the guy. The way he was behaving, that was an instant no. And I wasn't one to fuck my ex's best friend.

Then again, I never even—shut *up, Brooke. Don't let other people get inside your head.*

"Where's Reece?" Ming asked as soon as I reached him. He pushed a red plastic cup into my hand or tried to anyway.

The only guy I trusted to get me a drink was my fiancé. Plus, I wasn't even allowed to drink tonight.

"Parking the car," I replied.

"Who's your friend?" He nodded toward the bodies of

people, and when I turned around to look at Rina, I found her dancing with three strangers.

Oh, to be as social as her...

If she hadn't practically adopted me as her friend, I would've never even talked to her.

"That's Rina."

Ming smiled to himself, then slapped it off his face. "Is she single?"

Do people really go to these parties just to find someone to fuck? If yes, I was *very* glad that I was in a relationship.

Going out every weekend to be with yet another stranger sounded like an actual nightmare to me. I couldn't fathom how that was such a normalized experience.

Relationships were a great thing. Who wouldn't want to have that one person in their life who loved you unconditionally? That one person you could confide in? That one person who you could always count on?

Reece was all that to me. He made my heart flutter with love when I looked at him, even if he didn't look back. I could be myself with him, my *true* self—something barely anyone had ever met outside of my close family. He made life easier.

Who wouldn't have wanted a Reece in their life?

"She is," I answered. "But she's not into you."

Ming's eyes snapped to mine, shock on his face. His shoulders dropped, and his expression followed. "Not at all?"

I shrugged. "What do I know? I've only ever had one boyfriend in my li—"

"Exactly!" Ming wrapped an arm around my shoulder after turning me back toward the crowd. "You met *one* guy and were like 'Man, he's kinda cute. I'll keep him forever.' Teach me how you did that, Brooke. I want that." He pointed at Rina. "With her."

I laughed. "That's not how it works."

"I want her to have my babies." He leaned his head against mine. "How do I make her fall in love with me?"

Chapter Twenty-Five

Reece

"Hey, hey!" Fynn pushed a red cup into my hand as soon as I entered the Delta Chi house. "I was starting to think you wouldn't show up."

I set the cup down on one of the tables they set up for extra drinks and snacks that were already almost entirely gone.

It was fairly early for one of the frat parties, so it was a bit of a surprise to me to see the food almost gone. Then again, I didn't really care because I would've rather died than touched anything one of the members of Delta Chi prepared.

"Have you seen Brooke?" I'd been trying to find her for the past ten minutes, but she was *nowhere.* I looked inside the living room, the kitchen, the bathrooms, and even checked the backyard… but it was like she vanished from the face of the earth.

"Brooke who?" He took a huge sip of his drink. "Tonight's party night, Reecie-poo. Relax a little. Find a hot puck bunny and get freaky for once in your life. Fuck Brooke."

"That's my plan."

His mouth hung open. "I approve of cheating."

So badly I wanted to punch my fist into his average-looking face, then say my hand slipped or something, but I had to stay calm.

We had a huge game coming up next weekend in Boston. If I wanted to play, I couldn't afford to get into fistfights with anyone—especially someone who was also on the same team as me.

"I plan to fuck Brooke, like you suggested," I said. My eyes wandered over the crowd of dancing bodies, paying extra attention to anyone with blond hair to hopefully find my fiancée amongst them all.

I stayed unsuccessful.

"That's not what I meant."

"I don't care what you meant. And frankly, I've had it with your bullshit, Fynn. Just because your morals are in hell doesn't mean you can act like I'm as much of a fucked-up person as you are. I love Brooke, and whether you like it or not, we'll be together for the rest of our lives," I snapped and leaned closer to him, so there was no chance he was going to miss the next thing that left my mouth. "If I ever hear her name come out of your fucking mouth again, I'll shove your hockey stick so far up your ass, you'll taste the wood on your tongue."

With that said, I forced myself through the drunk and sweaty people to hopefully find my fiancée somewhere.

I tried calling her over and over, but she never picked up, which sort of made sense. It was loud as hell, so unless she had her phone in her hands, she wasn't going to hear it ring.

After making it outside onto the patio, I took a deep breath before deciding to give Ming a call. Perhaps I should've thought of that five minutes ago, but I was honestly more focused on reaching Brooke than him. Hopefully, she was with him.

Much to my surprise, Ming picked up on the first try. "What's up?"

"Seriously?"

"Where are you?" he asked just before someone screamed right into the phone, almost busting my right eardrum. "Sorry, that was Lane. He thought it'd be hilarious."

Lane was our goalie. For a year now, I thought he was the coolest guy on the team… I was starting to doubt it.

Who the hell screamed into someone else's phone because they thought it was hilarious? And the guy was older than me.

"Is Brooke with you?" I asked, deciding I could complain about Lane and my hurting ear after I located my fiancée.

"Sure is."

"Where are you?"

"I asked first." He sighed heavily into the phone, a bit dramatically. "Did you know your girlfriend has a very pretty best friend?"

"Rina?" I leaned against the exterior of the house, using all of my strength not to hit my head against the brick wall.

"Rina," he repeated back to me, dragging her name out in a soft tone. "Brooke's trying to teach me how to become you."

"Become *me*?" What was that even supposed to mean? "Why me?"

"Not *you*-you. But become like you."

Why? I thought Ming was a great guy, why would he want to change? "Ming… could you just tell me where you are? Please."

"You only want to know where I am so you can get to your girlfriend."

Perhaps I should tell Ming that Brooke and I were engaged so he'd stop calling her my girlfriend. "Exactly."

"We're in one of the bedrooms because it's quieter in here."

My pulse instantly picked up. "You, Brooke, and Lane?"

"Yup."

"Did anyone see you go in there?" I headed inside the house, once again wrestling myself through all those drunk college students.

"Yeah, a group of football players," he replied. "But we locked the door so nobody could come inside. It wasn't necessary because nobody even tried to kick us out or anything."

"No shit!" I snapped. "They think you're having a threesome!"

"Me, Brooke, and Lane?" Ming laughed. "Yeah, right. Brooke's like a sister to me."

Before I could reply, a guy from my hockey team swung an arm around my shoulders. "Did you hear that Lui and Vega are fucking your girl? Not sure if it's true, but it's said that Ming and Lane went into one of the bedrooms with her."

Great, people were already talking about it.

"Brooke's not good with crowds," I told Holden. "Ming just took her to a quieter place until I'd get here. And Lane is… Lane. That guy's always everywhere."

Holden nodded his head, eyes wide with sympathy. "Shit, dude. Word's going around that she's cheating on you."

"CHEATING?!" Ming shrieked into the phone. "Do they even know her? That girl's like disgustingly in love with you."

"Yes, thanks, Ming," I muttered but he couldn't hear as the music was still blasting.

"Lui's on the phone with you?" Holden laughed, then slapped his hand onto my back. "I'll take care of the rumors, you go find your girl, man."

"Thanks," I said. "Who told you about it anyway?"

"Ritchie," he answered. Of course it was fucking Fynn. "It was so weird. I thought you guys were tight. Lane's girl would murder every single person out there if he so much as thinks about another girl, so I was already confused as hell when Ritchie told me. And he should've known Lui's not fucking your girl either, especially since Brooke's like our unofficial team mascot."

My eyebrows drew together. "What?"

"Yeah. Carter, she's at *every* game. It doesn't matter if we're across the country, Brooke's there. So basically a mascot—wait, no. She's our cheerleader."

Well, he was right, in some odd way. Brooke never missed a game, even if that meant she had to skip school to be there. She usually brought Eden to games that were too far away so she wasn't alone on the way to and back from the place. She never went on a plane by herself.

But at least she showed up.

"If she ever doesn't show up for one game, we're gonna lose," he added. "So she's also our talisman. You got yourself a ruby."

I nodded slowly, unsure of what to say. "Anyway, I should go find them."

"Right." He slapped his hand to my back once more. "Tell her I said hi."

"Did you hear any of the things I just said?" Ming's voice came through the phone, reminding me that I was still on a call with him. "I ain't repeating it."

I sighed and walked around a group of girls because they refused to let me squeeze between them. "Come downstairs with Brooke, alright? I'm getting Rina so we can get the fuck out of here."

"But you guys just got here ten minutes ago."

"Yeah, and you already started rumors that my fiancée's cheating on me."

"FIANCÉE?!" Oh, right... I didn't tell him. "You're engaged?!"

"Can you give me Brooke?" I asked, and a moment later, I spotted Rina. She was dancing with five different guys at once.

Alright then.

"Actually, don't bother. Meet me downstairs in the kitchen. I'll get Rina." That said, I hung up the phone to make my way over to Brooke's friend.

Neither Brooke nor I were party people. We preferred to spend free weekends at home in bed and watch a movie or two, or five. We were both big on spending time with our families and thought that treating ourselves to a good meal from a high-ranked restaurant was worth more than spending a night in a way too crowded space with drunk people.

We were only here because of Ming since he didn't want to go to this disease-catcher party all by himself. But I was going to take that guy, drive his drunk ass home, and spend the rest of the evening with my fiancée in our shared apartment. It was such a waste of time coming here.

"Rina." I laid my hand on her shoulder, almost earning myself a slap but she stopped herself when she realized it was me and not one of the five guys surrounding her.

"Hiiii!" She took my hands, swinging them around in an attempt to make me dance. "You're so stiff, Carter. Loosen up, my God. You're such a grandpa."

Was that supposed to be an insult? "Thank you."

She laughed, let go of my hands, and continued to dance like nobody was watching. There were more than ten pairs of eyes on her—mine excluded—and I was almost sure it was mostly guys who were looking at her.

When I first met Rina, she seemed like a very innocent girl. She was covered in paint in a school that didn't offer art classes, perhaps that should've been a sign that she didn't have a single care in the world. But boy did I wish she was less confident right now.

"We're leaving," I told her, but had to repeat myself because she didn't acknowledge me.

"What, why?" Rina stopped dancing and let her arms drop. "We just got here. I'm having fun."

"Brooke's not a party person."

"Yes, I know." Her eyes rolled, then she turned toward one of the guys, took his phone, checked the time, and gave it back. "Aw, I thought she'd made it at least an hour."

"You can stay, but I'm taking Brooke home."

"No, it's alright. St. Trewery guys are weird anyway." She gestured for me to lead the way, so I did. "They're so... touchy."

"Juilliard guys are that different?"

"Nope." She hooked her arm into mine so she wouldn't lose me. I wanted to rip my arm out because a woman other than Brooke was touching me. But I wanted to get the fuck out of there. "We don't have much time for parties. Sure, one of the more popular students throws a party maybe once a month, but—"

I tuned her out, not because I didn't necessarily care about what she said—I didn't—but because I was far more concerned about the looks filled with sympathy I was getting as I walked past other students.

Guess they heard the rumors.

I was going to fuck up Fynn's face the next time I'd see him.

Chapter Twenty-Six
Brooklyn

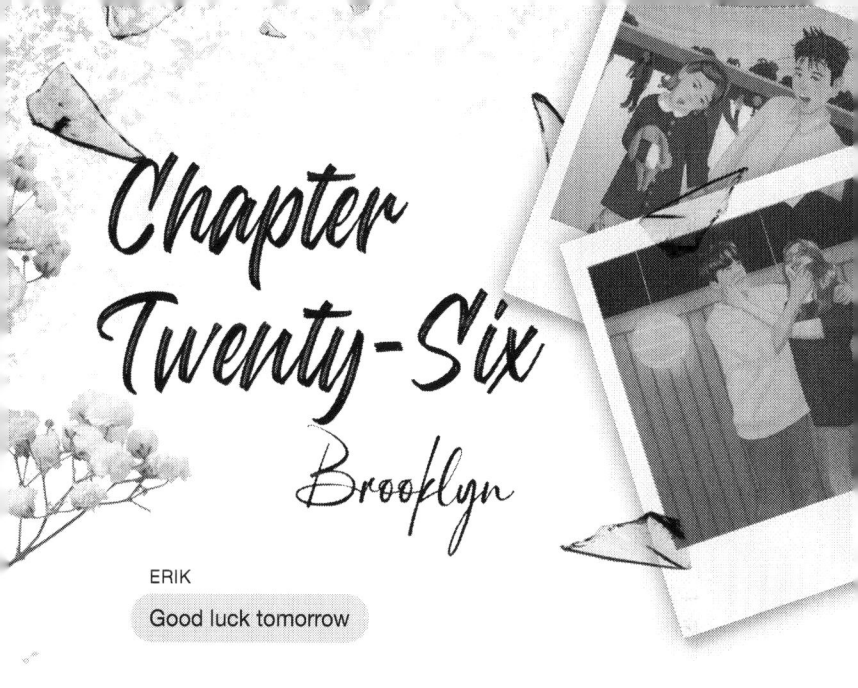

ERIK
> Good luck tomorrow

I stared at Erik's text as if it came from an alien. The only times he ever sent me messages were when he thought I was interested in his opinion about my on-ice performance. Or my eating habits. Or my relationship status.

Yet, I replied.

ME
> Thanks.

ERIK
> I don't think you'll make it far without me, but I thought I should at least wish you good luck

Now, that sounded way more like the Erik Reed I knew.

Just as I was about to type out my opinion for once, Ming pulled on my arm. "I think I see Reece!"

I looked up, scanning the crowd for my fiancé. And there he was, forcing himself past multiple drunk, dancing people. Rina followed close behind, though Reece had to pull her after him every now and then because she seemed to get lost every time someone glanced her way.

"Such a bummer that we're leaving already. It's just getting good," Ming said, sighing deeply. I think. It was pretty difficult to hear over the loud music.

My head was already throbbing, and I hadn't even been here for very long. I was starting to get thirsty, though, which wasn't good. The likeliness of finding some water at a party was somewhere in the negatives.

"Yes, a bummer," I replied sarcastically. I couldn't wait to leave this goddamn place. I didn't even want to be here in the first place.

Honestly, I was happy with a calm evening inside. Maybe doing some skincare with Reece, lighting some candles, and watching a movie before going to bed. It was my ideal night, but instead, we were here. In between drunk, sweaty people, some who were screaming, some who were almost stripping off their clothes on the stairs, and some who looked like they were seconds from throwing up.

"Hi." Reece sounded almost relieved when he stood before me. He gave me a soft smile, then cupped my face with his hands. "Are you alright, *mi princesa*?"

"Oh, my God." Ming dragged out a sigh. "It's official. I'll die before I could ever have a girlfriend. All because of you two."

I ignored Ming, as did Reece.

"I'm okay," I replied. "Are we going out of he—"

My phone kept vibrating in my hand, and it now reached a point where it started to annoy me.

Reece removed his hands from my face, watching me check my messages. I didn't even have to look at him to know he was watching me.

When I read Erik's name on my screen, all I wanted to do

was throw my phone into the nearest garbage disposal and destroy it for good.

Why was he suddenly texting me? And so much at once, too. It was strange and far from what I wanted.

Couldn't he pretend I never existed?

> **ERIK**
>
> I'm just saying, Brooklyn. Reece was decent once upon a time, but he's shit now.
>
> I saw the video from your practice session you posted last week.
>
> He sucked.
>
> You should've just quit the season and start back up with me next year.
>
> Reece is going to destroy your reputation

My eyes rolled, and that was the least bad reaction I had in mind. I was ready to scrub them with bleach.

> **ERIK**
>
> I'll be at the arena tomorrow to watch you fail
>
> Don't worry though, I won't film it or even mention your awful performance
>
> It's your boyfriend's fault anyway
>
> Let's just hope the judges won't disqualify you for having the worst skating partner in history

I took a deep breath, then slowly began typing out my reply.

ME

You're being quite the harsh judge for someone who broke both of his legs because he was too incompetent to keep a hold on me.

Oh, wait... you let go on purpose, hoping it would injure me.

Want to know what your problem is, Erik?

ERIK

I don't have any. And it's quite unfair how you use my injury as a flaw.

BROOKE

You view yourself as irreplaceable, when in reality, you're no better than an amateur. Actually, even an amateur has better catching skills than you do.

While I know you suddenly regain the ability to catch me, hold me up, or throw me in ways that allow me to actually stick the landing during competitions with judges present, it's not special enough to view you as irreplaceable.

Reece doesn't even drop me during practice. He wouldn't dream of it.

It took you two whole years to land an Axel without falling, while I've been doing Quadruple Axels with my eyes closed. Guess how long Reece took to relearn a Triple Axel?

2 attempts.

He stuck the Triple Axel on his second try after not having done a single jump since he was sixteen. What's your excuse?

You're the most replaceable person I have ever met.

"Is everything alright?" Reece asked, and when I looked up at him, I noticed how a little line formed between his eyebrows, his eyes glistening with concern. His head was slightly cocked, shoulders tense. "Who do I need to fight for you, *mi princesa*?"

The corners of my lips pulled into a faint smile. "Erik's being a jerk again, so nothing new. I'm alright, I promise."

"I hate that guy." He wrapped an arm around my body, hand resting on my waist. "Let's just get out of here. The fact that he lives in this house is disturbing."

I laughed. "He's home with his parents. He just got out of the hospital two days ago. I doubt any responsible parent would let their kid with two broken legs live in a fraternity home until their mobility is back to normal."

"Are we talking about Erik Reed?" Ming threw into the conversation. He now had a red cup of whatever beverage in his hand.

Where the hell did he get that from so suddenly?

"Yes," I replied, though sounding unsure.

"Hate that guy," he groaned before chugging down half of his drink at once. "Did you know he's related to Fynn?!"

My eyes widened in shock, my breath spiraling right out of my lungs. Reece's lips parted slightly in disbelief, his grip on me tightening.

"Ritchie?" Reece said. "No way."

"No, seriously! He told me."

"There's no way Fynn and Erik are related," I said, shaking my head as I didn't want to believe this could've been true at all. Fynn was an asshole anyway, he could've lied. "Erik literally once asked me who Fynn was when you guys showed up at the arena during our practice."

Ming nodded, then took another sip of his drink. "Yeah, they're like step-siblings, actually. They're keeping it a secret because, apparently, Erik can't stand Fynn. No surprise there, to be honest. Fynn's a dick."

"Erik isn't much better," I muttered. Thankfully, it was too loud for anybody to hear. "Aren't you and Fynn friends?" I asked, louder this time.

"Kinda," Ming replied. "I try not to engage with him as much. He's super weird to our Reecie-poo because of you. Like, dude, seriously, sometimes even I want to punch that guy in his average-looking face. I don't understand how Reece hasn't done it yet."

"I have," Reece said, laughing. "I'm just being smart about it. I punch the guy on the ice."

Ming smirked, tapping a finger to his left temple. "Smart, Reecie-poo."

"You're not seriously calling him 'Reecie-poo', are you?" Rina joined the conversation. "Now I wish I could drink, so I could forget those words ever left your mouth. I have to drive though, so I can't. Bummer."

"I can drive you home, Rina," Ming offered but all three of us instantly shook our heads.

"God knows how much you drank already," Reece said and took the red cup away from his best friend. "And you don't even have a license yet."

"Hey, I have my permit."

"Aren't you like… nineteen or twenty? Get your fucking license." Rina laughed and swung an arm around Ming, who didn't seem to mind it one bit. "Barely any girl's gonna want to chauffeur their boyfriend around. It's called Passenger *Princess*. Unless you identify as a woman, that's not you."

"If I get my license, will you go on a date with me?"

Reece covered my mouth before a comment that would've ruined everything could've made it past my lips. I tended to make comments to make an awkward situation less awkward. To be fair, I always made it worse, but at least I tried.

"Tell you what, Ming," Rina began. "I drive you home tonight, and in return, you can get as drunk as you want."

"How's that going to—"

Rina pressed her index finger to Ming's lips, stopping him from talking. "If I like the drunk you, I'll think about that date. But sober you is boring. So, let alcohol do the magic and take down your guard so I can see at least one reason why I should give you a chance."

"That sounds backhanded," Reece whispered right into my ear. I nodded in agreement. "Actually, it's not even backhanded. She straight-up told him he's boring."

I looked at my fiancé, laughing. "Yet Ming's stupid enough to agree," I said.

A moment later, Ming and Rina were making their way into the kitchen to get him some drinks.

I took a deep breath and leaned against Reece. "So, what now?"

His arms closed around my body, holding me tightly in his embrace. "Guess we're going to have to find a way to stay a little longer. I hope we can get them to leave in an hour."

I looked up, smirking. "There's an empty room just—"

Reece gasped. "Brooklyn Desrosiers-King," he said, then tsked at me. "Did you just imply that we should—" He leaned down and lowered his voice. "Get *a room* to pass the time?"

I shrugged. "That's what college parties are there for, no?"

"You already had one scandal tonight."

"Ah, well, one more with my fiancé won't hurt then."

Chapter Twenty-Seven

Brooklyn

Reece loosened his grip on me just to reach for my hand, and a second later, he pulled me toward the stairs.

I glanced back at the party, the noise and laughter fading into the background as Reece led me upstairs toward the bedrooms. There were some people up there, but far less than downstairs. Most of them were eager to use one of the bathrooms or hookup.

The air felt cooler up here, quieter, almost intimate in an unnatural way. Reece's hand was warm in mine, his touch soft and reassuring as he led me through the dimly lit hallway.

A few students glanced at us as we passed them, but none of them uttered a word.

As we reached one of the many bedrooms, Reece opened the door and popped his head inside to check it was empty. It seemed to have been occupied because Reece quickly shut the door again, shaking his head.

"That looked like it hurt," he said.

I didn't even dare ask what he just saw. "Maybe we should try another room?"

What If We Break?

Reece leaned down, pressing his lips to my forehead. "Sounds like a good idea."

We continued down the hall, passing a couple of closed doors with semi-loud music blaring from inside. It seemed like people were busy in them, so Reece didn't even stop to check if they were empty—he just assumed they weren't.

At the far end of the hallway, we finally found a quiet room. Reece turned the doorknob slowly, pushed the door open, and checked to see if it was empty. The room revealed a small but cozy space with a neatly made bed and a desk cluttered with textbooks and notes. It looked as if nobody had been inside before, at least not tonight.

My fiancé pushed me into the room, but as he was about to enter, he looked toward the other end of the hall. Suddenly, a mischievous grin tugged at his lips before he winked and finally followed me into the room.

"Who'd you wink at?" I asked as Reece closed the door behind him, locking it.

"Fynn," he told me. "He just came upstairs and looked at me, so I might as well provoke him a little."

"Because he's far from getting laid?"

Reece nodded. "He suggested it was a good idea that I fucked you tonight."

My eyebrows shot up. "What?"

"Well, technically he suggested I cheat on you and don't give a fuck about you, but you know? He said *fuck Brooke*, so..."

The idea of Fynn giving relationship advice was utterly absurd—especially since it was the worst 'advice' ever—and the thought of Reece taking it seriously was even more hilarious.

Reece loved me and certainly wasn't someone who'd

cheat. He couldn't even cheat on a test, what made Fynn think he was going to cheat on *me*?

"Can you imagine if I listened to Fynn?" Reece said between fits of laughter.

I shook my head. "Hell would freeze over before that ever happens."

As our laughter subsided, the sound of the music from neighboring rooms became more evident. It didn't matter.

Reece stepped closer, his gaze warm and filled with affection. "You know I would never listen to that idiot, right?" he said softly, his hand reaching out to cup my cheek.

"I know," I replied, leaning into his touch. "I trust you more than anyone, Reece."

His eyes crinkled at the corners as he smiled at me, a faint flush painting his cheeks. "I love you, Brooke."

"I love you too," I whispered before his lips met mine in a tender, loving kiss that was quick to turn needy and passionate.

As our kiss deepened, I melted into Reece's touch, my arms wrapping around his neck as he pulled me closer.

Slowly, we neared the bed, and only as the back of my knees hit the mattress, we broke apart.

"Are you sure you want this?" Reece asked as our eyes opened and our gazes met.

"As long as I can keep my clothes on." It was still strange to me that these guys from Delta Chi kept their rooms unlocked.

If I threw a huge party at my place, my bedroom would've been locked and I probably would've put up a motion sensor or something. The idea of a stranger having sex in *my* bed was disturbing.

And, alright, maybe Reece and I should've refrained from having sex in a stranger's bedroom as well, but... the overwhelming need to feel him inside of me clouded my judgment a little.

Reece looked at the bed for a brief moment, then his eyes wandered around the room. "Maybe it's for the best we don't sit you down on any surface. Who knows what was done to them before," he said, a hint of amusement sounding in his voice. "I don't want you catching anything."

The bed looked fairly clean, but I wondered what I'd find if I used a blue light to take a deeper look. There was a high chance I'd find stains that were best left unseen. The thought of that was gross enough to make me agree with my fiancé.

So, which part of the bedroom seemed like the perfect spot that didn't require me to sit on it?

"Maybe we shouldn't do this after all," I mumbled, feeling sort of bummed out by it. The possibility of getting caught had always been exciting for us, but perhaps a frat party was taking it a step too far.

"We don't have to do this," he said, and shortly after, his eyes lit up with something mischievous. Reece grabbed my hand and led me toward the wall-length window. His breath grazed my ear as he spoke up again. "But… you could have a great view of a party as I fuck you from behind."

I blushed at his suggestion, feeling a wave of adrenaline shooting through my veins at the thought of being so daring. We'd done scandalous things before, risked it in a bunch of different public spaces like the public pool, and the movies—if it was just the two of us in there, at school. The riskiest one was probably the treehouse in my parents' backyard when we were sixteen—the treehouse was gone now.

But the window at a frat party?

The window overlooked the backyard where the party was still in full swing, music thumping, people talking, and getting drunk.

The chances were slim of someone looking up and seeing us, but there was a chance of it happening.

Reece's hands slid around my waist, the warmth of his body seeping into my skin as he pressed soft kisses along my neck. "I'm pretty sure the windows are made of privacy glass. At least I couldn't see anything that was going on inside when I was out there."

"Pretty sure isn't a guarantee... and I don't know how much I like the thought of possibly being on the internet with videos or pictures like that."

He grabbed my hair, tilting my head back and forcing me to look at him. "Are you worried about your reputation, Ms. King?"

"Yeah," I replied. It was actually *our* reputation I was worried about, and what would happen if our families saw these online. It could've affected Colin's and my mom's careers, and maybe even gone as far as to ruin my father's restaurants. "I don't need strangers getting off on us."

Reece chuckled. "I promise, *mi princesa*, I'd *never* do anything that would lead to anyone but me watching you come on my dick. But if you don't want to risk it, that's okay, too. You decide."

He let go of my hair, allowing me to lift my head again. "We keep the lights turned off?"

"Yes."

That at least minimized the view on us.

"How sure are you that these windows are made of privacy glass?" I asked, watching two girls scream at each other.

"About eighty-nine percent," he answered, resting his chin on the top of my head. "Whoever's room this is doesn't have curtains, and I doubt he'd refrain from getting some if they were needed."

Reece had a point. Life without privacy seemed awful, and I could imagine it was already a struggle to get some of that if you lived in a fraternity. Surely the guy who stayed in this room didn't want to be watched all the time.

"Okay," I said. "Besides, what's one more scandal, right?"

Reece laughed, his grip on me tightening as his fingers dipped into my waist. "There won't be a scandal. As I said, your body is for my eyes only."

His hands slid underneath my dress, lifting the fabric up to my waist as his fingers gently traced along the underside of my breasts.

"Turn around," he whispered, his hot breath grazing my skin.

As soon as I faced him, Reece pulled my dress over my head, leaving me standing in nothing but my underwear and heels.

"Didn't we agree on keeping our clothes on?" I arched a brow at him.

"I figured since you're not sitting anywhere, it'll be fine." A smirk tugged at his lips as his gaze dropped to my exposed breasts. "Besides, your tits are pretty great to look at."

My eyes rolled as he threw my dress onto the nearby desk. "You have no shame, Mister."

He pushed me up against the glass window, my nipples hardening more and my back arching in an attempt to escape the cold surface. I could feel his erection through his pants, poking me just underneath my navel.

"I think you like that about me," he whispered, his voice raspy.

"Maybe a little bit."

He reached for the button of his pants, sliding it open

while keeping his eyes set on mine. "Oh, you know what? I think I even have a condom this time."

I smiled. "Really? That's a first."

He nodded proudly. "Just when you thought I couldn't surprise you anymore, huh?" One of his hands reached into the pocket of his pants, pulling out his wallet.

Something about the way he looked at me made me fear what he was about to reveal when he opened his wallet and pulled out that little square-shaped wrapper.

It turned out not half as bad as I feared.

"Seriously?" I chuckled as my eyes fell on the Trojan logo on the black wrapper. "Bareskin Raw? Might as well not use a condom in the first place then. These break so easily."

He handed me the condom just to lower his zipper. "You might be right about that. We could not use it, but I think it's worth a try seeing as I don't have tissues on me, and I highly doubt you want me to come on your body."

My eyes widened, my head shaking instantly. "Easily breakable condom it is."

It wasn't *that* easy to break... I hoped. It didn't break the last time we used one.

Reece dipped his head down, leaning in to press his lips against mine.

As we kissed, he reached down, pushing down his pants and underwear enough to free his erection. Taking the condom from me, Reece ripped open the wrapper and rolled the condom onto his cock.

When his lips left mine, all I wanted to do was move in again, taste him once more, but I also knew that we couldn't waste any more time.

"Turn around." His voice was laced with lust.

I did as he asked, turning to face the window. My eyes instantly landed on the backyard again, watching all these people who were oblivious to what was going on inside this specific bedroom.

A hand laid on my hips as he forced me to take a step back. "Hands on the window," he ordered, his voice low and commanding. I complied, feeling the cool glass beneath my palms, my heart beating heavily in my chest. "Good girl." My heart fluttered at the praise, and holy fuck, I didn't know that was possible. "Now, spread your legs," he whispered into my ear, sounding much raspier than before.

As I spread my legs slightly, Reece stepped back; the loss of his warm body made itself known immediately.

The icy temperature inside of the room was quickly forgotten when Reece traced a hand down my ass before hooking a finger into my underwear, pulling them aside.

His finger brushed against my opening, slipping inside, making me gasp.

Reece pushed me against the window, the side of my face pressing against the cool glass as he thrust his fingers into me. My lips parted, our eyes meeting as I looked over my shoulder.

"Don't hold back this time," he said as he added a second finger. "I want to hear you screaming my name."

I nodded, biting my lips as he continued to work his fingers in and out of me. My body arched, my breath leaving me in ragged pants as he worked me up to the edge.

A wave of intense lust surged through my body, building in intensity with each stroke. The feeling coiled in my stomach, threatening to consume me as moans escaped my lips, growing louder and more desperate with each brush of his fingers against my G-spot.

Every nerve ending was on fire, sending jolts of pleasure through me.

"Oh, Reece!" I cried, trying to catch my breath with every inhale.

His lips lay on my shoulder, his teeth gently grazing my skin. "Say it louder, baby."

My voice trembled with desperation as I repeated his name. "Reece!"

With that, he thrust his fingers into me faster, my moans spilling out louder and more frequently.

Each stroke pushed me closer to the edge of release, my legs slightly shaking.

Just as I couldn't take it anymore, my hips pushing back as I sought his touch, Reece pulled his fingers out of my cunt.

A soft, whimper-like sound elicited from my throat as the need for his fingers overpowered my senses. I was so close to coming, and he took it from me without hesitation.

"Reece, please," I begged, the painful ache in my stomach that was longing for release burning inside of me. "Please, I need you to—"

Before I could finish my sentence, I felt his cock sliding into me from behind, stretching me wide open.

A cry escaped my throat as my body adjusted to his size, my fingers turning white from the pressure I was applying against the window.

Reece laid a hand on my hips, sneaking the other one around my body to cup my breast, his thumb rubbing my nipple in time with his thrusts.

"God, you're so fucking wet," he murmured, his breath hot against my ear. "I can feel it dripping down my dick."

I whimpered in response, my body still trying to adjust to him inside me.

His hips moved in a steady rhythm, and I couldn't help the moans from spilling out of me with each plunge.

My nails tried to dig into the window in an attempt to

hold onto *anything*, but clearly, that didn't work. My heart was racing, thrumming so heavily in my chest that I could feel each beat.

Reece pinched my nipple, eliciting a sharp gasp from me, which was quick to turn into a pleasure-filled groan.

"You like that, Brooke?" he asked, his voice low and laced with seduction. "You like my cock stretching your tight little pussy?"

His fingers dipped into the skin of my hips as he pounded into me harder.

"Yes," I moaned, arching my back as I met his thrusts. "Reece, I..." My mind was blank for a second, my focus solely on the way his dick felt inside me, stretching me. "Faster, Reece."

He picked up the pace, driving into me with quick, hard strokes.

The glass beneath my palms vibrated with each thrust, and I leaned further into the window, feeling the chill against my skin. It was a welcoming cold this time, especially since my body was heating up more with every second.

Reece's grip on my hips tightened. "Fuck," he groaned. "I'm getting close, Brooke."

A shiver ran through me at the sound of his hoarse voice. I clenched around his dick as I fought my own orgasm. "Me too."

His thrusts became more erratic, his balls slapping against my pussy with each forceful move. The sound of our bodies colliding almost managed to drown out the music from the party entirely.

"I have an idea, *mi princesa*," he spoke quietly as he slid a hand around my body, his fingers working magic on my clit.

"You better not break that condom on purpose," I

breathed, though I honestly wouldn't have cared if he did. I was still on birth control anyway, and I was sure we would've found a tissue *somewhere* in this room. Or Reece could've stolen toilet paper from one of the bathrooms.

Reece laughed, a deep, hoarse sound that somehow managed to drive me even closer to my release. "I knew I should've thrown them out."

"Reece," I groaned, sort of madly this time while clenching harder around his cock. "Please, just… I'm so close."

His chuckle turned a bit devious this time, his grip on my hip tight enough to possibly leave a bruise before he pushed into me once more, hitting a particularly sensitive spot inside of me.

My body felt like it was on fire, every nerve ending going off like wildfires that even the cold window couldn't distinguish.

His fingers on my clit worked in sync with his cock pounding into me, driving me higher and higher.

I cried out his name, each moan louder than the next.

The room was filled with the sounds of our bodies slapping together, the thud of our skin, the wet sounds of our arousal, and the harsh, ragged breathing of two people who were apparently completely out of their minds.

"Come for me, baby," he growled.

As soon as the words left his lips, my body exploded into a million pieces. The instant orgasm rippled through my body, shaking violently as it took over every inch of me, making me scream his name. Whoever was in the rooms next to us or the hall heard me for sure.

"Fuck, that's hot," he panted, continuing to plunge into me until his cock twitched inside me, filling the condom with his cum.

Exhausted and limp, we collapsed against the window, gasping as we both tried to catch our breath.

My legs were shaking, my body still trembling as I found barely enough strength to reach behind me and pull his dick out of me. I turned around and wrapped my arms around my fiancé for a little more stability.

He held me tight, his heart racing against mine.

"I should get dressed," I said, though I didn't move.

"Yeah, probably." Reece let go of me, taking a step back. He removed his condom and tied it up, got himself all zipped up again, and then began looking around the room.

While he was looking for the trash, I made my way over to the desk, grabbed my dress, and threw it over my body.

"You alright?" Reece asked as he returned to my side. Guess he found the trash to dispose of the condom.

I nodded softly, shifting my gaze toward the window. I could see a faint imprint of where my body had been pressed against it. "Do you think we should leave a note so the guy can clean his windows?"

Reece pressed his lips to the top of my head, chuckling. "Nah, let him figure it out. Besides, we probably won't be the last ones leaving *something* in here."

I gave him a playful slap right in the middle of his chest. "You're quite something, Carter."

He winked at me before reaching out to cup my face and pull me in for a kiss. "And you, Brooke, are everything I need to survive."

I melted into the kiss, savoring the way his tongue explored my mouth.

"Oh, I have good news, by the way," he said, sounding all excited as he pulled away from the kiss. "The condom didn't break."

I laughed softly. Only Reece would get excited over that, but somehow, that just made me love him even more.

He found joy in such little things, it was impressive. Perhaps he should teach me how to do that someday.

"Great, so I won't have to tell my parents I'm pregnant in a few weeks." That still wouldn't have happened even if the condom broke, but whatever.

"Baby, we can't get you pregnant yet anyway," he said, rolling his eyes. "I promised your dad it wouldn't happen before we're married. I don't break promises."

My eyebrows drew together. "When did you promise that?"

"Like… when we were fifteen. We were talking, and then he made me promise."

My lips parted slightly in surprise and shock. "At fifteen?"

He nodded.

"So *you* told my dad when I lost my virginity!" Logically, it couldn't have been anyone but Reece anyway, but I never asked him to confirm.

"It slipped out, okay?" Reece held both of his hands up. "Colin just gave me *the talk* for the fourth time, and I went to complain about it to your dad. I might have mentioned me knowing all that already because… well, personal experience. Technically, I told him *I* lost *my* virginity."

"Yeah, to his daughter!" I couldn't help the slight chuckle that escaped me as I pulled him in for another kiss. "You sure know how to make my life interesting."

"It's my pleasure, *mi princesa*."

Chapter Twenty-Eight

Reece

"I want to sit in the booth!" Ming tried rushing toward his preferred seat choice, but I reached for his jacket, pulled him back, and shook my head.

"Brooke always sits there."

Ming frowned at me with confusion. "So? There's space for two."

"For Brooke and me, yes." I wasn't technically against not sitting next to my fiancée, but Ming really needed a helping hand with Rina. His little crush was so obvious, but he was a hopeless case on his own. "Now, off to the other side you go."

"But chairs are boring," he said, dragging out the last word. Ming wasn't drunk, but he was tipsy enough to turn into whatever he was right now—definitely not himself.

Rina laughed, shaking her head at Ming's ridiculousness. "Just take a seat, Dumbfuck. I'm hungry."

Ming covered his heart with a hand, sighing. "She already has a nickname for me."

"Not a great one, buddy." I slapped a hand on my best friend's shoulder, then made my way around the table.

After Brooke slid into the booth, I followed.

"Who's going to get our order when it's done?" Ming asked, looking at our receipt with the number 475 on it. "Bet we're going to have to wait *ages*."

"This is McDonald's, weirdo. The longest you're ever going to wait for your order is what? Ten minutes?" Rina dragged out an exaggerated sigh. "Have you ever been to McDonald's in your life?"

Ming turned his body toward Rina, smiling at her. "Of course, beautiful. But if you want, I can take you to—"

"I don't date weirdos," Rina interrupted.

Brooke leaned her head on my shoulder, stifling a chuckle. "Now more than ever, I'm super grateful that we didn't have a get-to-know-each-other phase. You simply spawned one day and adopted me as your friend."

My head whipped around, eyebrows drawing together as I pushed Brooke's head off my shoulder to look at her. "Did you just friend-zone yourself?"

Her eyes rolled as an amused smile tugged at her lips. "In case you forgot, we haven't *always* been a couple."

I shook my head, not wanting to hear of this. "You were mine the moment you were conceived."

"You weren't even slightly in the picture when that happened." She laughed. "I'm older."

"By a month."

Brooke shrugged. "That's older."

"Who says I wasn't a late boomer? Maybe I was conceived the same—"

"Wow," Rina's voice interrupted. "I take it back. You're the normal one." She looked at Ming. "Who would've thought?"

"I once spent an *entire* day with these two. That was a whole twenty-four hours of chatter that made zero sense to me. They're a different breed of human, I suppose. It's so weird, but man, they're so adorable," Ming replied.

"I don't even want to imagine it. Brooke used to tell me so much about Reece. At some point, I was convinced she was making him up. Like, honestly, nobody's as perfect as she makes him out to be." Rina looked at the screen that listed all the finished food orders. "Oh, our food's ready."

She was just about to get up when I told her to stay seated. "Brooke and I will get it."

"Why me?" Brooke groaned but got up and followed me either way. "I was just getting comfortable."

Interlocking her fingers with mine, we made our way over to the register. "Ming's trying to make a move on your friend. We shouldn't be there for that."

"Oh, Rina knows." She laughed. "He's more than obvious."

"Yeah, but we make him look bad."

"How so?"

I showed the guy at the register our receipt with our number on it to get our order, then turned back to Brooke as we waited. "Because it's *us*. We're perfect. We make everyone look bad."

"Here you go," the guy said before Brooke even managed to open her mouth.

I took the tray with our food from him. "Thanks."

"Enjoy your meal."

"Thank you," Brooke replied, smiling at him kindly. "We're not perfect," she then whispered as we made our way back to our table. "We fight. A lot."

"I can't remember the last time we did."

Brooke stopped in her tracks, crossing her arms tightly over her chest as she cocked her head at me. "Seriously?"

"Yup. Not a clue."

"This morning?" I shrugged in response. "We were fighting about going to this stupid party. Which, by the way, was super unnecessary because we weren't even there for two hours."

"Because of you."

Her head lifted in a slow nod. "You didn't want to go to that party either."

Yeah, I probably should've worded it differently.

I would've rather stayed at home with her than gone to that party, and I was actually really relieved that we could leave early, but that really wasn't the reason why we left.

Brooke walked past me, rushing toward the table. I couldn't even reach out to her because of the tray in my hands.

"Brooke!" I called after her. She turned around, looking at me, anger etched into her features. I couldn't even blame her for being upset as it really sounded like I was blaming her for leaving. "We left because you, Ming, and Lane started stupid rumors. I wasn't going to stay at a place where everyone was going to look down on you and say you've cheated on me."

The tension on her face faded as it was replaced with shock. "Cheated?!"

We stayed an entire hour after emerging from the bedroom, and the looks we got were… not nice. I was used to having eyes on me on the ice, but at school, I was invisible. Or I tried to be.

Despite Holden and a bunch of other guys from the team trying to stop the cheating rumors from spreading, once one started making its rounds, it was almost impossible to stop it. We now had to learn how to live with that shit being out in the open, at least for a few weeks until the rumors finally dimmed down.

Most people at the party were throwing disgusted looks at

Brooke. While she might've not noticed them because she was too busy telling herself nobody was judging her so she didn't have a panic attack, I noticed them. And I could interpret the looks just fine. I wasn't going to stay somewhere my fiancée wasn't wanted.

I nodded. "You and two guys in a room? With the door locked? What else would those who saw you walk in there think was going on? I mean, seriously, baby, everyone who saw us walk into that room was *very* aware of us having sex. They definitely assumed the same about the three of you."

Brooke stepped closer to me, keeping her voice down as she said, "They're your friends."

"This is college, Brooke. And we were at a party," I began. "We're no longer in middle school where hiding in another room means you're pissed off at your friends. Finding a room with someone else now means you're hooking up."

"I'm sorry…" Regret glistened in her eyes as she looked at me. "Reece, I swear, I didn't—"

"I know." It took everything in me not to drop the tray just to hug and kiss my fiancée. "You're too pretty to cheat on me."

Brooke's mouth opened and closed again, blinking at me.

"Seriously. Guys are intimidated by beauty," I added, forcing myself not to laugh at my speechless Brooke.

As we reached our friends, I set the tray on the table and Brooke seemed to have found her voice again. Sliding into the booth, she frowned at me. "You weren't intimidated by me."

I took my fries off the tray. "You weren't…"

Brooke stole my fries, holding them over the floor and threatening to drop them. "Finish your sentence, Carter. I dare you."

"What did Reece's fries do to you?" Ming asked, then shoved his veggie burger right into his mouth.

"He was going to say I wasn't pretty when we met."

"So not true," I vetoed, crossing my arms over my chest. "I was going to say that you just weren't intimidating, is all. My love for you was bigger than your empty threats. After all, I was ready to marry you right on the spot, remember?"

Honestly, I couldn't remember, but Colin told me that one of the first things I ever said to Brooke—aside from baby blabber—was: "We're getting married tomorrow." Tomorrow was now eighteen years ago, but technically, I never clarified *which* tomorrow it was going to be. Obviously, I meant tomorrow in twenty years.

Brooke laid my fries back down on the tray, then had the audacity to steal one and pop it right into her mouth. She had her own fries.

"Even your fights are adorable." Ming sighed, then looked at Rina. "I promise, my queen, I'll love you like these two idiots love each other."

"Oh, my God." Rina laughed, covering her face with her hands. "Just eat your burger, Ming. And stop annoying me."

"As you wish."

Rina took a sip of her sprite, then snapped her fingers once before turning her head to look at Ming. "And, please, stop flirting with me. You'll regret it."

I sorta felt like Brooke and I weren't supposed to be here for this. Basically all our lives, people were third-wheeling us… it felt weird being on the other side for once.

Was this still third-wheeling if Rina was about to turn Ming down?

"Why? Because you'd fall in love with me too quickly?" Ming retorted.

Rina shook her head. "I'm not made for relationships."

"Why not?" Brooke asked, reading my mind. If she hadn't asked, I would have. "Relationships are great. Well, minus the fights."

"Yeah... except when you're the kind of person who doesn't want to be at home all day every day," Rina said, now playing with her food. "I couldn't imagine not going on a new date every weekend. I need the thrill. And relationships are just... boring. What's there to do? You already know each other, and dates are just not that new anymore. They're not exciting—if they happen in the first place. After a while, the exciting crush feeling goes away and all that's left is *choosing* to love the other person. You see their flaws and get annoyed more easily. I mean, some couples don't even make it past the first three months because they were too stupidly in love to see the flaws right away. If all I see in my partner is their flaws, and maybe get a glimpse of the person I fell in love with every once in a blue moon, what's the point? It sounds like a nightmare to me."

"Relationships don't have to be boring," Ming muttered, the confidence in his tone far gone.

"No? Take Brooke and Reece as an example." She gestured toward us. "If it weren't for you begging Reece to come to a party, they would've spent all day inside their apartment, watching TV or something. What's there even to talk about anymore? They've been together since they were kids. I don't see how they could find a single topic to discuss other than picking fights. They love each other, you don't even have to look at them to see it, and while that's adorable, it's just... not exciting. I'm happy for them, but that's not what I want for me. They're choosing to love each other. They're choosing to stay together. And to be honest, if you really think about it, how unlikely was it for them to fall in love? When everyone in their lives was rooting for them, don't you think it's more manipulation and the fear of what their families would think if they broke up that's keeping them together?"

Rina's eyes ripped open when she realized what she'd just said, but it was too late to take back.

I could feel my breath getting caught in my lungs, but despite wanting to gasp, my entire system just shut down and left my head empty.

Everything inside of me tried fighting the intrusion of a thought I had refused to entertain ever since Brooke and I got together.

Sure, every once in a while I wondered if we really fell in love because we liked each other or if it was pushed upon us. However, every time that thought entered my mind, I shook it off because I didn't want to believe, not even for a single second, that Brooke could've ended up with some other guy if our families hadn't been so close.

Even now, I had no time to entertain the thought because Brooke jumped off her seat and I knew she was about to head right out of the building. She didn't react when Rina called her name. She didn't even grab her jacket or purse before making her way toward the exit doors.

I quickly gathered Brooke's belongings before reaching for my own, then looked at Rina for a brief moment.

There was regret etched into her features, but I couldn't empathize with her.

"It's okay not to want a relationship," I began. "But that doesn't give you the right to make assumptions about someone else's." I took my phone from the table and dropped it into Brooke's purse.

"I know. I'm sorry, I wasn't think—"

"You weren't." That being said, I finally went after my fiancée.

Chapter Twenty-Nine
Brooklyn

Neither Reece nor I uttered a single word, daring to address what Rina said, but she sent me about a hundred messages in the last thirty minutes, apologizing profusely.

I wasn't even mad at her. She simply said what I was sure almost everyone who met Reece and I thought. Besides, Rina was allowed to hate relationships.

That still didn't make the whole situation less painful to think about.

As a heavy sigh involuntarily left my lungs, I finally threw the kitchen towel onto the counter instead of picking up another wet plate that Reece just set down.

"God, I hate this," I mumbled, not thinking Reece was going to hear it over the noises of cutlery rubbing against one another. However, I was proven wrong.

"I take it your mind's been running wild with stuff that both agrees and disagrees with Rina?" he asked, setting down a clean mug this time.

"Yeah…"

Reece reached for a clean towel to dry off his hands, then looked at me. "Yeah, mine did, too."

Just by a millimeter, I felt my heart sink but I refused to

let it drop all the way and feel even more miserable before Reece got the chance to tell me what he was thinking. I learned a while ago that I had to let people speak their minds before I let my anxiety poison my thoughts.

Reece leaned against the kitchen counter. "Part of me wants to call Colin and your dad to tell them they're both assholes."

I chuckled softly but nodded my head because now that he mentioned it, I kind of wanted to do it too.

"They wouldn't deserve it though. Not this time anyway," he said, offering me a faint smile. "Because, Brooke, I had like an hour to think about this now, and... if you genuinely look at the whole situation, what exactly would they have done? Yes, Colin introduced me to you, but even if he hadn't done that when we were little, I would've met you eventually. There's no doubt in my mind that I would have fallen in love with you right on the spot even if I met you at thirteen for the first time. Or even later. We were just lucky that we got to meet earlier. That doesn't mean Colin and Miles *made* us fall in love. I don't even think that's possible."

"Manipulations," I said. "They could've... I don't know. Done something."

He held out his hand for me, and without thinking, I took it. Reece pulled me closer, turned me around, and then wrapped his arms around my neck.

"Do you love me?" he asked, his voice almost a whisper.

I nodded without hesitation. "Of course I do."

My love for Reece was one of the very few things in my life I had *never* questioned before.

As much as I loved figure skating, I'd sometimes wonder if I'd always wanted to make figure skating my profession. I even once questioned whether my dad was lying to me about Emory not being my mother. While I did dismiss that theory rather quickly because why would they lie about that, I still questioned it.

From the moment I realized I loved Reece, I had never questioned it. Not a single second in my life was I thinking we'd been better off as friends, or that my feelings were there because I'd been told to love him.

And I never questioned his love for me either.

"Do you think those feelings are there because your dad and his friends thought it'd be cute if we ended up together?" he asked.

I shook my head. "They said that?"

Reece chuckled. His right hand slowly slid down the front of my body and only stopped to press it flat over my heart, feeling it beating heavily. I didn't even notice it was racing.

"You didn't know."

"I didn't," I admitted. Yes, I knew Dad wasn't exactly surprised when I told him Reece was my boyfriend, and he later told me that they all figured it was going to happen, but I didn't know they said this.

"Then if you didn't know, *mi princesa*, why would you think they made you love me?"

"I don't know..." I covered his hand with my own. "Maybe *we* were too young to realize. Maybe they were being sneaky with pushing us closer together. Or maybe not that sneaky but we were too gullible and too naive to view you being around me all the time as their attempt of—"

"Brooke." Reece spun me around, laying his hands on my jaw to make me look at him. "I begged Colin to let me see you, even at the youngest age possible. I even begged your dad to let me go on vacation with your family when I was ten. We weren't dating then. If anyone was being pushy, it was me, not our families. Was there ever a day your dad told you that you *had* to see me? Or that you *had* to join the hockey team to spend more time with me when we were younger? Did your dad tell you that you *had* to quit Juilliard and transfer to St. Trewery?"

"Well, no, but—"

"And trust me, *mi amor*, your parents, my brother, or anyone else didn't force me to step in for Erik either. Or try figure skating. My dad and Colin drew the line when I told them I wanted to take ballet classes so we could spend *even* more time together."

A laugh bubbled in the back of my throat, but I didn't want to laugh so I tried my best to swallow it. "I couldn't imagine you wearing tights and pointe shoes," I said instead.

Reece's eyebrows drew together. "I would've looked hot in them."

My lips pressed into a thin line, the laughter now barely staying inside. "Mhm... sure."

"Uh, are you forgetting that I have to squeeze my muscly-self into a tight as fuck figure skating costume? That's basically the same, and I look hot in that thing." His thumbs brushed over my skin, a smile tugging on the corners of his lips. "Not as hot as you, though."

"It's not *that* tight. We sized you up."

"Yeah, so I don't actually have to suffocate," he said matter-of-factly. "Or would you rather I die on the ice? In your arms? In front of a crowd? On camera?"

"Now you're being dramatic." I stepped away from Reece, aiming to do anything but continue to look at him but he reached for my hand and pulled me back.

His eyes lingered on my engagement ring for a moment longer than usual for him. When he looked up again, all the playfulness from a second ago was gone—his gaze serious.

"You really don't have to worry about what Rina said, Brookie. We know what's true, we know that what we feel for each other is real. Just because Rina can't understand it doesn't mean we're not meant for each other," he said, then placed a kiss on my knuckles.

"So then we are boring. So we like to spend our time at home, talking, cuddling, and watching stupid movies we've seen a thousand times before. What's so wrong with that? We don't need parties and alcohol to enjoy the time we spend with each other. And, yeah, okay, perhaps we could go out on *official* dates more often, but we never did that. We still go out to restaurants, and I take you shopping, and we go to the movies, or do other stuff. It's just that these things are for *us*, and we don't share those moments with anyone. Just because we don't call it a date every time we go out doesn't mean it's not that. And I don't know about you, but I'd rather be comfortable with *you* than date another woman every other day," he added.

A relieved sigh drew from my lungs, followed by a tear that rolled down my cheek. Reece immediately cupped my face with his hands and stroked his thumbs underneath my eyes, wiping away my tears.

"Why are we crying? Did I say something wrong?" he asked, worry in his voice. His eyes were filled with panic, but it quickly vanished when I shook my head and smiled at him softly.

"No. God, no. You're perfect, Reece," I said. "Like, seriously, sometimes I'm not sure what I did to deserve you. You're too good to be true. It's as if I made you watch too many of those princess movies I used to love when I was younger. Then you took all the princes' personalities, threw them in a bowl, mixed them, and injected the mixture into your bloodstream to become the ultimate prince."

His eyebrows rose. "*Used* to love?" A chuckle slipped past his lips. "You're still making me watch them. You barely make it a whole day without watching a single movie with a princess in it."

"They're educational." I crossed my arms over my chest and looked away from him.

"What exactly is a Sleeping Beauty remake teaching you?"

"Uhm…" My eyes were back on my fiancé as I slowly took a step back because I knew I'd have to act fast once my next words left me. "That all men care about are looks. Prince Phillip basically fell in love with a corpse. So, it teaches that looks matter."

"Because that's what *picture-perfect* movies should teach little girls."

Reece would've fallen in love with me even if I hadn't had great genes, I knew that. Yet, I couldn't stop myself from saying, "Well, I found my Prince Phillip, didn't I?"

Reece's jaw dropped and a gasp fell from his lips. "Excuse me?" He took a step forward, I stepped back.

"You're excused."

I grabbed a candle off the table beside me, threw it at my fiancé, and immediately started running for my life.

Chapter Thirty

Reece

I pinched her hands down over her head, keeping her in place.

"Throwing stuff at me now, are we, *mi princesa*?" I chuckled, still in disbelief that my very own fiancée threw a candle at me just to have a head start. We both knew that there was no escaping me, especially when she ran into our bedroom instead of out of our apartment.

Brooke smiled back at me all innocently, pretending she had no clue what I was talking about. That damn smile almost made me lose my sanity. "I'm sure Prince Phillip would've been fine with Aurora throwing candles at him."

"I doubt it." My eyes traveled over my fiancée's beautiful face, my cock instantly making itself noticeable at her beauty. It was a curse, really.

If it were up to my dick, I would've fucked Brooke twenty-four hours of the day, every day.

How was I supposed to survive her when she was lying there in our bed, underneath me, so helpless and with that pretend innocent look?

She played her part well, tossing her head from side to side, trying to kick her legs as if she wanted me to get off her. But I knew her too well to fall for it.

If Brooke wanted me to let her go, she would've said it.

There was a spark in her eyes that said she was enjoying our little game. She might've even enjoyed it a little more than I did.

"I'm sure he wouldn't care. Prince Phillip is a man of honor; someone who loves Aurora deeply. He wouldn't give a flying fuck about a candle heading his way when he was the one who tempted her," she said, trying to sound convincing but I could hear the playfulness in her tone. "Maybe you need to be taught a lesson in chivalry."

She wiggled beneath me, her hips pushing up to meet my erection. I smirked, knowing that she was just baiting me more. The temptation to take her right then and there was almost too much to bear, but I resisted, wanting to make her suffer just a little bit longer.

"I'm also a man of honor and love." I leaned in closer, my lips brushing against her ear as I whispered, "But you think you're so clever, don't you, Brooke? You think you can outsmart me with your little games? Well, you're in for a surprise."

Brooke gasped, her eyes wide with fear and a hint of curiosity. I could tell she was eager to find out what I was going to do next, and honestly, so was I.

As I slowly sat up, I reached down, tugging at her dress until it settled around her waist, exposing her luscious thighs. "Do you know why Prince Phillip probably wouldn't mind if Aurora threw candles at him?" Brooke nodded, curiosity in her eyes. "Because he'd be as turned on as I am right now."

I could see the heat rise in her cheeks, her body trembling underneath me. "But you, Brookie," I said softly, my eyes never leaving her flushed face. "I'm no prince—but I promise you this, *mi princesa*: I'll make sure you know exactly how much I want you and how much pleasure I can bring you without ever having to resort to childish games or tossing candles."

With that, I let go of her hands and got up, walking over to our closet. I could feel her gaze on my body, confused and excited at the same time as she watched me open my side of the closet.

We didn't have any handcuffs, but I could tie her up with something else. As much as I loved Brooke's hands on every inch of my body, there was no way I'd let her touch me now.

I rummaged through the closet, searching for something to bind her with. My eyes fell on three silk scarves—one white, one a soft purple, one black—that I had bought for her on our last trip to Paris. It was the perfect choice.

With a smirk, I walked back over to the bed and crawled on top of her, pinning her down once again. Our eyes locked, filled with a mix of lust and anticipation.

I gently took the white silk scarf and wrapped it around her wrists, pulling them tightly together.

"What are you doing?" She sounded almost bored, but the hints of fear and curiosity of what was to come filtered out too easily for me.

"This," I replied, lifting her arms above her head and tying the scarf securely to the headboard. "And it's just the beginning of *your* lesson in chivalry, *mi princesa*. Now, you have nothing to distract you from the only thing I truly desire: you."

Brooke's eyes widened in shock, but there was definitely some excitement glistening in their depths. She knew that this was not like us, but I could tell that she couldn't deny the thrill that coursed through her veins at the thought of being bound at my mercy, never mind that I was merely teasing and pretending to be someone I wasn't.

With a sly grin, I moved down between her legs, my hands tracing the curves of her body.

After sliding her panties down her legs, her breath hitched when I reached for the black silk scarf, this time wrapping it around her ankles.

"What did you say about being a man of honor and love?" she managed to ask, her voice shaking slightly. "No man of honor would have to insist on dominance and control."

I chuckled, my fingers playing with the ends of the scarf. "Oh, Brooke, you've got me all wrong. This isn't about dominance or control. It's about showing you that I can give you the kind of pleasure that even a prince couldn't dream of."

I grasped the purple silk scarf tightly, pulling her knees apart and tying the ends to the footboard. The position exposed her completely, leaving her vulnerable and exposed.

Brooke's lips parted as she gasped. She looked like a beautiful, bound captive, and I never thought that would happen.

"I promise you, *mi princesa*," I whispered, my teeth grazing the shell of her ear. "I'll never hurt you, but I will give you every bit of pleasure you so desperately crave. And when I'm done, you'll understand what it means to truly be my princess."

With my hands trailing along her skin, I softly teased her sensitive areas, heightening the anticipation that was now evident in her eyes. She was breathing heavily, her body shuddering from the mixture of anxiety and excitement that filled her.

I hovered over her, laying my lips on her cheek and kissing my way to her mouth. "Now that you're so exposed and helpless, you can no longer escape my advances. Your body is mine to tease, to touch, and to explore. You will submit to my every whim, and you'll learn that I am indeed a man of honor and love, capable of giving you pleasure beyond anything you've ever experienced."

God, this sounded *so* unlike me... in fact, this whole thing was so unlike *us*. But it was also exciting in a way.

As I started to kiss her neck, her moans filled the room. She was trying to fight her aching need, but it was becoming more apparent that she was losing the battle. The longing in her eyes was now uncontrollable, and her breaths were coming faster and heavier.

I continued to tease her, running my fingers through her hair, kissing her neck, and trailing my tongue along her collarbones. Each touch sent shivers down her spine, and she was growing more and more desperate for my touch.

Sometimes, she'd try to pull on the scarves, try to reach out and lay her hands on my body, then she'd sigh or whimper when she realized she couldn't.

"Please, Reece," she begged, impatient. "Please, touch me. I need you so bad."

I smiled, feeling a rush of satisfaction from her plea. "You said I need lessons in chivalry, *mi princesa*," I whispered into her ear. "But I think you're very mistaken. *You* are the one in need of lessons, so I'm giving you one."

With that, I positioned myself between her legs, my erection harder than ever. I rubbed my covered dick against her pussy, feeling her wetness slowly coating the front of my boxers.

She could moan, cry out, and plead all she wanted. We were going to do this at my pace, and she was going to thank me for it.

Before I was getting my dick anywhere near inside of her, I needed to get my mouth on her perfectly perky tits, suck on her nipples, and play with them as I pleased.

"Is this what you want, Brooke? To be my prisoner?" I

asked, my voice rough. She moaned, her eyes fluttering shut as I trailed my fingers over her body, teasing her nipples before pinching them hard.

She couldn't answer, too busy enjoying my every touch. All she could do was buck her hips involuntarily against me, arch her back, and push her tits right into my face.

Her breasts were absolutely exquisite, and they felt like plush pillows under my hands, so soft yet firm enough to push back against my touch. I could feel her heart beating, see the gentle rise and fall of her chest, the slight flush of her skin, and the fluttering of her eyelashes as she closed her eyes.

As my hands grazed over her breasts, I couldn't help but groan at the softness of her skin. It was like velvet. And when I cupped her breasts in my hands, I could feel their warmth against my fingers. Her nipples were firm and responsive.

I lowered myself to her chest, eyes drawn to the soft curves and delicate skin. My tongue traced a path over her left nipple, lingering on the sensitive bud before giving it a gentle bite. The taste of her skin was sweet, like honey on a summer day.

"Then let me show you," I rasped, and closed my lips over her hard, strained nipple.

She cried out, her body learning a harsh, shocking lesson as I bit down on her nipple once more, her breasts jiggling beneath my lips. I then switched, sucking gently on the other one, teasing it with my teeth until I felt her arch against me.

It was an exhilarating experience, the taste of her skin against my lips, the sound of her breaths growing more ragged with each passing moment.

I couldn't help but smile as I continued to play with her body, knowing this wasn't even the best part yet.

As I continued to play with her tits, I could feel her body

melting against my own, her muscles relaxing as my fingertips grazed her silky skin.

I couldn't resist the urge to explore her further, even if it had been engraved into my brain a long time ago, and I slid my hands down, grazing her sides and trailing down to the delicate skin of her inner thighs. It made my cock twitch in anticipation, ready to plunge into her drenched, pink pussy.

But I needed to taste her first, let my tongue run over her pussy, tease her clit until she was screaming my name so loud the neighbors would complain.

Her hips bucked, her body seemingly alive with need as I kissed down her stomach, beneath her navel, to her smooth cunt.

I spread her legs wider, my thumbs rubbing against the outsides of her labia, teasing her swollen clit with the tips of my fingers. Her breath hitched, and her body tensed as I traced a path to her entrance.

"Are you ready to let me teach you, Brooke?" I asked, looking up at her.

She moaned, her eyes opening to meet mine. There was an intensity in her gaze that I had never seen before. For whatever reason, it made my heart skip a beat.

She looked so sexy when she was losing her mind, and her being naked and at my mercy certainly didn't make her look any less hot. Perhaps this was more torture for me than it was for her.

"Please, Reece," she begged, her voice shaking. "Please, I need you."

God, I liked the sound of that. "You're right, *mi princesa*. You do need me."

My tongue darted out, pushing right into her wet cunt. She tasted sweet and salty all at the same time, making my cock throb, feeling trapped in my pants and underwear.

I licked her harder, sucking her clit into my mouth and grazing it with my teeth.

Her muscles spasmed as I pushed two of my fingers inside her pussy, her wetness instantly coating them.

With every thrust of my fingers, her hips shifted and she tried to pull her arms down to touch me, just to get denied by a scarf that was holding her in place.

"Reece, oh, fuck," she screamed. "Fuck, that feels so good!"

I didn't want to stop; I couldn't get enough of her. My fingers pumped in and out of her, her pussy clenching around them. But I needed more, needed to feel her tightness wrap around my cock, gripping me, and making me see entire universes that didn't exist yet.

But there was no way I'd fuck her before she came at least once, so I continued to penetrate her with my fingers, flicking her clit with my tongue at the same time.

As she screamed my name, her muscles clamped down on my finger. Brooke tensed and quivered as her climax took over her body, the walls of her cunt contracting around my fingers.

I slowly pulled my fingers out of her pussy and sat up. Her eyes were heavy-lidded, her face flushed as she lay there, panting.

"Welcome to the world of chivalry, Brooke," I said with a smirk.

She stared at me, eyes clouded with post-orgasm bliss, her mind lacking words to talk.

While she was busy trying to catch her breath, I got off the bed and quickly stripped off my clothes. I then loosened the scarves around her ankles and wrists, freeing her.

"Get on your hands and knees," I demanded as I wrapped

my hand around my cock and gave myself a couple of strokes, getting ready to fuck her hard.

Brooke hesitated for a moment, her body still buzzing with the remnants of her orgasm, but when her eyes fell on my cock, she quickly complied with my request.

I watched as she positioned herself, her hips rocking back and forth with her ass in the air, inviting me to claim her.

My heart raced as I inched closer to her, my dick throbbing with need. With one hand, I guided my erection to her entrance, feeling the wetness that still covered my lips now coating the tip of my dick. I loved the way she tasted, loved the feeling of her body responding when I touched her.

As I positioned myself at her entrance, I took a deep breath.

"You good?" I asked, watching as she turned to look at me over her shoulder.

"Yes," Brooke replied, nodding. "I need you inside me. Right now."

I took that as her final permission. My heart was beating at a speed of million miles per hour as I slowly pushed into her, feeling her tight, wet cunt engulfing me inch by inch. I let out a groan, trying to control the feeling that was building up inside me.

Brooke let out a sigh, her body adjusting to my size. I held back for a moment, savoring the feeling of our bodies connecting.

"You feel incredible," I said.

With my hands on her hips, holding her steady, I pushed forward, burying myself inside her completely, feeling her muscles squeeze around me. Brooke let out a loud moan, falling forward into the pillow.

I pulled back slowly, dragging my cock along the walls of her pussy, listening to the wet, sloppy sounds our bodies created. I thrust forward again, feeling her tightness grip me harder each time, wanting more.

"Fuck, Reece," Brooke moaned.

"So tight, so wet, so good," I groaned, picking up the pace, my cock sliding in and out of her with ease.

She was dripping wet, coating my cock with each stroke, driving me wild.

Her body was moving beneath me, her hips bucking to meet my thrusts, her moans growing louder, more desperate. "Fuck me, Reece. Fuck me hard."

The words drove me mad, making me want to claim her harder and rougher than before. I grabbed her hips tighter, pulling her closer to me, and my thrusts became more violent and erratic. I pounded into her, my balls slapping against her skin with each harsh thrust.

Each time she tightened around my cock as I plunged into her, I saw stars. The need to feel her come again around my dick getting stronger with each time I slid in and out of her.

As her moans turned into gasps of air, Brooke clawed at the bedsheets, her nails digging into the material.

I knew she was close.

I reached around, finding her clit with one hand, rubbing it hard and fast, matching the rhythm of my thrusts. Her body tensed, her moans growing more desperate, and then, with a violent shudder, she came all over my cock.

"Fuck, yes!" I roared, feeling the walls of her pussy pulsing around my cock as she clenched and released in waves. I could feel her wetness running down her thighs, and I knew I wouldn't be able to hold back much longer.

I continued to thrust, relishing the feel of her cunt gripping my cock, her slick wetness, and the sound of our bodies coming together. The pleasure was overwhelming, and I could feel myself getting closer to my own release.

As I continued to plunge into her, she was begging for more, her voice hoarse and raw. Her pussy was still clenching around me from her orgasm.

Pulling out of her cunt for just a moment, I slammed back inside all at once. Brooke cried out, her body jolting with each powerful stroke.

"Oh, fuck, Reece," she moaned, her fingers clutching around our pillows. "I'm about to come again!"

That was all the encouragement I needed. I increased my pace a little more, my cock sliding in and out of her pussy with a slapping sound that filled the room.

My balls tightened, my orgasm building when her body shook with the shocks of her orgasm, and I knew I had to finish inside her, to feel her pussy grip me one last time.

"Fuck, I'm going to come," I growled, pounding into her harder.

"Do it, Reece," Brooke panted, her voice strained and gasping for air. "Fill me up with your cum."

Those words were the final trigger, and I let go, my cock pulsating inside her. My orgasm was intense, almost earth-shattering. My balls squeezed tight and released again and again, flooding her pussy with my hot cum.

Brooke moaned with each release, and after a short while, I collapsed on top of her, pushing her into the mattress.

She was shuddering underneath my body, my cock still buried deep inside her for a moment longer before I pulled out and rolled over, trying to catch my breath.

My heart was pounding like a drum, my cock still half-hard from the intense release, but that wasn't nearly as important as my fiancée.

I reached over and wrapped my arms around her body as I pulled her on top of me. Our lips met in a soft kiss, my heart exploding with love for her.

"Are you okay?" I asked, stroking her hair gently. Since I had never tied her up before, not making sure she was okay felt more than wrong.

"I'm okay," she replied, her eyes sparkling. "That was incredible."

I smiled, feeling my heart swell with happiness. "I'm glad. It's just the kind of thing that happens when we're in the world of chivalry, baby."

She laughed softly, snuggling closer to me. "I have to admit, I'm a big fan of this world."

"Apparently, so am I." I held her tighter, feeling her body shiver ever so slightly. "Wait here, *mi princesa*," I said and pressed a kiss to her forehead before laying Brooke down beside me and getting out of bed.

"Where are you going?"

"Getting a towel to clean you up."

Chapter Thirty-One

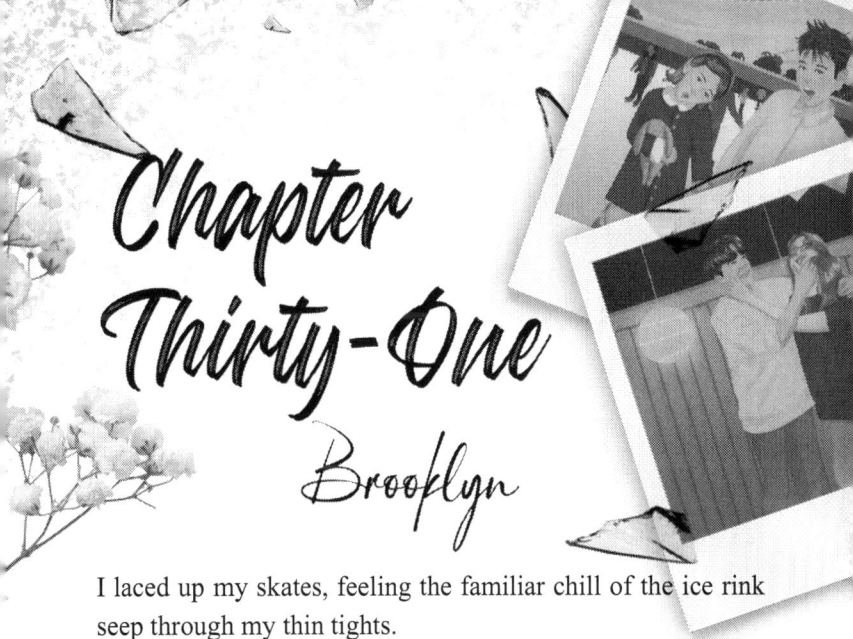

Brooklyn

I laced up my skates, feeling the familiar chill of the ice rink seep through my thin tights.

My heart was racing like a stallion as I glanced nervously at the scoreboard, the countdown clock ticking away the minutes until Reece and I's performance.

This was it. Our first figure skating performance together after almost five years. My first official performance of the season. The anticipation coiled right in my stomach.

Reece held a bottle of water out for me and offered me a reassuring smile, his blue eyes reflecting the overhead lights.

"You've got this," he said as I took the bottle from him. He sounded so steady and calm, like he had no care in the world, and like he wasn't nervous at all. "We've practiced countless times. Just focus on the routine and let the music guide you."

I nodded as I tried to absorb some of his confidence like a sponge. I wasn't sure how he of all people could be so calm right now. It was his first time back on the ice as a figure skater in ages, yet the butterflies in *my* stomach fluttered with persistent unease.

My eyes wandered over to my father who stood right next

to Ilya. They were both deep in conversation, which was probably the only reason why Ilya hadn't been standing right in front of me, telling me all sorts of things. He was usually the one who tried to calm my nerves, but I guess that he only did it because Erik sure as fuck wouldn't have.

"Hey." Reece brought a finger underneath my chin and lifted my gaze to his. "You'll make it to nationals. You're the best figure skater I know."

"You have to say this because you're my fiancé."

Reece shook his head. "I wouldn't lie to you, *mi princesa.*"

The soft glow of the arena lights enveloped me as I stood at the edge of the rink, the floor beneath my blades whispering promises of grace and precision.

The cool air kissed my cheeks as we stepped onto the ice, and I took a deep breath, trying to center myself. Before getting into position, Reece pressed a reassuring kiss onto my forehead and told me that I'd do amazing. While I believed him wholeheartedly, it didn't manage to erase all of my doubts.

As soon as the music started, the crowd's murmurs blended into a distant hum. My head snapped into focus and suddenly, it was silent. Not a single doubt clouded my mind.

With each glide and turn, I lost myself more and more to the rhythm, letting muscle memory take over. I landed my jumps and didn't mess up a single spin.

The first lift came seamlessly, Reece's strength lifting me effortlessly into the air. My body extended, trusting him not to drop me more than I'd ever trusted Erik. Adrenaline fueled my movements as we transitioned into our next sequence after he set me down gently.

Oh, but soft movements were going to get much rougher as our routine progressed.

My heart was beating in synchrony with the melody playing in the background. The cold air filled my lungs with every breath, cooling me while my skin was burning.

Reece and I's movements were synchronized as if we were one entity. Our connection intensified with every glide, each movement a silent conversation between us.

Reece's hand found mine, our fingers intertwining as he pulled me in just before I pushed him off me only for him to chase me again.

Ilya was right, Reece and I's performance had to be heartbreaking.

Each jump was executed with precision and poise. I could feel the air rush past me as I spun, my eyes only able to capture a blur of motion instead of whole objects.

My fiancé's steady presence guided me through each rotation, his support unwavering as we pushed the boundaries of what we knew we could achieve together.

As we neared the end of our routine, we came together in a final embrace. Our bodies pressed close as we glided across the ice in perfect harmony.

The audience erupted into applause; their cheers echoed through the arena as we came to a graceful stop at the center of the rink.

Breathless and exhilarated, I looked up at Reece only to find him smiling down at me. He looked so proud, even if his pride wasn't written all over his face. He couldn't hide his emotions from me.

Reece picked me up and spun us around twice before his lips crashed down on mine, kissing me in front of the entire audience. It wasn't an overly scandalous kiss, but it came to me as a surprise anyway. Usually, when we kissed, it was more intimate and not in front of a crowd.

Moments later, we were off the ice and Dad was throwing a blanket over my shoulders. "You did amazing," he told me and handed me my water bottle as he patiently waited for me to catch my breath.

"Thank you." I smiled up at him, but my smile vanished when I saw Reece from the corner of my eye. He stood there with Ilya instead of talking to his parents or even Colin. "Where is everyone else?"

I knew Emory was somewhere in the audience with my siblings as they preferred watching all pairs and not just me, so I wasn't worried when I couldn't see them. But back when Reece was still my actual partner, either Colin or Lily *always* showed up to be there for him after we were out there. Now, he was all alone.

Lucky for me, Dad immediately knew what I was asking without having to elaborate.

"Colin's at practice, but Lily's with Emory. She just didn't want to be back here with both Kayden and Kim," he told me. I didn't even have to ask about Kieren because he barely showed up *anywhere* unless Jamie agreed to go as well. "But she's probably already on her way back here."

I nodded and was about to jump off the bench to walk over to my fiancé when I noticed Lily making her way past a couple of figure skating pairs without interrupting any possibly important talks. She smiled at me when she noticed me looking, but she went straight over to Reece instead of stopping to talk to me first.

I was glad she went to him first.

Chapter Thirty-Two

Reece

"You did good, kid," Lily said before she forced me into one of her rare hugs. "Was it strange to be back out there after such a long time?"

I sighed, nodding softly before I pulled away from our hug. "I feel kind of bad about it."

"Why?" Her eyebrows drew together. "It's normal to be nervous after—"

"That's the thing, I wasn't nervous. I felt indifferent. Honestly, I thought I'd feel like dying because of my nerves but I was surprisingly calm about it all."

"Because you don't have anything to lose. You don't care about figure skating," she said.

"But Brooke cares. This is so important to her. She wants to go to nationals. I should feel *something*. If I'm not excited or nervous, how good can I really be for her?" I raked a hand through my hair in frustration. "I saw our points. We did pretty well, so I should be happy. I should be excited. If nothing goes wrong, we might even be in the top three today. But there's nothing."

Lily tilted her head at me. "Well, I'm sure you're excited

for Brooke. You're just not excited for yourself because figure skating isn't *your* thing. It's hers."

I hadn't considered that to be a possibility.

I was happy for Brooke. She did amazing, and I knew she was super relieved that we'd gotten such a high score. It just threw me off that I hadn't felt a single ounce of accomplishment for myself. No pride. It felt more like a task I got done.

One of many tasks.

"Is Colin here?" I asked. Talking about how indifferent I felt was pointless. It wasn't going to change and there was nothing I could do about it.

Lily shook her head. "He's at practice. But I recorded everything so I can show him later." She got up onto her tiptoes, laid her hand on my head, and started messing up my hair like she used to do when I was younger. "Ah, he'll be so proud."

I swatted her hand away. "Hey, I'm an adult now. My sister-in-law is no longer allowed to mess up my hair."

Her eyebrows rose. "You lived in my house for seven years. I helped you hide your bad grades from your brother. If I want to mess up your hair, I'll do that."

Brooke had tears in her eyes, yet I still felt indifferent.

Even as we were sure we were in the top three, standing on the edge of the rink and waiting for the judges to announce the third place, I felt nothing. Sure, we could've placed way lower, so low that we weren't even worth mentioning, but my gut feeling knew we were somewhere in the top three.

After a while, figure skaters could easily determine where they were ranked—if only an estimated rank. Multiple factors made it easy to figure it out.

Our performance and the crowd's reaction were too good not to be ranked at all, so we had to have been in the top three. I wasn't even really anticipating finding out what place we got.

I knew I was supposed to be excited and scared at the same time. I used to feel those once upon a time, but not anymore. My heart was with ice hockey, and no matter how hard I tried to be excited to have placed this high on the first try, I just couldn't feel anything.

In the back of my mind, I was grieving my hockey career. When I offered to be Brooke's partner, I knew what I was getting myself into, but it only just dawned on me.

I was missing our fifth game this season. And it was the second game I missed because of figure skating. I hadn't even told Brooke because I knew she'd feel bad if she knew.

While I wasn't planning on joining the draft next year, scouts' eyes were still on me. Colin told me the teams were watching me, if only because of my last name. What if he was right and they now noticed how I was skipping out on games and being the worst teammate *ever*?

What if that was why Pike thought it was better had I been single?

No distractions.

No putting hockey last.

I loved Brooke more than anything, but fuck, knowing I was voluntarily risking my career, something I'd been dreaming of since I was a kid, just to make her happy was sitting heavy in my stomach.

I'd be happy for her, I'd celebrate her victories with her, for her, but what about me? What about my dreams?

Brooke next to me exhaled deeply, her hands clasped tightly together, her gaze fixed on the judges' table as the arena filled with a pulsating energy. Anticipation crackled in the air like electricity.

Once upon a time, my heart would've been racing in rhythm with the thrumming beat of the music echoing throughout the arena, but it was now beating to a different song.

The announcer's voice reverberated through the speakers, cutting through the buzz of the crowd. "Ladies and gentlemen, please welcome your third-place winners… Natalia Kozlova and Alexei Romanov!"

Brooke reached for my hand, gripping it so tightly that she might as well have been cutting off the blood circulation to my fingers. "Oh, my God," she muttered under her breath. She was still holding back her excitement.

Top two.

And still nothing.

"We might've actually gotten first place," Brooke said, looking up at me. "Erik's going to be pissed."

"Yeah." I nodded slightly. "He'll be furious."

"I haven't ranked this high in years!" A little excited shriek slipped out. "I told you that you'd do amazing!"

I sighed. "You did."

"Ah, pssht! They're about to announce…"

"Please welcome your second-place winners," the announcer spoke through his microphone. The words seemed to echo endlessly, each syllable stretching out into an eternity, prolonging the agony of anticipation.

I braced myself, my muscles tense, praying not to have placed second for Brooke's sake.

"Brooklyn King and Reece Carter." His words hit me like a blow to the gut, stealing every ounce of oxygen left in my lungs.

Brooke's hands loosened, her shoulders sinking as she closed her eyes to take a breath.

The words hung in the air, a mix of relief and disappointment washing over me like a wave.

Well, these were certainly emotions... but only because I knew Brooke was going to feel awful.

Second place.

Not first. Not the gold medal that had been Brooke's singular focus for weeks on end, but second.

I was relieved Brooke was placed at all, but second place...?

It was an achievement, no doubt, but in the competitive world of figure skating, second place was just short of the ultimate goal.

You were the first loser—good enough to rank high but not good enough to win.

The disappointment washed over me in a wave, threatening to engulf me entirely. If I felt bad about second place, I could barely imagine how Brooke felt.

I forced a smile, a facade to mask the bitter taste of defeat that lingered in my mouth. When I looked at my fiancée, she had tears in her eyes. Her lips were turned downward, but within seconds, Brooke shook off her sadness and plastered a smile onto her face.

Applause erupted from the crowd, a cacophony of cheers and whistles that served as both a celebration and a reminder of our first place as losers.

I took Brooke's hand and we skated onto the ice to get our medal. Silver, the color of failure.

We took our final bow, drowning out the applause thundering around us. We hid our true emotions behind a smile so bright that nobody would ever think we weren't happy about our placement.

Despite the pang of indifference inside of me, I knew what losing felt like. I knew how awful second place felt, and just because figure skating had never been my true passion didn't mean I was okay with losing.

My mind drifted from the glittering arena into the dimly lit confines of a hockey rink.

I pictured myself clad in my jersey, the number 17 largely displayed on the back, with the familiar weight of the hockey stick in my hands and the adrenaline-fueled rush as I charged towards the net. The place where I felt alive, on the ice during a hockey game. The place where every stride, every shot was a testament to my dedication and skill. Nothing had to look pretty or be executed neatly and with too much precision.

I saw myself at the Frozen Four, sirens shrilling through the arena as the timer ran out and my team lost. Second place. The first loser.

Now, that was painful, so I knew second place in figure skating was as well.

"We'll get first place next time," Brooke said quietly, nudging me softly. "Being the best would be great, but we'll have more chances. This was just the first—a practice run if you will."

"What? Oh, yeah, sure. Practice run."

Chapter Thirty-Three

Reece

"You're late," Coach spoke harshly as I rushed into the film room to watch some tapes. "Again."

"I'm sorry." For the first half of November, I hadn't been early for practice a single time. I wasn't even *on* time. Either I was stuck in a gym with Brooke, going over stunts and whatnot to improve our performance and tweak a few things, or I was at the arena… just not with my team.

Like today. I was on the ice when my teammates were starting to show up. I was still on the ice when Coach said we were watching some tapes before going over a new strategy for tomorrow's game.

I was still on the ice when they were in the film room.

"This is unacceptable, Carter." Coach paused the video. "You used to be one of the top players on the team, and now I'm not even sure it's worth keeping you on the team. You're unreliable. Your head's far from in the game when you're on the ice. You're a no-show to games. You fell from the top right to the bottom. And for what, Carter?"

Well, I couldn't tell him that it was because of my fiancée and her dream to make it to the Grand Prix. Then again, Coach knew I was skipping to skate with Brooke.

"I'm sorry, Coach. I'll do better," I promised, unsure whether I could keep it.

As the captain, I knew I had let the team down, especially with playoffs getting closer. I had to find a way to balance my commitment to the team and support Brooke in achieving her dream.

It was harder said than done, though.

Coach's gaze lingered on me for a moment, his disappointment palpable. "I hope so, Carter. Because if you don't step up soon, I'll have no choice but to bench you or even let you go entirely. This team needs players who are fully dedicated, not ones who have their priorities elsewhere."

His words hit me like a slap in the face. I knew he was right, though, so I couldn't have been mad even if I had wanted to.

I had been neglecting my responsibilities to the team, and it was time I at least tried to be a better captain again.

"Now, take a seat," Coach commanded, pointing at a chair in the front row.

I nodded, the weight of his words still sitting pretty heavy in my stomach as I found my seat among my teammates.

The room was silent as Coach restarted the video, dissecting our previous game play-by-play. Every mistake, every missed opportunity, was magnified on the screen, a harsh reminder of how far we had strayed from our potential.

The next time Coach paused the video and zoomed in, it was me on the screen. I could feel Coach's disappointment way before he commented on what I did wrong at our game two days ago.

"This moment right here, this is where you could have turned the game around for us. But instead, you let it slip right through your fingers," he said, making sure to look right at me.

I felt a wave of shame wash over me as the video resumed, and I had to watch the replay of my missed shot which could've been the game-winning goal. Looking at it now, I could see how easily I was able to score, but in that moment, my head was too busy worrying about Brooke's competition the following day.

I clenched my jaw, trying to maintain a stoic expression as Coach continued to insult me. But I deserved it.

By the time we were done watching tapes and going over tomorrow's game plan, I knew I had my work cut out for me. I knew I had to make the game count, win it, and prove to everyone on the team that I was worth still being their captain.

Guess that didn't work out.

"Why can't we get this right?!" Brooke groaned in anger as she dropped down on the ice.

Her frustration was evident in every inch of her body, her chest rising and falling rapidly with each heavy breath she took.

I took a quick glance at the clock, sighed, and then crouched down next to her, laying a hand on her back as we both stared out onto the empty rink.

"We'll have to try again," I said softly. "And I'm sure we'll get it next time."

She turned to look at me, her eyes filled with a mixture of determination and exhaustion. "But when, Reece? Championships are in January, and we're nowhere near ready. We couldn't place first even *once* all season."

It was always the second place; always the first losers.

I checked the time once more, slowly getting frustrated

with myself. I had to be at Manhattanville College's hockey arena in less than two hours. Actually, I had to have been there already. The game was starting in less than two hours.

"It's not like we don't rank at all, *mi princesa*. Perhaps we just need to add one more stunt... that might fix the problem. Second place is awful, but it's *almost* first place, there's just something missing in our routine, obviously."

Brooke stared at me for a moment. "You really think adding another stunt will make the difference?"

I nodded, trying to sound more confident than I felt when I spoke. "Absolutely. We just need that extra wow factor to push us over the edge. We're so close, Brookie. I know we can do this."

She let out a deep sigh. "I guess we can try it. We have nothing to lose at this point."

My eyes fell back on the clock, and in that moment I just knew I was going to miss my game... again.

I was letting them down again.

God, I was the worst captain the St. Trewery ice hockey team had *ever* seen.

Brooke seemed to notice my distraction and followed my gaze, and as her eyes settled on the clock, they widened in realization.

"Reece, your game!" She jumped to her feet. "You're going to miss it if you don't leave like right now."

I nodded but it was mostly to myself. "It's okay. Even if I left now, Coach would be so furious with me for being late again that he'd bench me. It'd be hours wasted on a bench that I could be spending with you, working on getting you that win."

"But this is hockey, Reece," she said, her voice tinged with concern. "Your team needs you. And hockey is important to you."

I stood up, brushing the ice off my pants as I took a deep breath. "It's alright, I promise."

Chapter Thirty-Four

Brooklyn

I laced up my skates, each pull of the laces echoing the tightening knot in my stomach. Looking up, I watched the Zamboni glide over the ice a couple more times. We got to the arena late, past official closing hours, but Dad was paying the owner quite a bit of money to allow us to be here whenever we wanted before opening and after closing hours.

Practice was important for us, and due to college and ice hockey, we had to sacrifice our resting time. We had a late competition yesterday, so we slept in this morning and chose to be at the arena in the evening.

The ice rink was bathed in a soft, ethereal light, casting shadows across the already pristine surface. It wasn't going to get any smoother than that.

It was our sanctuary, the place where magic was meant to happen, where our dreams were meant to come true. But tonight, the atmosphere was thick with tension.

By the time December came around, Reece and I still hadn't *once* ranked first. Always second.

His hockey team won so many games, I couldn't even count them anymore. And I was so happy for him, they deserved a great season, but I was also getting *so* frustrated with always being second.

We were two months away from the championship.

Reece was leaning against the boards, his eyes fixed on his phone. I bet his mind was miles away—Chicago most likely. He was missing a game tonight to be here with me. I couldn't have been more grateful. Anyone else would've told me to fuck off and attend their game, but not Reece.

I told him he should go, but he refused and I certainly couldn't force him onto that plane. As much as I tried to reason with him, he insisted that practice with me was more important.

I felt really bad that he was missing his game.

Yet, despite him *choosing* to do this with—*for* me, his annoyance was palpable.

He was lost in the world of hockey stats and schedules. It became obvious that his attention drifted further from figure skating and ranking higher with each passing competition. Even when we were on the ice for practice, he wasn't concentrating as much anymore.

"Reece," I said, trying to keep the frustration out of my voice. "We need to focus. We can't afford to slip up. Second place is painful enough as it is, we don't need to sink *even* lower."

He glanced up, his eyebrows furrowing in annoyance. "I know, I know. I can't help it, okay? You know that I have a meeting with Anthony tomorrow. He's probably going to tell me the same things Pike did: that I have to focus on hockey or else not a single team will want to draft me. Or that he's sick of being my agent. Do you know what happens when he quits? I won't have an agent. Do you have any idea how important agents are for hockey players? My chances of getting drafted without him are far too slim to even think about him walking away from me. And he's already my second agent."

I bit back a response, the words hanging unspoken in the chilly air. I understood his fears, his ambitions, and his dreams of making it big in the hockey world. Following after his brother had been his goal forever.

But what about *my* dream?

He *promised*.

What about the countless hours we'd already spent perfecting our routine, pushing ourselves to the limit, only to fall short time and time again?

And especially today, I told Reece to go to his game. I would've followed him like always when they played in a different city or state. He was the one to insist we practice more for figure skating.

"It's just practice anyway," he added and finally laid his phone on the bench. "Be glad I'm here."

My hands balled into fists, anger flooding my bloodstream but I bit back any of the bad words lingering in my mind. With a resigned sigh, I got up and stepped onto the ice. The familiar chill sept through the fabric of my clothes, and suddenly, I wished I hadn't left my jacket on the bench.

Sure, I could've gone back to get it, but I was a little afraid that Reece would laugh at me. Maybe he thought I was stupid for forgetting it because I should've known better by now.

Reece followed me onto the ice, his movements mechanical, lacking fire. If this was hockey practice, he would've been lighting up the entire arena with his enthusiasm.

As he stopped in front of me and looked at my arms, his eyes rolled. "No jacket today?"

I was going to shake my head, embarrassed to admit that I forgot to put it on, but when my gaze fell and I caught a glimpse of my hands, I remembered that Reece and I were supposed to be a team. He was still my fiancé. I shouldn't have been embarrassed to make a mistake in front of him.

So, I took a breath and said, "I left it on the bench and only just realized."

He chuckled slightly, but not in a condescending way. "Do you want me to get it for you?"

See, Brooke, everything's fine. It's just the chemicals in your brain acting up again.

"You don't have to, but thank you."

Reece smiled at me, then skated off to get my jacket.

Once Reece was back with my jacket and I was finally freezing a little less, we started with our basic warm-up routine, gliding across the ice in what used to be perfect harmony just a couple of weeks ago.

It might've looked flawless, but beneath the surface, the perfect harmony was fractured. Each movement was marked by unspoken tension. With every move, I could feel Reece's frustration simmering just below the surface, a volatile energy threatening to erupt at any moment.

As we were about to move into our first set of jumps, I stopped abruptly. I looked at Reece, defeated by his unwillingness to take this seriously tonight.

"Honestly, Reece, if you're not even going to put effort into this, why bother showing up at all?"

"Well, I'm sorry that I have a bunch of shit to worry about," he said, his voice harsher than usual. "I'm skipping an important game to be here. I'm messing with my career to be here. I'm trying to push myself beyond my abilities to get that stupid first place for you. What else do you want me to do?"

"Because it was me who forced you to do all this, right? I begged you to be my partner, hadn't I? Every morning I wake up just to ruin your stupid ice hockey career, don't I?" My eyes rolled without my permission.

"Brooke, that's not what I—"

"Just forget it!" Tears were building up in my eyes, blurring my vision so hard I could barely even make out Reece's facial features. "If you're too busy worrying about your precious hockey career to care about being mentally present during our practice, which you insisted on, then just leave. I get it, hockey is important to you. You deserve to be out there with the pros one day, and I really, *really* hope you get there someday. I'm sorry that figure skating, something you *volunteered* to do, is taking you away from the one thing you truly love in life. I gave you the option to go to your game tonight, but you said no. That's not on me. So now you don't get to be mad at me for ruining your career when *you* are the one who's making all these decisions. Yet somehow, you don't even bother to see that, do you?"

"Brooke—"

"If my presence in your life and my dreams are causing you so much trouble, why don't you just leave me?!"

"Woah there," Reece said, suddenly laying his hands on my shoulders. I didn't even notice him getting closer. "I know this is your anxiety talking mixed with the pressure of needing to succeed, but you saying this hurts anyway, okay? You *know* I love you. And you know I care about you and your dreams. And you know that your presence in my life is the best that's ever happened to me. Just because I have a bad day, week, or even month does *not* mean I no longer want to be with you, okay?"

Only now did it really dawn on me what I had said. Yes, I heard myself speak, but I couldn't control what came out of me before it did.

You'd think after twenty years on this earth, I finally

learned to control this... I got better, outbursts like these didn't happen as often anymore, but I suppose I still slipped sometimes.

"I—Reece, I'm so sorry... I don't—" Tears streamed down my face as I collapsed onto the floor. "I don't know why I said all this. I didn't... I didn't even mean most of it."

"I know," he said, lifting me off the ice. Reece held me in his arms, my legs and arms wrapped around his body. "And I promise you, Brooke, I'll give it my all tomorrow at the competition. But tonight I just need to *be*."

"Okay," I mumbled.

"I *am* choosing to miss hockey for you, and I'd choose to do this for you over and over again, but that doesn't mean I can just brush it under the rug as well. Going pro is still important to me, and I can't just ignore or stop feeling bad about risking it to be here."

"I'm sorry you're missing another game because of me." I felt awful about it. Truly. I knew how much hockey meant to him. I should've known he was putting a lot on the line to help me.

Somehow, between all the eagerness to make it to nationals and being sure Reece was my ticket to get there, I overlooked how much he was sacrificing for me. I wasn't exactly sure how it slipped my mind or why I couldn't see it until now, but I also knew it had to change.

We had to find a way to balance it both. Find a way to ensure Reece wasn't going to get in trouble with his team or agent—if it wasn't too late for that already—while he could still help me. Or I'd just have to get myself disqualified from this season and pray that I could skate with Erik or someone way better than him next season.

Chapter Thirty-Five
Reece

"What are you doing here?" Colin asked as I walked right into his house without prior notice. Ever since I moved out, I told him when I was stopping by, no matter the reason why. I didn't today. "Aren't you supposed to be, I don't know, with Brooke and preparing for your competition in a few hours?"

I sped past my brother, rummaging through his living room cabinets. "Brooke's at home—uhm, well, her old home." I shook my head, trying to focus. "She's with her family, I mean. You know, the house across from us right now."

Colin chuckled. "Could've just said she's with her parents."

"I tried and failed." I moved on to another cabinet, still not finding my stupid papers. "Anyway, I will race to the arena and meet her there this time."

"You know, it's not good to be so distracted before a stressful day like today," he said. I heard him stepping closer to me before eventually, he laid a hand on my shoulder and stopped me from looking through all of his cabinets like a crazy person. "What exactly are you looking for, Reece? This is still my house, maybe I know where it is."

Looking at my brother, I sighed heavily. "Do you remember when I signed with Pike, he told me to create a portfolio with all my stats? Like all my hockey wins and losses over the years?"

Colin nodded. "He can look them up online."

"That's what you said back then as well, remember?"

"I do, and I still think it's stupid you had to do that."

He wasn't the only one who thought it was stupid. I wasn't even sure why Pike needed this information. I understood having been watched since high school, but he even wanted my middle school stats and whatever games I played *before* middle school.

And as Colin said, he could just look them up online.

"Yeah, well, I need that portfolio. I left it here when I moved out because I thought it wouldn't get lost then, but I have no idea where I put it," I said. Anthony asked me to bring the portfolio to our meeting so he could have a look at it. I was certain he just wanted to make fun of Pike. "So, that didn't work."

My brother looked at me, watching as he raked a hand through his hair. "Honestly, the only one who might know is Lily."

"Yeah, but she's not here." As far as I knew, she was currently on set for the next movie she was directing. She should've been home later though, but that wasn't helping me now. "I'm not surprised to hear you have no idea where *my* stuff is. You're barely home. It's a miracle you know where the kitchen is."

"I'm only ever in there for the kids anyway, and they show me the way, so I don't *need* to know, do I?" he joked. Though, he really wasn't in the kitchen a lot. He usually ate whatever Lily made or stole food from Miles. I did the same though, so I couldn't even make fun of him.

Speaking of Colin's kids, Kieran decided to show up at that very moment. He looked at me first, then at his father.

"Dad, can we go to the bookstore?" Kieran asked. "I have nothing more to read, and JJ's sick so I can't even go over to Uncle Ron's house to play with him."

"Didn't your mom get you a new book just yesterday?" Colin asked in return.

Kieran nodded. "So? I finished it." He looked at me again, smiling this time. "Mom put your folder with your portfolio in my room so Kim wouldn't accidentally use the papers to draw on."

That was smart.

"And why don't I know about this?" Colin inquired, probably feeling pretty stupid right about now.

"I don't know, Dad." He stepped closer to his father, then suddenly wrapped his arms around Colin, looking up. "Can we go to the bookstore now? Mom always says that reading is good, and we don't say no to good things."

"I'll just let you discuss this all by yourself and get my stuff," I said and immediately fled the scene.

Was Colin going to take Kieran to the bookstore? Totally, and if only because it meant that Kieran was going outside—in public—for once.

Ten minutes after heading into Kieran's bedroom, I finally found the folder with my portfolio. Okay, I would've found it faster had Kim not been spending most of that time clinging to my legs.

Kieran's bedroom looked like the most organized grandpa lived there. He had tons of books neatly stored on his bookshelf, barely any toys around, and I saw some kind of math book on his desk. It was a ninth-grader mathematics book. That kid was ten, and he was doing more math than I'd ever bothered to learn.

I had good grades, but I was pretty sure Kieran was acing all of his classes. Jamie, his cousin, was a whole other subject. Honestly, I was convinced Kieran was taking Jamie's tests and doing his homework just so he wouldn't be held back.

"Uncle Reece's Cups?" Kim sat down on my foot, once again swinging her arms around my leg to stop me from leaving.

I looked down, refraining from rolling my eyes at a three-year-old.

"Yes, Kiwi?"

"Daddy and I come watch your hockey today," she told me.

"Really?" I said, earning myself a convinced nod in return. "Are you sure you're not already asleep at that time?"

My game didn't start until eight PM, and Kim was usually asleep by six.

"I sleep now, and then I and Daddy go to hockey, okay?" She held up her pinky, and though I truly doubted she was going to be awake for my game, I hooked my pinky finger with hers.

"Deal."

Within seconds, Kim let go of my leg, stood up, ran across the hall, and right into her bedroom.

"DADDY! I NEED MY JAMMIES!" she yelled. "UNCLE REECE'S CUPS SAY IS OKAY WHEN I GO TO THE HOCKEY GAME! I HAVE TO SLEEP NOW, AND THEN I BE AWAKE!"

Closing the door behind me as I exited Kieran's room,

Colin was already in the hallway and heading toward his daughter's room.

Colin rolled his eyes at me as if his daughter growing up and evolving a love for ice hockey was my fault. Surely not his, right? He was the professional ice hockey player in the family, but it was my fault nonetheless.

"Why would you tell her to sleep *now*?" Colin asked. "Do you know how exhausting three-year-olds can be at a sports game? Especially at a time when they're supposed to be sleeping."

I nodded. "You have three kids, and Lily took me to every single game of yours—well, the ones she went to anyway. I sat in a room with all the players' partners more often than you could even begin to imagine. That was a room full of little, crying kids, and parents—and Luan, sometimes even Miles and Emory—being *desperate* to find a way to get them to either stop crying and watch the game, play with the other kids, or fall asleep in someone's arms."

Colin chuckled, shrugging at me. "Considering that I'm usually on the ice when all that happens, that's not my problem."

"Considering that I'll be on the ice when Kim gets restless, it's not my problem either." I looked into Kim's bedroom, watching as she used her bed as a trampoline, rather impatiently waiting for her father. "Kim will be fine, I'm sure of that. Look how excited she is."

She hadn't been to many of my games. Mostly because she was still very young, but also because she went to enough of Colin's games that Lily didn't want her to go to mine anymore. Hockey games were super stressful for little kids, and far too loud for their ears.

Colin peeked into the room, sighing softly. "Kimi, stop jumping on the bed."

"Okay, Daddy." Kim plopped down, giggling.

"Oh, before I forget to tell you," Colin began, looking back at me. "Mom and Dad are coming tonight as well. They landed about two hours ago and should probably be on their way to their house by now. It was supposed to be a surprise but I know how much you hate it when they show up without telling you first."

It wasn't that I *hated* it, but I just wanted to know when my parents were here.

Since they moved to Spain, it didn't happen often that they watched me play in person. Knowing they were there made me want to be better. For them. I wanted to score for them. Make them proud.

While I knew they watched my games on TV every time, them being there in person was different.

Chapter Thirty-Six
Brooklyn

"Then I was thinking, what about…." I swiped to the next page of my PowerPoint presentation, and suddenly a picture of an enormous castle showed up on the TV. "*Château de Challain.*"

Grey's face didn't waver, however, Luan started to laugh hysterically.

"Man, it's a good thing we're not paying for that wedding, huh, Grey Davis?" Luan said and nudged his husband in the side with his elbow.

"You don't like it?" I asked, my smile fading. My eyes wandered over to my father, who'd been silently crying as I broke down half of the money I was planning to spend on my wedding dress.

Reece and my wedding wasn't even in sight yet. In fact, we hadn't even talked about it ever since we'd gotten engaged, but that didn't stop me from planning our wedding.

"It sounds… expensive," Luan replied. "But amazing."

I looked at Grey, waiting for his thoughts.

"It's certainly you," Grey said. "What does Reece think about it anyway?"

I took a seat on the floor in front of the TV. "We haven't

talked about it yet." I was fully planning on talking to him about it. I wouldn't make any decisions about our wedding without talking to him about them first. The problem was that he barely had time to sit down with me just to talk.

"Don't you think Reece should be okay with your plans first before you have your mind set on a really expensive wedding in a castle?" Dad asked.

"And a wedding dress that looks like it weighs about as much as you do," Grey added.

"Let the girl dream!" Luan groaned, rolling his eyes. "It's her wedding. Reece doesn't have a say in it."

"He's a Carter," Aaron threw into the mix. "Carters don't have shit to say, they just pay for it. I mean, do you seriously think Colin had a single say in his wedding except that he was getting married? I don't think so. Why would Reece have more rights?"

"That's why I love you." I grinned at Aaron. "You're always down to insult the Carters with me."

Before Aaron could reply anything, Dad cut in. "Brooke, I'm not saying I wouldn't pay for all of it, but I know you. You're saying you don't care about what Reece thinks now, and then you'll cry yourself to sleep for the next ten years, wondering if Reece is mad at you because you didn't ask him if *your* dream wedding was okay with him."

A slight, dreadful shiver ran down my spine. Dad was right. As much as I always tried to ignore that unwell feeling in my stomach, and make decisions based on what *I* wanted, it would haunt me in my sleep for years.

It got easier the older I got, but major decisions like a wedding were definitely going to give me a bad time if I decided all this by myself.

I could picture the venue, could imagine how amazing our day was going to be... but the ache in my stomach was also slowly creeping in to ruin it all already. The fear, those voices that were occupying my head would never leave. Not until the day of, or soon after. A wedding was a huge thing, and I couldn't live with myself, thinking Reece didn't like it.

It was a good thing I only wanted to know what my family thought about my plans before I spoke to Reece about them and made amends. The castle in France was just one of many ideas.

But what if I asked him, he agreed, and still didn't like it? Oh, God.

What if he'd just pretend to like it? What if he didn't even want to marry me in the first place? What if—

No. No, stop this.

I clutched the sides of my head, closing my eyes to drown out all of these what-ifs, but they just wouldn't stop.

What if he doesn't like the venue?

What if getting married isn't nearly as magical as you imagine?

What if the vision of our wedding day isn't what he had in mind at all?

It was like a never-ending storm, a tornado of thoughts that I knew I shouldn't have listened to, but it was impossible to drown them out. Each thought was more irrational than the last.

What if, soon after getting married, Reece wants a divorce because you suck at being a wife?

What if he says no at the altar?

What if he doesn't even show up at the wedding?

What if the wedding was the beginning of your ending?

"Brooke," Dad said as he gently cupped my face with his hands. I didn't even notice he had crossed the room, let alone sat down on the floor with me. "Take a deep breath."

I nodded slowly, trying so hard to breathe in, but it felt like my lungs were boycotting, refusing to let oxygen inside.

My body felt so heavy all of a sudden. Every slight movement took so much effort and used so much of my energy that not moving at all seemed like the best option.

"Everything will be okay," Dad's soothing voice cut through to me once more. "You don't even have a date set yet. There's plenty of time left to talk about everything. You can plan the day out down to the last second of it. And you know Reece loves you more than anything. He'll love the day as much as you will."

He pulled me into his arms, hugging me tightly. The familiar scent of his perfume offered a sense of comfort, tricking my brain into thinking everything was alright.

"Reece is just leaving Colin's place," Aaron said, and almost instantly, my head shot up, and my eyes were on the window. "Do you want me to get him?"

"He has a meeting with his agent," Grey answered before I could.

I watched as Reece rolled his eyes at whatever Colin said. And I still watched when he bumped fists with Kayden to say goodbye. At that, a slim smile tugged on my lips.

Kayden was seven now and way too cool for hugs, so he insisted.

"How do *you* know that?" Luan asked.

Reece exchanged a few more words with his brother before finally turning around to walk to his car. Colin didn't close the door, though. He was waiting for Reece to drive away as always.

"Because I have ears, baby. Sometimes, I listen when you talk," Grey replied.

"SOMETIMES?!"

Laughter erupted, but I didn't join in.

My heart skipped a beat when Reece stood in front of his car, but instead of unlocking it, getting inside, and driving away, he turned around and looked toward my dad's house.

The air in the living room felt heavy, almost suffocating, and the voices around me were merely a hum in the distance at this point.

Kayden ran back out of the house, and while I couldn't hear their conversation, I was almost sure Colin told him to come back.

He hugged Reece, causing my fiancé to flinch before he laughed and picked Kayden up.

A smile played on his lips as they talked.

Reece didn't know I was watching, he couldn't have seen it either, as Dad and Emory insisted on smart windows way before the plans for this house were even done. Yet when he looked away from Kayden and back at Dad's house, it was like he was looking right at me without being aware of it.

My heart skipped a beat, and soon after, it was racing as if it was trying to break free from my chest.

I couldn't explain it, but it was like he found me. As if the house was a crowd and he found me in it. It was as if he possessed some extra sense, attuned only to the rhythm of my heart.

In that moment, time seemed to freeze entirely. The world faded away until there was only him and me, bound together by an invisible thread of love.

It was in the way his eyes softened, and his lips curved up by just a tiny bit. And the way his head tilted sideways as he looked at his own reflection in the window, not knowing I was right there, watching him. Like he could see right through the tinted glass.

Everything will be okay, a voice in my head whispered as I looked at Reece a little longer.

What If We Break?

Despite the chaos surrounding us, there was a sense of serenity in his presence.

Reece managed to calm me down when I just looked at him, and he didn't even know. He made me feel cherished beyond measure, and I had no idea how I could ever tell him about it.

As he finally let Kayden back down and looked away from my dad's house, he waved at Colin one last time and got in the car.

Chapter Thirty-Seven

Reece

I'd meet Brooke at the arena after I met with Anthony. It was very unusual for us as we always showed up to competitions together. We even showed up to my games together, never mind the fact that Brooke had to wait for *hours* until the game started.

I was just hoping it wasn't going to throw off our performance today. I was a bit superstitious when it came to my games—figure skating competitions were no different. We had a routine we stuck to every time, but we had to switch it up today.

At least we were lucky enough that today's competition was close by.

After messaging Anthony over and over again, asking what this meeting was about, he finally caved and told me. I was relieved, to say the least. However, that off-feeling in my stomach never dissipated.

Anthony wanted to talk to me about what my plans were if the Rangers wouldn't draft me. I hadn't been thinking about it much as I was sure I still had at least two years of school ahead of me before I needed to make a decision, but I suppose he wanted an answer now.

Honestly, it was stupid either way because I couldn't pick the team I wanted to play for. Sure, I had my preference, obviously, but if a different team wanted me and nobody else, I had no other choice.

Even if the Rangers drafted me, it wasn't a guarantee that I'd stay with them forever. They could trade me whenever they wanted unless I had a contract that stated I couldn't be traded, which definitely wasn't going to happen any time soon.

Colin had one, as far as I knew anyway, but it took almost a decade until his contract was changed, and he was no longer tradable. Guess they just didn't want to lose one of their best players on the team. Aaron and Grey had safe spots as well. Okay, seeing as Grey was the captain, it would've been odd if they suddenly decided to just trade him anyway.

I left Colin's place thirty minutes ago and was now approaching my agent's office building when my phone started ringing. I was going to ignore it, but when I saw it was Lily calling, I couldn't. She rarely called me.

Wasn't she on set, anyway?

"Hello?" I said as I picked up. She stayed quiet for a while, which had me worried. "Lily?"

If she needed help with something, she wouldn't have stayed quiet. And she would've called Colin first, especially since he was at home today. And if something happened on set, she still would've called Colin first.

"Lily?" I tried again, but she stayed quiet once more. I was about to hang up, convincing myself that this was an accidental call, when I heard a sharp intake of breath.

"Uhm... Reece?" She sounded distressed.

"Yeah?" My eyebrows drew together in confusion.

"Are you with someone right now?"

Such an odd thing to ask. "No. I'm about to head into a meeting with my agent. Why, what's up?"

"Uhm…" I heard her taking a deep breath. This was so unlike her. "Is there any way you could come to the New York Presbyterian Weill Cornell Medical Center?"

I looked at the entrance doors to Anthony's office building. "Is Colin okay?"

He was just fine when I left. I wasn't even sure if it was possible for something to happen to Colin and him being at *that* hospital within thirty minutes of me leaving his residence. The hospital was about an hour away from his house—might be more depending on traffic.

"Oh, uh, it's not about Colin… uhm… it's—"

"Is it Brooke?" My stomach churned as the unsettling thoughts of something bad possibly having happened to Brooke sank in, a heavy weight settling in the pit of my stomach. It felt like my insides were twisting and knotting, a sickening sensation spreading through my body like a creeping vine.

"N-no. It's your dad," she said. "Your parents were in an accident. Your mom's fine, but…" Lily struggled to find words, but she honestly didn't need to say much more for me to understand what she was trying to tell me.

"Is he dead?"

She was quiet again. All I could hear was heavy breathing, some muttering and stumbling until she finally found her voice. "Not technically?"

"Not technically?!" What was that even supposed to mean?

"Yeah, uhm… Reece, I think you should come to the hospital as soon as possible."

My mind was racing, trying to comprehend the magnitude

of what I'd just been told while my stomach was battling to keep my breakfast inside of me.

I could feel a headache building up, a knot in my throat, and a stinging in my eyes, but I had no idea what exactly I was feeling at that moment. It was everything and nothing at all.

It wasn't just nausea, that I could tell. It was a sense of the ground crumbling beneath my feet. It was a dreadful realization that, no matter what happened, my life was never going to be the same again from this day forward.

Life had thrown me a curveball I wasn't prepared to catch.

"Did you call Colin?" I asked. I wasn't sure what to say, my mind was blank, but I suppose Colin had to know. She had to have called him first, right? They were married. Of course she called him first.

"He's on the phone with your mom. It's why I'm calling, not Colin."

"Okay," I breathed out, unsure of what else to say. "I'm on my way. Could you meet me outside?" I turned around and walked back to my car. Screw that stupid meeting, it was probably unnecessary anyway.

"Yeah, sure," she replied, then stayed quiet again for a beat before adding, "Reece? Drive safe, okay?"

"I will." Or I would try to. Luckily, the hospital wasn't that far away from Anthony's office, so I didn't have to turn a long drive into something rather short. It'd take me maybe fifteen minutes, or thirty with New York's traffic.

I hung up the phone, ripping the door to my car open. After starting the engine, I called Brooke because... just because.

Brooke might've not been the closest to my parents, but she still deserved to know. I wanted her to know. I needed her at the hospital because I couldn't possibly go through this without her by my side to catch me when I fell.

I tried to reach her about fifty times, but she never picked up her phone. I tried calling Miles and Emory, but neither of them picked up either. But of course they wouldn't. They were probably already on their way to the arena, or had just gotten there.

By the time I reached the hospital parking lot and got out of the car to race to the entrance and find Lily, neither of them had been picking up or calling me back.

I started to spam Brooke with messages in hopes that she might peek at her phone soon and call me back, but I knew better. She rarely used her phone before a competition. Brooke was always so focused on figure skating, she didn't want to get distracted by anything. Not even important calls.

But I didn't understand why neither Miles nor Emory picked up either.

From afar, I could see Lily standing in front of the main entrance, pacing back and forth. She was on her phone, probably on a call with Colin or someone else.

Oh, God… if Colin was on his way, was he going to bring the kids?

I wasn't even sure what would've been better—children being there to possibly watch their grandfather die, or staying home and just being told he passed.

My pace slowed down as I got caught in my mind, trying to think back to when my sister died. Would I have preferred having been there? Would I remember if I was? Maybe I was there, I just had no recollection of it.

I was almost four when Eira died, surely I should remember *something*, but I didn't.

Sometimes, when Colin or our parents talked about Eira, I remembered a few things, like her playing with me and making me laugh. She used to sing me a song, but I didn't remember it, I just knew she did it.

But I couldn't remember her dying. Or her funeral, which I was sure I attended. Hopefully. Or I was too young and stayed with Brooke and her grandparents or Emory.

Aiden—who was the oldest of us all—was entirely wiped from my memories. I couldn't remember a damn thing about him, but that didn't surprise me, seeing as I was a literal baby when he died.

"Colin's on his way," Lily told me as soon as I reached her. "They'll be like an hour because traffic seems to be terrible today."

Lily was breathing quite erratic, her eyes were red and puffy. Tears stained her cheeks, and she kind of looked like her life had been sucked right out of her soul. I'd never seen her like this.

She hadn't even been crying this much when her mother died from liver cancer a couple of years ago, and as far as she told me, my dad was still alive.

Truthfully, I didn't know what to do. The only person I was good at consoling was my fiancée, and that was only because I knew Brooke. I knew what made her feel better, and I knew how to make her smile, and how to distract her mind.

But I didn't know any of those things about Lily. I wasn't even sure I knew how to do these things for myself.

"Is he dead?" I asked again, unsure of how to understand her distressed state. If Dad was still alive, surely she wouldn't have been as upset, right?

Was *I* supposed to be this upset?

I mean, yes, I could feel my breakfast wanting to come back out of my stomach every other second, and my heart was hammering like crazy inside of my chest, but I wasn't crying or anything.

"I... I don't know," she admitted, sobbing. "The doctors aren't exactly talking to me."

"But you said—" I stopped myself from talking. It really didn't matter what Lily said before, it wasn't going to help the situation now, either. "How are you here? I thought you were on set."

I followed Lily inside the building, into the ER.

"Yeah, I was, but I left early because I was planning on being there for your competition... and on my way back, I—" Lily wiped her tears away, taking an unsteady breath. "Your dad called me because he wanted to make sure he got the right arena for your competition so they could be there. And then suddenly... I heard tires screeching, followed by a loud crash, and shortly after, the call end—"

"Mamá," I called out as soon as I saw my mother standing in the middle of the ER, clutching my father's jacket close to her chest.

She turned around, looking right at me. Unlike all the other times I'd seen my mother, her eyes were empty, devoid of every emotion possible. She wasn't even crying.

Mom had blood in her hair, as well as some splatters all over her clothes. Her wrist was bandaged up, and she was wearing a shoulder immobilizer.

I rushed toward her, but suddenly every step felt like my feet were made of concrete.

"Reece." Mom's voice broke when she spoke, her bandaged hand quivering as she brought it up to her face to cover her mouth. "Oh, Reece."

I fell into my mother's arms, completely forgetting about her injured shoulder, and she didn't remind me of it either.

Upon hearing her sob as her mostly okay arm wrapped around me, I finally broke, too.

Tears dripped from my eyes, and my heart sank deeper with every passing second. It felt like my whole world had suddenly tilted off its axis.

My mouth felt dry and my throat constricted, making it hard to swallow. Dread settled in my chest, the nauseating feeling from earlier returning.

"Are you okay, Ma?" I asked, not knowing what else to say. It was a stupid question, I'd realized. Of course she wasn't okay.

"Your dad. He…" Mom tried to take a deep breath but collapsed instead. If I hadn't been holding her, she would've fallen to the ground. "I think… I don't think he'll make it."

Chapter Thirty-Eight

Reece

It had been an hour since I got to the hospital.

Colin sat across from me with his wife and their kids, trying his best to stay positive. He kept assuring all three of them that their grandpa was going to be alright, even though he didn't know if that was true.

Every time Mom tried to tell us what happened, she started to sob uncontrollably so that both Colin and I eventually stopped asking. It was a car crash, so much we knew.

Back in the ER, I overheard the two police officers talking to a doctor who was exiting the room the other guy involved in the accident was kept. The guy died on impact, apparently, but I wasn't sure if he caused the accident.

Dad was in surgery, but nobody could tell us when he was expected to get out—merely a broad estimate. Something between two to seven hours, they said. Maybe more.

"Did you reach Brooke yet?" Lily asked, and I immediately shook my head. She still hadn't called back. "Miles?" I shook my head once more. "Anyone?"

"Nope." A heavy sigh left my lungs. "Competition starts in thirty minutes... I should've been at the arena like thirty minutes ago. Earlier, actually, but whatever."

Colin looked up at me at the same time as our mother did. She was still crying but far less sobbing now.

"You should go," Mom said. "Your dad wouldn't want you sitting here and missing your competition, no less your game later."

"Yeah, right." I laughed humorously. "I'm not fucking leaving."

Kim gasps. "Don't say that word, Uncle ReeRee."

"Sorry."

"Reece," Mom said in a defeated tone, kind of like a sigh, but not really. "You can't put your life on hold just because your father's might have come to an end."

Did she listen to herself?

Perhaps I was hearing wrong. My ears appeared to be working just fine, but maybe they weren't.

I looked toward my brother, hoping he was going to say something helpful. Anything would've sufficed, but he kept quiet and just looked at me like our mother was right.

I couldn't believe it.

A blunt chuckle slipped past my lips. "You can't be serious."

"You shouldn't be sitting around and waiting for bad news, Reece," Mom said.

"But I am!" I got off my seat, needing to walk around, even if it was just two steps back and forth. "Dad's in surgery, and God knows if he's ever making it out of there alive. Fuck, even if he does, who's to say he will still be alive two hours later, huh?! He could die any moment, and then where was I? In the arena, doing stupid jumps and whatnot on the ice instead of being here with him."

"If I had been glued by Eira's side the moment I learned that she was going to—"

"Fuck this!" I yelled, interrupting my mother. "Did she

die too young? Sure, I'm not saying she didn't. But Dad's not Eira. Dad doesn't have cancer, and we didn't have *years* to come to terms with his death. I didn't even fucking know Eira, okay? So please, just stop using her or Aiden as an excuse for everything."

"I'm not using their deaths as excuses," Mom said, sounding offended now. "But because of them, I know that you cannot just sit arou—"

"Mamá," Colin interrupted, shaking his head at her. "I know you mean well, but you have to stop."

"You carried on with your life just fine," she said. "Instead of spending the last few days Eira had with her, you were constantly…" Mom looked at Lily, who now had her eyes closed as if she was waiting for some sort of secret to be revealed. "Well, going on dates with Lily."

Kieran rolled his eyes as if he was *so* over the whole topic. He was acting like he was hearing this exact story for the tenth time this year.

"Yeah, I did spend a lot of time with Lily when I should've been there for Eira. I still visited her, though," he said. "I left Lily to die just so I could be with Eira."

My eyes were instantly back on my sister-in-law, shocked and confused at what Colin just said. I didn't even fully understand what he was saying. Lily was alive, and she was fine? What did he mean he left her to die?

"Reece has every right to miss out on one stupid competition and one stupid game to be here. You don't get to tell him how to live or when to hit the breaks for a moment. Truthfully, I'd rather he stayed here. He might seriously regret leaving, and you never know what this regret might do to him," he continued. "Just because I could leave without regret doesn't mean he can. He isn't me. Reece is his own person.

And this is still our father you're talking about. If Reece wants to stay, he will stay."

I wanted to agree with him, and I would have, but at that very moment, my phone started ringing. Thinking it was Brooke *finally* calling back, I was disappointed to see it was only Erik.

Erik was calling me.

What the fuck?

Rolling my eyes at my phone screen, I picked up and started to walk away from my family. There was no need to let them hear whatever bullshit Erik was about to tell me. That guy was incapable of saying anything smart, but it made sense… he was Fynn's brother after all.

"To what do I owe this pleasure, Erik?" I asked, refraining from sighing.

To my surprise, it was Brooke's voice coming through the phone. "Where are you?"

Chapter Thirty-Nine

Brooklyn

My leg was shaking uncontrollably as I stared at the entrance doors of the arena. Reece and I were on in an hour and he wasn't here yet. Surely his meeting couldn't have taken this long.

Dad tried reasoning with me, telling me that there was no need to worry. Reece was probably just stuck in traffic. Today's traffic was something else, I knew that, which made the whole thing even scarier.

On our way to the arena, we'd gotten in almost two accidents. Minor ones, mind you, but still. Whatever was going on today was crazy.

"Why don't you just call him?" Dad asked, trying to be helpful. It wasn't helpful at all.

"I forgot my phone at home." It was lying on the coffee table in the living room.

Oh, God... what if Reece tried to call me because he'd gotten into an accident, and now he was dying because I didn't pick up?

Dad's phone was dead, so I couldn't even use his to try and reach my fiancé. Mom was already in her seat, watching the whole competition with everyone else. Nova was desperate to see the whole thing only because she had a crush on one of the skaters, and she didn't want to miss her.

"I'm sure he'll get here any minute," Dad said, then leaned down and pressed a kiss to the top of my head. "I can try and find Emory. She could call him."

I shook my head. "Knowing Mom, she definitely left her phone at home just so she didn't have to give it to Kim."

Kim *loved* playing games on Emory's phone. Lily and Colin wouldn't give her one, so she always opted to ask Sofia and Emory for theirs.

"Eden definitely has his phone," Dad said. "I can try and find him, but that might take a hot second."

I chuckled, even if it was just briefly. "He's probably trying to flirt with one of the skaters or their sisters. He'll think it's embarrassing if you suddenly show up and ask him for his phone."

"One more reason to go there." Dad shrugged. "That kid hasn't made raising him easy."

"Well, I didn't want him to begin with."

Dad tilted his head at me, raising his eyebrows.

"He's okay." My eyes rolled, a smile tugging on my lips. "I'm still your favorite, though, right?"

"I love all of—"

"Nope." I covered my ears with my hands, not wanting to hear him finish that sentence. "I'm the original, Dad. You *have* to love me the most. I won't accept anything else."

I could see him laugh before turning around and making his way back to all the other skaters, probably in hopes of finding my brother.

Eden was a good kid. A bit exhausting at times, but good. He had a huge problem with wanting to impress everyone around him, including our parents, and he was deadly afraid of disappointing anyone he loved.

And ever since Eden learned that there was a whole crowd of girls out there he could impress instead of just random ice hockey fans, he was always on the go to find a new victim of his charms.

Teenagers, am I right?

As I was waiting for my dad to return, I kept staring at the entrance doors in hopes that my fiancé would finally get here, but it was hopeless at this point.

He stood me up.

Then the doors opened, but it wasn't Reece who entered, it was Erik. His casts came off exactly six weeks after the incident, which was good for him. He could walk again… well, to an extent. He was re-learning it as far as I knew.

At huge events like these, he was still bound to his wheelchair.

But that wasn't what had caught me off guard. It was *who* was pushing that wheelchair.

I was baffled. All the words in my head in both languages I was able to speak left my brain in just one second.

Her green eyes were burning holes into my body as she stared at me, waiting for any sort of comeback. There was none.

She put her blonde hair up into a tight bun, her makeup flawless. She wore a grey suit, looking all business-like. Millie looked like she had her whole life together, caring for her sick child. She was acting like the ideal mother, as if she hadn't abandoned her own daughter the moment she was born.

Millie couldn't have been Erik's mother, at least not biologically. Unless I had a twin I never knew of, but Dad would've told me.

Perhaps she was only working for Erik's family. Who knew?

But there was no other logical explanation for her pushing Erik's fucking wheelchair.

It didn't matter anyway. This woman could've died on the spot for all I cared. So then she knew Erik, perhaps she even adopted him, or maybe she was his stepmother, it didn't matter. Millie just threw me away to raise someone else's kid. No biggie.

Yet, despite telling myself how little I cared, I couldn't seem to tear my eyes away from them. How she laughed when Erik spoke, and how she helped him open a can of coke because he still struggled with that.

There was something strange happening inside of me, but I really didn't want to explore those feelings.

Millie was dead to me. I had Emory, my mom. And I didn't need some woman in my life who figured staging her own death so she didn't have to raise me was a good idea. I hated her.

But—

"Woah, what's Mom doing there with Erik?" my brother asked as he suddenly came up beside me. Our dad wasn't in sight, and I wondered why. Actually, it was good Dad wasn't here. "Wait, that's not Mom. Mom's hair is longer and—"

"It's Millie," I muttered.

"Shit." Eden kept looking at her for another two seconds before his head snapped to mine. "Are you okay?"

"Yeah," I said, smiling at Eden. "Why wouldn't I be?"

"Uh, because your mom is literally being all... motherly with Erik. That guy is your age, she could be his mother for all we know. Which is *so* fucked up, dude."

"She's not my mom." My eyes were back on Millie, watching as she walked over to some guy in a suit. I knew that guy, he'd been at Erik and my skating practice a couple of times. While Erik never confirmed it, I just always assumed it was his dad. "She's just... a fucked up woman."

"A woman who's kissing Erik's father." He laughed. "It's like watching Mom kiss another guy. That's so gross."

I slapped my brother, but unfortunately, not as hard as I could. "Don't fucking say that."

"Brooke, they look the *same*. It's just an observation."

"A gross one at that." I sighed. "You know Mom doesn't like being compared to her." Which made a lot of sense. I wouldn't have wanted to be compared to someone like Millie, either.

Someone who was sick enough to cause pain to her own twin sister, who had admired her so much. Someone who literally stole her sister's boyfriend and made her loathe herself. And that was only like a year before she faked her death.

To be fair, I should've been thankful for her in a way. If she hadn't disappeared for five years after I was born, I wouldn't have had the best family imaginable now. She did us a huge favor.

"Do you think I should say hello to her?" Eden asked. "Would she even recognize me?"

I looked at my brother, narrowing my eyes. Eden was a carbon copy of our father. "No, Eden, I don't think she would. Why don't you go try it out?"

He was about to take a step forward when I reached for his shirt and pulled him back. "Don't you dare."

"But you said—"

"That was sarcasm, idiot."

"I knew that," he muttered, crossing his arms over his chest. "It was just a joke."

Yeah, sure.

"Where's Dad? Didn't he send you here?" I asked.

What If We Break?

Eden cocked his head at me, and his eyebrows drew together. "Dad? I haven't seen him since we got here."

"So he's probably still looking for you."

"Why?"

"Do you have your phone? I need to call Reece," I said instead of answering his question. At the end of the day, it didn't matter why Dad was looking for him. Besides, my reply was technically the answer.

"Obviously." He pulled out his phone and handed it to me without any further complaints. "I just realized Reece isn't here yet. Pretty unusual for him."

I nodded to show my brother some sign of acknowledgment, but I was a bit too focused on finding Reece's number. "Why don't you have Reece's number saved in your contacts?"

He chuckled. "I do."

"Well?"

Eden tsked. "He's *Brother-in-law*. You should've been able to find that one."

My eyes snapped up to him. Was I supposed to find this adorable or weird? Reece and I weren't married yet. We didn't even talk about it anymore. "Very… creative."

"Thank you. I was very proud of that one."

"Sure." I scrolled to *B,* and when I finally found Reece's contact, I was so close to hitting the call button when Eden's phone turned off.

"What?" My brother snatched his phone away from me, hitting the screen over and over again. "NO!" He kept tapping the screen. "How am I supposed to save all these cute girls' numbers now?!"

More importantly, how was I supposed to call my fiancé now?

"Fuck this," I muttered under my breath as I got up from the bench and made my way over to Erik.

Chapter Forty

Brooklyn

"Could I use your phone for two minutes?" I asked, not bothering to greet him. Erik wasn't a fan of greetings anyway.

Since I didn't greet him, I didn't say hello to Millie either. I wouldn't have even if I said hello to Erik.

As a matter of fact, I wasn't even paying attention to her in the first place.

Suddenly I wondered if Erik knew Millie gave birth to me. Perhaps that was why he was so determined to hurt me when we were still skating partners. I was going to ask him about it another time.

"What for?" Erik asked, smiling up at me cockily. He knew I would've never asked him for *anything* unless it was super necessary.

"I have to call someone."

"Call who?"

"None of your business," I replied.

"I think it is, Brooklyn," Millie said. "It's his phone."

I took a deep breath, trying my very best not to punch her right in the face. "I need to call Reece."

"Use your own phone," Millie replied. "Isn't your oh-so-great father paying for your phone bill, or why do you need to use my son's phone to call that boyfriend of yours?"

Wow, she really was as horrible as I pictured her to be.

Before I could reply, Erik spoke, which was fortunate for me because I wasn't sure what was going to come out of my mouth next.

"I told you he was going to ditch you eventually." It shouldn't have surprised me that he was, once again, assuming he knew everything. "But sure, call him."

I held out my hand, waiting for Erik to hand me his phone.

"Your whole family constellation isn't good for you, Brooklyn. Dating your father's friend's brother? Ridiculous. But you refused to listen when I tried to talk to you," Millie said, shrugging at me.

My lips parted slightly as I tried to speak, but I realized that no matter what I had said, it would have just fueled her stupidity.

Who was she to tell me anything about my direct family or who I considered part of my family? She didn't even know anyone but my parents, at least not that I knew. And even if she had known my parents' friends once upon a time, they hadn't been in touch for at least twenty years.

"Erik told me all about how awful that guy is to you. What was his name again? Reece? He grew up around your father, so he really can't be that much of a good guy."

"Oh, shut up, you whore." I decided to simply take Erik's phone from him as he made no attempts to hand it to me on his own accord. I couldn't have cared any less about what either of these two was going to say or think about me at that moment. "If my father really was such a bad guy, how come he didn't fake his death to get out of raising me?"

She remained silent, looking at me with some form of shock in her eyes.

"And not that it's any of your business, but my *fiancé* treats me just fine. In fact, your stupid kids could *never* be half the man Reece is." That said, I walked back to my brother, still keeping Erik's phone though.

Since I knew his passcode, I simply allowed myself to unlock Erik's phone and call my fiancé. Truthfully, I wasn't sure if Reece would pick up since he couldn't stand my ex-skating partner, but I had a bit of hope he would.

I waited and waited, and just when I thought he would ignore the call, Reece picked up.

"To what do I owe this pleasure, Erik?" he said, sounding just fine to me.

I could feel the anger that I was truly trying to contain bubbling up, and unfortunately, I didn't manage to let the steam evaporate before I spoke. "Where are you?!"

Reece was silent.

"Are you at least on your way already? It's the traffic, isn't it? God, it's so horrible today."

I was met with even more silence.

Why was he so quiet?

Sure, Reece very rarely, nearly never raised his voice toward me, and I wasn't expecting him to yell back at me... but some form of reaction would've been nice.

"Anyway, I guess I'll hang up then and give this stupid phone back to Erik and his god-awful stepmother, who, by the way, happens to Millie. Did you know that? She's been giving me shit about you not being here, but that doesn't matter, does it? I just needed to be sure you haven't gotten in some—"

"Accident?" His voice was way quieter this time. "I'm fine, Brooke."

My hands started to shake at the sound of his voice. Something was wrong. "You don't sound fine."

All of my anger suddenly disappeared, replaced by something that made my lunch do not-so-funny things inside of my stomach.

God, I was such an awful fiancée, wasn't I? Instead of asking if he was okay, I immediately started being rude to him.

"Are you okay, Reece?" I asked carefully, not sure if he'd even tell me now. He said he was fine, but really didn't sound it.

"I think my dad's going to die," he told me after yet another few seconds of silence. "Pretty soon."

"What?" Panic now mixed with all that regret inside of me, which was far from a great combination.

I looked up at my brother to see if he could hear the conversation through the phone, but judging by the confused look on his face, I assumed he didn't. It was quite unfortunate because I had hoped Eden could just… I don't know, tell me I was dreaming this whole conversation.

"What do you mean?" I pressed.

"I'm at the hospital right now because"—his voice broke —"my dad was in an accident with my mom. Mom's fine, but…" I gasped softly, covering my mouth with my hand in shock. "Dad's in surgery, and I don't think he'll get out of there alive. The last update we'd been given wasn't good."

"I… Reece, I'm so, so sorry." Tears swelled in my eyes as I felt my heart sink deeper with every second that passed. "Which hospital are you at?"

"Hospital?!" Eden muttered in disbelief. "I'll get Mom and Dad. We're leaving."

"New York Presbyterian Weill Cornell Medical Center," Reece replied.

"Okay. That's not that far. I'm on my way, okay?"

"No, wait," Reece began, then cleared his throat before continuing. "I'll be at the arena in twenty minutes."

"Baby, you don't have to come, it's okay. I'm sorry for yelling at you, I—"

"I know," he interrupted. "But I want to be there. My mom is right, he wouldn't want me to miss the competition or my game for him."

"But if he's… dying… that's a different thing, Reece. That's not *just* being in the hospital."

"Yeah, but if he's dying, it wouldn't matter whether I was in the hospital waiting room, wasting my time, or I'm on the ice with you or my team. Honestly, I think he'd rather I'm on the ice than doing nothing."

"Are you sure?" I asked, the unwell feeling in my stomach refusing to settle. "We can skip today, Reece. Don't worry about the competition or your game. Everyone will understand."

"The distraction will be good for me," he insisted. "I can't stay here. I'm losing my mind."

"Okay." I still thought he should've stayed at the hospital, but I couldn't force him to stay there. "Please, drive safe."

"I will, *mi princesa*," he replied. "Will you wait outside for me?"

"Of course. I love you."

"I love you."

Chapter Forty-One

Reece

Brooke and I were lucky that we weren't supposed to be on the ice for another two hours, so when the initial twenty-minute ride over to the arena turned into forty, it wasn't half as bad.

The first thing I did when I saw my fiancée standing in front of the arena was to just hug her. In Brooke's arms, everything seemed a little less painful. She was the steady that kept me sane, the support I really could've needed back at the hospital.

But I had her now, and that had to have been enough.

"I am so, so sorry, Reece," she whispered as she buried her face deeper into my chest. I wrapped my arms tightly around her, never wanting to let go.

"It's fine," I replied. "I'm fine."

"Baby, I know you're not." Brooke looked up at me, but I just couldn't bring myself to look her in the eyes. As much as she tried hiding those tears in her voice, I knew they were there… and if I saw them, I'd crack, too.

All I wanted was to go inside that stupid arena, get changed, and be done with this whole day, but even if we'd rushed it now, time wouldn't have passed quicker.

"Did you tell your dad?" I asked, needing to prepare myself for possible impending hugs.

"Eden knows. He was with me when I called you."

"Right." I finally allowed myself to look at my fiancée, slightly pulling away from our hug to give myself a better view of her. "What's that stuff you said about Millie and Erik?"

Brooke's red-rimmed eyes rolled. "It's not important right—"

"Please, just tell me," I practically begged. "It'll keep my head occupied for a bit."

She sighed softly. "There's honestly not much to say. Apparently, she's his stepmom, and she's not very fond of you. I don't quite understand why she cares so much about our relationship when she couldn't even bother to be my mother."

"I'll ask Ming to get some information out of Fynn. I'd ask, but I doubt Fynn would even want to speak to me."

"Their whole family dynamic confuses me," she admitted. "I mean, Erik is Millie's stepson... and Fynn's Erik's stepbrother. But Fynn can't possibly be Millie's biological son as he's older than me by a few months, and I'm pretty sure Dad would've told me if I had a twin brother. It's... weird."

"Fynn looks nothing like your dad or Emory anyway." Aside from the blond hair and the green eyes.

"I love how you compare him to Emory, not that stupid woman." She smiled at me softly, it wasn't as bright as always, but given the circumstances, it was more than enough.

Brooke's smile was something so extraordinary that I couldn't get enough of it. It melted parts inside of me that I didn't know could turn into liquids. It was so captivating, it almost brought peace to my racing mind.

"That woman's not worth mentioning," I said to which Brooke nodded in agreement. "Let's go inside, *mi princesa*. I still have to get changed."

Chapter Forty-Two

Reece

"Oh, that's fucked up," I muttered under my breath as the first place was announced.

The air in the arena was electric, charged with the cheers of the crowd. It felt all so distant, muffled by the raging storm inside of me.

Brooke and I stood there, side by side on the podium, our hands tightly intertwined, as the words repeated on a loop inside of my head.

In first place, with a performance that left everyone speechless, are Brooklyn Desrosiers-King and Reece Carter.

They were haunting me like demonic whispers coming from deep inside a forest.

I couldn't be happy about it. All this time, I'd been pushing myself to be better for Brooke, to win at least once just for her... why now?

Why on a day like this?

The win was meaningless.

The gold medal hung around my neck, heavy with the weight of expectations to deliver a better performance next week in Colorado Springs.

I glanced at Brooke, wanting so desperately to feel that

calming wave hit me when she beamed a smile at the cameras. Her eyes sparkled with joy and pride. She deserved this so much, but I couldn't share that joyous moment with her.

Dad was supposed to be here, watch this moment, see us win. He was supposed to sit in the crowd and cheer us on, but he was probably still in surgery.

He was the man who had taught me everything I knew about skating and ice hockey. He was the one who supported me the most when I picked up figure skating for Brooke and said it might benefit my hockey performance. He watched every game, and every competition, even when he couldn't be there in person.

I'd always get a call from him once everything was over. I'd always hear the pride in his voice and it felt so strange knowing he wasn't going to call this time. It felt wrong that he didn't watch me today.

He was fighting for his life in the OR while I was standing on this stupid podium, basking in the glory of the first place, when all I really wanted was to be by his side.

How could I celebrate when he was slipping away from me, and every moment spent on the ice without him watching me felt like a betrayal?

My hands clenched into fists, my jaw tight with frustration.

"We can leave any second," Brooke whispered to me, making sure to cover her face from the camera so nobody would try to read her lips at a later time and cause unnecessary drama. My dad once told us to do this when we were younger. "We'll head straight to the hospital and—"

I bowed my head as the national anthem began to play, trying to hide the tears that threatened to spill over. "I have a hockey game to play."

"Reece…"

"It'll be good for me," I argued again. It was a few hours spent with my mind being anywhere but with my father.

Brooke squeezed my hand, her touch warm and comforting, but it only reminded me of what I was about to lose. "Okay."

When the anthem ended, I forced myself to raise my head, plastered a smile on my face just to please the cameras, and pretended that I was just fine. I was happy. I was proud of my win. I was… perfectly fine. But inside, I was crumbling with every breath that I took.

As we stepped down from the podium and made our way off the ice, we were greeted by Brooke's dad, as always.

My fiancée almost fell right into Miles' arms, shrieking with excitement, and smiling with pure happiness as her dad told her how proud he was of her, how well she'd done.

It was like someone was stabbing a knife right through my heart over and over again. I would never hear my father tell me how proud he was of my accomplishments ever again.

"I'll just go get changed," I muttered as I walked past Brooke and Miles, heading straight toward the locker room. If I had to pretend to be just fine for another goddamn second, I was going to lose it.

Chapter Forty-Three

Brooklyn

We made it to the arena for Reece's game with five minutes to spare. Reece rushed inside to get changed, so I couldn't even wish him good luck, but that was okay. He had worse things to worry about than winning a game or waiting for me to wish him luck.

His coach seemed angry, but kind of relieved that Reece showed up at all. He'd been skipping a few more games for me recently. Each time he did, I felt awful about it, but even if I tried to make him go, he always found a different excuse to stay at practice with me.

Now, I was trying to find my best friend, who had been waiting for me for a while now, and when I found her in a seat next to Erik, I was a little taken aback.

He was probably here to support his stepbrother in the game, but it was still odd seeing him here. Erik never showed up to the games before. At least I'd never seen him.

As I approached Rina, ready to greet her, Erik took the first word. "Brooke, can we talk?"

Brooke? He usually used my whole name to speak to me.

"Do I have a choice?" The last thing I wanted to do right now was argue with Erik.

What If We Break?

"Not really, because I really think you should hear me out." He cleared his throat before he continued. "Look, I didn't know she's your mother."

I looked at Rina, her eyes wide with shock and confusion. She was going to need context, but that was going to have to wait another few minutes.

"Millie's not my mother," I said. Disgust crept up on me just at the thought of ever considering such an awful person as her to be my mother. "She gave birth to me, that's it. She has honestly done more for you than she has for me. In fact, for the first five years of my life, everyone thought she was dead because that's what she made everyone believe. So, don't call her my mother again, got it?"

He nodded softly. "That's awful."

"Yeah, whatever. It's not like you care. You treated me like shit, Erik. I'd honestly rather someone run away from me than hurt me purposefully."

Erik got off his seat, sighing. "You're a good skater," he told me. "And a good person. You have a great family and an even better boyfriend. You have everything anyone could imagine. I was jealous of you, Brooke. It's the only reason I was ever mean to you."

Wow. That was pathetic. "Cool, that doesn't excuse your behavior."

"I know. But I'm not here to discuss this anyway. I just wanted you to know that I didn't know you were biologically related to Millie. She just married my dad a few years ago, and she never mentioned having a daughter. If you're going to hate me, and you have every right to do that, just know that I didn't mistreat you because she told me to."

"I appreciate you clarifying that, Erik," I replied, somehow feeling the slightest twinge of sympathy for him.

"Also, I can't stand her either. Maybe that might make

you feel a little better. Millie's awful. I have to accept her because she's married to my father, but the things that come out of her mouth are... terrible. And she's such a gold digger. My dad can't see it, but she definitely only married him for his money."

I raised an eyebrow. Erik seemed genuine, but it was hard to trust someone who had been so cruel to me in the past.

Perhaps he really wanted to make amends in his own strange way, though.

"Okay. Thanks for telling me that," I said cautiously. I didn't know what I was going to do with that information, but it made me feel a bit better about the situation.

Erik basically just confirmed to me what I'd always known. I didn't gaslight myself into believing Millie was a terrible person—she actually was.

"Oh, and one more thing," he paused, looking hesitant.

"What?"

"Fynn isn't her kid either. I bet you're curious about that, so I thought I might as well tell you. His dad died when he was ten, and since he didn't have any other family but Millie, she took him in."

I took a moment to process everything.

With every little detail Erik revealed to me, Millie sounded more and more like the worst person that ever walked this earth. How could she leave her newborn daughter for "freedom" and not wanting to take responsibility, but then ten years later take in a kid who wasn't even hers?

"Okay," I spoke in a whisper. "I appreciate you telling me all this, but Erik... I need you to stop talking now."

Erik nodded. "Yeah, anyway, I should probably get going then. If you ever want to know more, you know how to reach me. I'll see you at your next competition."

"You'll be there?"

"Of course. I wouldn't want to miss seeing you fail."

"Why is Reece so aggressive today?" Rina asked, stepping away from the boards to reclaim her seat next to me. "He almost hurt Ming."

Rina was right, Reece was pretty aggressive on the ice tonight, but it also earned them five goals in the first round, four of which were Reece's doing. Their opponents barely got a chance to get the puck on the other side.

Five goals was… insane.

It was great for all St. Trewery fans, yet I couldn't help but wonder if they'd still be so happy about Reece's performance if they knew *why* he was able to do all this. Alright, they probably didn't give any fucks because all that mattered was the team's win.

"Since when do you care about Ming?" I asked, hoping it was going to prevent me from having to talk about Reece and his behavior.

"I don't," she replied, sounding a bit panicky. "We're friends, is all. I don't want my *friend* to get hurt."

I laughed. "He plays ice hockey, my love. He's going to get hurt."

Her head snapped over to me. "Really?"

Rina was *so* not an ice hockey person, it was obvious. But it was just about time that I finally had someone to watch my fiancé's games with… other than my family, of course. She'd have to learn the rules of the game, but I could teach her.

Just not today.

"Rina, this isn't your first game. You've seen how violent it can get out there," I said, tapping my fingers on my thighs.

"Yes, but I thought that was just a one-time thing," she

admitted, to which I instantly tilted my head at her. "I mean, seriously, Brooke... If it was really *that* violent and dangerous, surely you wouldn't want your boyfriend to be a hockey player, right? That'd be stupid. What if he gets seriously injured or even *dies* on the ice?"

I shrugged. "Serious injuries happen all the time, death not so much. Besides, who am I to tell my *fiancé* what he can and cannot do? It's his passion."

"You think differently because you grew up with hockey players all around you." She looked back toward the ice, and if I had to guess, her eyes were glued on Ming, not the puck. "You're used to the violence."

"It's really not that bad," I told her, resting my head on her shoulder. "Reece's brother once broke his arm during a game. It healed. Getting that injury looked worse than it actually was. You'll get used to it."

"Mhm..."

A smirk pulled on the corner of my lips. "But it's not like it should matter to you, right? Ming is *just* a *friend*."

Rina shot up from her seat and made her way back to the boards to get away from me. "What? Yes. You're right. Just a friend." She pointed toward Ming who was currently getting pushed against the boards while Crews, one of the opponents, was continuously beating the poor guy. The refs tried to pull Crews away and de-escalate the situation, but it took them a hot second. "What did the guy do that for?! Ming didn't do shit!"

"It's just how it is."

"But that's not fair! Crews should get fired or... or blocked for the game. Whatever it's called."

My lips pressed into a thin line as I tried not to laugh. "He's getting a penalty, and our team's going into Power Play for the time being."

"What's a penalty? And what's a Power Play?"
Oh, Jesus… This was going to be one long game.

They won. Of course they won today.

Reece could barely find the strength to be happy about placing first earlier, which I assumed was a mixture of being devastated about his father dying and because he just didn't care about figure skating as much as I had. I thought he was going to be at least a little excited about winning his game and scoring the most goals *ever* in a single game… but his face was blank the entire time.

Reece was off the ice almost the second the timer ran out, he didn't celebrate with his team, didn't wait for anyone—not even Ming. I wasn't sure if he'd show up for any interviews, but if I had to guess, he wasn't going to talk to *anyone* tonight.

"I'll go find Reece, okay? I'll see you tomorrow," I said as I hugged my best friend goodbye before rushing toward the locker room. Was I supposed to be inside the locker room? No, but that never stopped me before.

As I stood in front of the locker room door, I looked around myself to make sure that nobody could see me before I snuck right into the room. The team was still on the ice anyway, so I knew it was just Reece in there which meant knocking wasn't necessary.

Reece wasn't by his cubby, but I could hear the water running, so on my way to the shower room, I went.

"Reece?" I called as I rounded the corner to the showers. "Please tell me you're alone in there." In theory, I knew he was alone, seeing as everyone else was still celebrating on the ice, but I preferred to receive a definite answer.

"I am," he answered, and I could swear there was a hint of amusement in his voice.

With his confirmation, I walked into the shower room and looked around to locate my fiancé. He was tall enough to look over the shower stalls, which was quite fortunate for me right now.

"What are you doing here?" He leaned his arms on the top of the door, cocking his head at me.

"I just thought you might want some company. Or a hug."

"You in my shower will lead to a different kind of hug, *mi princesa*. And I don't think that's very appropriate right now." A smirk pulled on his lips and mischief gleamed in his eyes.

I knew he was hurting, but he looked almost happy in that moment.

"You should hurry up a little more anyway. We have a long way home." It was too late to stop by the hospital and visit his dad. As far as I'd been told, Tobias was in a critical condition but no longer in surgery.

Reece sighed softly. "I think I'll stay at Colin's tonight—if that's okay with you, I mean."

"Of course."

"You know, we're engaged, so Colin can't say you're not allowed to stay there with me."

"Did he ever say—" Both of our heads snapped toward the door as chatter started to echo through the room.

Panicked, Reece opened the door to his shower and pulled me inside.

"I'm getting all wet!" I shrieked as my clothes began to soak with water.

"It's okay. I have a change of clothes for you in my car." They were all his clothes, I was sure of that, but it didn't matter.

I shook my head at him, eyes wide with horror as the voices got louder. "You can't keep me in here for like... hours. Wet."

"Say wet one more time, Brooke, I dare you."

"Wet."

"You're lucky we're not at home right now, otherwise I woul—"

The voices got louder, but since I knew my head wasn't looking over the door or the sides of the shower, I didn't bother to duck down.

I never understood why they didn't just install entirely closed-off showers instead of half walls. The doors and walls started at the bottom of the floor, so nobody could see our feet, but they only went up like five feet something. Like I said, taller than me, but not high enough for tall people.

Reece turned my face toward him, leaned down, and quickly pressed a kiss to my lips before he pushed my head down and forced me to kneel.

"If anyone leans over, they'll still see the top of your head," he explained when I looked up at him, frowning. "Ah, fuck, don't look at me like that from down there."

"What the fuck, Carter," someone said as he obviously entered the room.

I froze in place. In theory, I knew I wasn't visible to anyone, but if, for some very weird reason, someone opened the door... what would they think I was doing?

I knelt in front of my fiancé—my *naked* fiancé, who seemed to find this whole thing a bit more exciting than I thought.

If I wanted to, I could've easily done something to annoy Reece a little, but I figured I was going to be nice today and just wait this out down here. My knees were going to be dead by the time all of Reece's teammates were gone, but it was a price I now had to pay for sneaking inside the locker room.

Reece leaned forward, resting his arms back on the door as he looked at whoever tried to talk to him. If I hadn't turned my head away in that very second, I would've had his dick in my face.

"Where was all this enthusiasm two days ago?" the guy asked. It wasn't Ming, that much I knew. "You have a massive fire inside of you and you only now decided to let it out? How dare you?"

"It's not always there," Reece replied.

"We won, Reece, eight to zero. That's *huge*. What was the difference tonight?"

"Had a fight with Brooke, I was just mad." While I was sure the smugness in his voice wasn't audible to his teammate, I could very much hear it. I figured he wasn't going to talk about his dad yet, but seriously? A fight with me? "You know how it is, right, Denton? Girlfriends. They're so dramatic for nothing."

Alright, that was it.

I reached for his cock, wrapped my hand around his shaft, and held it a bit tighter than what was possibly comfortable.

Reece winced slightly and tried to cover it with a cough, but Denton noticed anyway.

"You good?" he asked.

"Yes, sure," Reece replied. "Just... a random sharp pain in my, uh... side. I probably overdid it tonight, is all."

I looked up just in time to see Reece looking down at me, giving me a warning look. He shouldn't have done that. Telling me not to do something only made me want to do it even more.

So, with a mischievous grin on my face, I loosened my hand and stroked it up his cock. I sat down on my knees with as little movement as possible and started to slowly move my hand up and down his dick. Reece shifted slightly, but he tried not to move too much so it wouldn't attract any attention.

"Coach was too scared to take you off the ice," someone else said, the voice much deeper than Denton's. "He was sure we'd lose if he took you off for too long."

"He would've been right," Reece answered, sounding much more strained this time.

We'd never done something like this before. Okay, that was a lie. We'd had sex in plenty of public spaces, but never with people in the same room as us. I'd also never touched Reece with someone else around. It always seemed weird, but right now, even if I wanted to stop, I wasn't sure I could've brought myself to do it.

The shower on my right turned on, as did the one on the left side of me a moment later. I wasn't sure what I thought happened in the men's shower room, but I expected less chatter. These guys were *talking*.

Someone else then decided to talk to my fiancé, but that didn't stop me from taking the tip of his cock into my mouth.

Chapter Forty-Four

Reece

I was going to die.

If my performance out on the ice wasn't going to bite me in the ass in a few moments, I was almost sure my fiancée would.

"Do you guys remember that time we drove down to NYU and snuck into their locker room?" someone on the team asked. I was a tad too busy to care which one of the guys was talking.

"When we stole the cap's 'lucky socks'?" Denton, in the shower beside mine, laughed. "We killed them on the ice that following weekend."

Brooke held my dick firmly in her hand as I could feel her tongue swirl around the tip.

My breath spiraled right out of my lungs, and it took everything inside of me not to look down. If I made any sudden moves, my teammates would've known something was up, and that certainly couldn't have happened.

"Did any of you see who broke my stick?" someone asked. "Three hundred dollars down the fucking drain. And it was a new one, too. I want that guy to pay me back."

Don't look down.

Brooke moved her hand, dragging it up and down the length of me slowly.

Don't look down.

She slid her thumb over my tip, gliding it along the slit.

There was nothing sweet or delicate about the way she jerked me off, rushed movements, torturous pauses after every other stroke to tease me.

"I think it was Anderson," someone replied.

My lungs were burning with the need to breathe, but I couldn't. I had to stay focused and remember not to move or let any sound get past my lips, there was no time for breathing.

It got even worse when her lips closed around my tip, and I let my head fall forward onto my arms, almost biting myself to keep me from letting out a tortured groan.

"Guys, did you hear that Estrada quit hockey?" Denton asked, laughing to himself.

Her hand worked me over as she kept licking the tip of my cock, driving me insane.

My balls slowly began to draw up, the pleasure she was causing pulling them tighter and tighter with each stroke, each lick.

My heart was hammering inside of my chest, begging me to step away. But instead of moving, I tried to focus on the conversations around me. It didn't work.

"The guy that just got married?" Ming asked in return.

"Yup. Apparently, his girlfriend, well, his now wife, refused to marry him until he agreed to quit."

I should've stopped her. I should've turned the shower colder and stood underneath the icy stream for the next three business days. Scratch that. I should've called a priest and gotten us both dunked into some good old holy water.

But as much as I tried telling myself to reach for my

towel and get the hell out of here, I couldn't move. My feet were glued to the floor, not just because I couldn't leave for Brooke's sake, as someone would've discovered her if I left the shower.

There was something strangely exciting about the fact that someone would've just had to open the door or look over the shower divider, and they would've seen exactly what was going on. The worst part about the possibility of getting caught was the fact that it made every touch, every stroke, and every lick feel so much more intense. So intense, I had to grit my teeth.

Don't look down.

My eyes closed when Brooke took my dick deeper into her mouth. Her nails trailed up my thighs, moving past my hipbones as she touched every inch of me that she possibly could while still keeping her presence unknown.

I grabbed the top of the shower, my fingers probably turning white from the pressure, but I couldn't help it. I was hard as steel, refusing to give in to the need burning in my balls because if I came with my teammates around, Brooke would've made sure I'd *never* forget it.

"You good, Reece?"

I flinched at the sound of his voice, head jerking up to see who was talking to me, just to find Fynn staring right at me.

Brooke released my cock, wrapping her hand back around the length of me to ensure I stayed hard while I was sure she was panicking right this moment.

"You look like shit," he added. "One would think after a game like today, you'd look… happier."

God, how I hated that guy, but even the sight of him didn't manage to soften my dick. There was only one way I was going to get rid of my erection.

"I'm fine," I forced out, noticing how six other guys were staring at me with concerned looks. "Just... in pain."

And what a pain it was. A very torturous, burning kind of pain that was going to end up feeling better than a win. A pain that could get me kicked off the team if the wrong people found out about what was happening.

Brooke's lips closed back around the head, but this time, I couldn't help but shift my hips, jerking forward. I regretted it immediately as I could hear the faint sound of her gag over the showers running. If I could hear it, I knew Fynn, who was standing barely a foot away from me, could hear it too.

"What was that?" he asked, his eyes narrowing at me suspiciously.

"My stomach," I replied, trying to sound confident in my answer. "I haven't eaten all day."

Finally, I looked down, just to find my fiancée grinning up at me before taking me deeper, sucking on me like I was fucking candy.

Think about something disgusting, Reece. Like...

"Well, the team's going out for a drink, if you want to come," our Goalie said from across the room. "Bet there'll be pizza."

I looked back up, clearing my throat. "It's fine. I have something important to do."

Like getting revenge on my fiancée. Very important.

"Whatever," Fynn muttered as he walked away and left the shower room.

Dexter smiled at me before following Fynn. The more guys were leaving, the better. Only two remaining, as far as I could tell anyway.

Brooke worked me even further down her throat, one hand grabbing my balls to massage them just to make me question my sanity.

"*Fuuuck*," I groaned quietly, hitting my forehead against my arm. I was ready to shoot my cum down her throat, and it took *everything* in me not to do that.

The two remaining showers in the room turned off, leaving my own to be the last. I was usually quick to shower because I wanted to head out as soon as possible, but I suppose I was going to be the last to leave tonight.

"Try not to get a concussion," Ming laughed before exiting the room, Denton following close behind.

Brooke and I were alone now. Anyone could come back at any moment, but that didn't stop me from finally turning my entire attention onto my fiancée.

Looking down, I pushed my fingers into her wet hair, holding her head still as I thrust my hips, fucking into her mouth. "You're mean." I forced myself in a little deeper, smirking as she gagged. "But, God, how I love your mouth."

My fingers curled tighter in her hair as my balls drew up in pleasure, my heart racing.

"You're doing so good for me, Brooke." My head dropped back, my lips slightly parted, balls clenching. "Oh, *fuck*."

A low groan left me when the delirious pleasure released, my orgasm ripping through my body like a tidal wave, spurting cum down her throat.

As much as I wanted to enjoy this moment for a bit longer, the sound of laughter from the other room was quick to bring me back down to earth.

"What am I going to do with you?" I asked as I pulled Brooke up to stand, my voice rather breathless.

She smiled at me. "Something adventurous, I hope."

"God, I love you." My hands cupped her face, leaning in to kiss her when someone suddenly cleared their throat.

My eyes snapped over to the entrance, finding Ming

standing there all serious-looking. He had his arms crossed over his chest, head cocked, and eyebrows raised.

"You look plenty fine all of a sudden, Carter," he said. "You're even glowing."

"It's a miracle," I replied, wrapping my arms around my fiancée as she leaned forward to press her face into my chest. Ming knew Brooke was here anyway. No need to pretend she wasn't. He couldn't see her, and if he could, it was only the top of her head.

"Sure." He nodded. "I suppose my question can wait another day. You seem a bit occupied."

Well, I was fine now, but I would've survived some more alone time with Brooke. Or perhaps I wouldn't have. Who knew?

"How's your shower, Brooke?" Ming asked.

"Oh, God," Brooke muttered, slapping her hand to my back when I chuckled. "It's... refreshing, really!"

"I'll get the guys out for you," Ming laughed, rolling his eyes at me before he turned around to walk away.

"We appreciate it!" I called after him.

Ming would never let me live this down.

Chapter Forty-Five

Reece

"Do you want breakfast?" Colin asked as I came out of my old bedroom and into the kitchen at barely five in the morning. It had become my new daily routine.

I shook my head. "I'm not hungry."

He played with his scrambled eggs on the plate for a little while longer, then dropped his fork. "Me neither."

I walked over to the refrigerator and took out a bottle of water. It was all I was able to swallow without it coming right back up again.

"Sleepless night, I take it?" he asked in an attempt to make conversation, but I didn't reply. Getting a good reply from me was a rarity these days.

My eyes were on his food, and my empty stomach was begging me to take just a tiny bite, but I couldn't. I wasn't sure why Colin made scrambled eggs only for him to not eat them, but I couldn't blame him either.

Everything felt so surreal lately—as if I was trapped in some sort of game and someone else was controlling me.

Dad had passed away. He died on the first night after the accident, which was now a few days ago. The funeral was set to be in a couple of days, but the closer we got to that day, the less I felt.

Part of me didn't want to believe he was truly gone, that I'd never see him again, never hear his voice again, never get another hug and an "I'm so proud of you" after a hockey game again.

Surely it was all just a bad dream, and he was safely inside his house in Spain, and he would call me any second. He couldn't have been dead. I was only twenty years old, parents are supposed to be alive at that point in their child's life. He was supposed to be there for my wedding. Dad was supposed to be the greatest grandpa to my kids.

But deep down, I knew he was gone, wanted to grieve and find my way back into my old life, laugh, play hockey, and be happy… but the whole goddamn way back, there was nothing but a pitch-black forest with misleading signs.

With every passing day on this planet without him, each step I took felt heavier. My heart felt emptier, as if a huge piece of it was missing.

My games felt different. Skating practice with Brooke felt different. Even breathing and being alive felt different.

Colin took the loss better than I did. He was grieving, and he wasn't as happy as before but was still functioning. Each day I watched him be the greatest dad ever, laugh with his kids, and talk to his wife without tears in his eyes. Then suddenly, I'd catch myself wondering if his kids would have to live almost their whole lives without him as well, and if Lily would become a widow at not even fifty.

I could lose my brother in ten years when Kieran turned twenty, if not earlier.

As it seemed, our family was doomed to die young, so it wasn't even that unlikely to happen.

What if I died young? I didn't want to marry Brooke and

leave her a widow in her twenties. And I didn't want her to have my babies just to raise them all on her own because I couldn't make it past my early thirties.

It wasn't fair to her.

"Do you think you'll die too early?" I asked, our eyes meeting.

He frowned at me in confusion. "Why would I?"

I shrugged. "Kind of seems like it's a thing in our family."

"Death is unpredictable, Reece," he said. "There are no age restrictions, and it's not usually up to us when we die."

"But that wasn't my question, was it?" I leaned back against the kitchen counter. "Don't you ever just think about it? Like, seriously, Colin, you've seen two of our siblings die at a young age, and now Dad's dead way too early. Mom's probably going to die next week just for the sake of fucking with our family. I never met either of our grandparents because two of them died the same year I was born, the other two died when *you* were young, and I wasn't even anywhere in sight yet. Our aunts and uncles? Never fucking met them. To me, it's a miracle you're still here."

"Reece."

"Have you ever talked to Lily about it? I mean, seriously, I wouldn't be surprised if you dropped dead right this second. How would Lily raise three kids all on her own? Would she find a new hus—"

"Lily and I don't talk about death," he cut me off. "We don't mention it, we don't even think about it. And even if I died tomorrow, she would never get remarried."

"How would you know?" I raised my eyebrows at him, crossing my arms over my chest. "She's still young and good-looking. Lily could have a new husband by next week if she wanted to."

Colin leaned back in his chair, looking at me with

narrowed eyes for a whole minute before he cleared his throat and spoke again. "You're scared you're going to die early, and Brooke's going to be all alone, aren't you?"

My expression fell, my heart beating faster inside my chest. I clenched my jaw as I dropped my arms and balled my hands into fists.

"How could I not?" I walked over to my brother and took a seat across from him. "Obviously, I wouldn't want her to move on because she's mine, but I don't want her to be alone either because I know that makes her anxious. And what if she does find someone else, he'll never know her the way I do, so he couldn't ever make her as happy as I can. And what if…"

I kept on talking about a million different things that'd be completely absurd if I died and Brooke was still alive. I wasn't sure for how long I kept coming up with theories, and reasons why nobody was ever going to be better for her than I was, but I noticed that each time a new thought passed my lips, my brother's expression softened. Eventually, he even smiled at me, which seemed pretty odd to me.

Colin smiled a lot, sure, but not usually when I was freaking the fuck out. Wasn't he supposed to… I don't know, tell me everything would be all right?

While my brother's smile didn't keep me from talking, his following words sure managed to do it.

"Did you notice that not a single thing you're saying mentions any sort of fear of *your* death, but what would happen to Brooke if you died?" Colin said, slightly cocking his head at me. "I don't think you're worried about death itself or dying young, Reece. It's leaving Brooke behind that truly scares you."

"I guess…" A heavy sigh left my lungs. "But, Colin,

don't you think that's what's going to happen? It's an obvious pattern in our family."

He kept quiet once again, but not for very long. It was maybe ten seconds, but it felt like the longest ten seconds of my life.

"I used to think about it a lot," he admitted. "After we found out that Eira would die from her cancer, and then Aiden died. I thought about *you* a lot. I was convinced I'd lose you, too, but I never thought that I might die next week or something."

Oh. Well, I suppose that sort of explained why, growing up, Colin had been keeping an eye on me more than anyone else. Before I moved in with him and Lily, Colin used to call me every day just to speak to me. If he wasn't on the road, he stopped by at home every evening. Sometimes, he'd even take Brooke and me out for ice cream because I didn't have time for him otherwise.

Even after I moved in, he called me after or before each of his games just to talk. And since I'd moved out, he still called me daily.

Perhaps it wasn't sheer interest in me and my life after all.

"How do you live with that?" I asked. "How aren't you losing your mind after everything?"

Colin shrugged. "Because it's life. It's unpredictable. You can take as many precautions as you want, never leave the house again, and still die tomorrow. We have two options; live every day like it's the last, or spend the rest of our lives worrying about the day we die and never truly living in the moment. It'll end in death either way, but it's much more fun not to worry about the ending," he said. "There will be so many ups and downs in your life that you'll have to learn to thrive through a bad time. It's going to fucking hurt, yes, but eventually, you'll find a way to live with it. And you have to

What If We Break?

remember that you'll *never* have to go through anything painful on your own, Reece. You have an entire army of people around you who love you so much, and while they won't be able to make the pain disappear, they will help you through it. And they will help you get back onto your feet when you're ready to try."

While all that sounded like the most reassuring and probably most real stuff I'd ever heard my brother say… it did little to console me.

Chapter Forty-Six

Reece

Life was great.

I had been staying at home for a week now; no hockey, no skating, no responsibilities. I was thriving. It was the least stressful time I'd had since like… kindergarten.

The TV was turned on, playing some kind of show I didn't care about, but it was entertaining enough to keep it on. I held a can of an espresso martini in one hand and the remote in the other, just in case I wanted to watch something else. I wasn't going to move just to switch between channels.

Ever since we moved here, I hadn't once turned on the TV, but it had been my best friend for the past couple of days now.

It was early in the morning, so coffee was very necessary —the alcohol too. Good days only ever happened if I was drunk, so I had to start early.

"Hey, did you finish…" Brooke trailed off, a deep sigh drawing from her lungs as she stood in the middle of the room. "I guess you didn't finish your work."

Since I'd been at home all week and didn't plan on going back to college for at least another one, Brooke talked to our professors to get my assignments so they had *something* to grade.

I had the entire week to finish this project for our sports analytics class. It was super boring, and honestly, I was too busy thinking about what I wanted to drink next to care about that assignment.

I leaned back on the couch, sipping from my espresso martini before responding to my fiancée. "Work? What work?" I asked casually and nudged the papers on the coffee table off onto the floor to hide them from her, but more importantly, my view. If I had to look at that pile of papers for a second longer, I was going to get a headache.

Brooke raised an eyebrow at me, crossing her arms over her perfect chest. "The project for Dr. Lessley's class? The one that's due tomorrow?"

I flashed her a charming grin, trying to distract her from the mess of papers scattered on the floor. "Oh, that project. Yeah, don't worry about it, baby."

Her eyes narrowed at me, clearly questioning something about me or whatever I said. I didn't care. Even if she didn't believe I was going to start working on that stupid project—I really wasn't—I couldn't have cared less.

"Reece, you can't just blow this off. It's worth a significant portion of your grade," she scolded me, sounding almost exactly like my father when he was upset about my grades.

Oh, my dad. Right.

He was the reason I was in this mess in the first place. If he hadn't died, I wouldn't have been sitting at home and trying to distract my mind.

But, hey, life was treating me very well recently, aside from the fact that I couldn't even call my dad to talk to him anymore. Whatever, right?

I pushed the thought of my dad away, not wanting to dwell on it. Instead, I focused on Brooke, who was still standing there, arms crossed, and looking more serious than ever.

"If that stupid project is so important to you, then you do it." I averted my gaze back onto the TV, continuing to sip on my drink.

"Fine." She walked in front of the TV, kneeling down to pick the papers off the floor. "Did you at least eat something before you opened that espresso martini?"

I shook my head. "Empty stomach, baby." I held the can up. Food hadn't been on my mind in a hot minute. The only times I ate was when Brooke forced it down my throat. "But the good news is, I can still see the buttons on the remote."

Brooke got off the floor, the papers now neatly stacked in her hand. She shot me a disappointed look before heading into the kitchen. I didn't bother to look, but I could hear her opening some cabinets and rummaging through our fridge.

When she returned a moment later, throwing a pack of cookies at me, I caught it with a surprised laugh.

"You'll need something more than just alcohol and caffeine to survive," she said, her tone harsh as she walked over to the couch, snatching the remote from my hand. She turned off the TV, silencing the background noises.

How rude of her. "I was watching that!"

"You can continue to watch that shit once you eat."

I groaned loudly, throwing the cookies across the room. "You know what I also need to survive?" I asked, not expecting a reply. "A dad who's alive."

Brooke's expression softened at my words. "I know, Reece, but you still have to eat *something*. All week you've been getting up, grabbing a bunch of drinks, and rotting away on that couch. And if you haven't been on the couch, it was because we were naked in bed together."

I smirked at the mention of us naked. "Are you leaving for classes soon?"

She nodded. "In ten minutes, but stop changing the subject. I'm worried about you, okay?"

I reached for her hand, pulling Brooke down to sit on my lap, kind of forcing her to straddle me. I wrapped my arms around her, leaving kisses on her neck.

Her skin tasted so sweet in comparison to my drink, and I couldn't get enough of it, my worries melting away as she leaned into my touch. My hands were on her ass, squeezing gently.

God, I was so lucky to have her in my life. Brooke was the best. She was the kindest person I knew, loved me endlessly, was the most beautiful woman I'd ever seen, and her body was a true work of art.

Every curve, every freckle, every scar was perfect.

I kissed her lips, smiling against her mouth as her fingers tangled into my hair. Her hips rocked involuntarily against mine, and my dick responded to her movement instantly.

"Stay home with me," I murmured, laying my lips on as many inches of her skin as I could reach. "We can fuck all day and night instead of worrying about stupid assignments and attending boring classes."

Brooke let out an ironic laugh. "Someone's got to get *your* work done."

"Tomorrow." I kissed down her neck, biting lightly. "I need you, Brooke."

She shivered as I snuck my hands underneath her oversized knitted sweater, aiming for her bra. Her breath quickened, eyes fluttering close as I played with the clasp, not opening it.

"I..." A gasp fell from her lips as I shifted my hips, rubbing my erection against her. "I could go in late, but only if..."

I traced my fingers down her spine, grasping the end of her sweater where it met her pants, and slowly lifting it. Her body tensed but she didn't stop me, so I continued to pull the sweater up until it was around her waist.

"If what?" I whispered, my mouth close to her ear.

Her hands cupped my face before her lips brushed against mine. "If we're going to have breakfast together *before* we do anything else."

I laughed softly. "Alright, deal."

Brooke's eyes widened as if she didn't think I'd agree. "Okay... yes, sure. That's awesome!"

For a moment, we sat there in silence, her sweater bunched around her waist, and my hands on her body. She looked almost guilty, but I didn't know why.

"I have an even better deal," she said, offering me a smile that didn't quite reach her eyes. It was odd, but honestly, I was too fucked up to worry about any unspoken feelings. If she wanted me to know what was on her mind, she would've told me.

"Shoot."

"I go in late for my classes every day, and in return..."

Oh. I understood her deal.

"You want to fuck before classes every day? Now that's something we can arrange." I smirked at her, expecting her to blush or at least smile, but instead, her expression dropped for a second.

"Uh, yeah... that. And since you know classes are super important to me, we should at least have a daily breakfast together. You know, to make up for me running late to have sex with you."

I raised an eyebrow, intrigued yet also suspicious of her deal. It sounded a bit different, but I couldn't quite make out what was odd about it. So, I shrugged it off. "You've got yourself a deal, Ms. King."

Chapter Forty-Seven

Brooklyn

"I'm going out with Ming and Rina. Do you want to come?" I asked as I entered the living room, knowing Reece was going to say no.

It didn't matter that he would reject my offers. I still wanted to make him feel at least a little included. Perhaps if I kept asking him to come, he'd say yes eventually.

"Nah, I'm good." He waved me off, not even bothering to tear his eyes away from the TV. "Get me a whiskey from the pantry before you leave, okay?"

I sighed softly, used to Reece's dismissive responses by now.

Grabbing my purse from the hook by the door, I made my way over to the pantry, retrieving one of the three remaining bottles of whiskey he requested.

I closed the pantry door with a soft click, feeling a pang of sadness for my fiancé. He used to be so full of life, but ever since his father's passing, he turned into nothing but a shell.

As I reapproached him, I set the bottle down on the coffee table, not bothering to pour him a glass since I knew he was just going to drink straight from the bottle after I left anyway.

Reece glanced at the bottle of whiskey, a flicker of emotion crossing his eyes before he masked it with a nonchalant expression. His hands trembled slightly as he reached for the bottle, his fingers wrapping around it tightly.

He didn't say thank you, but he rarely did anymore.

"I'm leaving then," I told him. "Or do you need something else before I go?"

"No, I'm good," Reece replied. He was staring at the TV, watching some kind of commercial that was *far* from interesting, yet he made it seem like the most exquisite form of television ever.

His blue eyes were empty, not an ounce of emotion glistening in them. He looked almost haunted, I could barely recognize him.

I hesitated for a moment, my heart aching for him. "Reece, please talk to me," I practically begged. "I know you're hurting, and I want to help you through this."

He met my gaze then, the lack of emotion turning into anger. "I don't need your help, Brooklyn."

A lump formed in my throat as frustration built within me.

All I wanted was to help him, to be there for him when he clearly needed someone. But Reece had built a wall so high around himself, that it seemed impossible to reach him anymore.

I knew he was struggling, drowning in grief and self-destructive habits. And as much as it pained me to see him this way, I couldn't force him to accept my help.

Taking a deep breath, I tried my best to shake off the sadness that was slowly creeping up on me. "Are you at least going to spend Christmas with your family?"

Reece's jaw tensed at the mention of Christmas.

It was anything but a joyful holiday for the Carters this year, I knew that, but he could at least show up, right?

"I don't know, Brooke. Maybe."

I nodded softly, knowing better than to push further. "Just know that they miss you."

"Whatever." He gulped down a huge sip of whiskey.

"Rina and Ming are waiting downstairs," I muttered as I went to grab my jacket, aware of the fact that he wasn't even going to bother to respond.

As I slipped on my jacket, I couldn't help but steal one last glance at Reece. His shoulders were slumped, not a single hair was in place, and I was sure he'd been wearing the same shirt for a week now.

As I opened the door to leave, I heard Reece call my name, so I turned around. For a moment, I hoped he was going to ask me to wait, tell me he was going to take a shower and come with me… but instead, he simply said, "Have fun with your friends."

Well, it wasn't what I hoped for, but I'd take it. Reece hadn't said anything like that in what felt like years. Small steps, right?

"Ming's your friend, too, you know?"

Reece let out a humorless chuckle. "Yeah, well, I doubt he wants to be my friend right now."

I frowned at him, hating the disgusted tone in his voice. "Reece, he cares about you. We all do. And Ming asks about you all the time."

He shrugged, once again avoiding my gaze. "Don't turn this into a lecture now, Brooklyn."

I nodded softly, holding back on, what he claimed to be, a lecture.

"I love you," I whispered, not expecting a reply before I left the apartment.

Chapter Forty-Eight
Brooklyn

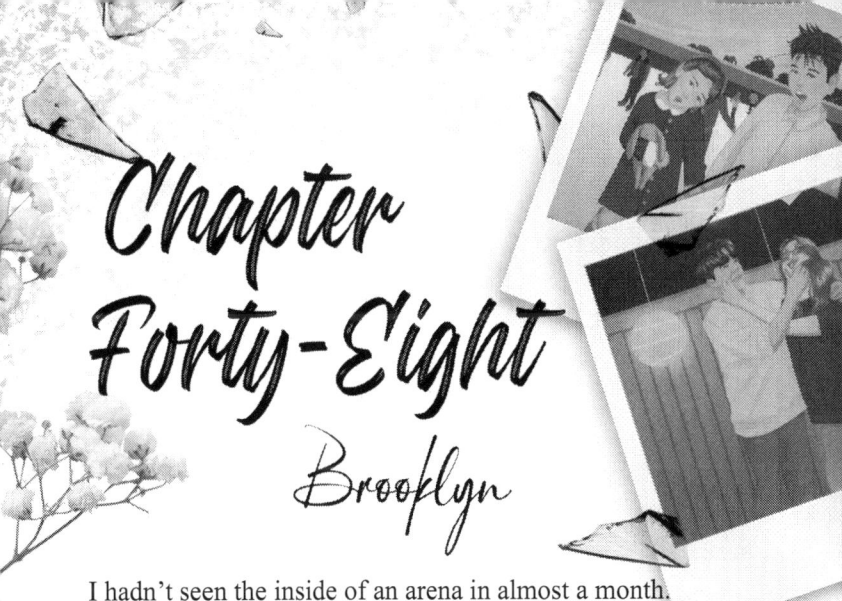

I hadn't seen the inside of an arena in almost a month.

Ever since Tobias passed, Reece didn't bother to leave the apartment, not even to take out the trash or just breathe in some fresh air.

I was kicked out of the competition since I hadn't attended a single one in a month, and though it stung at first, I was kind of glad figure skating was one last thing I had to worry about.

I understood Reece was struggling, so it would've made me a bad person had I gotten mad at him for being a no-show for practice and competitions. Actually, he wasn't even a no-show since I *knew* he wouldn't have come even when he promised he would.

Watching him break every promise he made was painful, but I had no way of knowing what his father dying did to him. Sure, I saw he wasn't okay, and I tried my very best to cheer him up... but he didn't want my help.

All I knew was that if my dad died, I wouldn't have known how to function either.

But I worried about him so much.

Since his father's funeral, Reece had been keeping to himself—to an extent, anyway.

If Reece wasn't attempting to fuck me every other hour, or I shot him down, he was drinking. A lot.

He didn't attend his classes, no hockey at all, and, as already mentioned, no practice with me either. He skipped so many of his games and practices that his coach threatened to kick him off the team if he didn't come back next week.

With every passing day, he turned more and more into a ghost. He drank so much more that just last Tuesday, I had to ask my dad to spend the night at our place because I couldn't watch my own fiancé all by myself.

He barely ate, and if he did, it was only because we compromised, even though I somehow managed to convince him that it wasn't a compromise so he wouldn't feel bad about it. I offered to be late for classes every morning just so we'd have an extra hour in bed together, but in return, he'd have to eat breakfast with me. I did the same after classes and for dinner as well.

It felt like no surface of our apartment was safe anymore, and I hated it. I hated it so much that I started to stay out with Rina and Ming longer. I went to visit my family for hours without him because I knew that if I asked him to come—and he'd actually agree, which he never did—he'd just find a moment to drag me into my old bedroom to fuck me there.

I never thought I'd ever say this, but I was *so* done with having sex. I needed a goddamn break, but I didn't know how to tell Reece without making him feel bad about it.

It's not that I didn't want to have sex with Reece. I proposed the deals in the first place, and if I said no, he didn't complain and accepted my decision. I simply wasn't built for sex *at least* three times a day, every single day. It was more sometimes.

With a shaking hand, I unlocked the door to our apartment, taking a deep breath because I knew what was about to happen.

Only that instead of smelling alcohol and finding Reece glued to the sofa, he was standing in the kitchen, cooking.

He immediately looked at me as I entered our apartment, smiling brightly.

"Hi," he spoke softly. "How was school?"

I dropped my bag by the door, slipping out of my loafers, and taking off my jacket. "Okay, I guess."

After hanging up my jacket, I turned around just for Reece to stand right in front of me. Startled, I looked up at him.

"Did you take notes?" he asked, grasping my chin with one hand.

I held my breath as I nodded, waiting for him to kiss me. Waiting for that kiss to get more passionate until I found my dress on the floor and his hands all over me. To my surprise, he only quickly, softly pressed his lips on mine before making his way back to the stove.

He didn't taste like alcohol this time.

"I was thinking about picking college back up," he told me. "At least give it a try, you know?"

"Really?" I followed him into the kitchen, leaning against the refrigerator. He hadn't mentioned anything about college in weeks. The assignments I brought home for him, I did all the work because he just wouldn't. The last thing he needed right now was failing his classes as well.

"Yes. I'll even go back to hockey next week."

"You are?" Why didn't he tell me that he was thinking about it? Reece usually told me *all* of his thoughts, even if they made no sense. He used to say that even if he didn't make sense, I'd find a way to make it sound like he did, so he always told me everything.

We could've been deadly silent, and out of the blue, Reece would start babbling about super random things that popped up in his head. Why didn't he tell me about his plans earlier?

"Yup. I'll need your notes, though, so I don't look stupid."

"Of course." It was a good thing that we had the exact same classes. Somehow I knew it was going to come in handy one day.

Reece pushed the pan aside and grabbed two plates from the upper cabinets. Meanwhile, I went to get some forks and two glasses and set them down on our kitchen table. It wasn't a very big one, but it was enough for both of us. Though the huge bouquet of dried flowers was in the way, so I set it aside in the living room while we ate.

"I was at the cemetery today," he said as he set both of our plates down opposite from each other. Reece pulled back a chair for me, then pressed a kiss to the top of my head as I took a seat before he made his way around the table.

"You were?" My eyebrows rose in surprise.

Thinking about it, he looked like he left the house. He was dressed and didn't smell like alcohol, so he took a shower. His hair was cared for, and not because I did it for him. He looked like the old Reece, the one before his world came crumbling down.

He even smiled.

I hadn't seen Reece smile in so long.

"Yes." Reece reached a hand over the table, holding mine. His thumb brushed over my knuckles, then he kissed the ring on my finger. "We should go on a date."

"Hold up." I wanted to pull my hand away, but I feared

that if I did, he'd feel rejected in a way, so I didn't. "I mean, yeah, sure, let's do that."

His eyebrows fell. "But?"

"No buts." I laughed awkwardly. "I just... I wanted to ask about you going to your dad's grave. That's huge, Reece."

He let go of my hand. "Yeah, I guess."

"Did you go alone?"

He nodded. "I wanted to wait for you and ask if you'd come with me, but I realized it was going to take a couple more hours, so I just went alone."

I smiled at him softly, proudly.

I was waiting for that relieved feeling to kick in, for me to feel like my life was going to go back to normal... but it never came. There was a voice in the back of my head, whispering *just you wait*. It wasn't over, I wasn't even sure the ending was in sight.

I wanted to help Reece so badly, but all I did was cover for him. I always covered for him, even when we were younger. It was wrong, I knew that, but I felt awful just thinking about making him look bad in front of our families.

He asked me not to tell anyone that he didn't leave the apartment or that he drank a lot. I should've told someone when it started, or at least when I noticed it was getting bad. Now I was a bit too afraid to tell someone because Reece was in too deep.

There was a chance he was going to leave me if I got him help, but that was better than him destroying himself. Then again, he promised he was getting better, that it just took him a minute longer than expected.

I believed him when I shouldn't have.

"It's not a big deal," he added, brushing off going outside like it was nothing.

It was a big deal, but I wasn't going to say this aloud. If

he wanted to downplay his accomplishment, I had to go with it for now. The last thing I wanted to do was startle him and set him back somehow.

It looked like he was doing better today, so perhaps he really was trying.

"So, uh... our date?" I said, hoping it was going to light the mood again. We hadn't gone out in so long, I could barely remember the last time we spent quality time together.

Almost instantly, Reece smiled again. It was a little odd, but I was just glad he seemed okay-ish for once. "Do you remember the first ever *real* restaurant your dad took us to?"

"I don't think I could ever forget it." I laughed.

We were about six years old when Dad thought it was a good idea to take us to a fancy restaurant that wasn't his own. Truthfully, it wasn't *my* first, at least, I didn't think so, but that particular day just stuck with me.

Dad ended up getting kicked out because Reece and I tried to climb up the walls. They had Victorian-like 3D patterns on the walls, of course we were going to try and climb them.

"I figured it'd be cool to go there again, so I called the restaurant and got us a table for tomorrow evening," he said.

Oh. "Tomorrow evening?"

"Uh-huh." His soft smile faltered. "Why? What are you doing tomorrow evening?"

"I, uh... I promised Nova I'd go to the movies with her at five." It was my attempt to stay away from home for longer, especially on a Saturday when I didn't even have classes to catch a break from Reece.

It was sad, I admit. What kind of awful fiancée would beg her ten-year-old sister to hang out with her just so she didn't have to be at home? Me, apparently. But now that Nova was excited for the movies, I couldn't possibly cancel.

"The movies?" Reece narrowed his eyes at me. "Which one?"

"The one on 34th Street. Not sure what it's called." I pushed my pasta around with my fork, avoiding looking at Reece.

"So, in the middle of Manhattan?" He chuckled disbelievingly. "You'd rather drive like forty minutes from Staten Island to Manhattan for a stupid movie when there's a movie theatre like ten minutes away from your dad's house?"

"Nova chose it."

"By the time your dad gets home from dropping you off, he can turn around and pick you back up."

I looked up again, sighing. "Reece, please, it's really not that deep. Dad has a restaurant close by anyway."

His eyes rolled, but I wasn't sure why.

What did I say wrong?

Was it because I didn't invite him? But he never cared about that before, and I was allowed to spend time with my siblings without him.

Or perhaps it was because I didn't ask him to drive us like I usually did.

Or he was looking right through me, knowing this was my attempt to get away from him for a while. I rarely went to the movies, especially in crowded ones, he knew that. And if I did go, Reece was with me to make sure I was okay.

A wave of panic washed over me, but I really tried to keep my cool. I didn't want to upset him even more.

"Uhm... I can cancel on Nova," I suggested.

Reece shook his head. "It's alright. We weren't supposed to be at the restaurant before eight anyway. Let's just meet there then."

"Are you sure?"

His smile returned, soft as the one from before. His eyes

were filled with pure love, not an ounce of malice in them. He seemed mad a second ago, but now he was perfectly fine. My guts told me something was off, but the way he looked at me told a different story.

I was taught to trust my gut feeling, but how could I when my gut feeling was constantly betraying me? Reece was the one person I knew who never had any bad intentions with me.

I was overthinking this again, I realized.

This was Reece we were talking about, my fiancé, the love of my goddamn life.

He was safe. I was safe with him.

"Of course," he said and reached for my hand once more. "I love you. I want you to have a good time with your sister, *mi princesa*. It doesn't matter how we both get to our date as long as we're there together."

The next thing I knew, Reece abandoned his food and walked around the table again. He pulled my chair back and pulled me up on my feet.

My eyes fell onto my mostly full plate, then his. We barely touched our food.

"Reece," I said, my voice strained as he held me tightly in his embrace. His lips laid on my neck, kissing me. "We barely ate."

"It's okay," he muttered, then looked right at me and cupped my face with his hands. "We can eat later."

"I'm pretty hungry." I wasn't actually since I went out for lunch with Rina and Ming, but I was sure Reece hadn't eaten anything since breakfast.

He leaned down and pressed his lips on mine. "Me too," he spoke quietly, then kissed me again right after. I could feel him smile into our kiss.

Reece's hands slid down my body, then he picked me up, my legs automatically wrapping around his hips. His teeth grazed my neck, his hot breath rolling over my skin and leaving goosebumps behind.

He carried me to our sofa, setting me down first before crawling on top of me, settling between my thighs. "But I'd rather eat something else."

"Reece." My voice came out like a breathless exhale, thin and ragged.

He looked at me, worry in his eyes. "Are you okay?"

I nodded. "Of course," I said, stroking my hands up his back.

"But?"

God, how was I going to say this without hurting his feelings?

"But I... I just think we don't have to have sex like three times a day, every day," I said. Perhaps being rather forward with it was going to be the best option.

Reece sat up, looking at the turned-off TV for a moment. "Yeah, you're probably right."

I pushed myself up to sit, wanting to rest my head on his shoulder but refraining from doing so. "It's not that I don't wan—"

"It's exhausting," he interrupted. "Isn't it?" His head turned toward me, tears in his eyes.

I haven't seen him cry since his dad's funeral.

My eyes closed as I inhaled deeply, nodding softly. "So exhausting, Reece."

"I'm sorry." He leaned his forehead against my own, taking shallow breaths. "I'm so sorry, *mi princesa.*"

My arms wrapped around his body, holding him so tight to my own that I wasn't sure if it was my heartbeat that I felt or his. "It's okay."

"I love you, Brooke," he mumbled, crying. "God, I love you so much. I'm so sorry."

Chapter Forty-Nine

Brooklyn

"Are you sure you don't want to wait in the car until he gets here?" Dad asked once more as I stood underneath the roof in front of the restaurant, hiding from the rain.

It was raining so heavily, I could've been taking a shower out here.

"Yes, Dad." I exaggerated an eye-roll, a wide smile plastered on my face. "Reece should be here any minute."

"Just making sure." He was worried. I knew that. Reece hadn't been the most reliable recently, but after yesterday, I was more than confident in him. He was going to show up on time, and we were going to have a super adorable date.

Before Dad picked me up to take Nova and me to the movies, I'd checked with Reece to make sure tonight was still on. He seemed excited about our date, said he couldn't wait.

"Just go!" I laughed, waving him off. "You're embarrassing me."

Dad gasped, covering his heart with a hand. "I expected this kind of behavior from your siblings, Brookie, not from you." He sniffled, wiping away fake tears, which the couple walking past my father's car seemed to think was strange. It was certainly not normal... except that it kind of was on brand for my dad. "You promised that you'd never think I was embarrassing."

I covered my face with my purse, trying not to die right on the spot. "Just gooo."

"And to think that I was considering you to potentially be my favorite child..."

The rain had gotten heavier over the past hour, and I still stood outside the restaurant, waiting for my fiancé.

They'd probably given away our table by now, so even if he still showed up, we weren't going to get dinner. Truthfully, I wasn't even up for a date anymore.

I was cold and my makeup was most likely running down my face from all the crying I'd been doing the past thirty minutes.

At this point, I was only still waiting here because there was a little bit of hope left inside of me. Maybe he told me the wrong time, or maybe he somehow thought we were meeting up an hour later. I didn't want to think he forgot about me. Reece never forgot about me and our plans before, so admitting it might've happened now was the last thing I wanted to do.

"Ma'am?" someone said from behind me. I turned around, looking at the hostess, who offered me a sympathetic smile. She looked like she was in her mid-forties. "Don't you want to come inside?"

"No, it's alright." I tried smiling back at her, but my muscles refused to move.

"Are you sure?" She handed me a cup, some kind of tea, I assumed. "It's pretty cold out here."

It was January and I stood here in a short dress. I had a jacket, but it started to do little to warm me.

I took the tea from the hostess and thanked her wholeheartedly. "My fiancé should be here any minute."

She nodded slowly. "You've been standing here for an hour and a half. I don't think he'll show up anymore."

My shoulders sagged, and a deep sigh drew from my lungs. "I don't think he will either," I admitted. "But... I don't know. He's never stood me up before, and we've known each other since we were like two."

Was this oversharing? Probably, but it was better than calling my dad and telling him Reece didn't show up.

Dad knew Reece was struggling, he just didn't know how bad it really was.

Things had to change, I knew that. I also knew that I was going to have to call my mom or my dad to pick me up... and once they did, I *really* needed to tell them what was going on.

They could help me help Reece.

"Did he tell you he'd be late?" she asked.

No, he didn't. In fact, Reece hadn't even tried to reach out to me, not a single message or call. Nothing. But I wasn't going to tell her that. "Maybe he got caught up at work." That definitely wasn't the case.

"Maybe."

"I should go..." I handed her the now half-empty cup. "Thank you, though. I really appreciate it."

"Of course."

Chapter Fifty

Reece

My eyes ripped open as I heard a key jiggle in the door.

I looked out of the window, seeing it was pitch black outside. As my phone lit up beside me, drawing my attention to the time, a rush of panic flooded through my veins.

Fuck. Brooke.

My heart was racing, knowing very well that I fucked up big time. It was too late to throw away all of the liquor bottles on the coffee table, too late to make it seem like I'd accidentally fallen asleep.

Brooke stepped inside, but she didn't even look at me.

The door slammed close behind her as she threw her keys onto the cupboard. She didn't say a word, just walked inside and headed straight to our bedroom.

"Brooke?" I called but got no reply.

Sitting up, I grabbed two of the beer bottles and went to throw them away just to clean up a little, but I was frozen in place when I heard the door to Brooke and my closet. It was a very distinct sound that Brooke had asked me to fix weeks ago but I hadn't gotten around to doing it yet.

I set the bottles down on the kitchen table and then made my way down the hall to our bedroom.

She was just changing into something more comfortable, I was sure of that. And she was just mad that I slept through our date, that was why she ignored my presence. Maybe she thought I was still asleep.

But then why did this feel so wrong? Why did something feel completely off?

As I stood in between the doorframe, my heart sank so deep that I was almost sure it wasn't even inside of my body anymore.

There was a suitcase on our bed and Brooke was throwing her clothes into it one after the other. Tears were streaming down her face, and loud, shaky breaths left her lungs. Her movements were uncontrolled and messy—I realized I brought this mess into our lives.

There was no way Brooke would leave just because I missed one date. The past weeks had been a blur but even so, I knew that I must've done something to *truly* upset her.

The alcohol most likely wasn't even the worst part of it all. And God, if my brain wasn't as clouded and I could access my memories, perhaps I could narrow these past weeks down to all the shit I've fucked up and find a way to apologize, but I couldn't. It was a mix of blurred actions and awful-tasting drinks, all of which were currently trying to come back up again.

What was I going to apologize for?

I stood there, paralyzed by the sight of her leaving, my mind swirling with regret and self-loathing.

The image of my fiancée, the love of my goddamn life, packing her bags and getting ready to leave me; anger, hurt, and sadness etched into every inch of her face was now burnt into my memory.

How the fuck did I let it come this far?

"Brooke," I said quietly. Saying her name was like poison on my tongue, like I didn't deserve to say her name anymore.

She wiped away her tears, acting like she didn't hear me but I knew she did.

"Brooke," I repeated louder this time, my voice rough with emotions. She paused but didn't turn to look at my face. "I'm sorry."

She continued to throw two more dresses into her suitcase before she broke down entirely, taking a seat on the floor in front of the bed. Her sobs tortured me, but I deserved it.

All I wanted to do was walk inside the room, take my fiancée into my arms, and hold her tightly, but I doubted she would've wanted that right now. Honestly, I wasn't even sure I still had the right to even look at her.

"I've been a mess," I told her, unsure if she was listening. "I haven't been myself since my dad passed."

The truth was, I'd been drowning. I knew it, I could feel it. Every day since he'd passed, I felt like I was suffocating, and I didn't know how to make that feeling stop.

His death hit me harder than I anticipated. The pain of losing him, coupled with the pressure of wanting to help Brooke succeed and worrying about my own career, became too much to bear.

The only way I knew how to make it stop was by reaching for all those bottles, numbing the ache in my chest.

When that wasn't enough anymore, it was sex I figured would help. Alcohol numbed the pain, sex silenced my brain. It seemed easy, like a good deal, but in my haze of grief and intoxication, I overlooked the only person who stuck by my side this whole time. I shut Brooke out when I needed her the most.

Now, as I looked at her, every word we'd exchanged in these past weeks felt like a mistake. I was lying to her. I was using her kindness, her love, to fuel myself, not realizing I was draining her in return.

How do you apologize for failing to show up, not just tonight, but for weeks? How do you apologize for taking your own fiancée for granted when all she wanted was to help?

"I'm sorry," I repeated. Words were failing me, and even if I had the entire dictionary memorized to offer her the most poetic apology, it wasn't worth it. Brooke shouldn't accept *any* of my apologies, no matter how great they sounded.

Brooke finally looked up at me, her eyes empty, tired. "I get it," she said, shrugging to herself. "Losing someone sucks, Reece. I get that. And I tried *so hard* to be there for you. I tried *so hard* to function when I had to watch you lose yourself more and more with every day, knowing I couldn't do shit about it. But I can't keep doing this."

I took a shaky breath as the weight of her words hit me like a punch to the gut. "I know, and I'm sorry. I'm sorry I didn't show up to our date, and I'm sorry that I messed up today and all those other days before."

"Messed up?!" She chuckled ironically through her tears. "Reece, you made me believe you were doing better. I lied to Colin for you, just so he wouldn't worry about you. I lied to my dad because of you! This isn't messed up, it's awful."

Brooke got back up onto her feet, pushing all of her clothes into the suitcase to make it fit. "I waited for you for almost two hours in the pouring rain only because I didn't want to lose hope. You've *never* stood me up, Reece. Not even once. Now I get home, and you're half-dead on our sofa, drunk off your ass. The whole date was *your* idea, not mine! How could you do this to me? How could you do this to yourself?"

"I don't know," I admitted. I wanted to fall to my knees

and beg her for forgiveness... but I was frozen in place. "God, Brooke, I have no fucking clue what I'm doing."

"Yeah, I got that." She zipped up her suitcase and then looked at me once again. "I understand you're grieving, and I understand that this has to be awful for you. I'm willing to be patient and wait this out, Reece, really, I am. I'm willing to be there for you and love you enough for the both of us for a while, but I can't do this anymore when you're not willing to meet me halfway. Even a quarter of the way would be fine. You're not trying anything. You don't even want to get better."

Tears blurred my vision as it finally dawned on me that I was about to lose her for good. That zipped-up suitcase, her emptier closet, her tears, and her words... she was done. And it was all my fault. I couldn't even blame her for leaving.

"I-I know." I cleared my throat in an attempt to stop the stabbing pain in my heart from making itself noticeable through my voice. "Please, Brooke... I'll do better. I'll change. I will get help. Just..." My eyes fell on her suitcase, my nerves shaking at the way she wrapped her hand around the handle. "Please don't go."

She looked up at the ceiling, this time trying to blink her tears away.

"I need you, Brooke. I... I can't do life without you."

Her chest rose as she took a deep breath before she lowered her head and met my eyes again. "Mom and Eden are waiting in the car. I have to go."

"They can go back without you." I finally stepped into the bedroom, making my way over to her with long strides. As I stood right in front of her, I so badly wanted to touch her and hug her, but I couldn't.

I knew one hug of hers was going to make me feel better, but there was a good chance that my hug would've just hurt her even more. For the life of me, I couldn't cause her more pain.

"Please don't go..." I whispered, pleading. "Don't leave me."

Brooke laid her hands on my face, her icy fingers stroking underneath my eyes. "Luan will spend the night here," she told me. "So you're not alone."

"I don't want *him* here. I need *you*."

She shook her head at me. "You need to get better, Reece. And you're not going to get better with me around."

"That's not true." I covered her hands with my own, pressing them harder against my skin. "You're all I need."

"No. No, I'll just cover for you. I'll keep finding ways to make me feel better about how miserable you are instead of *helping* you. I'd buy you more alcohol, I'd let you fuck me just so you'll eat, and I'd try to get you to talk about it, but you will find a way to change the subject. I'd wait and wait for you to magically wake up one day and be the old you again. And that would only make everything worse. Me leaving and allowing you to find a good way other than sex and alcohol to cope is my way of helping you. And it's the only way I know how to." She smiled at me, or at least she tried to. "I tried being there, Reece. I tried listening, I tried talking to you, I tried letting you rot and use *me* whenever you wanted... but that's not going to work anymore."

"I need you to get better, Reece," she continued. "Because I love you, and the fact that you're hurting is killing me. And because you're throwing your entire life away right now. I couldn't care less about skating and winning, but it's your *dream* to play for the NHL. And if you don't get back out there soon, you'll never get the chance to try and get drafted. Not only will you hate me and everyone around you, you'll hate yourself. So, please... please let us try *this*."

What she said made sense, even in my intoxicated mind, but that still didn't mean I could live without her. "I can't just not see you or talk to you for days, weeks, or even months. I would go insane. Even more than I am now."

I wasn't going to survive this.

Since I moved in with my brother and his wife, I'd seen Brooke every single day of my life. She took off from school to be on the road with me if I had a game, and I followed her wherever she had to go for skating competitions. We went on vacation together with each other's family. The only times I didn't sleep over at her place was because she stayed at Colin's with me.

How could I possibly go from that to not even speaking to her anymore?

Brooke snuck her arms around my body, pressing her head right into my chest. I swung my arms around her as well, holding her tightly, not ever planning to let go. If I didn't let go, she couldn't leave.

"We'll see each other tomorrow," she said. "My parents and Grey will get rid of anything alcoholic, so you wouldn't even be tempted to reach for it. Luan will watch over you like a hawk. And Colin and your mom will be there to talk if you want to."

Okay... okay, I could maybe survive one night without her.

Wait. Brooke mentioned something about Elliot having gotten some kind of award for something. I knew she mentioned something like that, but I couldn't remember what he'd done to get an award.

They were celebrating it, apparently, so it must've been huge.

Wait, Luan? "Why would Luan stay with me anyway?"

"Because he's the only one who knows what it's like to

genuinely want to drown your feelings in alcohol. He'd be more helpful than Colin."

Oh, right. I knew that.

"Didn't my mom go back to Spain?" I asked, finally registering that part.

How come I didn't know she was in New York?

I felt Brooke shake her head. "She isn't ready to go back. She's been staying with your brother."

How the fuck didn't I know this?

How couldn't I know that my *mother* never left the country again?

"She probably isn't going to go back either," Brooke added. "Aaron's helping her look for a small little house in Staten Island, somewhere close to Colin. The Mansion's too big for it being just her, and she said Spain without your dad is too painful."

I nodded slowly, trying to find that piece of information somewhere in my brain. Surely I'd been told about this before... how didn't I remember any of this?

"We can meet up sometimes," Brooke said, taking a step back from our hug just to look at me. She held both of my hands, and I was so goddamn thankful she didn't fully let go yet. "Maybe not all by ourselves at first though."

"Why?"

"Because I'm afraid that if we're all alone, you're going to drink again because you know I'd hide it for you. You know I'd lie for you, Reece," she answered. "I'm afraid that I'll mess up, ruining your progress. I'm afraid that even if I stopped you from drinking in my presence, you'd just do it when I'm not there. And what if I keep saying no to sex, huh? What if you get frustrated with me because of that, and you'll do something stupid?"

"I wouldn't cheat on you, Brooke."

"I know." She sounded sure of that. "But I also don't want to risk anything. It's going to be easier to relearn control with as minimal temptation around you as possible. It's better to go at this slowly but surely."

"Okay." My head bobbed as I tried to find it in my heart to agree with her. My head thought it all made sense, but my heart just didn't want to see her leave. "But I'll see you, right? And we'll talk on the phone?"

"If you need to, yes."

"Okay… I can do this." Hopefully.

I had to be able to do this.

Chapter Fifty-One
Reece

Everything was hurting: my arms, my legs, my stomach, even my eyes, and especially my heart.

Was this what dying felt like?

I lay there on the cold, hard floor of Ash's, Luan and Grey's son, bedroom, pain searing through every fiber of my being. Memories flooded my mind—of laughter, of times when everything was great, when Brooke was in my arms and I could feel her love for me.

Each time my thoughts included Brooke, the pain in my body faded, but the moment I couldn't feel anything anymore, my brain decided it was time to throw my deceased father into the mix.

I closed my eyes, clutching my stomach, and letting out a low groan. I forced myself to take slow, deep breaths, trying to find a way to push through the pain.

The room was silent, and all I could think about was how badly I needed a drink. Alcohol was going to make the pain bearable. It was going to make me forget. It was going to numb the ache in my soul.

But I had to stay strong for Brooke, for my family, but most importantly, for myself.

I pushed myself up to sit, gritting my teeth. The room spun for a moment, but I clenched my fists and waited for the dizziness to pass without throwing up.

Suddenly, a knock appeared on the door, and before I even managed to speak, Luan already knelt in front of me.

He unscrewed a bottle of water and then handed it to me. "You need to stay hydrated."

I took the bottle from him, my fingers trembling slightly as I brought it to my lips. The water felt surprisingly refreshing as it slid down my dry throat.

"This is the worst you'll be, I promise," Luan said as he took the now empty bottle from me, screwing the cap back on. "You just have to stick it out."

I nodded weakly, grateful for Luan's help these past three days. He spent the past days in the same room as me all day long, just to ensure I didn't sneak out to get a drink from *anywhere*. Every twelve hours, he'd tell me how great I was doing, and while I didn't feel like I was doing great, his support kept me going.

Sure, I wished Luan was Brooke instead, but the longer I went without an alcoholic drink, the more I understood why she couldn't do this with me.

I barely remembered anything from the past weeks, but I knew I was using Brooke big time. I knew she tried to be there for me, she tried to talk to me and get me to stop drinking, but I didn't let her help me.

The guilt of how I treated her clawed at me, and though the grief of losing my father caused a significant amount of pain now that I had to feel it, mistreating the love of my life hurt so much more. She didn't deserve that.

"Can I take anything? Like… painkillers?" I asked, sounding so weak, I could barely recognize my own voice.

"I don't recommend it," he replied. "And you're not *phys-*

ically in pain, anyway. I know it feels like it, but you're not. All this pain you're feeling, they're symptoms of withdrawal. Also, they're normal pain from grief. Painkillers won't actually help you."

"So, it's all in my head?" I looked at my trembling, sweaty hands. "I'm not sure if I can handle this, Luan."

He took my hands in his, smiling at me softly. "You're stronger than you think. Getting sober sucks, and it's horrible... but you will feel *so* much better once you're past the first couple of days. It's only getting better from here."

I knew he'd been through this before, I should've trusted him, but my mind was clouded with doubt and fear. What if I was never going to get better?

I'd been told that I was lucky since I hadn't been drinking for years and only a few weeks, but I certainly didn't feel lucky.

"Remember who you're getting sober for, Reece," Luan said when he noticed my hesitation. "It's not for Brooke. It's not for Colin. It's not for your parents. You're getting sober for yourself."

"Right." I took a deep breath, trying to muster whatever strength I had left in me. "How long am I going to feel this way?"

"Just a couple more days."

"Day*s*?" Oh, God.

"Yeah... but, as I said, today is the worst day you'll have to endure. You'll already feel better tomorrow. It's still going to be tough, I won't lie, but better."

"Okay." I got this. I could do this, hopefully. "And then... I can see Brooke tomorrow?"

He chuckled lightly. "If you want to."

"Yeah, I want to."

Chapter Fifty-Two

Brooklyn

The first week was the worst, but Luan had already told me that it'd be the worst one.

Luckily, Reece wasn't technically an alcoholic. He wasn't always drunk after his dad passed, more often than not he only had a drink or two a day to stop his thoughts, but sometimes he drank so much that he blacked out.

It was still bad, but not the worst possible situation.

And it was a good thing it hadn't been years, just slightly over a month since it started.

Luan said it was going to be easier to get that under control than stopping an alcoholic from drinking. And I had faith in him.

Still, Reece looked like a ghost of himself in that first week. He'd called me multiple times a day starting on day four, and sometimes he refused to video chat because he didn't want me to look at him.

Reece told me that he didn't have any cravings per se, but he got nervous when he didn't have a drink that day. He was constantly tired, and sometimes he'd call me in tears, begging me to make this pain stop.

Colin got him a therapist, and as far as I knew, Reece had a session with him every other day.

I wanted to be with Reece all week long, but I knew it was for the best if I stayed away. At least for now. We'd try a sleepover at my dad's place in a couple of days just to see how he'd react.

Sure, we could just go back home but we'd be all alone there, and that was a bit scary. Like I told him, I'd lie for Reece even if I shouldn't and I was so afraid to make everything worse. At my parents' place, we had my parents there as well as my siblings, so it was easier not to give in to him.

It took me way too long to get help, just because I believed Reece's drunken lies, and I wasn't going to make that mistake again.

"Are you going over to Grey's later?" Mom asked as I walked into the living room at six in the morning. Why was she awake already?

"I'm not sure." I took a seat next to her, resting my head on her shoulder just to see what she was doing this early. She was drawing... but of course she was. "I don't really feel like socializing today."

"That's great." She chuckled softly. "You can go hide with Grey."

"Wasn't it *his* idea to host Taco Sunday at their place?"

Emory nodded. "We all knew he'd regret it. But he's actually just hiding from Luan because Luan has *awesome* last-minute ideas for Sage's birthday."

"What's he plan—" I didn't manage to finish my question before Grey came storming into the house.

"Your husband still asleep?" he asked, barely even nodding a hello.

"He is," Mom replied, laughing. "Why?"

"That dumbass promised to help me cut all the taco

toppings. I'm gonna wake him, and then I'll kill him." Instead of marching toward my parents' bedroom, Grey made his way over to me first. "Good morning, Princess." He placed a kiss on the top of my head. "How are you doing?"

"Why don't I get a good morning?" Mom asked, sounding offended.

"Because I'm mad at your husband," Grey replied. "So, anyway, how are you, Brookie?"

"My husband is Brooke's father…"

Grey shrugged, looking as indifferent as ever.

"I'm okay, I think," I finally replied. "How is Reece today?"

Luan took Reece home to his place instead of staying at our shared apartment. It made more sense that way since Luan had two kids to look after. Sure, Grey was home this past week, but he'd be gone almost the entire next week.

I bet all the kids in this family couldn't wait for their dads to finally retire after this season. Though, perhaps it was also a bit sad. I was going to miss watching Colin, Aaron, and Grey play.

"I'll let you know when he wakes up," Grey answered.

"He's still sleeping?" That was new. He'd been awake fairly early all week.

"Yes. Luan thinks Reece is finally starting to get some rest. He's a lot less nervous and anxious for sure."

"That's good," I said, slightly more relieved by the news. I was expecting bad ones.

"Anyway, I got to wake your dad now." Grey cracked his knuckles as he made his way to my dad. "MILES!"

"So, what's it like sharing your room with Ash?" I asked, looking around Ash's room. That kid was being *spoiled*, but so was Sage.

It wasn't the first time I'd been inside either of their bedrooms, but it never failed to blow my mind.

Ash had an entire collection of signed soccer balls on one of his walls, and the one opposite was covered with ice hockey sticks. Signed, of course—but Grey had easy access to those anyway, so it wasn't *that* mind blowing.

The kid was only six and he had a whole shelf of awards from science fairs and whatever else he was currently interested in. I was a little jealous, not going to lie.

"I wouldn't know. Ash refuses to sleep here with me. He says I snore," Reece replied, rolling his eyes. "But that can't be possible, right?"

I cocked my head at him. "Well..."

We laughed, and God, did I miss laughing with Reece together. It was the first time we'd seen each other in person since I temporarily moved out. He didn't go to my brother's celebratory party for getting an award, but I kind of expected that.

Reece looked better, a bit healthier. He smiled more, and his eyes weren't as empty as they were the last time we'd been together. I couldn't tell a difference, but Luan and Grey told me that Reece had been eating twice a day these past three days, which was great. Still not enough but it was better than nothing. And he wasn't even forced to eat—he wanted to.

"You never complained about me snoring before, so I'm not trusting you," Reece said, shrugging.

"I grew up having to listen to it, baby. I'm used to it." He didn't actually snore, but if he did, I was certain I would've been used to it by now.

Reece fake gasped, shaking his head at me as he laughed.

It felt good to hear his laughter again. I never thought I could miss someone's laughter, especially Reece's because I was used to hearing it daily, but this right now just showed me how much I took for granted.

Suddenly, Reece pulled me onto his lap, keeping his left hand on my hip. "Anyone ever tell you how pretty you are?"

His free hand approached my face just to tuck a strand of hair behind my ear.

I smiled at him, my cheeks getting warmer. "Not in a while."

"That should be a crime," he said and tsked. Reece leaned in closer to me, his lips brushing my own before he added, "You're the prettiest woman in the whole universe, Brooke."

"Thank you." I smiled into our kiss. As much as I wanted to continue kissing Reece, I knew that if we didn't stop now, it would go further and I wasn't sure if I was ready for it yet.

I could tell he was doing a bit better, but I didn't want to risk anything. What if we moved too fast and he fell back into old patterns? Perhaps it was better to wait another week or two before we took it a step further.

Just when I was about to bring my hand between our faces, Reece pulled away. His eyes bore holes into my soul with the intensity of his stare. His lips were turned upward, if only a little.

"Let me take you out," Reece spoke softly. His hands moved up to my waist, holding me. "I'll pick you up tomorrow morning and we'll go have breakfast together."

My eyebrows drew together slightly. "Breakfast?" We'd barely ever gone out for breakfast before. If we went out to eat, it was usually around dinner time.

"Yes." His hands moved underneath my shirt, his thumbs brushing my skin, but it wasn't anything sexual—more innocent than I was used to. It felt nice to feel his skin on mine again. "I'll pick you up at eight, then we'll go to your dad's restaurant and have breakfast together."

I chuckled lightly but quickly covered it up by clearing my throat. "You do remember that Rêverie doesn't open until six pm, right?"

He nodded. "I don't think I'm ready to go elsewhere... and your dad said it's okay. He'd open for us. As usual."

"It's better than just having breakfast at my parents' place, huh?" I cocked my head at him, a smile tugging on my lips.

"More private, with no kids around. Just the two of us."

"And my dad in the kitchen."

Reece shrugged. "I'd rather he's around us than some random guy who has a crush on you."

I leaned my forehead against his, trying my best not to laugh. "You'd survive someone else having a crush on me."

"I would, but only because I know you'd choose me. In fact, I think it'd boost my ego more than yours because like... fuck, I can barely comprehend my luck. How was *I* lucky enough for you to fall in love with me? And knowing it's *me* you love? It's the best fucking feeling in the whole world."

"To be honest, I expected a little more jealousy," I said, not really meaning it. Reece and I had been together long enough to know that we'd *always* choose each other, no matter what.

I trusted my fiancé. If he wanted to hang around ten different girls every day, then so be it. At the end of the day, he would come home to *me*.

Actually, ten different girls every day would overstep a line, but since that never happened, it didn't matter.

Reece cupped my face with his hands and smiled at me all sweetly. "Do you want me to fight the guys who have a crush on you?"

I nodded once, still not meaning it but I was sure Reece knew I was joking.

"I'll tell them they can never speak to you again, okay?" His smile turned into a mischievous smirk. "Then you'll kiss me, and everything will be alright."

My eyes rolled. "I was thirteen, Reece. Let it go."

"Never." He shook his head. "If you hadn't told whoever the fuck wasn't allowed to speak to me, that she, in fact, wasn't allowed to speak to me, I would've never kissed you. And we wouldn't be engaged now."

"You would have... one day."

Reece wrapped his arms around me, pulling me closer into his embrace. "You're right. I would have kissed you eventually."

Chapter Fifty-Three
Reece

Not once in my life had I been nervous before picking Brooke up to go on a date. It was always easy for me—I'd pick her up, and I knew we'd have a good time. There was no way I could mess up. We'd laugh, joke around, and then eventually, I'd come up with a stupid idea and Brooke would keep me out of prison.

Today was different. It was probably the most important date we'd ever go on. If I messed up today, I was sure our relationship wasn't going to survive it.

I needed Brooke in my life though, more than I needed oxygen, so fucking up wasn't an option.

It's just breakfast, I tried to tell myself. Surely I couldn't mess up one stupid breakfast. It was only an hour or two until I'd take her back home and we'd go back to not seeing each other for a couple of days.

When I asked my therapist if I could move back in with Brooke, he said that it'd be better to move toward it slowly. He thought it was better for Brooke and my relationship if I figured out how to stand on my own feet again and avoid the risk of using my fiancée as an anchor once more.

Yes, Brooke held me together, and I honestly wouldn't

know how to function without her, but my therapist had a good point. If I continued to use Brooke to get through the days, I was only putting more weight on her and ruining everything. The last thing I wanted was to destroy Brooke just so I didn't fall apart. And I knew that she'd catch me if I fell again, even if that ruined her completely.

As I crossed the street with a bouquet of baby's breath—Brooke's favorite flowers—in my hands, my knees weak, and my breath barely finding its way out of my lungs, I kept telling myself that it was just breakfast.

God, if this was even *remotely* what Brooke felt like on a daily, I had to figure out new ways to distract her because this was awful.

With a shaking hand, I knocked on the front door and barely a second later, Nova opened the door for me.

Her eyebrows were raised, her hands on her hips, and her curly, blonde hair hung in a perfectly styled ponytail as always. It was a little odd how she looked so much like her older sister yet not at all. Nova's expectant look was definitely more intimidating than Brooke's, and she had only recently turned eleven.

"Reece," Nova said, sounding a lot less friendly than what was usual for her. I had to give it to that little kid, when it came to anyone hurting her siblings or parents, she was going to be a pain in the ass. Nova could be very rude if she had to be.

And she wasn't stupid. She probably knew that things weren't all sunshine and rainbows between Brooke and me, considering that my fiancée moved back home for a while. Not for long, I was sure. Once I was doing better, we'd be going back to our apartment. But until then, Nova was going to make my life a living hell, I could feel it.

Or at least give me a hard*er* time.

But I came prepared.

"Nova." I pulled a single white rose out of the baby's breath bouquet—it was the only place I could store it—and handed it to the little unimpressed girl in front of me.

She took the rose but her expression didn't falter. "Bribery doesn't work on me, Reece's Cups."

"I know. That's why it's not bribery."

"Then what is this?" Despite trying not to react too much, she still smelled the rose.

"Just a rose for a cute little girl."

Nova snorted a laugh. "As much as your crush on me is flattering, you're engaged to my sister, Reece."

I did not have a crush on her, for very obvious reasons. She was a kid for starters, and I was very much in love with my fiancée.

"Oh." I covered my heart with a hand. "You're right…"

"And I don't even like you right now."

I nodded. "I understand. Your rejection wounds me, Ms. Desrosiers-King, but I shall survive."

She laughed, then instantly wrapped her arms around me for a hug. "I missed you."

"Have you?" I chuckled and I could feel Nova nod against my body. "Didn't seem like you did just a minute ago."

"Because you hurt my sister, Reece," she told me. "But you're like my brother. How could I hate you? Yet I have to dislike you for Brookie's sake, but like… I still love you, you know? But you hurt her big time, and so I should hate you."

"Yeah, I feel the same way about myself."

She looked up at me, furrowing her eyebrows. "You do?"

"Yup. I don't think I'll ever—" Before I got to finish my sentence, a little cat tried to sneak past us. It was probably for the best that Purrito decided to interrupt. I shouldn't burden a ten-year-old with *my* problems.

"Purrito!" Nova laughed and picked him up. "You sneaky Mister." She tsked. "Always trying to escape. Don't you like any of us?"

Without even glancing at me again, Nova walked inside the house, leaving the door open for me. Guess that was the usual *come in*.

"Oh, good, you're here," Emory said as soon as she spotted me make my way past the living room to get to my fiancée.

It was a miracle Brooke hadn't been waiting by the front door for me.

"Yeah? I said I was going to come pick Brooke up, hadn't I?"

Emory nodded, smiling at me but there was something that didn't feel right about it.

"She wasn't sure I meant it, huh?" I sighed softly, but honestly, I had no reason to feel any sort of bad about it. I wasn't even *allowed* to take it badly. By the way I'd been acting for weeks before she moved out, it probably wouldn't have surprised her if I stood her up again.

But I was getting better. Slowly.

"Brooke was certainly hoping you did," she told me, sympathy in her voice. "You can't blame her for worrying."

"I know." I took a step toward the stairs when all of a sudden, I stopped moving entirely and looked at Emory again. "Did you ever think I wasn't good enough for Brooke?" blurted out of me before I even knew I was wondering about it.

Ever since I'd been living with Luan and Grey, once or twice staying at my brother's place again, I'd been thinking Brooke deserved way better than me. However, while I was beating myself up for hurting her, I didn't actually think her parents thought of me the way I had been thinking of myself lately.

Emory shook her head. "You've always put her over *yourself*, Reece. Seeing you in a different light just because you've encountered a pretty rough path in your life wouldn't be right. And losing someone pulls out different reactions in everyone. Some take it a little better than others. You're not suddenly a bad person just because you lost yourself for a little while, especially after something like this."

"So Colin keeps saying."

"You should listen to your brother more often."

"Perhaps I should." My eyes fell to the flowers in my hands, reminding me of why I was here. "I'll go find Brooke now, otherwise she'll probably think I forgot about her."

"Last time I checked on her, she was still getting dressed. I'm not sure she even knows what time it is."

I chuckled. "Sounds like Brooke."

Chapter Fifty-Four

Brooklyn

I was going to lose my goddamn mind.

Looking back at the pile of clothes on my bed, I couldn't help but roll my eyes. In the past god-knows-how-many-minutes, I'd been trying on outfit after outfit, and none seemed to look right.

It was just breakfast, nothing fancy, and yet my clothes seemed to have built a mind of their own and collectively decided to make me look bad in every single piece. Not even my go-to outfits—a short skirt with black tights, loafers, a cute shirt, and a jacket, plus jewelry—were working today.

I was going crazy.

"Urgh." I fell onto my bed next to the pile of clothes. "Fuck this, I'm not going."

But I couldn't just *not* go, I knew that. If Reece showed up without forgetting about me, there was no way I could tell him we couldn't go because my clothes were doing unfunny things to my body today.

In fact, if I told him this, he would tell me all the reasons why it was all just in my head and how I looked good in everything I tried on. Perhaps I needed his input after all.

Upon hearing a knock on my door, I looked up but didn't bother to move at all. The door was unlocked either way.

"Brooke?" I heard Reece's voice. "Can I come in?"

Within seconds, I sat up on my bed, holding my breath.

He was here. He didn't forget about me.

A smile tugged at the corners of my lips, and for whatever reason, my chest felt lighter—not as tight anymore.

"Since when do you ask permission to enter my room?" I chuckled, cocking my head as I watched the door open slowly. "You usually just barge right in."

His head poked into the room. "I didn't think it was appr —Brooke, you're in your underwear."

I looked down at myself, laughing. "Yeah… I couldn't find an outfit. But on the bright side, I *am* wearing *something*."

"Not a lot." He finally walked into the room, closing the door behind him.

For just a second, my eyes widened at the sight of him. Reece wore a suit which he only did for special occasions and his hockey games as it was required. He looked so good in a suit, yet I wasn't quite sure why he'd wear a suit for breakfast. Perhaps this was just his way of showing me that he was being serious.

I would've totally been underdressed.

Reece held a hand behind his back, but I knew he bought me flowers. He used to get me flowers at least once a week, and if they somehow died earlier than expected, it was more than once a week. I kind of missed it.

"Not a lot is better than nothing." I shrugged.

My gaze was fixed on Reece's arm, waiting rather impatiently for my flowers. He must've noticed because I could hear him chuckle, followed by him revealing a beautiful bouquet of white baby's breath.

As a gasp left my lungs, my eyes snapped up to meet his blue ones. My heart wanted me to jump off my bed and run into his arms, but I was frozen in place, just taking in the sight.

The tiny white blossoms seemed to glow against the black fabric of Reece's suit. A warm, fuzzy feeling spread through my chest as he smiled at me softly.

Oh, how I missed his smile—the old smile. The smile that wasn't malicious or seemed to only be there because he knew that it would lead to other things if he pretended to be alright for me. It seemed real, honest, and even a little better than yesterday.

"You got me flowers?" I grabbed the next best shirt from beside me and threw it on before I got up.

"It was long overdue," he replied while I was looking for a black skirt in the pile of clothes. "Between all that drinking and trying not to appear lost, I somehow forgot to ensure the one thing you could always count on—having fresh flowers."

"Reece." I finally approached him. "It's okay. They're just flo—"

"Please don't make excuses. It's not okay, I know that," he said. "It'd be a different story had I been too upset to get flowers or was too deep into grieving that I couldn't physically leave the apartment. But I was simply too drunk and too unbothered to get them. They're not the same excuses, *mi princesa*. The latter doesn't deserve understanding."

Perhaps not, but I didn't want to talk about this right now.

With a delicate smile on my lips, I took the bouquet from him, my fingers brushing against his, sending a tingle up my arm. I brought the flowers to my nose, inhaling the faint, sweet scent. It was what I liked about these flowers—that their scent was so faint.

Roses gave me a headache, as did a lot of other too-strong-scented flowers. Baby's breath was perfect, and they looked cute as well.

"Thank you," I whispered, feeling my eyes well up.

Reece took my left hand in his, eyes briefly falling on the engagement ring I refused to take off before they were back on my own. No matter how hurt I was, I couldn't bring myself to take it off. We were still engaged, and I was positive that we'd find our way back to a peaceful life together. We were certainly trying.

And it was going great so far.

Then again, it was our first time going out since we'd been staying at separate places.

"I'm sorry, Brooke," he said, his voice carrying sincerity. "I want to make things right between us, no matter how long it will take."

"I know." Reece had apologized a lot since I temporarily moved back home, but he'd never said anything about wanting to make things right. Then again, it was quite obvious he would want to do that.

The Reece I knew could barely make it two hours without talking to me. While our conversations were short these days, I knew it was because he was learning to get back on his feet, not because he didn't want to speak to me. Each time he called me in the evening, Reece wouldn't greet me with a *hello*. Instead, he'd say *I missed you.*

"Is my dad taking us to Rêverie?" I asked as I made my way over to the dresser. I laid down the flowers, unsure of where else to put them. The only vase I had in here was gone, and I just assumed Mom or Nova took it. It didn't matter anyway, as I hadn't planned on moving back for all too long.

"No," Reece replied. I could hear him walk around my room, but I didn't bother to look at him as I had to get ready. "He's already at the restaurant, I believe."

What If We Break?

"So... who's driving us?" I slid into my sheer, black tights, then reached for some white socks.

"I am."

Finally, I looked up at Reece, and I was almost sure he could see the worry etched into my face had he looked at me. He was too busy folding the clothes on my bed to pay any attention to my expression.

He didn't have to fold my clothes, but the gesture was highly appreciated. I *hated* folding clothes. Ironing them or doing the laundry in the first place, no problem. But folding? Nope.

"The entire way?" I asked carefully. It wasn't the shortest drive, and under different circumstances, I wouldn't have even questioned him, but given his recent history, forty minutes seemed like a long time. I didn't have a driver's license, but driving a car sure looked like it wasn't the easiest thing to do.

Reece chuckled lightly. "It's alright, Brooke. I promise."

"Alright. Good." I grasped my favorite pair of black loafers and slipped into them.

Making my way over to my makeup vanity, I took a seat and just stared at myself in the mirror for a second. I didn't need a lot of makeup today, it was just breakfast at my dad's restaurant. A still-*closed* restaurant. Surely some concealer and mascara would suffice.

Opening one of the drawers, I was hoping to find my makeup but instead, I was greeted by my old straightener that I hadn't touched in a while. Almost immediately, flashbacks from Reece and me getting ready for our first official date came flooding into my brain.

Somehow, this morning felt the same as it did back when I was thirteen.

"Reece?" I said as I closed the drawer again and tried the

other one. Finally, I found my concealer. "Do you think you still know how to straighten hair?"

I taught him back when we were fifteen. I used to straighten my hair a lot back in middle school and high school because I thought it made me blend in with all the other girls better. Sure, I wasn't the only one with textured hair, but all the popular girls had straight hair—or at least straightened them. While I had no desire to be popular at school, I preferred not to get bullied for standing out so much.

Blonde hair and curls? Yeah, that screamed for all sorts of drama. I never understood why it was such a big deal, but whatever.

I loved my curly hair now, and that was all that mattered.

While I was doing my makeup for school, Reece used to straighten my hair, which allowed me to wake up at a reasonable time and not two hours earlier.

At seventeen, I stopped straightening my hair, and if I did, I'd done it myself.

"Why do you want to straighten your hair?" Reece asked in return, not quite answering my question. "Your hair is beautiful just the way it is."

A smile crept onto my face, cheeks getting slightly warmer.

Through the mirror, I watched him get up, turn around, and make his way over to me. He laid his hands on my shoulders, eyes meeting mine.

"I don't," I answered. "I just wondered if you still know how to do it."

"I don't think straightening hair is a skill that can be unlearned." He leaned down and pressed his lips to the top of my head. "Besides, I had the best teacher ever. There's no way I could forget what she had taught me."

My eyes rolled, but the smile on my face refused to disappear. "Flattery won't help you today."

A smirk pulled on his lips, and there was something playful in his eyes. "We'll see about that."

Chapter Fifty-Five

Reece

"Oh, and could you please make sure the fruit platter is prepared without strawberries? My date's highly allergic," I said, to which our waiter nodded and began to scribble it down on his notepad.

Brooke giggled at my request, and when my eyes laid on her beautiful face, I watched her shake her head softly. "You know we're the only ones here, right? And my dad's in the kitchen. He's not going to put strawberries on our plates."

While I knew Miles wasn't going to serve her some, I would've requested no strawberries at any other restaurant. This was supposed to be a date, and since Brooke always forgot to mention her allergy or make sure her fruits didn't include strawberries, I had to make sure to mention it.

I might've taken the easy way out by asking Miles to open Rêverie for us, but that didn't mean I could afford to make mistakes. Necessary or not, I was on the safe side by mentioning it.

"He might not put strawberries on our plates, but I still had to say something... just in case he forgot," I replied.

"The day my dad forgets I have an allergy that will most

likely kill me, I'll have to assume he suffers from memory loss."

"You never know when the day might come." I shrugged while Brooke chuckled.

Since we have now ordered our breakfast, I set the menu aside. The menu was a handwritten piece of paper with *very* limited options to choose from. Rêverie didn't usually serve breakfast. In fact, they didn't open this early, so it was a miracle Miles even prepared a menu for this morning.

As we waited for our food to be served, Brooke and I couldn't stop talking. She told me all about what she did the past weeks when we were apart in much greater detail than on our phone calls. And in return, I told her about my progress, even when I was sure Luan and Grey kept her updated at all times.

There were times when I talked to her about my progress on the phone, but I was usually more interested in hearing Brooke talk, hearing her voice, and allowing her to distract me for an hour a day. But I suppose hearing my side of how I was doing rather than Luan or Grey's view of it was still a huge difference.

She held my hand as I spoke and smiled at me with pride as if fighting my way back into some version of my old life was a huge accomplishment. Perhaps it was.

By the time all of our breakfast was served by the one single waiter Miles had asked to work early, Brooke had begun talking about what I'd missed while I was... physically present but far gone in my head.

It was a lot to process, but I suppose it was better for me to find out about my possible expulsion from St. Trewery's hockey team now rather than later. Apparently, Colin even took his time to talk to my coach, which old me would've probably been pissed at, but at this point, I was just glad Colin could buy me some more time.

"Ming asked about you," Brooke told me as she used her fork to play with her scrambled eggs instead of eating them. "Obviously, he's heard about the news, which to be fair, wasn't that unlikely, seeing as it was plastered all over the Rangers' social media. I didn't want to lie when Ming asked how you're doing, but I also didn't want to tell him how unwell you've been, so I told him that you just need a bit of time to yourself for now."

Brooke went out with Ming and Rina a lot while I was rotting away on our sofa, which I sort of remembered. At least it didn't sound too unfamiliar hearing about it.

I nodded to myself, unsure of what else to do or even say. I expected Ming to be worried. Well, perhaps not worried but definitely slightly concerned about my well being seeing as I skipped out on *a bunch* of practices and classes, not just one or two, or even a whole week. It had been over a month.

But either way, I never meant for Brooke and my date to turn into her updating me on everything I've missed. I genuinely wanted to spend time with her without thinking about the past weeks. She lived through it, I existed. There was no need to talk about it now.

"Perhaps you should give him a call whenever you feel like you're ready to talk to anyone but our families." Brooke finally set her fork aside just to take a sip of her water. "By the way, he refuses to let anyone sit in your spot at the cafeteria." She chuckled softly. "I tried to sit there last Tuesday, and I swear, he almost yelled at me. Well, not *yelled* but he didn't sound like the usual, preppy Ming like I know him. Guess he really misses his best friend. I get it though, you're his ice hockey wife."

My eyebrows shot up, a hint of laughter bubbling inside

of me but I didn't dare let it out yet. If I laughed, Brooke would stop talking, and I really enjoyed listening to her speak. "His ice hockey wife?"

"You know what? That would be an understatement. You're his wife. Period."

I nodded slowly, carefully, like I didn't quite want to grasp what she was implying. "So, he's my... husband?"

"Nope." Brooke shoved a forkful of her scrambled eggs into her mouth. "You're his wife."

"But I—if he's my wife... and I'm his wife? I don't understand. Why isn't he my husband?"

She sighed heavily, rolling her eyes. "Because WAGs are usually women."

"Luan's not," I argued.

"Because there's no such thing as WAG in male version, which, frankly, is stupid because there are quite the number of gays in professional sports these days. But anyway, let's not get political." She pushed her hair behind her shoulders to keep it from falling into her food. "Luan's also a wife. If Luan—and all the other guys—belongs to all the wives and girlfriends, so do Ming and you. Easy as that."

"Who says Luan belongs to them?"

"All the Rangers' partners who have adopted him as part of their group... and Grey."

We held eye contact for no longer than a second before we both burst into laughter.

Unfortunately, I couldn't enjoy the moment because I was rudely interrupted by my phone ringing.

Just to check it wasn't important, I glanced at my phone only to find my agent's name spread across the screen. My eyebrows dipped for merely a second, but I suppose it was long enough for Brooke to notice.

"Something wrong?" she asked, her voice more high-pitched this time which told me she was worried.

I looked up, shaking my head. "It's just Anthony. He'll probably tell me he doesn't want to work with me anymore or something." Frankly, I wasn't even allowed to be mad about it.

Brooke reached a hand across the table to hold mine. "Pick up. It could be good news too. Or perhaps he just wants to ask how you're doing."

"Maybe." My eyes were back on my phone, my thumb hovering over the accept button but there was a moment of hesitation.

What if he was about to tell me bad news? It could ruin my entire mood. And what if that was going to set me back?

Then again, Anthony wasn't anything like Pike. He was more understanding, and Colin told him what was going on.

So I picked up.

"Carter," I said, hoping to sound neutral.

"Reece, are you seated right now?" Anthony sounded much happier than usual, it was strange. He wasn't broody by any means, but cheerful?

What an odd question as well.

"I am?"

"Good," he said. "You will want to sit down for what I have to say. But first, how are you?"

"I've seen better days," I answered honestly.

I felt Brooke's thumb brush over my knuckles, instantly drawing my attention to our hands.

There was no reason why a woman's touch should make a guy feel at peace when there was a whole storm inside of him, but somehow Brooke managed to do just that to me.

When her eyes were on mine, her love for me was palpable. When her hand touched my own, every nerve in my body calmed instantly. When she was around, breathing made sense again.

Only with her, I could live.

She was the antidote that made life's poison bearable.

"Of course. I am very sorry about your loss," Anthony said, the cheery tone gone and replaced by sympathy.

"Thank you."

"Now, I understand this might be an awful moment to call, but I have news that is supposed to make you happy."

"Okay?" My eyebrows drew together in confusion. Anticipation filled my body, and though every instinct of mine wanted me to walk around the room, Brooke's touch kept me seated. "What is it?"

"The Rangers want to draft you," he told me.

My heart stopped beating and for a split second, my lungs were giving in and there wasn't any oxygen coming through.

This was impossible.

"But I haven't even entered the draft yet," I managed to say, my voice barely above a whisper.

Brooke cocked her head, confused. Hell, *I* was confused.

"I know, Reece," Anthony replied, his tone once again excited but more serious this time. "They reached out to me shortly after your father's passing but I figured it was an even worse moment to call you."

"Yes, but that doesn't explain why... how?"

"They don't want to risk losing you to another team. The Rangers have been keeping an eye on you for a long while now, and they obviously see a lot of potential in you. This isn't just about talent though, it's about legacy."

So Colin said, but I barely wanted to believe him.

I felt a lump in my throat, my heart was racing, but somehow I couldn't seem to be happy about it. There was no way this was real.

"Anthony, I haven't played a single game in almost two months. I didn't even show up to practice. Even if I accepted now, surely they don't want me anymore after not seeing or hearing anything about me in so long," I said.

Each word hurt to say out loud, but it was the truth. Ice hockey was ruthless, not only on the ice. There was no space for breakdowns. Fuck, most players didn't even care about being sick, they still showed up. You'd have to force them off the ice and chain them to their beds in case of an injury.

Okay, it wasn't *that* bad, but it might as well have been. Not a single player wanted to miss a game, and I happily skipped them for weeks.

"Yes," he said and cleared his throat. "Your absence was noticed but they understand it must be difficult for you to lose your father at such a young age. Your father was a beloved member of the Rangers, Reece, they share your pain. Surely not as deeply as you, but either way, they understand."

Yeah, it was impossible to feel as beat-down by my father's death as I felt.

Dad was their head coach for decades. He brought many wins, tons of trophies, and so many smiles. He trained those who were fortunate enough to play under his guidance well.

He was a great coach, but he was everything to me.

Dad taught me how to skate, how to handle a puck, and how to get a feel for the ice underneath my skates. He taught me how to stop, how to sneak past opponents, how to score. Everything I knew about ice hockey, I knew thanks to him.

Losing him was the hardest thing I'd ever faced.

But perhaps this was one last lesson he wanted to teach me.

The New York Rangers. Being part of the team I'd been dreaming about playing for since I was three years old.

"I don't know what to say," I admitted, pulling my hand

away from my fiancée's just to run it through my hair. "This is everything I've ever wanted."

"There's no contract yet," Anthony said. "Well, there is a contract, but if you sign it now, your NCAA career is over."

"What about college?" Colin would kill me if I quit college for hockey. Dad didn't allow him to quit, so why would I be allowed to?

"As I said, only if you sign the contract now, you'll become ineligible for NCAA hockey. However, it'd be effective immediately upon signing. You'd have a secure spot with the Rangers if you sign now. You'd be officially playing for the NHL then, which means no more college because you won't have much time for it. You could do online college," he replied. "For full transparency, if you don't sign the contract now, there is a chance that another team might request you before the Rangers do once you're ready to play for the NHL. They said you'd be their first choice, as of now anyway, but the whole drafting thing is a bit more complicated than that, as you may know. The choice is up to you."

Up to me.

This shouldn't be up to me.

Looking at my record of recent decisions, I was in no position to decide whether to play for the NHL or finish my studies.

Chapter Fifty-Six

~~Brooklyn~~

My fiancé clutched my hand tightly as we listened to Aaron list all the cons and pros for Reece to quit college and pursue his NHL career earlier than initially planned.

It had been a couple of days since Anthony called, and while Reece wasn't under any stress and could take his time to decide, he figured that choosing sooner rather than later was only beneficial. For one, he could concentrate on his studies if he decided not to sign the contract. After all, Reece wanted to go back to his classes next Monday.

But if he decided to sign the contract, he no longer even had to think about college. However, St. Trewery did allow students to take their courses online as well, so that was another aspect to consider. Reece could still finish college despite playing for the NHL, he just wouldn't attend a lot of classes anymore… if any.

Ming and Rina showed up for emotional support, but neither of them dared to utter a word. To be honest, Rina had no idea what was going on, she only came because her boyfriend asked her to and because I was here.

Oh yeah, apparently, Ming somehow managed to make her fall for him after all. I totally called it.

"Wouldn't you agree?" Aaron asked Colin after finishing his rant about all the pros of playing for the NHL. Aaron had found a lot more pros than cons, which was to be expected. Colin, however, looked at the whole situation a bit more carefully than Aaron had.

"Sure, but that still doesn't mean Reece should *quit* college," Colin replied. "We all—" His eyes moved to my father beside me, and instantly, his usual mocking grin spread across Colin's face. "Well, we all except Miles—"

"Rude," my father muttered under his breath, making me chuckle.

"—know how much pressure NHL players are under. Especially right now, it'd be best for Reece to take it slow." Colin's eyes fell on his brother for a brief moment, probably making sure Reece didn't get offended by what he said. "He could have an awful Rookie year, and what happens then? He could realize the pro league isn't for him, and he just quit college. What's he gonna do then?"

Aaron looked at his list on the TV, sighing before he added *Reece's mental health* to the cons list.

"I could always restart college, I guess?" Reece threw in. "Or take online classes. But online classes suck."

"There's a reason I wasn't allowed to quit college. I could've started playing for the Rangers at eighteen," Colin said, earning himself just a few gasps in return. Lily was pretty much the only one who didn't look surprised. "Oh, come on, you guys. You didn't seriously think I wasn't offered a contract the second I turned eighteen. My father was their head coach at that time. Of course the Rangers wanted to get me on their team the moment they could."

"Way to make us feel good about getting drafted at twenty-one," Grey said. "You were just waiting for the day you could finally drop this, weren't you?"

"Obviously." Colin winked at his best friend, beaming a smile. "I didn't want—"

"Guys, this decision is much easier to make than you think," Lily said, interrupting her husband before he could become any cockier.

Suddenly, every single person in this room was staring at Lily, some more intensely than others.

"How so?" Reece asked. "It feels pretty impossible to me."

"You'll see." Lily smiled softly, taking the iPad away from Aaron just to delete the cons and pro list. "Colin?"

"Yes, *mi sol*?"

"If your dad hadn't intervened, would you have chosen to play for the NHL rather than start college?" Lily asked. I bet she already knew the answer, though.

Reece rested his head on my shoulder, sighing heavily. I didn't know where Lily was going with this, and I suppose my fiancé had no idea either. I couldn't imagine it being an easy decision to make.

"Fuck yeah," Colin said, sounding a bit offended that she even dared to ask such a stupid question. "I was ready to sign the contract."

Lily nodded, then slightly turned her head to look at Grey. "What about you?"

He shrugged. "I wouldn't have been allowed to do it."

"Welcome to my life," Colin chimed in, nudging his best friend in the side.

"Okay, but in a perfect world, you would've chosen hockey over college?" Lily queried, earning herself a convinced nod in return. "That means all of you—"

"Excuse me. You forgot to ask what I would've done," Aaron interrupted, crossing his arms over his chest in protest.

"I know your answer." Lily tsked. "Anyway. All of you

would've chosen the NHL in a heartbeat if you could have." She looked at Reece again, her head slightly cocked, and a sympathetic smile on her lips. "You're hesitating, Reece. Hesitation says a lot about someone's true desires."

"You should know," Aaron muttered, just to get lightly slapped by his wife, and turn into the receiving end of seven death glares. Why they all took it so seriously, I didn't know, but perhaps it was better that way. "Sorry. I wasn't thinking."

I looked at my fiancé, finding him deep in thoughts. He stared blankly ahead, so inanimate, one could think he'd fallen asleep or that he might be physically present yet mentally in a faraway land.

But I knew Reece. He could've been in Neverland with his thoughts, yet the moment I moved by just a millimeter, he was right with me. He proved my point when I accidentally loosened my hand around his as his head snapped toward me instantly.

"Are you okay?" he asked, concern in his voice and eyes. He looked so defeated, so exhausted from everything, yet he still worried about me accidentally loosening my grip.

I smiled at him before I leaned in and placed a soft kiss on the left corner of his mouth. "Not as long as you're still in pain."

A sigh drew from his lungs, his hot breath rolling over my skin.

Reece didn't reply, instead, he stood from his seat and pulled me up as well. As I and everyone else in this room looked at him with confusion, he declared, "I can't just trust my own gut feeling. Brooke and I need to have a little conflab and then I can decide what I want to do."

That said, he pulled me down the hall and right into his old bedroom.

Chapter Fifty-Seven

Reece

Lily was right, even if she hadn't technically claimed to be.

If I was ready to play for the NHL right this instant, there shouldn't have been a single doubt in my mind.

Did I want to go pro? Fuck yes.

Did I want to play for the Rangers? Preferably, but it wasn't like my spot was secure, even if they drafted me. The NHL could trade me any day without talking to me about it first unless my contract said otherwise. That little piece of writing—not getting traded—wasn't as easy to get, though.

They could also always decide I wasn't NHL-worthy and then make me play for the AHL, or even worse, the ECHL.

I could sign that stupid contract right now and it still didn't mean I'd be going out on that ice with the team. It wouldn't guarantee that I'd be getting any ice time for the foreseeable future.

Was potentially getting benched my entire first year truly worth ruining my NCAA experience for me? I liked my college team, we were great, and I didn't plan to leave them before my graduation next year.

One year could change a lot, I knew that, but I was already guaranteed to get drafted next year. Maybe they'd still want me next year, and even if they didn't, it wasn't going to ruin my life.

It would sting, sure, but spending my senior year with my team, and attending college with my best friend in the whole wide world was worth so much more than a career. Collecting as many memories with Brooke as I could was more important to me than the NHL—they could wait another year.

"Reece, I'm not going to tell you what to do," Brooke said, genuine concern in her voice. Her eyebrows were drawn together, yet her gaze was soft.

"I don't want you to," I replied and laid my hands on either side of her jaw. "I already know that I'm not going to sign the contract."

"You're not?" Surprise covered her features.

I shook my head. "Ever since we started talking about college in high school, I knew I wouldn't play for the NHL before I graduated. We have plans all year, Brooke. What about your birthday? You wanted to go to Bali. I already booked the whole trip, and I sure as fuck won't cancel the vacation of your dreams because I start my first official NHL season that month. And I know I ruined your figure skating season, so I *need* to be there for the next one."

"But…" She clung to my wrists, her breathing quickening. "Reece, it's okay. I don't want you to risk anything for me."

"It's not about you. And it's not that I *never* want to go pro," I told her. "I just want to get my degree first. I want to go to some more stupid college parties that we're both going to hate so endlessly much that we'll leave again after thirty minutes. Maybe it's crazy or even stupid not to sign the contract, but either way, I don't want to force myself to do something that I'm just not ready for yet."

Brooke loosened her grip on my wrists, her arms dropping to either side of her body as her face drained of any sort of emotion.

"I want to enjoy my last year with you, *mi princesa*. I want to enjoy my life for one more year before I'm constantly on the road with whatever team I may end up with. And in case we'll have to move to a whole other state because I don't end up playing for the Rangers, I want to enjoy that last year in New York," I added, even though I was almost a hundred percent sure Brooke didn't need any more reasons to be convinced that I was sure of my decision.

However, her silence made me nervous.

Brooke displayed little emotion in her eyes, let alone on her face. No expression whatsoever; No happiness, no anger, not even disappointment, or uncertainty. There was nothing. She looked almost frozen in time.

If I had counted the seconds, I was sure it would've been at least half a minute until her lips curved upward. In that moment, a relieving breath drew from my lungs.

Brooke's opinion was the one I valued the most, and certainly the only one that could make me change my plans in a heartbeat. If she thought I'd make a mistake by not signing the contract just yet, I was making a goddamn mistake.

"Well, it'd be nice to move back home before we get anywhere near your plans," she said and took a tiny step forward until her body was pressed right against mine. Her arms snuck around my torso, her head colliding with my chest.

"You don't think that's stupid or irresponsible?" I asked, my voice shaking in fear that she might've thought less of me now.

"No, Reece." She shrieked when I picked her up, her legs wrapping around my waist. "I'm so proud of you."

"What if I won't get to play for the Rangers?"

I walked us over to my dresser and sat her down, keeping my hands on her hips.

She sighed softly, slightly tilting her head. "Then I guess we're moving."

"What about figure skating? Or your family? You hate not being around them."

Brooke chuckled. "Reece, I've been ready to move to a whole other country with you since we were like ten. Not staying in New York won't kill me." Her hands slid from around my neck down my chest. "And I could never skate for a living. The stress isn't good for me, I don't think. Maybe I'll give lessons instead, sounds like much more fun."

"God, I love you so much." I leaned down and pressed my lips to hers. I never intended for this kiss to turn into a full-blown makeout session, so I was quick to pull away. Brooke, however, seemed to have had other plans.

"I know you do." She smiled. "I love you, too."

She leaned back in, her lips brushing mine before she opened her mouth to grant me access. Even if I had tried to tell my brain to stop, it wouldn't have listened.

My tongue swept inside to rub against hers, and I instantly felt her shiver. Brooke's delicate fingers snuck into my hair, her nails slightly scratching my scalp.

When a moan left her mouth, it took all of my self-restraint not to sneak my hands underneath her skirt and rip her tights apart. Or to push her underwear aside and slide a finger or two inside of her.

While I managed not to undress her, I couldn't bring myself to stop kissing her. Fortunately, yet also unfortunately, Brooke pulled away first.

"Are you okay with getting married in a castle?" she asked, catching me so off-guard, I started to laugh.

Leaning down, my forehead rested on her shoulder as my

own shook with laughter. It didn't take long for Brooke to lightly slap her hands on my back to make me stop.

"This is a serious question, Reece. I have a wedding to plan."

"I'm sorry," I said with a chuckle, still trying to calm myself down. As my head lifted and my eyes were back on hers, I finally managed to control my amusement.

Somehow, I expected Brooke to grin at me or smile, but she looked as serious as she did when she was scolding me for making us late for class.

"You're being serious," I noted.

"Of course I am." Her eyebrows drew together, offended. "I wouldn't joke about our wedding, Reece. You know I've been ready to switch my last name to yours for at least a whole decade."

Take a deep breath, Reece. No more laughing—no smiling either, no matter how adorable your fiancée is.

"Yeah, but I always just assumed we'd get married in a castle, *mi princesa*," I answered honestly. "I've had to listen to you talk about princesses since the day you were born. Our wedding would be the only day you get to live that movie-princess-life, even if it's just for a day. Of course we're getting married in a castle."

Even before I had finished talking, Brooke had been smiling so widely that I was a little afraid she was going to rip the corners of her mouth.

God, she was just the most adorable person in the entire universe, and nobody was ever going to convince me otherwise.

"Good," she whispered as her lips brushed mine again. "Because we have to book the venue *way* in advance, so I went ahead and did it like last week."

"Of course you did."

Epilogue

Reece

One Year Later – Age 21 (May 2039)

"How's Brooke doing?" I asked while looking at myself in the mirror, trying my best to tie the stupid tie around my neck.

Since we were expected to wear suits before our games, I knew how to tie these stupid ribbons, but for some very unexplainable reasons, my hands were shaking and my fingers refused to do what they were supposed to do.

Why was I nervous anyway? I was ready to marry Brooke since the day I could remember, so how dare I be nervous?

I mean, I was only marrying the love of my goddamn life and she'd have my last name in like… two hours. No biggie, right?

Wrong.

It was the biggest fucking deal ever.

How was I of all people lucky enough to marry *the* Brooklyn Desrosiers-King? The most beautiful, nicest, sweetest, and best person to ever walk this godforsaken planet.

"I think she's having a party with her bridesmaids," Colin

told me as he stepped closer. He was just checking on her for me. "I'm not allowed to enter the room, so Lily insists."

"Her bridesmaids," I chuckled. Brooke's bridesmaids were Emory, Lily, Sofia, Rina, and Grey. As far as I knew, she even convinced Grey to wear a purple suit, which I couldn't wait to see. I don't think I'd ever seen Grey in anything but black clothing. "Is she freaking out?"

Colin shook his head. "Honestly, I think you're more nervous than she is." He turned me around to face him and then swatted my hands away from my necktie, taking over for me.

"Why are you nervous, Uncle Reece?" Kieran asked as he walked up to us. For once, that kid didn't have a book in his hands. It was a miracle. "Don't you want to marry Brooke?"

I cleared my throat, taking a step back when Colin finally finished tying the ribbon around my neck. "Of course I do. It's just... I don't know. You're too young to understand."

Colin chuckled, then quickly covered it up with a cough. He tapped his right hand on my shoulder, whispering, "Prepare to be lectured."

"Too young?" Kieran's eyebrows shot up. "I'm already twelve. I'm like six years away from marrying someone, though that's pretty unlikely. Unlike you, I don't need to marry someone to fill a void in my life. I have my books, which, for your information, keep me company *and* make me smarter. But even if I were to marry someone at eighteen, I wouldn't be nervous. Nobody's forcing you to marry Brooke. Then again, I guess nervousness isn't just a sign of fear or worry. It might be a good thing to anticipate what the future with someone you adore might hold." He looked at his dad, cocking his head. "Were you nervous to marry Mom?"

"Me?" Colin pointed at himself, eyes wide with surprise. "Uh... no. Well, yes, but no."

"Dad..." Kieran sighed heavily, shaking his head. "What will Mom say when I tell her that you weren't nervous to marry her? Mom's the best. If nervousness is an important factor for marriage, then you should've been nervous."

"Yeah, Carter. You should've been nervous," Aaron added from across the room. I totally forgot he was here as well. For the past hour, Aaron had been asleep on the king-sized bed. "Didn't even ask me for my blessing."

"He was supposed to ask Grandpa, Uncle Aaron," Kieran corrected. "So, technically, your blessing would've been useless unless Grandpa was dead."

"Did Gramps give his blessing?" Jamie asked curiously, suddenly sitting up beside his father.

When did Jamie get here, anyway? The last update from the kids I got was that Jamie, Elliot, and Nova were running around the castle to check it out.

"He did," Colin answered. "But that's not important now. Today's about Reece and Brooke."

"One more question," Jamie announced, now looking at me. "Did you get Miles' blessing to marry Brookie? If so, do I need Miles' blessing to marry Nova?"

"Nova?!" Kieran's jaw dropped and I swear, his eyes were about to pop right out of his head. After making his way over to his cousin, Kieran grasped Jamie's arm and made him follow him out. "We're going to have a *loooong* talk about this, Jamie. Nova? Seriously?"

"Great, with the kids gone..." Colin turned to all of my groomsmen, which, to be honest, were also just family and Ming. Brooke and my wedding was small but expensive. "I need all of you to leave as well. I have important matters to discuss with my brother."

Important matters? I swallowed thickly at the thought of whatever that was.

Colin might've been my brother, but that guy could scare me like no other.

Ah, shit, he was probably going to threaten me because if I ever broke Brooke's heart, he was going to murder me. But I already knew that, and frankly, if I ever broke Brooke's heart *again*, I'd ask him to do it.

As soon as everyone left the room, Colin seemed a bit more on edge. It wasn't like he was about to explode or anything, he wasn't angry, either. He appeared almost nervous.

"Are you okay?" I found myself asking. Suddenly, the heavy weight in my chest that had caused my lungs to malfunction just a minute prior had lifted all on its own.

What the fuck was Colin about to tell me that made him look... like this?

"Of course," he replied as he walked across the room and over to that mysterious box he'd brought with him. When I'd first seen it and asked about it, Colin refused to tell me what was inside. "You have a first look with Brooke, right?"

I nodded. "Why?"

"Just wondering." Colin picked up the box. "I have something for you, or well, you have something for Brooke. Either way, I promised someone I'd give this to you on your wedding day."

My eyebrows drew together in confusion as I watched Colin carry that box to the bed and set it down. "How does that make any sense?"

"All right, so... little back story. When you were born—"

"Oh, God." My hands shot up to my face, fingers rubbing my temples. Any story that started with *when you were born* wasn't a good one.

"No, listen. When you were born, we kind of already knew

that Eira was sick. We didn't know *how* sick but that doesn't matter because ever since Eira knew she was sick, she started to really cherish every second she had with you. From the moment you could walk and started to pick random objects off the floors, she came up with a really interesting idea."

"Should I be scared?"

Colin chuckled as he shook his head. "You probably don't remember but the first *ever* flower you picked off the ground wasn't for Mom or Eira, it was for Brooke. Miles, Eira, and I took you to a park and when Eira saw you picking that flower and giving it to Brooke, Eira immediately begged Miles to make sure Brooke wouldn't lose it because she wanted to collect these for you."

My eyes fell to the box on the bed. It wasn't huge by any means, but it wasn't small, either. There was no way there were flowers inside of that thing, right?

"Before Eira died, she asked me to continue to collect them if I could, and she wanted me to give these to you when you got married." He picked the box back up and handed it over to me. "So, that's every single flower you ever picked off the ground and either already gave or planned on giving to Brooke from the first up to the very last I'd gotten my hands on."

Walking over to the bed, I set the box down and opened it, finding a good-sized, perfectly arranged bouquet of dried flowers. These weren't just everyday flowers like daisies that you could simply find almost everywhere. There were some roses, indigo, tulips, daffodils, and tons of others that I couldn't even name.

I couldn't even remember picking any of these.

"I still have boxes of roses and whatever those white flowers are that you keep getting Brooke in the attic." Colin nodded toward the bouquet of dried flowers. "But I figured these were more interesting."

Not the prettiest bouquet, but the most interesting, indeed.

"You can't turn around yet," I heard Brooke say when she finally got out on the balcony. Once again, she knew me better than I did because the second I heard steps coming from behind me, I was ready to turn around.

"This isn't fair, *mi princesa*." My heart was pounding with anticipation, eager to look at my bride, knowing it was likely going to be the death of me.

She chuckled in return. "I just have to adjust something, then you can look."

"I can adj—"

"No, I have to look perfect before you see me," Brooke interrupted.

"Baby, you look perfect in a burlap sack. A misplaced hair won't ruin your look now," I said, yet I waited impatiently for her okay.

"Stop, I'm going to cry!"

For months I'd been waiting for this moment—when I could *finally* see the love of my life in her way too expensive wedding dress. It felt like the dress had been the center of attention in most of everyone's conversations for *weeks*, and I was the only one who had no idea what kind of dress Brooke got. I wasn't even allowed to be in the room when they all talked about the dress.

For all I knew, Brooke could've gotten a sleek, purple dress just to throw me off. I doubted it but it was a possibility.

We were getting married in a castle in France, spent *thousands* on this stupid location, only for Brooke to wear a

What If We Break?

simple dress? Yeah, that was impossible. She must've planned something big, so now she had to look perfect when I first got to see her.

She would've looked perfect no matter what she was wearing.

"Just... one more second," she said, her voice quieter this time.

I began to fidget slightly, adjusting the cuffs of my shirt without ruining the delicate flowers in my other hand. I tried my best to conceal my nerves and took deep breaths to keep the excitement that bubbled inside me under wraps.

My breath got caught in my lungs when Brooke laid her hand on my shoulder. "You can turn around now."

I turned around without hesitation, and the moment my eyes met hers, every ounce of nervousness I seemed to have a moment ago evaporated into thin air.

Brooke, my beautiful Brooke, stood in front of me in her *enormous* white wedding dress. The world stopped spinning as I took her in: her anxious but radiant smile, the delicate lace of her dress, her beautiful makeup, her perfectly styled, curly hair, and the tiara she wore which was attached to the longest veil I'd ever seen in my entire life.

She was even more breathtaking than I had imagined.

But what captivated me the most were her eyes; the way they sparkled with unshed tears, and that perfect smile of hers.

"Brooke..." I whispered, a mix of emotions forming a lump in my throat. "You look..." How was I supposed to describe perfection other than showing Brooke a picture of herself? "Like a real-life princess."

Her tears began to fall as her smile widened and her rosy cheeks deepened in color. "You don't look so bad yourself."

My hand reached out to gently touch her cheek. "You're

the most beautiful person I have ever seen," I said, sincerity in my words. "I can't believe I get to marry you."

Brooke leaned into my touch, her eyes closing for a moment as she savored the warmth of my touch. "I can't believe it either," she whispered softly. "I've been dreaming of this day for so long."

"Almost eight years."

She shook her head. "Almost twenty years."

How had it been almost twenty years since we first met?

According to my brother, I'd definitely fallen in love with Brooke right then and there. I couldn't even remember a single day in my life that I hadn't loved Brooke.

When she looked at the flowers in my hand, her expression softened even more but I could tell that she was a little confused.

"Oh." I held up the bouquet, my throat clogging up with tears. "Apparently, Colin's been collecting as many flowers as he could for years."

"Colin?"

"Yes, on my sister's orders." My gaze fell to the flowers in my hands. "Well... he collected all of the flowers *I* picked for *you*." I looked back up into Brooke's eyes, clearing my throat. "From the very first I'd ever picked to the last. Colin said that Eira thought it might be cool to have them."

Brooke's lips parted as she sucked in a sharp breath. Her fingers trembled as she reached out to take the bouquet. "I love them."

"Maybe we can put them somewhere in our apartment? Or, though I'm not sure if it isn't too late for it already, we could press them super flat and put them into a picture fra—"

"I want to use them," she cut me off.

My eyebrows drew together, not quite understanding what anyone could use dried flowers for. "Okay?"

What If We Break?

"We can try framing them, or do anything else, but I'd like to use them as my wedding bouquet."

I smiled at my bride. "Baby, I'm sure you already have *fresh*, super expensive flowers."

"Yes, but these are better," she insisted. "They're not the prettiest anymore, and perhaps the mismatch doesn't look all that aesthetic... but they're meaningful."

"You know you don't have to use them, right? I just wanted to give these to you before we got married." They were meaningful, sure, but I knew that Brooke spent months trying to find the perfect flower arrangement for the venue which would also complement her and her bridesmaids' bouquets.

"Reece," she said with a hint of amusement in her voice. Amusement was better than tears, especially since I was sure her makeup took *hours*. "I don't care if they don't look perfect. To me, these are the best flowers I could *ever* have. Each of these flowers got us a step closer to where we are today. They're like your unvoiced promises that we'd be getting married someday. And *someday* happens to be today. So then our wedding pictures won't feature an aesthetically pleasing bouquet, but at least we know it was meaningful. And just think about the stories we can tell when anyone sees these pictures and asks us about the flowers."

How could I not love her?

I laid my hands on her waist, pulling her body right against mine. "God, I love you so much, Brooklyn," I said shortly before I pressed my lips to hers softly.

Was I allowed to kiss her before the wedding? I didn't know, and I couldn't have given any more fucks at this moment.

A wave of Brooke's perfume lingered in the air as I leaned my forehead against hers. She smelled mostly like vanilla, but I could swear there was a slight hint of something floral in there as well. She didn't usually like floral scents, but her perfume was an exception. It was the best scent I'd ever known, and luckily for me, she rarely switched it up.

"I love you, too," she whispered back, those tears echoing in her voice once again.

"You're not allowed to cry, baby. This wedding cost your parents, my mom, and Colin a *fortune*. The makeup was a good portion of that price."

She laughed, and God, how I loved that sound. I could happily live with hearing that one for the rest of my life.

I could stand here for hours just holding my Brooke in my arms, and I would've been the happiest man alive. And perhaps I wouldn't have cut this short but we had a wedding to attend, and fuck, was I excited to marry her.

"Are you ready to do this?" I asked as I pulled back slightly, my hands now cupping her face as I stared deeply into her eyes.

A tender smile pulled on her lips, tears still glistening in her green eyes. "With you, I'm ready to do anything."

THE END

ALSO BY JOELINA FALK

Unfrozen Four Series:

Nine Days #1

Eight Weeks #2

Seven Months #3

Six Years #4

Tartarus Club Series:

A Taste Of Light #1

A Taste Of Darkness #2

NY Sweethearts Series:

What If We Break? #1

Follow me on social media to stay up to date with new releases, bonus content, have a chat with me, and more.

Instagram: @authorjoelinafalk

TikTok: @authorjoelinafalk

Website: www.joelinafalk.com

For bonus content of her books, head over to: https://www.joelinafalk.com/bonus-content

Printed in Great Britain
by Amazon